"Read *The Mark* and you will [...] new talent, Jason Pinter, [...] page-turner you won't be [...]"
—JAMES PATTERSON

"A first-rate debut from an author who dares to take the traditional thriller in bold new directions."
—TESS GERRITSEN

"An excellent debut. You are going to love Henry Parker, and you're going to hope he survives the story, but you're not going to bet on it."
—LEE CHILD

"A harrowing journey—chilling, compelling, disquieting. A remarkable debut."
—STEVE BERRY

"This is a top-notch debut.... Fast-paced, gritty and often raw, *The Mark* is a tale you won't soon forget."
—MICHAEL PALMER

"From first line to last, the story rockets through a city rife with corruption and tangled loyalties, where one man holds the key to salvation...but only if he can walk through fire. A stunning debut by a major new talent!"
—JAMES ROLLINS

"Jason Pinter has made a substantial contribution to the thriller genre with *The Mark*, a fast-paced, addictively suspenseful thriller."
—ALLISON BRENNAN

Praise for Jason Pinter's

The Mark

"*The Mark* is a stunning debut!
It's *Front Page* meets *The Sopranos*,
with more than a little Scorsese thrown in."
—Jeffery Deaver

"Jason Pinter's riveting debut novel, *The Mark*, is lean,
fast and furious, with a tinge of classic noir and a voice
all its own. It's *The Fugitive* for the new millennium. Pinter
is among the best of a new generation of thriller writers,
and I look forward to reading more from this extravagantly
talented newcomer—and the further adventures of his
irresistible hero, Henry Parker."
—Joseph Finder

"Jason Pinter has a wonderful voice. *The Mark* captivated
me from the first. A page turner from the get go—I loved it."
—Heather Graham

"A high-octane debut, *The Mark* introduces Jason Pinter
as a major new talent in thriller fiction.
It's a brilliantly executed chase novel but it's also a
heartfelt exploration of honor, ambition and courage."
—Jeff Abbott

"Breathless, poignant and fresh...
Jason Pinter's debut thriller, *The Mark*, is a story
of good intentions gone wrong and what happens when
cub reporter Henry Parker, Pinter's charming and guileless
protagonist, finds out the hard way what it's like to be *in* the
headlines instead of writing them."
—P.J. Parrish

JASON PINTER

THE MARK

MIRA®

ISBN-13: 978-0-7783-2489-8
ISBN-10:   0-7783-2489-3

THE MARK

Copyright © 2007 by Jason Pinter.

www.MIRABooks.com

Printed in U.S.A.

For Susan
I only hope my words fill these pages
like you fill my heart

ACKNOWLEDGMENTS

I would like to thank:

–Joe Veltre, who supported this book from the beginning, offered invaluable insight and found the perfect home for it. An agent I can truly call both a friend and a consigliere.

–Linda McFall, who has been the kind of editor every author dreams of: encouraging, indefatigable and patient to no end. Because of you *The Mark* is a better book and I'm a better author (not to mention a preferred customer at 1-800-FLOWERS).

–Donna Hayes, Dianne Moggy, Margaret O'Neill Marbury, Craig Swinwood, Loriana Sacilotto, Stacy Widdrington, Maureen Stead, Katherine Orr, Marleah Stout, Cris Jaw, Ana Movileanu, Rebecca Soukis and everyone else at MIRA Books who got behind *The Mark* and published it with a passion and intelligence second to none.

–The authors who donated their invaluable time to reading advance copies of *The Mark* and offering truly humbling words of praise.

–The readers and booksellers who continue their passionate support of the literary industry, and were brave enough to invite a first-time novelist to tell them a story or two.

–Rick Wolff, Rick Horgan, Jamie Raab, Carrie Thornton, Steve Ross, Kristin Kiser and all my colleagues at Hachette Book Group and Crown Publishers who allowed me the privilege of working on both sides of the desk.

–M.J. Rose and Sarah Weinman. If there are two people out there who are more generous, love books as much, and do more for the industry, I'd like to meet them.

–Brett Battles, J. T. Ellison, Sandra Ruttan and the rest of the Killer Year crew. Great friends and partners in crime. I hope 2007 is full of all the murder, mystery and mayhem we hoped for.

–Clark Blaise. Keep on truckin'.

–Mom, Dad and Ali. Thank you for your never-ending love and support, I'm not a good enough writer to properly express my gratitude. Every day my eyes open more to the unflagging love and support you've shown my whole life.

–Susan. My life. My love. My inspiration. I can't imagine where I would be without you (though it would probably involve bumping into walls while wearing mismatched clothing). I am the luckiest man in the world, and I will spend the rest of my life trying to make you as proud and happy as you make me.

Prologue

Right as I was about to die, I realized that none of the myths about death were true. There was no white light at the end of a tunnel. My life didn't flash before my eyes. There were no singing angels, no thousand virgins, and my soul didn't hover and admire my body from above. I was only aware of one thing, and that was how much I wanted to live.

I watched the shotgun, moonlight glinting off its oily black barrel. The stench of death was thick. The air smelled of cordite, ripe and strong, blood and rot choking the room as everything grew dark around me. My panicked eyes leapt to the body at my feet, and I saw the spent shells scattered in a spreading pool of rich, red blood.

My blood.

There were two other men alive in this room. I'd met them each once before.

Five minutes ago I thought I had the story figured out. I knew these men both wanted me dead, knew their reasons for desiring my death were vastly different.

On one man's face burned a hatred so personal, just looking at him felt like the grim reaper had come for me. The other man held a cold, blank, businesslike stare, as though my life was merely a timecard waiting to be punched. And couldn't help but think…

Human emotion was formerly an obsession of mine.

Guilt.

Passion.

Love.

Courage.

Lust.

And fear.

In my twenty-four years of life, I'd experienced them time and time again.

Experienced everything but fear. And over the last three days, all the fear I owed the house had been paid back in spades.

Traversing the black and white of human emotion was my passion, finding the gray between was my calling. Seeking out man's limits and limitations and conveying them to the masses, it was my insulin. I moved to New York because I was given the chance to experience these emotions on a grander scale than I ever imagined. Here I had a chance to uncover the greatest stories never told.

The bullet in my chest sent cold sparks rippling down my spine. The right side of my body was numb, every breath felt like I was sipping mud through a crushed straw. When the slug entered me, tearing through my flesh, my body sent flying like a broken puppet, I expected to feel a blinding pain. White searing heat. Waves of agony that crashed against my body like vengeful surf. But the pain didn't come.

Instead I was left with the terrifying sensation that there was no sensation at all.

As I lay dying, I tried to imagine the precious moments I might lose if that black muzzle fired again, its orange flame illuminating the darkness, death traveling so fast my world would end before the realization even hit me.

Was I meant to have a family? A bigger apartment than the shitty, overpriced rental, now with crime-scene tape crossing the door? Was I meant to have children? A boy or a girl? Maybe both? Would I raise them in the city, where I so eagerly arrived just a few months ago?

Maybe I'd grow old and get sick, die of natural causes. Maybe I'd step out from the curb in front of Radio City Music Hall and get hit by a double-decker bus filled with tourists, digital cameras snapping pictures of my mangled body as a bicycle cop directed traffic around my chalk outline.

But no. Here I was, Henry Parker, twenty-four years old, weary beyond rational thought, a bullet mere inches from shattering a life that had seemingly just begun.

And if the truth dies with me tonight, I know many more will die as well, lives that could have been saved, if only…

I can't run. Running is all I've done the past seventy-two hours. And it all ends tonight.

My body shakes, every twitch involuntary. The man in black, his face etched in granite, grips the shotgun and says two words. And I know I'm about to die.

"For Anne."

I don't know Anne. But I'm about to die for her. And for the first time since it began three days ago, I have nowhere to run.

I want my life back. I want to find Amanda. Please, let it

end. I'm tired of running. Tired of knowing the truth and no
being able to tell it. Just give me the chance to tell the story
I promise it will be worth it.

1

One month ago

I watched my reflection in the doors as the elevator rose to the twelfth floor. My suit had been steamed, pressed and tailored. My tie, shoes and belt matched perfectly. I nervously eyed Wallace Langston, the older man standing next to me. My brown hair was neatly combed, the posture on my six-one frame ramrod straight. I'd bought a book on prepping for your first day at a new job. On the cover was an attractive twenty-something whose dentistry probably cost more than my college tuition.

Security downstairs had given me a temporary ID. Not yet a member of the fraternity, still a pledge who had to prove his worth.

"Make sure you have your picture taken before the week's up," the husky security guard with huge, red-rimmed glasses and a personality-enhancing cheek mole told me. "If you don't, I gotta run you through the system every day. And I have better things to do than run it through the system every goddamn day. You get me?"

I nodded, assured her I'd have the photo taken as soon as I got upstairs. And I meant it. I wanted my face on a *Gazette* ID as fast as the lab could develop it. I'd take it to Kinkos myself if they were backed up.

When the doors opened, Wallace led me across a foyer with beige carpeting, past a secretary's desk with the words *New York Gazette* in big, bold letters mounted on the wall. I showed her my temporary ID. She smiled with an open mouth and chewed her gum.

Wallace pressed his keycard against a reader and opened the glass doors. As soon as the silence was broken, I thought how strange it was that all my hopes and dreams were embedded in one beautiful noise.

To an outsider, the noise might seem incessant, cacophonous, but to me it was as calm and natural as an honest laugh. Hundreds of fingers were pounding away, the soothing rattle of popping keys and scribbling pencils drawing a smile across my lips. Dozens of eyes, all staring at lighted screens with type the size of microorganisms, reading faxes and e-mails sent from all over the world, faces contorted as though the telephone was a human they could emote to. Some people were yelling, some softly whispering. If I hadn't clenched my jaw trying to project confidence, it would have hit the floor like I'd stepped into a Bugs Bunny cartoon.

"This is the newsroom," Wallace said. "Your desk is over there." He pointed to the one unoccupied metal swivel chair among the sea of tattered felt, showing how every day I would be wading through greatness. Soon I'd be seated at that desk, computer on, phone in my hand, fingers rattling at the keyboard like Beethoven on Red Bull.

I was home.

If you're in media or entertainment, New York is your mecca. Athletes count the days until their debut at Madison Square Garden. For classical pianists, Carnegie Hall is their holy ground. Professional stripper—sorry, exotic dancer—yeah, New York is their Jerusalem, too.

It was no coincidence, then, that this was my holy land. The newsroom of the *New York Gazette*. Rockefeller Plaza, New York City. I'd come a long, long way to get here.

I briefly wondered what the hell a twenty-four-year-old with little more on his résumé than the *Bend Bulletin*, was doing here, but this was everything I'd worked for. What I was destined for. Wallace knew what I was capable of. Ever since my first page-one story in the *Bulletin*, the one that was syndicated in over fifty papers around the world, Wallace had been following me. When he heard I was accepted to Cornell's prestigious journalism program, he made the three-and-a-half-hour drive to take me out for lunch. And during my senior year, before I could even start to look for jobs, Wallace made me an offer to join the *Gazette* full-time.

The newsroom needs some new blood, he'd said. *Young, ambitious kid like you, show the skeptics out there that the next generation has its head on straight. There are other papers in this city, but if you want to chase down real stories instead of celebrities on vacation, you'll make the right choice. Make your mark, Henry. Make it with us. Plus, our first-year salary is five grand higher.*

I drank three bottles of champagne that night, and passed out in John Derringer's shower with a Bic mustache and sideburns.

I felt Wallace's hand against my suit jacket. I hoped he didn't press too hard—my threads probably cost less than Wallace's haircuts. Yet though Wallace was my professional benefactor, the top shelf on my wall of professional hero worship was permanently occupied. That man was seated just a few feet away. But as far as being indebted to a person, right after my mother giving birth, Wallace hiring me was a close second.

We snaked through the skewed chairs and cups of cold coffee, past writers who were too busy to tuck their chairs in. This was how they worked. I loved it. I knew not to interrupt a reporter on deadline, and sure as hell didn't expect them to move. I was here to purify the blood of the newsroom, not to disrupt its flow.

I recognized some of the writers. I'd read their work, knew to look for their bylines. It was scary to think of them as my new colleagues. Not to mention how seldom they appeared to shave or shower.

I wanted them to respect me, *needed* them to respect me. But for now I was just a mark. A newbie. The guy all eyes would be on to see if he produced.

And then I saw him. Jack O'Donnell. Then Wallace pulled me forward and I remembered to breathe.

As we walked by, I let my hand swipe O'Donnell's Oxford blue shirt sleeve. A silent brush with greatness. I couldn't have been any less subtle than if I'd taken out his latest book, asked for an autograph, then smacked him across the face with it. Talk to him later, I told myself. Follow him to the bathroom. To lunch. Offer to shine his shoes, raise his kids, whatever.

Man. Jack O'Donnell.

Five years ago, if someone had said I'd be working fifteen feet from Jack I'd have kicked his ass for mocking me. A few years ago, Jack O'Donnell was profiled in the *New Yorker*. I had a copy of the article at home. I taped one page above my desk, underlined one quote, the quote that threaded its way through every story I ever wrote.

News is the DNA of our society. It shapes how we think, how we act, how we feel. It dictates who we are and who we become. We are all beneficiaries—and by-products—of information.

Many people, myself included, credited the first injection of this strand of DNA to William Randolph Hearst. Hearst took over the *San Francisco Examiner* in 1887 at the tender age of twenty-three. The only guy who made *me* feel lazy.

Hearst was the first to truly sensationalize print media, splashing his newspapers with big, bold headlines and lavish illustrations. Conspiracy mongers blamed Hearst for inciting the Spanish-American war with his constant editorializing on the Spanish government's civil rights atrocities. As Hearst reportedly said to illustrator Frederic Remington, "You furnish the pictures and I'll furnish the war."

Since then, it almost seems like journalism has taken a step backward. The scandal at the *New York Times* proved that. Some people laughed it off as an isolated incident. Others who knew their stories couldn't hold up to scrutiny quietly updated their résumés. And I followed the whole thing shaking my head, trembling in anger, wanting to shake up the system.

And if Jack's quote was accurate—as I believed it to be—when that blood became tainted, it could spread disease through every capillary of society. Liars and fabricators and egos the size of Donald Trump were popping up like rats in the subway, from men and women who were supposed to report the stories, not *be* the stories.

Just last week, a junior reporter at the *Washington Post* came to work jacked on amphetamines, two pots of coffee, with a deadline in six hours for a thousand-word story he hadn't written a sentence for. He cranked out the piece then returned home, punched his girlfriend, and took a header out of their fifth-story walk-up. Just more fuel for the fire.

I wanted to be the antidote, to pick up Jack O'Donnell's mantle, polish the surface and carry it with pride. I wanted to extract the venom that had poisoned journalism, to bring some credibility back to the newsroom in the wake of these lies. Jack O'Donnell had given me an unbreakable faith in what a good reporter could accomplish. And now here I was, within coughing distance of the legend himself. Time to put up or shut up, Henry.

After bobbing and weaving through jackets slung over chair backs and pens rolling along the floor like plastic dust bunnies, we arrived at my desk, a smile on my face as if it were opening day at Yankee freakin' Stadium. My desk was right by the window, overlooking the veranda that in the winter became Woolman rink. Prime real estate, baby. I could watch the multilingual tourists snapping away at the beautiful golden sculptures and international flags, people gazing at the fair city as though they never knew such architecture and panache existed. Sunlight poured over my workstation, glowing off the fresh-scrubbed walls, and I couldn't help but feel blessed.

"Welcome to your new home," Wallace said. "Comes fully stocked with, well, everything you see here."

"Any assembly required?" I asked.

Wallace leaned in, whispered, "Some of the old-timers, I guess you can count myself in there, keep a flask in their desk." I didn't know what to say. Was he serious? Wallace laughed, clapped me on the back. "You'll fit in just fine."

He leaned over and tapped the shoulder of the woman whose workstation was adjacent to mine. She spun around, her swivel chair well-oiled and squeak-free, and glowered at me. She was slim, blond and quite attractive. Late thirties, early forties, with a "what the hell do you want?" look on her face so convincing I couldn't help but think she practiced it in the mirror. She wore a pink tank top and black Capri pants, her hair pulled back into a ponytail. No wedding ring. And from the looks of it, no bra. If Mya asked what my co-workers looked like, I'd have to lie.

"Paulina," Wallace said stepping aside, allowing her to view me in full. "Meet Henry Parker. This is his first day on the job."

Paulina shriveled her nose. "He's taking Phil's old desk."

Wallace coughed into his hands, slightly embarrassed. "Yes, he's taking Phil's old desk."

Paulina scanned me as if reading a computer printout. Finally she extended her hand. I shook it, her grip limp and apathetic.

"Welcome to the mad house, new guy," she said.

"Thanks. I'm excited to…"

"Tough luck taking Phil's old desk. You tell him what happened to Phil, Wally?"

Wallace sighed. "No, I haven't had the chance yet."

Paulina shrugged. "Bad karma, Henry." She looked at me inquisitively. "Henry. That's a strange name for such a young man. How'd you get saddled with that?"

"Saddled? I…"

"What, your parents didn't like you?" My eyes hardened. Paulina could tell she'd dug too far, and her face became all twinkles. "I'm just playing with you, Henry. You've got a fine name. I like things that are different." She looked up at Wallace, apparently satisfied with my answers. "This is the kid from Oregon, right?" She looked at me again. "Wallace told me you were, quote, a *prize find*. That right?"

I tried to ease the tension. "Yeah, Kmart was having a blue- light special on junior reporters. Wallace got me at twenty-five percent off." Paulina's eyebrow cocked and she shook her head. Wallace turned away in shame. I gave myself a mental slap.

Paulina said, "That's not funny, Henry. You haven't been here long enough to get away with making shitty jokes."

"Sorry. From now on, only funny jokes."

"Or no jokes," she said.

"Or no jokes."

She smiled, much warmer now.

"Good." Paulina held up a pen, its nub chewed to a quick. I noticed several pairs of shoes under her desk. Shiny red dress shoes, worn sneakers, broken-in Birkenstocks.

"If you're smart, you'll keep a few good pairs of shoes around the office," she said. "You never know what kind of story you'll have to chase at a moment's notice. You need to be prepared at all times." Wallace nodded. I made a mental note to bring in my old Reebok pumps.

"Best of luck to you, Henry," she added. "Wally's a good guy. Listen to what he says."

"Absolutely."

Paulina turned back to her computer and began typing away.

"She's a fine journalist," Wallace said softly. "Paulina, here, found our hero of the day six times this month alone."

"Seven times, Wally," Paulina said. "If you fuck that up on my performance review I'll call my lawyer."

"Hero of the day?" I asked.

"Every day has a hero," Wallace said. "It's our page-one feature, the main attraction, the story that sells papers. One day it could be the war, the next it's the elections, the next it could be a man who keeps a Bengal tiger in his apartment as a pet or a celebrity discovered screwing his babysitter."

Paulina added, "Every day has a different hero. Simply put, it's that day's biggest news. Every day needs a hero. Without one, there's no news. We don't sell papers, the *Gazette* brings in no money, we all get canned, you're back in bumblefuck Oregon before the month is out. Plus, whichever reporter reports the most heroes over the calendar year gets a pretty nice bonus. So get cracking. There are a lot of rocks out there to turn over."

Wallace said, "Don't worry. You'll have your chance. For now, though, try to observe how your new colleagues work. It'll be hard to gain your footing and find your voice. Just remember everyone here started out exactly where you are.

Mickey Mantle was an Oklahoma boy before he came to the Yankees. Pretty soon, you'll be finding your own heroes for us." He became serious, leaned in closer. "We're counting on you to find ones that matter."

Paulina chimed in, "Unlike Phil."

Wallace nodded resignedly. "Yes, unlike Phil."

I decided not to inquire about this Phil. It was newsroom gossip and I hadn't earned the right.

"Well, have a seat," Wallace said. "See how the old desk fits you."

Watching Wallace to see his reaction, I settled into my new chair. The seat wasn't meant for comfort, rather for a body that was constantly fidgeting, moving around. Designed more to keep you awake than keep you relaxed, and I was sure my spine would hate me for it.

"Well?"

"It's perfect," I said. Wallace laughed.

"Bullshit, but you'll get used to it. Let's have lunch Thursday. HR will send you info about benefits and 401k. Give me a holler if you need anything." Just then a voice rang through the office. Wallace's secretary.

"Mr. Langston! Rudy Giuliani on line two."

He muttered, "Shit, he's probably pissed about the piece on page five." Wallace gave me a quick pat on the back. "And Henry?"

"Yeah?"

"Don't wear a suit and tie again. You're a journalist, not a stockbroker. Lesson number one, your sources will want to feel you're on their level. Not a level above them."

As I settled in, Paulina turned to me, a cagey look on her face.

"And one more thing," she said.

"Yeah?"

"Remember one thing, and make sure you remember it good in every story you write. Ninety percent of this job is reporting good versus evil. And without evil, we'd be out of a job."

2

"Is a good space," Manuel Vega said, inserting a nicked key into the lock. He met some resistance, smiled as though it was intentional, then jarred the door open with his shoulder. After seeing—and rejecting—twelve apartments in barely a month, I prayed this one would fit in my budget. Not to mention fit me.

The stench of mildew immediately attacked my nose. Flecks of white paint spotted my coat where I brushed against the doorframe. A rasping noise, like the death throes of an elderly marsupial, emanated from the radiator.

Putting my hands in my pockets, I gritted my teeth. "And this is how much?"

"Nine seventy-five a month. Six months rent paid in advance."

It was manageable. Plus this was the only apartment I'd seen remotely in my price range and still on the island of Manhattan. Most were double the price and equal in size to my baby crib. Right now this apartment, nestled on the Northwest corner of 112th and Amsterdam, whose lone streetlamp seemed to share an electrical outlet with every hair dryer in the city, was the only one I could afford without turning tricks. And if I was going to work at a newspaper, a New York paper, I didn't want to live anywhere else but in the city. If I was in, I was in all the way.

The last three weeks I'd been squatting with my girlfriend, Mya Loverne, at her apartment. Every second spent together was filled with palpable tension. We counted the moments until I finally got my own place. Most couples couldn't wait to move in together. We couldn't wait to be apart. I had eight grand in my bank account, savings from summers spent writing for the *Bulletin* back in Bend and odd jobs I took to offset my financial aid at Cornell. It took all my strength to go home after each semester ended, but I couldn't afford summer housing. I could live for free in Oregon. I could live with being a ghost in my own home. That was the only way I could stay sane, slipping in and out without saying a word to the man on the couch, or the woman who couldn't do anything to stop him. Eight grand was all the money I had in the world. I sure as hell wasn't expecting any monthly stipend from the man I stopped calling Dad a long time ago.

Mya was a 2L at Columbia. Her father, David Loverne, was the former dean of Fordham law, had made a killing sitting on the Internet bubble and selling right before it burst. Needless to say, her ticket was punched a long time ago. The first two years of our relationship at Cornell were a dream, and just like a dream they ended before we knew what happened. The third brutal year felt like the cold sweat residue from a nightmare that never really ended. Mya was a year older. She moved to New York when she graduated. I stayed in the frigid barrens of Ithaca and watched our relationship freeze.

It was just a few months ago, this past February, that our relationship was dealt a mortal wound. Since then our pulse had slowed, the gangrene of that horrible night spreading and poisoning us. We hoped things would get better when I moved to the city, like a couple in a failing marriage that decides to have a child in the hopes that it will "bring them together."

I found Manuel Vega on Craigslist. The announcement was in tiny lettering, as though embarrassed to compete with the bigger notices with bolder font.

"So you've seen the apartment. Now you rent the apartment," Manuel said. He pulled a piece of paper and pen from his pocket, held them out to me.

"Whoa, hold on a second, chief. What if I don't want to rent it?"

"What's not to like?" he said, as though personally insulted. "You have four walls, ceiling. Refrigerator even."

How could I argue with that logic?

The price seemed reasonable, even for such a uniquely odorous pad, and I had no other options. Manuel even offered to cram himself into the fridge to prove its square footage. I politely declined.

After briefly investigating for vermin, and finding none visible, it was time to get down to business. I needed the space. Maybe space would bring Mya and I closer. And maybe there were gold bricks buried along with Jimmy Hoffa in the walls.

"So, six months rent, up front. That's a lot," I said, sighing. Unbelievable. I was on the verge of shelling out over two-thirds of my savings for an apartment that looked like the only witness to a teen horror flick.

"Up front. You pay down payment now."

"*If* I take the apartment," I said. Manuel shrugged and nibbled a fingernail.

"You don't take now, someone will tomorrow."

"That right?"

"I place the ad yesterday, amigo. You the third person to see it today. You write check today, maybe I tell the others to scram."

"Damn," I said, a little too audibly. "Is there a cable hookup? Is the apartment Internet-ready?"

"Of course," Manuel said, a toothy grin spreading over his face. "You have all the Internet you want."

"All right," I said through gritted teeth. "I'll take it."

I took the papers, read them over.

"You fill these out now, have a certified check for me tomorrow for the first six months. Six thousand, eight hundred seventy-five dollars."

"You mean five thousand, eight seventy-five."

"Yes, right. And you don't pass your credit check, I put ad back in the paper."

I nodded, followed Manuel downstairs to an office on the first floor. He took a seat behind a squat metal desk littered with papers and empty candy wrappers. I filled out the application, my chest swelling when I filled in the "employer" field. When I handed it back to Manuel, he turned the page around, pointing to that very space.

"This," he said. "Who you work for?"

"The *Gazette*," I said. "You know, the newspaper."

"You take pictures?"

"No, I'm a journalist. I'm going to be the next Bob Woodward." Manuel eyed me, eyed the form.

"Woodward?"

"You know, Bob Woodward? *All the President's Men?*"

"Yes, the building has very good woodwork," Manuel said, tapping the wall behind him.

No sense explaining. Soon enough, everyone would know. The newsroom at the *Gazette,* that was my Batcave. This apartment would be my Wayne Manor, the shell covering the hero underneath. Though I doubt Wayne Manor housed mice the size of beagles.

"You'll like it here," Manuel said. "Just like home."

Yeah, I thought. Just like home. Like the home I wished I'd had, instead of a clapboard box where the only noises were a faulty sink and the venom spewed from the man who called himself my father. Home. At last.

I went straight to Mya's once we finished the paperwork. Before moving out I wanted to celebrate, spend one last night in her bed. See if those familiar sparks could be ignited one last time. I called ahead to propose a celebratory dinner, but she replied with a curt, "Henry, I have finals next week. Dinner will take hours. If you want we can grab something from Subway."

I declined. I'd eat on the way.

She met me at the door wearing a red bathrobe, her blond hair stringy and wet. She smelled great, fresh. I wanted to gather her up, hold her like I held her when we first met. When nothing else mattered and real life seemed so far away. I placed my hand on her arm, rubbed it gently.

"Henry, I just moisturized."

"Sorry."

"It's okay, it's just…"

"I know." She sighed, smiled faintly.

I took off my sneakers and lay them outside her door. She sat down on the bed, her lips pursed, and crossed her arms over her chest.

"So tell me about the new place."

"Well, as far as I know nobody's ever died in it." Mya didn't seem to find me funny today.

"Come on, seriously. What's it like?"

"Well, it's in Harlem, 112th and Amsterdam. The building won't win any awards from *House and Garden,* but the utilities work, I have room to live, the door locks and that's all I need."

"Is it clean?"

"Well," I said, choosing my words carefully, "I'm not sure clean is the word. But it's livable."

"Do you expect me to come over?"

"I was hoping you would, being my girlfriend and all."

Mya stood up and walked to the open window. She stared out across the street. The night sky stared back, cold and uninviting, as she chewed her nails.

"I thought you stopped chewing," I said.

"I did for a while. Just came back."

I could feel the brutal static between us. Why were we together? Just because we'd weathered the storm and were content to hit dry land? Or did we really think we had a chance? That maybe we'd remember those first nights, when every moment was the only reality we needed?

Staring out the window, Mya said, "I hope your apartment works out for you."

"What's that supposed to mean?" And this, I knew, was the end.

"That's all I mean. I hope you like your apartment. Don't try to analyze so much."

"No, there was something in your voice. 'I hope you like your apartment, but…' I just want to know what the 'but' was."

Mya turned around. Her hair fell around her shoulders, her skin shined.

"I wonder sometimes, Henry."

"Wonder about what?"

She turned back around. "Nothing."

"Don't do that, that thing where you ask a question and then say it's nothing."

"It's not worth talking about."

"Yes it is. It always is." I walked over to her, put my hands on her shoulders. She shivered for a moment, then relaxed.

"Sometimes I think about things."

I knew where this was going and felt a knot rise in my stomach. My hands fell off her shoulders and I took a step back. Then her voice got soft, quiet. "Things have been different. I think you and I both know that."

"I know it has."

"It's been like this since…"

"Since that night."

"Yes," she said, sighing. "Since that night."

I sat down on the bed, wrapping my arms around a lace pillow. I looked up at Mya, could see the faint scar on her cheek. It was barely noticeable unless you knew it was there. I knew it was there.

"I just think about that night and wonder if it was an omen, you know. A sign." I nodded, knowing too well what she was saying.

"So what do you suggest we do? End it now, right when things get hard?"

"This isn't hard, Henry. Hard is what's going to happen when I graduate from law school and you're working night shifts at the *Gazette*. School and work take up time, but—" she paused "—they're really only stepping stones. I just don't want to slip up before I graduate. I don't want to lose focus."

"This isn't—we aren't—a stepping stone. If we work hard we'll find a way to make it work. I know things have happened." I hesitated, my voice catching, a lump rising in my throat. "Bad things. But we can get past them."

"Maybe," she said, uncertainty coloring her voice. "But when I'm a lawyer and you're a…journalist or whatever, we'll have even less time to talk things out. At some point we need to step back and really wonder if it's worth it." I knew I shouldn't ask. It wasn't the topic of discussion. But it burned me, and I had to.

"What do you mean a journalist or whatever?"

"I just mean when your career is on track. When you're doing whatever you want to do." I shook my head, tossed the pillow onto the headboard, where it lay at an awkward angle.

"You've never had faith in me."

"That's not true. I've always stood by you."

"That's easy to do in college, easy to say when you're not even there. But what about now? Would you stand by me now?"

Mya's face grew cold, all the life fell away from her. "Don't you ever *dare* talk to me about not being there."

Mya stepped forward and put her arms limply around my neck. She pressed her lips against mine, then removed them. I left moments later.

The next time I spoke to Mya, three men wanted me dead.

3

If I was less ambitious, none of it would have happened. But I was stubborn, impatient. I like to think all great minds are. But I never dreamed ambition might cost me my life.

My fourth day at the *Gazette,* Wallace offered up my first reporting assignment. It came at the perfect time, too. Mya and I hadn't seen each other in days. I was in desperate need of a pick-me-up. And an assignment did a better job of that than a six-pack.

When Wallace called me into his office, the possibilities flew through my head. I knew the stories Jack O'Donnell was reporting. Sometimes when I passed him on the way back from the Flavia machine, I'd look over his shoulder and see the words on his computer.

For the last six months, Jack had been working steadily on a story so big, the *Gazette* was planning to run a week-long feature upon completion. I knew what the story was. Everybody in the office did. Jack had risked every source and even his life to dig it up. Jack was investigating the brewing war between two organized crime families, a story that first took shape twenty years ago when O'Donnell wrote a book chronicling the resurrection of the New York *Cosa Nostra,* personified in the form of John Gotti. The book sold almost a million copies and was made into a film starring James Caan. When I was a teenager back in Bend, I bought a tattered copy at a used bookstore. It sat on my shelf like a trophy. And now, years later, in the wake of Gotti's death, O'Donnell was exploring the new wave of organized crime— the men fighting over the crumbs of an empire, trying to create their own dynasties in the wake of Gotti's Rome.

Due to public outcries, even the mayor had acknowledged it with hyperbolic platitudes, calling the unrest an ugly river of bile trying to flow up out of the sewers and erode the peace of the last decade. I wrote that quote down.

Following Gotti's death, mob activity in New York had all but vanished. But recently bodies had been turning up, each punched with more holes than a drug addict's memoir. Talking heads got worked up on Fox News, warning us that the sleeping giant had awakened. A man was shot dead outside a famous Chinese restaurant. A fire broke out at a tailor shop in the meatpacking district. There were murders so ghastly the papers tripped over themselves to see who could color it in the purplest prose.

The two men assumed to have picked up the slack were Jimmy "The Brute" Saviano and Michael DiForio. While I'm all in favor of creepy nicknames, "The Brute" seemed a little too overt for my tastes. Too in-your-face. Like a guy nicknaming himself "Killer" in the hopes it would make up for the fact that one of his testicles hadn't descended.

The Saviano family had started out small. More like a crew with a couple dozen loyal thugs who knew their chance to pocket six figures was only possible through the noble profession of cracking heads. Guys more loyal to the amenities of the lifestyle than to Puzo's *Omerta*.

But once Gotti's crew folded, his men searched for a new start, another strand of crooked DNA. Most shifted allegiances, promising obedience to Saviano.

The other family, the one that seemed to be instigating this 21st-century war, was led by Michael "Four Corners" DiForio, who'd inherited the mantel from his father, Michael, who'd inherited it from *his* father, Michael. Clearly originality wasn't what put the family on the map.

In my opinion, the nickname "Four Corners" was much more effective than "The Brute." It referred to DiForio's preferred disposal of his enemies, via the act of literally cutting him—and sometimes her—limb from limb and sending them to the four corners of the earth. Obviously nobody had informed DiForio that the earth was round. After all, it really is the thought that counts.

I knew I had to cut my teeth before getting close to stories of that caliber. Yet in the back of my mind I hoped Jack might have heard some good things, come across my clips from Bend. Maybe he'd need help with research, someone to make a few phone calls, pick up his dry cleaning, whatever.

Wallace called me into his office on a Thursday, and I was pretty sure he could see my heart beating through my shirt. The thin smile on his lips meant he surely had a hard-hitting story for me. Something from the top of the pile. Uncovering some deep-rooted corruption that helped the common good. I had no sense of entitlement and wasn't driven by ego or narcissism. I just wanted to be the best damn reporter the world had ever seen.

My chin dropped when he handed me a white index card. A name, telephone number and address were scribbled on the front. Without looking up Wallace said, "I need an obituary for tomorrow's paper. I want to see copy by five o'clock."

I stood there for a moment, scanning his face for sarcasm. Maybe Wallace had a sense of humor. Nope, nothing.

"All right," I said, pulling out a notepad and pen. "Who's…ahem…Arthur Shatzky?"

Wallace scratched his beard. "Arthur Shatzky is—was, I should say—a classics professor at Harvard until he retired about fifteen years ago." Wallace looked at me, tented his fingers and breathed into them. "Write something nice, Henry. Jack O'Donnell was an old student of Arthur's."

I wrote down the info, my heart slowly sinking. Not exactly front-page material.

"And Jack didn't want to take the story?" I asked. Wallace laughed.

"Jack O'Donnell is a national treasure. He writes what he wants, when he wants. He hasn't written an obituary in forty years." Wallace stood up, clamped his hand on my shoulder, squeezed it gently. "Everyone's got to start somewhere, Henry."

I offered a weak smile and returned to my desk, making an effort not to drag my heels. Paulina shot me a quick glance that didn't go unnoticed.

"So what'd Mayor McCheese want?" she asked.

I sat down, said, "Gave me an assignment."

Paulina's eyes perked up. I sensed jealousy and shook my

head. "Don't get worked up. He's got me writing an obituary for one of O'Donnell's old professors."

Paulina sniffed, then blew her nose into a tissue that she let float to the floor.

"Been here one week, you're already writing for O'Donnell." She seemed more than a little peeved. "You get a few stories syndicated out of some Podunk paper in Bumblefuck, Ohio…"

"Oregon."

"Same place. I've been syndicated around the *world*, Hank. And Jack's barely said two words to me in ten years." She took a sip of black coffee. "And now they have a flavor of the month who probably gets carded at the movie theater."

I held it in. Kill them with kindness. "It's just an obit. I'm not writing it 'for' Jack." Paulina let out an exasperated sigh, turned back to her computer. She spoke without bothering to look at me.

"They'll be saddling up and riding you, Henry. Oh, yes, they will. But that bronco's gonna buck like you wouldn't believe. So keep that golden-boy trophy nice and polished, otherwise they're gonna pawn it and sell it to the next kid who walks through the door and can spell right."

If I wanted to make a career out of writing obituaries, I was off to the right start. Two weeks later and the sting had been taken out of death. It refused to sink in any deeper than my computer screen. First Arthur Shatzky, then a painter named Isenstein I'd never heard of, then an electrician who'd fallen down an open elevator shaft.

There are four steps, Wallace told me, to writing a good

obituary. First, their name and occupation. Second, the cause of death—even if they fell down an elevator shaft, make it sound tragic. Third, use one quote each from a former business associate and family member. Fourth, list the immediate surviving family. If they have no family, list the companies and committees that will lose their leadership. A life boiled down to a template.

I respected the dead, but in my opinion hiring a promising young journalist and making him write obituaries was like hiring Cassandra and having her make coffee. Screw ego, it was the truth.

On my third Monday, Wallace came over to my desk, interrupting my obituary of an architect whose sleep apnea had finally caught up to him.

"Henry," he said, "I have a job for you."

"Yeah? Who died now?"

Wallace gave a hearty laugh. "No, nothing like that. You've seen Rockefeller Center, right?"

"I'm vaguely familiar with it. We do work here."

"So you've seen those spiders they have out front, right?"

I didn't like where this was going.

"Uh, yeah, I have." The arachnids Wallace was referring to weren't real spiders, but huge twenty-foot monstrosities some *artiste* had constructed out of what looked like metal from an old barbecue. The only people interested in this "art" were visor-wearing tourists and small children who climbed it like some playground out of Stephen King's nightmares.

"I want three hundred words on the artist and sculptures. Minimum of two quotes from bystanders. Copy for Wednesday's edition."

I heard Paulina stem a chuckle. Rather than leaving, Wallace stood there, waiting for a response.

"I think he's got a problem with the assignment, Wally." Paulina. Chiming in at the perfectly wrong time. Wallace raised his eyebrows. I avoided eye contact with both of them.

"Is that true?" he asked. I said nothing. Paulina was right. I hated writing obituaries and I sure as hell didn't want to interview bumpkins from North Dakota about metal insects the size of commercial airliners.

"You want me to be honest?" I asked.

"It would upset me if you weren't."

I looked at Paulina. She was pretending to type.

"I don't think I'm cut out for this piece. No offense to spiderphiles, but to be honest you're really not getting my best work right now. And I think you know that."

Wallace put his thumb to his lip, chewed at the nail.

"So you're saying you'd rather work on more interesting stories." I nodded. This was thin ice. I was asking the editor in chief of a major metropolitan newspaper for, essentially, more responsibility. After less than a month on the job. There were probably a thousand people who'd kill to write obituaries at the *Gazette,* but I'd worked damn hard to get here and screw it, I could do better.

Finally Wallace said, "I'm sorry, Henry, really, but this is all I have right now. Believe it or not, these stories are important. You want…" But all I heard was *blah blah blah,* trust me, *blah blah blah.*

"You see what I'm saying?" Wallace asked. I couldn't hear Paulina anymore; she was in full eavesdropping mode. I didn't move, didn't nod. I knew what he was saying, but in my heart I didn't believe it. Then right as I was about to open my mouth, an unexpected voice rang out through the newsroom.

"I have something Parker could help me with."

Three heads turned to stare. The voice belonged to Jack O'Donnell, and he was staring right at me. Thankfully I peed after lunch.

A slight laugh escaped Wallace's lips, and with a flamboyant wave of his hand he directed me toward the elder reporter.

Before I could even register that Jack O'Donnell—Jack *freakin'* O'Donnell—was talking to me, my legs had stumbled over to his desk. He was leaning back in his chair. A light gray beard coated his face. His desk was covered in Post-it notes and illegible scribblings. A photo of an attractive woman at least twenty years his junior.

"So you're looking for more action?" he said. My chin bobbed and I muttered a "Yes, sir" beneath my breath. I could smell tobacco and coffee coming off his breath in waves. I wondered if I could bottle it and bring it back to my desk.

O'Donnell slid his hand under a pile of paper and removed a notepad. He scanned it, then ripped off the top sheet and handed it to me.

"Not sure if you've heard, but I've been working on some copy about criminal rehabilitation." I nodded again, kept on nodding. "You all right, kid?" I nodded some more.

Jack sighed an *okay* under his breath. "What I'm doing is profiling a dozen ex-convicts, a kind of 'where are they now' of the scum of New York. Then hopefully tie that into a larger investigation about the criminal justice system and its effectiveness, or lack thereof." More nods. I was getting good at it.

When I asked, "What do you need me to do?" my voice cracked worse than a fifteen-year-old working at the drive-thru. I coughed into my fist. Repeated myself in a much deeper tone of voice.

O'Donnell tapped the paper, underlined the name, address and phone number on the page.

Luis Guzman. 105th and Broadway.

"I'll call Mr. Guzman to tell him an associate of mine will be coming by for an interview. I've already spoken to his parole board, and they've confirmed it with Luis. They put pressure on ex-cons to do this kind of thing, put a happy face on the correctional programs. Don't be afraid to lean on him if he's reluctant to talk. I simply don't have time to interview all twelve of these people by deadline. Give me the transcript and pick out some choice sound bites. Then give copies to me and Wallace. You get what I'm looking for, I'll give you an 'additional reporting by' credit on the byline."

"Wait, so I'll be working with you on this?"

"That's right."

"Directly with you on this?" O'Donnell laughed.

"What, you want me to push you around in a stroller? Guzman did a few years for armed robbery, but records show he's been a model citizen since parole. Half a dozen good, usable sound bites, and you're done. Think you can handle that?"

I nodded.

"I'm assuming that's a yes and you don't have Tourette's syndrome."

"Yes. To the first question."

Jack looked me over, clapped his hand on my elbow. Wallace liked the shoulder, O'Donnell the elbow. When I got my first page-one story, maybe I'd slap people on the neck to be original.

"You do this right, Henry, I might need some more additional reporting down the line."

This time nodding felt right.

4

I lay awake that night, my mind swimming with memories I wished could be forgotten, swept from my head and air-brushed from reality. But that would never happen. The dreams would haunt me for years. The helplessness I felt that night months ago would never leave. Yet any nightmare paled in comparison to the truth.

It was in February, about three months ago. I was finishing up a term paper, trying desperately to boost my GPA a final few tenths of a point to impress employers, as though a tenth of a point was the difference between the *New York Gazette* and the *Weekly World News*. Three sleepless nights in a row and my brain was stringing up yellow tape and preparing to go on strike. Mya and I had been fighting all week. Something about unreturned phone calls. She was in New York, I was in Ithaca. It doesn't matter now.

Hang-up after hang-up, words we'd eventually regret. At eleven forty-five with Flaubert in my mind and sleep deprivation settling in, Mya called me childish. To say it was the straw that broke the camel's back is like the skipper on the Titanic saying "Oops."

I called her a bitch. I told her I was sick of our relationship. I was tired of her crap. She said I was an asshole. I told her she was right. And then I hung up on her.

I memorized the last page of blurry text and let my eyelids mercifully close. And I wondered, not for the first time, if it was worth it.

Then at 2:36 a.m., a time now branded in my subconscious, my phone rang. I answered it. It was Mya. I said hello. I heard heavy breathing on the other end, the sound of shuffling. A whimper. She was crying. About us, surely. But there were no words. I hung up without thinking twice. And then I turned my phone off.

The strains of "Love Me Do" woke me at seven-thirty. I laughed at the irony of the lyrics. I barely remembered last night's phone calls.

After swigging from a cup of cold French vanilla, I turned on my phone. There were four messages waiting for me. I felt a twinge of guilt as I dialed voice mail. I remembered hanging up on Mya while she was crying. The girl who'd shared my bed so many nights, who'd asked me to make love to her, who held my hand when I needed it. How could I have been so cruel?

The first message froze my blood. It was filled with static, the words nearly unintelligible, but I could hear enough to make out a voice amidst the confusion.

It was Mya. And she was crying.

Please, Henry, oh, God, please pick up….

And then the call ended.

In a panic I listened to the next three messages. Two were from Mya's parents, the last one from my father.

I had to get to the hospital.

Suddenly I was hammering on door after door until my friend Kyle answered. In tears, I convinced him to lend me his car. I drove down to New York at 90 miles an hour, double-parking in front of Mount Sinai hospital. Kyle's car was towed as soon as I ran inside.

"Mya Loverne," I told the receptionist. She punched a few keys on an old computer, anger and frustration building in me with every wasted second. I sprinted to the elevator and rode to the sixth floor, my body shaking, tears pouring down my face. When I found room 612 I bowed my head and entered. I steeled myself for the worst, but the vision inside will remain carved in my brain until the day I die.

Mya's face was covered with sterile white bandages, her skin pale and dry. Her mother and father were kneeling beside her, holding her hands, stroking her arm. I could tell they'd been crying all night.

An IV was punched into Mya's forearm, drinking from a clear plastic tube. I could barely utter the words *I'm sorry* before I completely broke down.

Mya had been attacked. She'd called me for help at 2:36 a.m.

And I had hung up on her.

She'd gone to meet friends for a drink, her mother said, and was looking for a cab when a man grabbed her and shoved her into an alley. He stole her purse, slapped her across the face, then decided he wanted more. He ripped her skirt and punched her in the stomach. All the while her lover—*I love you, Mya*—was ignoring her. The man took his time, unzipped his pants. Mya managed to press the send button on her phone. It automatically redialed my number. That's when I hung up. A man was gripping his hard penis while my girlfriend lay bleeding. And I was trying to go back to sleep.

Thankfully Mya carried a can of pepper spray on her keychain. She managed to get a shot off before he could…

I love you, baby.

Oh, God.

Reeling from the spray, he punched her in the face and broke her cheekbone. Then he ran. And she lay there. Bruised. Broken. Crying in the street. And I slept peacefully.

The doctors reset the bone in surgery. The scarring would be faint. At least there was something to be thankful for.

Mrs. Loverne took my hand as I knelt down, my tears spilling onto the cold linoleum where they vanished into the tiles. She smiled weakly, told me it wasn't my fault. I couldn't bring myself to look at Mya's father, and from his silence I knew he didn't want me to.

Then Mya was awake. She was medicated, barely coherent.

"Baby," I said, my lower lip trembling against my teeth as my entire body shook and shook and *goddamn you fucking bastard, look what you've done.*

"I'm here, baby," I said.

"I called you, Henry," she whispered. "You weren't there."

I nodded, my eyes stinging. I took her hand, squeezed it, felt nothing in return.

Because I was there. She cried for help, cried for me, hoping I could do something.

Anything.

And I had hung up on her.

Mya had to wait for an ambulance, alone and beaten in an alley. I was asleep when her parents called me, when my own miserable father left a fuming message asking why Cindy Loverne woke him at four in the morning. I could have saved her. I could have helped her. But I didn't. I chose not to.

The next night I found myself on the very same street corner where Mya's blood had stained the concrete. A fifth of vodka was my only company as I waited in the dark, searching the face of every stranger for a hint of menace, an awkward glance, some sign that said *I did it, come get me, asshole, make me pay.*

Two days later I sat with Mya while, in a deadened, monotone voice, she helped a police sketch artist create a composite. She didn't remember much. The resulting picture could have been any man who ever lived. I called every hospital within fifty miles looking for a white man, between twenty-five and forty, five foot ten and six foot two, who might have checked in with a broken hand, with singed eyes from the pepper spray, even a dick caught in a zipper. All roads turned up empty, all channels parched dry.

Deep down I know if I'd been there, he wouldn't have lived. Mya would have been safe. But I hadn't been there. And that was something I had to live with.

That night made me question everything. I had turned my back on the girl I loved—*said I loved*—without a second thought. From that point on I knew I would always be there for her, for anyone, because I could never turn my back again. That, I told myself, was the only way I could live with it.

5

I grimaced at my latest statement, and wondered if the bank laughed every time they saw my meager deposits. I could pay half my current rent and find a studio twice as big in Brooklyn or Queens, but as long as I didn't mind crackers and an apple for lunch, the aura of living in the city made it all worthwhile.

Getting used to the random, spooky noises in my apartment was a different matter. Every night I heard the scratching of tiny claws, water dripping from invisible pipes. Work allowed me to focus. Thank God, because everything else would drive me insane.

I was living the life I'd wanted ever since the first time my father told me I wouldn't amount to shit. My mother standing in the kitchen, smiling like we'd just returned from a fishing trip with nothing but tall tales. Always smiling, like a wax sculpture with a pulse. Distant. Not uncaring, just removed from reality. Some people get lost in their demons. Me, I preferred to turn the tables, let anger fuel my fire. Every word my father said was gasoline. My own resolve was the match.

And now I had the chance to work with a legend. O'Donnell was well into his sixties, but his face was full and bright, cheeks lined and reddened by age. At the keyboard his fingers flew and his eyes were like gateways into another world. By trusting me with an assignment, Jack had given me a taste. And once I got a mouthful, it would bring out the best in me.

When I arrived at the *Gazette* I grabbed a tape recorder from the A/V room, went to my desk and dialed Luis Guzman.

A man with a thick Hispanic accent answered, "Hello?"

"Hi, Mr. Guzman, this is Henry Parker from the *New York Gazette*. Did Jack O'Donnell tell you I'd be calling?"

"*Sí.* He said a young associate would be getting in touch about an interview. Would that be you?"

"That's me. Do you mind if I stop by today for a few minutes? It won't take long." There was a pause, hesitation.

"I don't know, Mr. Henry. Today's not so good. I have an appointment later."

He was evading the conversation, just like Jack said.

"What time is your appointment?"

"My appointment? It's, ah, seven o'clock."

"So you won't mind if I come at six then."

I heard mumbling in the background. A woman's voice said something that sounded like *No*. Then Luis came back.

"Mr. Henry, I can talk for just a few minutes if you come over at six, but you can't stay for long. I cannot miss my appointment. Is for the doctor."

What kind of doctor had appointments at 7:00 p.m.?

"It shouldn't take long, Mr. Guzman. You'll have plenty of time." More mumbling. A door slammed.

"If that's so, then come on over. My wife and I will be here."

"Great, see you tonight."

At a quarter to six I left the office and flagged a cab. As the cabbie zigzagged through traffic, I read the quickie bio Jack had given me.

In 1997, Luis Guzman was arrested for armed robbery after he and an associate named Jose Ramirez Sanchez walked into a Chase branch and pulled two semi-automatics. Sanchez got nervous and shot a clerk. Both men were sent to Sing Sing. Guzman did three years. Ramirez Sanchez was stabbed to death in his cell.

When I arrived at 105th and Broadway, I rang the buzzer, wondering why Luis had seemed so agitated on the phone.

The building didn't look as if it met the hand of a janitor too often. The floors were dusty and smudged, and the lobby décor consisted of three flower pots whose flowers had come from needlepoint rather than seed. I checked the directory encased behind a dirty pane of glass. The superintendent, Grady Larkin, lived in apartment B1. I jotted this down, just in case.

I rode the elevator to the second floor. The hallway was wallpapered in light green with vertical beige stripes. The doors were gray and most of the hinges looked old and rusted. The light fixtures cast a soft glow. There was a strange quiet in the building like a hospital waiting room, awkward and forced. Walking down the hall I noticed that several doors lacked nameplates and the carpeting in front wasn't dirty like the others. The apartments were obviously vacant.

I found apartment 2C and knocked once. Before I had a chance to collect myself, the door opened.

"Mr. Parker?"

The man in front of me was big. That was my first thought. *Damn this guy is big.*

Biceps are a misleading measure of strength. You can tell a person's true power from their forearms. Luis's looked like half a dozen ropes had been wound together and then singed.

He was wearing a white undershirt, tucked into a pair of gray suit pants that looked freshly ironed. A small piece of tissue was matted to his chin where he'd cut himself shaving. A thin scar, barely noticeable, ran horizontal over one eyebrow. A prison wound sewed up poorly. His goatee was perfectly groomed, his cheeks smooth and moisturized. He smelled like a botanical garden had thrown up all over him. There was a kindness in Luis Guzman's eyes, as though all evil thoughts had been sucked completely dry. Then his eyes flickered, and Luis glanced into the hallway. For an instant, I swore there was fear in his eyes. I checked the hallway; it was empty.

A layer of flab had settled like frosting over his midsection. Luis Guzman had probably been well-toned in prison, where months were counted in dumbbell repetitions, but since being released Luis's appetite had returned.

I eyed his natty attire. Must be an expensive doctor to warrant this kind of dress code.

"Hi, I'm Henry. We spoke before."

"Yes, so nice to meet you, Mr. Henry." Suddenly Luis's hand was gripping mine. Tight. I gritted my teeth and hoped he'd let go before my knuckles were ground into paste. When he eased up I made sure my bones were intact. Luis's iron grip was effortless, easy as a pat on the back. "And that beautiful *mamacita* is my wife, Christine. Say hello, baby."

"Hello, baby," she said with a sly grin. Christine had honey-colored skin, with long brown hair and deep green eyes. She sat on an overstuffed couch, holding a pair of knitting needles, her hands working fervently on what looked like a baby's sweater.

"So, Henry," Luis said, a contemplative look on his face. "Señor O'Donnell tells me you have a few questions about my jail time." Luis smiled. His teeth were perfectly straight, a little too white for a man who had eaten nothing but prison food for three years. He must have had serious dental work.

"That's right," I said.

"Well, come on in, make yourself at home."

He draped a trunk of an arm around my neck and led me to a freshly varnished pine table. The apartment was tidy, well kept, but it had a sterile cleanliness. There were no photos, no trinkets, no paintings or posters anywhere in sight. Except for Christine's knitting, it felt more like a place of business than a residence.

Luis pulled a chair out for me as I set up the tape recorder. For a moment he seemed unnerved by its presence, then calmed a bit.

"So, Mr. Henry, what you want to talk about? Let us begin, I have only a few minutes before my appointment."

"No problem, thanks again for doing this."

"Oh," he said, laughing. "I don't do this for Jack. My parole officer tells me it keeps me respectable looking."

"Of course." I clicked the recorder on. "First off, would you state your name and date of birth for the record?"

Luis cleared his throat theatrically.

"My name is Luis Rodrigo Guzman. I was born on July 19th, 1970."

"Okay, Luis, what's your most vivid memory of your time in prison?"

Luis sat back in his chair, then suddenly stood up. He went into the kitchen, poured a glass of water. He offered it to me. I politely declined. Taking a long sip, he rested his elbows on the wood and spoke softly.

"That's a tough one. But I have to say the RTA."

"RTA?"

"Rehabilitation through the arts. It's a program they have up in Ossining. They bring in instructors to help us to get in touch with ourselves by being creative. Not in a dirty way."

I nodded. "Go on."

"Once a year the inmates, almost all guys in maximum security doing twenty-five-to-life, but a few others thrown into the mix, the RTA helps them put on a play. My first couple years I made fun of the guys who did it, said prison made them into fags."

I noticed Christine's gaze harden, her brow furrowed.

"So my last year inside I said what the heck, if I did it I might get points for good behavior. So I auditioned for a Kentucky Williams's play called *The Glass Menagerie*."

"Tennessee Williams," I corrected.

"What's that?"

"Nothing. Go on."

"So I audition for the part of the 'Gentleman Caller.' A week later the director, this big *cholo* named Willie who's in for double homicide, tells me I got the part. The gentleman's real name is Jim O'Connor, but the audience don't really know him by that. So we're rehearsing three hours a day, really busting our asses. At first things are kinda jokey, you know, 'cause we have guys playing the part of girls. So in the play, I'm supposed to go out with this girl, Laura—played by my buddy Ralph Francisco. Even go so far as to kiss Ralph on the cheek. Laura's a cripple who's been waiting her whole life for something good to happen, and spends her whole time polishing these little glass animals. So she finds out my character's engaged, and it just kills her. Soon as I walked off stage opening night, I busted out crying. We did four shows. The first three were for the general population, but the last one we did it in front of five hundred people from the outside. I'm talking wives, parents, children. It was the best night of my life."

Luis's voice was soft, but the emotion was unmistakable. He dabbed at his eyes, took another sip of water, then continued.

"Anyway, this play, it's about what you want and what you can't have. Made me think about why I was inside in the first place. I always wanted something I couldn't have, and then when I thought I had it, turns out it was nothing but bullshit. That's my most vivid memory, Mr. Henry."

For a half hour, Luis poured his heart out to me. He laughed, cried, but never asked me to turn the tape off. I learned how he met Christine at a Harlem poetry reading after his release. How she was knitting clothing for a child they hadn't yet conceived. That he worked as a security guard and pulled in $23,000 a year, before taxes. I learned that he was the happiest man in the world because he was supporting the woman he loved under a roof he paid for.

When he mentioned the apartment, a small chime went off in my head. Christine didn't work. The apartment, I estimated, based on my own home's pitiful dimensions, was a solid thousand square feet, at least. Not bad for a guy barely above the poverty line.

At six-thirty, Luis stood up and clicked off the tape recorder.

"And now I need to get ready for my appointment." I stood up as well. He took my hand and ground more metacarpals into powder.

"Thanks, Luis, it's been a pleasure."

"All mine, Mr. Henry. So, Henry wants to write newspaper stories. Well, I wish you all the best of luck."

As I left I watched Luis close the door, his eyes disappearing as the bolt latched home. Right before it closed I saw that fear again. And saw there was more to this man than even Jack O'Donnell knew.

Sitting in the back of a Greek diner, shoveling souvlaki into my mouth, I listened to the tape of Luis's interview. Tomorrow I'd transcribe it for Wallace and Jack, highlighting the best parts. This was my chance to prove I could hunt with the big boys. Jack O'Donnell, a living legend of the newsroom, would review my work for his story. There was some great stuff on the tape. But the more I listened, I couldn't help but listen to the trembling in Luis's voice. Something was eating at him while we talked.

The more Luis spoke in that quivering tone, I knew he was holding back. He'd lied about the doctor's appointment—hell, I'd done the same thing to get out of work before—but Luis was dressed to the hilt, like he was preparing for a wedding or a funeral. And I didn't buy for a second that he could afford that apartment on $23,000 a year. There was more to this man than what I'd caught on tape.

I needed to know more, to pry out of Luis Guzman what caused the fear behind that voice. But Jack had given me an agenda. I did what he asked, no more, no less, but it didn't sit right. There was more to Luis Guzman, and I had to find out what it was. Christine would be home. Maybe she could shine a light.

Stuffing the tape recorder and notebook into my backpack, I left the diner and headed back to the Guzmans' apartment. I walked into the building on the coattails of another tenant who was kind enough to hold the door. I only had one chance to do this right. Christine might be reluctant. I might have to lean on her, tell her it was in Luis's best interests. Hopefully she'd answer me honestly, thoughtfully, and then I could give Wallace and Jack the full picture.

The elevator opened and I strode toward apartment 2C with visions of a firm handshake from Jack O'Donnell and a pat on the back from Wallace Langston. I felt warm, invigorated, and knew I was doing my job right.

And that's when I heard the screams.

6

Christine. She was screaming.

And then there was silence.

I heard a deep, baritone voice from inside apartment 2C. The voice was enraged, but the words were muffled. Then another bloodcurdling shriek sent shivers through my body.

Christine.

I stood in front of the door, afraid to move.

Could Luis be beating her? No, it wasn't possible. I'd looked into his eyes, saw that violent life had left him long ago. But for most criminals, rehabilitation lasted only as long as chance. All it took was one moment to plunge back into the abyss.

Then I heard the voice again, more clearly. It wasn't Luis. No, Luis had a thick Hispanic accent. This was a different person altogether. The voice was crisp, American. No Latin inflections.

I heard a loud *thunk,* like the sound of wood hitting wood.

Oh, Jesus, oh, God…

My feet were rooted to the floor. This was none of my business. I wasn't supposed to be here. My job was done. I already had what Jack wanted. Nobody would think worse of me.

Then I heard it again. Another *thunk,* and a muted scream. Mya.

That night, sitting by her bedside at the hospital.

I called you. You weren't there.

I called you, Henry.

The screams grated my flesh. I heard Christine sobbing. Then the hush of another man's voice, pleading. This voice had a Hispanic accent.

Luis.

Then the American shouted, and I heard another *thunk.*

I was alone in the hall. Nobody else wanted any part of this. An evil quiet had set in, because nobody dared to stop it.

And then there was silence.

Maybe it was over. Maybe I could go back to the comfort of my bed, sleep off the terrible night and prepare to turn in my interview. Luis and Christine would be fine. Surely it was all a misunderstanding. Deep down I knew I would have helped if they needed it.

I called you, Henry.

Then Christine screamed again, and my thoughts were shattered. And in that moment, I knew what I had to do.

I set my backpack down. I took a deep breath. Then I knocked on the door.

"Luis!" I shouted. "Christine? Is everything okay?"

My words were met with silence. Then the sound of footsteps. The American was talking, his voice soft but firm. I could turn back, recede into the shadows, and whoever was inside wouldn't know the difference.

Or I could be strong. Like I should have been for Mya.

And so my feet remained bolted to the floor as the door swung open. And in that moment, my life changed forever.

Thankfully I'd gone to the bathroom before leaving the restaurant, because when the door swung open there was a gun aimed right at my head.

"Who the fuck are you?" the man said, his narrow eyes surprised, taking me in.

He stood a hair over six foot two and outweighed me by a good fifty pounds. It wasn't all good weight. His midsection was soggy, lines creasing his face like he'd fallen asleep on chicken wire. His hands were rough, calloused. Two of his knuckles were bleeding. He looked like he hadn't slept in days.

I gulped down saliva, coughed on it, and forced myself to breathe.

"I said who the fuck are you?" His spittle pecked my cheek.

"Leave him alone!"

It was Christine, wailing from inside the apartment. I looked past the man with the gun and saw Luis sitting in a chair. His arms and legs were handcuffed and bloody. His suit was spattered with red, his tie unraveled. His face was shellacked with cuts and bruises. Blood leaked from several openings. Then I saw Christine. She was tied to the radiator.

"What…" was the only word I could muster. The man with the gun leaned in, peered at me.

"You got some business, kid?" I waggled my head, neither a nod nor a shake. "Then get the fuck out of here."

He pushed the door closed, turned back to his captives. Without thinking, I blocked the door with my foot.

The man waited a moment, cocked his ear, then turned back to me. His gun was still raised, his finger gently tapping the muzzle. In Bend I wrote about guns and violence many times. I recognized his weapon as an old-school .38 caliber. A six-shooter.

I called you, Henry.

"Let them go," I said as defiantly as possible. It must have come off well, because he lowered the gun a fraction of an inch. Christine was working fervently at her bonds, rubbing them back and forth along the edge of the radiator. Our eyes connected for a moment, then I looked away. I didn't want to clue him in.

"Kid's got balls, Luis." He let out a small laugh. "You know him?"

Luis's head bobbed and he mouthed something unintelligible. His cheeks were swollen, his head lolling like a screw unfastened from its mooring.

Seeing Luis bleeding, helpless, watching Christine flail at her bonds, seeing this man, this animal, I felt a fire burning in my stomach. After Mya was attacked, all I wanted was a venue to prove myself, some way to prove I'd never turn my back again. Drunken bar fights and remote staredowns meant nothing. And so here it was. Standing directly in front of me. Wearing a trenchcoat and holding a loaded pistol.

Stepping into the apartment, I gritted my teeth and said, "I'll call the cops. Right now." I took out my cell phone and opened it.

The man stepped back like I'd slapped him. He was trying to gauge my resolve, to see if I truly had the balls to turn my back and make the call. I looked into his eyes for a moment, then started dialing.

"Okay, kid," he said, amused. To my surprise he held up his hands, gun included, like a kid being held up in a game of cops and robbers.

"Don't go doing anything stupid, kid. I'll leave peacefully."

"My name's Henry," I said, jaw muscles clenched.

"Henry," he said with mock admiration, adding a faint laugh. "That's an old man's name."

I said nothing.

"So, Henry, now that you've terrified the bad guy I guess I'll go crawl into a hole and cry myself to sleep." He turned to face Luis and Christine. Christine stopped working her bonds and looked up at him.

"Just leave us alone!" she cried. Luis struggled lamely against his ropes, but the man had no energy left.

"In time, hon. In time."

"I don't see you leaving," I said.

"Don't have a fucking heart attack, I'll leave." Then he whipped the gun around and pointed it at Luis's head. "But not until I get what I came here for."

Christine spoke softly, her will crumbling. "I told you. We don't have it."

"Bullshit!" he roared. "If you don't tell me where it is in five seconds…" He looked back at me and smiled. "And if you do tell me, I'll leave. Just like I promised Henry."

Saliva spilled down Christine's lips as she spoke. "Please, I swear, we don't have it."

"One."

Christine's body tensed, a helpless wail escaping her lips.

"I'm calling the cops," I said. "Right now."

"Go ahead," he said. "This'll be done in four seconds anyway. You think they'll be here in four seconds?" Then he added, "Two."

"Please don't do this," Christine sobbed. "Please just listen...."

"Three."

Christine was frantically working her bonds, rubbing them harder and harder against the radiator. The ropes were fraying. She was almost free.

Then the man stepped forward and whipped his pistol against Luis's head. His neck snapped back and blood poured from his temple.

"Jesus Christ!" Christine screamed. "Oh, Jesus, oh, Jesus." She rocked back and forth, reaching for her wounded husband. "You leave him alone!"

"Four."

There was no thought process, no weighing of right and wrong. As soon as the man counted four, I drove my shoulder into the small of his back, sending him sprawling forward. The gun flew from his grip and landed by Luis's feet. I kept driving until his head collided with the wall, a whoosh of air escaping his lungs. The man groaned. He swung an elbow that glanced off the top of my head, rattling me.

Luis was babbling, bubbles spraying red foam over his lips. Christine was working her ropes like a handsaw.

I dove for the pistol, my stomach smacking on the hardwood floor. Then it was in my hand, my finger sliding through the trigger guard, when I felt a sharp pain as he kicked me in the ribs. I doubled over, fire burning through my side. The gun fell from my grasp.

I looked up at Luis, his eyelids fluttering, barely coherent. Suddenly, I was fighting for three lives.

As I struggled to get to my feet, the heel of his palm struck me in the solar plexus. The wind knocked out of me, I dropped to a knee and gasped. The man touched a finger to his nose, saw it come away red with his blood.

"You little fuck," he said. "You had the chance to mind your fucking business. I didn't want to kill you, you brought this shit on yourself."

He bent down and reached for the gun. I leapt up, stomped on his wrist with my heel. A sharp crack reported as the bone snapped. He cried out in pain and stumbled back, cradling his maimed appendage.

Again I went for the gun, but he kicked it away, skittering it between my legs until it came to rest by the door. For a second neither of us moved. I was closer to the door.

I went for the gun but a massive shoulder slammed me against the door. The hinges groaned, and the door buckled. I grabbed a fistful of hair, pulled hard. The man screamed.

He stepped back, wrenching himself free. Again I went for the gun, and again was driven into the door, my head slamming viciously against the metal. This time, the hinges gave way.

The door collapsed outward, and we toppled into the hallway. His two hundred and fifty pounds fell on top of me like a mushy sandbag. I felt a sharp pain in my ribs where he'd kicked me, every breath like a knife in my lungs. I was dizzy from the blow to the head.

The man rolled onto his back as I pushed myself up. When I got to my feet, I noticed that everything was silent.

Then I saw the gun pointed at my head.

"Stupid fuck," the man said. His right arm was folded across his chest, sling-style, while his left was fingering the trigger.

I stopped breathing. My mouth went dry. I could be dead in less time than it took for my heart to beat.

"Wait," I said.

"I didn't come here for you," he said, breathing slowly. I could tell from his eyes that he'd killed before. There was no fear, no hesitation. If he wanted me dead, I was dead. There was no moral ambiguity to it.

I gritted my teeth. Tried to think of something to say. Something that might dissuade him. Something poignant that might reach him.

Instead, the only word I could muster was "Don't."

He smiled. Blood stained his teeth.

I closed my eyes, thought of that night. Mya.

There was a yelp, and the thunder of a gunshot. I expected a ripping pain to tear through me, but when I opened my eyes Christine had managed to free herself from her bonds and was hanging on the man's back, her fingers clawing at his face. The gun had discharged into the ceiling, pieces of plaster sprinkling down like snow.

As she pounded his head with her fists, red nail polish chipped and flaking, purplish ligature marks on her wrists, the man struggled to free himself. He leaned over and rammed Christine into the wall, back first. She whimpered and crumpled to the ground.

Again he aimed the gun at me and I charged. We both fell, and my hand closed around the gun's muzzle. My heart felt ready to burst as I climbed on top of him, my knees straddling his chest, trying to pry the gun away. He was stronger. The gun was swinging back toward me.

To beat him, I needed leverage. To take him off guard.

I relaxed my grip, and as the gun lined up with my chest, I rolled over, heard a small gasp as he lost balance. I didn't know where the gun was pointed, but suddenly I had a better grip. My fingers searched frantically for the trigger guard.

Just as my finger entered the smooth, circular hole, I felt his meaty finger join mine. On the trigger. Then his finger tightened its grip.

There was a tremendous explosion, and a flash of light burned my eyes. The gun propelled itself into my shoulder, knocking me backward. I got to my knees, surprised to find the gun in my hand. Finally I had control. I looked for my target.

He was lying on his side. And he wasn't moving.

A faint curl of smoke wafted from a tattered hole in his raincoat. A pool of blood began to spread out on the floor beneath him.

"Oh fuck," I said. "Oh fuck, oh fuck, oh fuck."

The gun clattered to the floor. I looked around the hallway, saw faces peeking out of doorways. I locked eyes with an elderly woman, who quickly shut her door when she saw the carnage. Christine picked herself up, wincing as she touched the back of her head. She limped over and looked at the man. Terror was etched on her face, as though she were being lined up before a firing squad.

"*Dios mío,*" she said softly, crossing herself. "He can't be…we didn't have it…"

"Is he…" I whispered. Christine said nothing.

I knelt down, my legs like cooked pasta. The man's eyes were wide open, his mouth frozen in an *O* shape. A thick slab of tongue lolled in his mouth as I fumbled for his wrist, pressed my fingers against his veins. Nothing. I felt my wrist, just to make sure I was holding the right place, and felt blood coursing through my body faster than I thought possible. Gingerly stepping over the spreading pool of blood, I pressed my fingers against his fleshy, unshaven neck. Nothing.

"Oh…my God," I said, standing up, stumbling backward.

"Is he…" Christine said, nodding at the body.

"I think so."

"Oh, sweet Jesus," she whimpered. "God, no." She should have felt safe now that he was dead, but the look of terror in Christine's eyes was even greater than before.

Luis was still slumped in his chair. Christine stumbled past me into the kitchen, returning with a carving knife. She began slicing through her husband's bonds. I caught my breath, dizziness spreading over me, the lifeless eyes of a corpse boring a hole in my back.

"What are you doing?" Christine yelled.

I said, "Shouldn't we…"

Sirens blared in the distance. My blood ran cold.

"Go!" she cried, tearing rope away from Luis's wrists. "Get out of here!"

I stumbled back, picked up my backpack and charged into the stairwell. I took three steps at a time, pain shooting through my body with every breath.

I burst into the warm night. Nothing made sense. I broke

into a full sprint, headed south down Broadway and didn't stop until my lungs were on the verge of bursting.

I ducked into an alleyway, saw a homeless man sleeping under a cardboard box. My head throbbed. I couldn't run anymore. I sat down, and pulled my legs up to my knees. I heard faraway sirens, and the blackness overcame me.

7

Joe Mauser couldn't sleep. His torso was warm under the covers. His legs were naked, cold. He eyed the finger of scotch on his nightstand. He left one there every night. Sometimes it worked. Often it didn't. And often he found himself going for a refill.

Sitting up, Mauser squeezed the sleep from his eyes and looked at the clock—4:27 a.m. He flicked on the antique lamp that was a gift from Linda and John for his forty-fifth birthday. It was a reading lamp, they said. Only thing he read by that light was the proof number on the bottle. The only other item on the nightstand was his Glock 40.

Joe lifted the scotch and took a small sip. He felt the liquid burn under his tongue, considered turning on the television. Sometimes watching QVC put him to sleep. Maybe scan the movie channels. No, that wouldn't work. Only things on this late were titty flicks and infomercials.

His legs were sore. Early morning runs. He'd lost twenty pounds over the last six months, working off a few years of complacency. Down to two-ten. Not terrible, but on a five-eleven frame dropping another twenty would do him good.

Early morning runs were easy when you didn't sleep much to begin with.

He switched off the lamp and closed his eyes, hoping sleep might meet him halfway. Just as he felt darkness descending, the shrill ring of the telephone shattered any chance he had of slumber.

Cursing, Mauser turned the light back on and picked up the receiver.

"Yeah?" he said.

"Joe? I wake you?" Mauser recognized the voice of Louis Carruthers, his old friend and the NYPD Chief of Department. Carruthers held the job since '02, the fourth Chief of Department since 1984, back when it was referred to as Chief of Police.

"No, you asshole, I just got home from the bowling alley."

Joe and Louis had been partners for three years in the NYPD. Then Mauser left to join the Feds down in Quantico, while Louis continued up the ladder. They met for drinks once or twice a year, but those occasions were always planned out weeks in advance. Louis calling this late, Joe didn't think it involved sitting on bar stools and shoveling snack mix down their throats.

"I'm uptown at 105th and Broadway," Louis said. "We've got two assault victims on route to Columbia Presbyterian. There's one more, and he's…he's not making it. Joe, you need to come up here."

"So you got a stiff up in Harlem," Mauser said. "And you call me at the butt crack of daylight for what?"

He heard Louis take a breath. He was struggling to get it out. "The victim, he took a .38 in the chest. He was gone when we got here. We don't want to move him until you have a chance to come up here, Joe."

"Is it the Pope?" Mauser asked. "'Cause if it isn't the Pope or the President or someone really important, I'm going back to bed." He heard deep breathing on the other end. Muffled speaking. Louis trying to cover up the phone.

"You should come down here," his friend said. "105th and Broadway. Follow the squad cars. It's apartment 2C."

"Is there a reason I should give up a good night's sleep to check out a random vic that's not even under my jurisdiction?" He paused a moment. His heart began to beat faster. "Lou, is this call personal or professional? Should you be calling the bureau?"

"I thought you should hear it from me before I do. Joe," he said, his sigh audible over the phone, "we have an ID on the victim."

"Who is it?"

"Please, Joe. I don't want to tell you over the phone." Mauser felt a flash of pain shoot through his stomach. It wasn't the scotch. Something in Louis's voice.

"Lou, you're scaring me, buddy. What's going on?"

"Just come down here." Mauser swore he heard the man choke back a sob. "A lot of the guys haven't seen you in a while. They'll be glad to know you're coming." Then he hung up.

Three minutes later Joe Mauser had on his leather jacket, a pair of beaten khakis, house keys snuggled in his pocket. Gun strapped to his ankle holster.

Stepping into the warm May night, Federal Agent Joseph Mauser cinched up his coat and walked to his car. He turned on the radio. Listened to two talking heads argue over whose fault it was that the Yankees lost. He drove uptown, a gnawing feeling in his gut that the body he was about to see would mean many more sleepless nights lay ahead.

8

You wake up in a sun-dappled alley. Your ribs hurt. There's a knot on the back of your head that throbs nonstop. You feel dizzy. A man wearing a cardboard box for a blanket blinks at you, his eyes adjusting to the sight of this stranger sharing his alley. His beard is frazzled and dirty. His hands look like he's worked in a coal mine for twenty years. You think it has to be a dream. There's no rational explanation. You have a bed. You live in an apartment paid for with your money. You have direct deposit. You have a MetroCard. You may or may not be in a relationship. You have a college degree. You have parents you fled three thousand miles to get away from.

You stand up. There'll be milk in the fridge, day-old coffee in the pot. It must be a dream. Where will the day take you?

Then you remember the corpse lying at your feet. The pool of blood you avoided stepping in. The kickback as the gun fired into the man who came this close to killing you and two other people.

And then you know it wasn't a dream.

The homeless man stared at me as I wiped the dirt from

my hands on a discarded newspaper. He held a crinkled coffee cup that held a nickel and three pennies.

"You new here?" he asked. Four rotted teeth jutted out from his black gums. "If you're new here, you gotta pay a toll. I'm the tollbooth collector. Have been for two years. Last guy died. Tragedy. You can't live on this block unless you pay the toll."

I absently went for my wallet, then thought better and headed toward the street. A voice behind me yelled, "Hey, you didn't pay the toll!"

Morning had broken. The sun was hot and bright. A beautiful early summer day. I checked my watch. It was eight fifty-three. I was due at work in seven minutes.

Every breath brought pain. I stopped in front of a building with a waist-high brick outcropping. Lifting up my shirt, I saw a mild discoloration under my armpit. Nothing too bad, nothing broken. Just black and blue where I'd been savagely kicked.

As I stood there, regaining my composure, winking away the dizziness, visions of last night came to me like a swarm of locusts. A man was dead because of me. Whether I'd pulled the trigger or not—it was all so fast, but I remember his finger in the trigger guard—I was responsible for another man's death. It hadn't sunk in yet, merely hovering around the fringes of my subconscious.

I tried to help Luis and Christine. And now a man was dead. In my heart, I knew I wasn't to blame. He could have killed them both. He would have killed me.

My first stop had to be the police. They'd understand the situation, know the Guzmans were in mortal danger and I acted in their defense. He had the gun. He attacked two people. If I hadn't been there, he might have killed them. I was a hero. My picture would be in the papers, bold-faced copy that could never be erased.

Pride swelled in my chest as I stumbled down the street. I checked my backpack, took out my cell phone. It wouldn't turn on. It must have broken during the fight. I looked for a pay phone to call 911. Then I began to notice something odd.

Pedestrians were staring at me, vague recognition on their faces, mouths pursed like they were trying to pick someone out of a lineup. An unsettling feeling crept over me, but I dismissed it, assuming last night had shocked my senses into overdrive.

But still…

The body kept popping up in my head like a jack-in-the-box with a busted spring.

A man was dead because of me, and nothing else mattered. Two people were hurt, severely perhaps, hopefully being tended to. But there was still an 800-pound elephant in the room. What was that man looking for last night?

He was at their apartment with a purpose. Christine seemed to know what he was talking about, but denied having anything in their possession. Luis was incoherent. But still, she knew…

Perhaps there was a story in all of this. Maybe I could talk to the Guzmans, find the answers to the questions I'd gone back for last night. Approach Wallace with the story of a lifetime. A story few reporters my age would have the guts to go after. It could make my name. Maybe there really was a silver lining in all of this.

But first I needed to call the cops. The truth had to be told.

I found a pay phone on the corner of 89th and Broadway next to an aromatic delicatessen, and stepped into the booth. A couple walking a tiny dachshund eyed me suspiciously. The man, wearing a visor and Black Dog shirt, put his arm around the girl and hurriedly ushered her away, dragging the yelping dog behind him.

Something was wrong. New Yorkers weren't shocked that easily. It's not like I was covered in blood, or tarred and feathered. If anything I was a bit disheveled, but nothing to elicit that kind of reaction. Something spooked them, but I couldn't figure out what. My heart began to beat faster.

The deli on the corner reminded me of how hungry I was. Maybe I'd get a bagel after setting the record straight. Food would feel good. Something to fill the empty feeling in my gut.

Looking through the deli's window, I saw an Arab man with a thick mustache and thinning hair talking on the phone. The hole in my stomach seemed to spill out burning acid when I noticed that he was staring at me as he spoke, his mouth moving in exaggerated, cartoonish gestures. Flamboyant nods. He mouthed the word "yes" several times. His eyes were deadlocked with mine.

I was going crazy. That was the only explanation. After last night, paranoia was a normal response. My senses were overloaded, jumping at the slightest buzz. There was nothing to be worried about.

Deep breaths, Henry. Everything would be fine.

I picked up the phone and dialed 911. One ring and a woman's voice picked up.

"9-1-1 emergency response. How can I help you?"

"I…"

Then I saw it.

My mouth fell open. My saliva dried up. I forgot to breathe.

This wasn't possible.

Oh, my God. Please, no.

No.

Slowly I sank to my knees, tendons and muscles melting. My breath came in short bursts. My head felt light, as though a helium tank had been emptied into my skull.

I heard a tinny voice from the receiver.

"Hello? Sir? Hello?"

The phone fell from my hand and swung aimlessly.

The man in the deli had hung up the phone, but his eyes were still fixed on me.

Run.

A woman walked by, chirping on her cell phone. Her eyes found mine, a flicker of recognition in them, then she picked up her pace and rounded the corner. Fear. There was fear in her eyes.

"I'll call you back," I heard her say.

Run.

The man in the deli had come outside. He was holding a baseball bat. Three younger Arab men were standing in front of the store with their sleeves rolled up. They were all staring at me.

Run.

My eyes reverted back to what had caught my attention in the first place.

A newspaper vending machine sitting on the corner. Fifty cents on a weekday. I had no change on me.

I walked over to the newspaper rack in front of the deli. The Arab men watched every step I took.

"Just leave," one of them said.

"Take what you want and go," said another. The owner gripped his bat tighter.

I grabbed a newspaper from the top of the pile.

This was impossible. It couldn't be happening. Looking at the front page, I felt like someone had scooped out my insides and replaced them with hot lead.

Staring back at me was my face. I recognized the picture from my driver's license.

Next to my smiling, youthful grin were two words, printed in big, black, bold letters.

Cop Killer.

9

Blanket walked through the wrought-iron gate, said hello to the ugly guy whose name he could never remember—fucker always wore a beret like he was Irish or something—and heaved open the unmarked wooden door. He ducked down so as to not smack his head—the last lump was subsiding, thank you very much—and was met by Charlie, the odor of heavy designer impostor cologne pouring off him in waves.

"Charlie."

"Blanket." The two men shook hands and exchanged a brief and solemn embrace.

"I assume Mike's seen the paper."

"Never seen the guy read the *New York Times* before. Think he spent twenty bucks buying every paper he could. Spilled his Folgers all over the carpet, first time he seen it."

Blanket took a cigarette from his pocket, lit it. "I'm guessing that saying he's pissed is a mighty understatement."

"Pissed was two hours ago. Wait'll you see what he is now."

Blanket sighed as they went down the metal steps, his

boots echoing in the narrow stairwell. Blanket knew full well that Charlie resented him, resented that he'd climbed the ladder so quickly. More responsibility equaled more cash. Charlie had been dealt the short end of the stick, a measly nine-hundred-square-foot apartment in Soho, none of the high-heeled women who circled Blanket's apartment like vultures after a massacre. Cash was a sign of importance, a symbol of respect. Blanket started out as a page, running picayune errands for greasy tips. He spent too much money on spiffy ties from Barney's, showing off to his friends who'd been weaned on *Goodfellas*. The salespeople had been reluctant to wait on such a young kid. Until he whipped out that money clip crammed with fifties. Blanket still had most of those ties, frayed and worn, now ugly as sin. They were a reminder of just how far he'd come.

When they reached the bottom of the stairwell, Charlie knocked four times, then twice, then three more, and a large door swung inward. A beefy man in a turtleneck—ironic since Blanket didn't think he had a neck—nodded slightly and ushered them along.

The corridor was sparsely lit, a filmy yellow sputtering from a few low-wattage bulbs. Blanket walked behind Charlie, Charlie looking over his shoulder every few feet as though worried Blanket might fall behind.

"What's your man say about the Parker kid?" Charlie asked.

"I think I'll save that for Mike," Blanket said irritably.

The loathing wafted off Charlie, almost as strong as his cologne, and just as repugnant.

"The fuck. You can tell him but you can't tell me?"

"Exactly."

"Asshole," Charlie whispered.

Blanket grabbed Charlie by the shoulder and spun him around. Charlie resisted, and Blanket clamped down hard on the man's neck, squeezing his fingers around his collarbone until the man's knees buckled.

"Get the fuck off me!" Charlie yelped, his fingers struggling to break Blanket's grip. Blanket eyed him sadly, like a dog who didn't know any better than to pee on the rug. Charlie looked like he'd spent about thirty seconds in the gym his whole life. Probably couldn't bench-press his dick. Blanket could probably do biceps curls with the pudgy little dumpling.

"You know this, but I'm gonna remind you again since your thick fucking head seems to have missed the memo." Blanket relaxed his grip on Charlie's shoulder. "I don't say shit to you. I decide what you need to know. You make one more comment like that, I'll be scraping your balls off the bottom of my Cole Haans." Charlie groaned. "You get me?"

"I got you. Now let go."

Blanket let Charlie hit the floor. He got up, wiped his knees, rubbed his shoulder.

"You have anger issues, man. You gotta control that…."

"Are you saying something?"

"No, Blanket. I ain't saying nothing."

Blanket smiled, ran his fingers along the dusty brick corridor. He could hear voices from the other end, a mixture of panic and calm. Blanket took a deep breath, swallowed the phlegm in his throat. He knew he was about to walk into a buzzsaw. Meetings like this didn't happen often. Seeing Michael DiForio in such spur-of-the-moment circumstances was like spotting one of those rare white elks or Haley's comet or some shit.

They came to a metal door, green with rust, a grated slat on top. Blanket knocked. The slat opened. A pair of eyes popped into view.

"Hey, Blanket. Charlie. Mike's waiting for you."

"I was afraid you'd say that. How bad is it?"

"He forgot to eat breakfast this morning."

"Fuck me, that's bad."

The man gave a nervous laugh, threw back a dead bolt and opened the door.

A large mahogany conference table was set up in the middle of the nondescript gray room. It smelled of ammonia and dust. The table looked out of place, like a de Kooning on the wall of a prison cell. Water pitchers lined the table. There was no alcohol. This wasn't a social gathering. A dozen men were seated, and appeared to be in various states of unease. All older men, gray hair slicked back and oily. Dull ties. Questioning eyes. Waiting for answers. One man sat at the head of the table, facing the doorway. His green eyes were serrated blades.

"Blanket," Michael DiForio said.

"Boss."

Blanket looked at the man's face: thin nose, arched eyebrows. Olive complexion. Trim in his tapered suit. He looked hungry. Now sixty-one, more athletic than most men half his age, Michael DiForio was vying to lead his family and usher in a new era of prosperity. Like Gotti before him, DiForio was a legend in his hometown, and a savvy real estate developer to boot. Everything about the man commanded respect, and in return he would offer his friendship. He was smart, ruthless, vicious, but always in control. Except for today. Today, DiForio looked like a man who, for the first time, had to question everything.

Now Blanket stood opposite this man, and all eyes waited. Michael finally spoke, his voice calm.

"What's the news?"

Blanket cleared his throat and tried to speak in a confident voice.

"Well, my sources told me…"

"Fuck the pussyfooting. Speak."

Blanket toed the floor, looked up.

"The cops don't have Parker yet. That's a fact. He fled the scene before the boys in blue showed up. This morning some towel head at a meat market called 911, claimed Parker stole a newspaper after threatening his sons. Cops're combing the area, but they couldn't find a doughnut if they fucking sat on it. Rumor has it since they killed a cop, the Feds will be called in soon."

DiForio looked like he was about to swear, then held back. "Have they locked down the building on 105th yet?"

Blanket nodded. "Place is tighter than my old lady."

"*Fuck*," DiForio spat. It startled Blanket, this sudden loss of composure. DiForio rubbed his temples. "What are Parker's outs?"

Blanket scratched the back of his neck and looked at Michael. "Well, Port Authority's out of the question. There's no way he's buying a bus ticket out of New York without a thirty-eight going up his ass. Airports, not a chance. Guy's a college grad, figure even nowadays that's worth something, so he's too smart to try and use a passport."

"What else?"

Blanket coughed.

"The Path could be a tough one. They're sending cops to cover entry points at 33rd and Union Square, but there's a definite chance he could have made it to Jersey." The Path was an underground train service running to and from New Jersey. It was as hard to monitor as the subway system and ran just as often. There were several stations in the city, and a constant, bustling stream of crowds. "The kid doesn't have any relatives there, maybe some college friends, who knows. Definitely nobody who'd take a bullet or get sent to lockup for him."

"He got a girlfriend?" DiForio asked. Blanket stayed silent. Michael stood up, pushing his chair back. Metal scraped against metal. His voice effortlessly thundered in the small room. "Blanket, does he have a girlfriend? Boyfriend? He like transvestites?"

"Actually, boss, I'm not sure about that yet. Cops're checking phone records, my man at the 24th said he'll tell me whatever they find, but they're still looking. We're not gonna know anything until they do."

DiForio picked his chair up and heaved it across the room. A dozen pairs of eyes watched it fly over their heads and clang against the wall. Michael walked around the table and approached Blanket, his chest mere inches away.

Dom Loverro stood up. The man weighed three hundred, three-fifty easy. Body fat percentage hovering around ninety-five. He said, "Mike, you want us to take care of it? Find this prick Parker?"

DiForio looked at him with contempt. "If I need a fat asshole to walk up behind a deaf and dumb guy and hit him in the back of the head with a crowbar, I'll let you know. I need to chase down a fugitive thirty years younger than us, something tells me I'll need a guy who can see his toes."

"Mike?" Blanket said.

"The package from that junkie shutterbug," DiForio said. "Where is it?"

Blanket's heart caught in his throat. He blinked rapidly, felt sweat leaking through his pores. "The cops don't have it. It wasn't at the scene."

DiForio slowly turned around, taking two steps away from Blanket. Then in the blink of an eye, he spun around and slapped Blanket across the face.

Spit flew from his lips. He tasted salty blood, wiped his mouth with the back of his hand, took it in stride.

"So, would you find it safe to say that since Luis Guzman doesn't have my package, and the cops don't have it yet, either…you see what I'm getting at you stupid fuck?"

Blanket spit a cluster of blood and phlegm onto the concrete. "Parker," he said. "He must have taken it last night when he ran."

DiForio nodded. "Blanket?"

"Yeah, boss?"

"Call the Ringer."

Blanket felt a shiver, an electrical pulse, course through his body. A smile crept over his busted lip. He felt no pain, only a sense of satisfaction. At that moment, Blanket wouldn't have traded places with Henry Parker for all the riches on earth.

10

Federal Plaza felt like 3:00 a.m. during a graveyard shift, everyone walking around like zombies. Many of the agents knew the man who died last night. And they were all looking to Joe Mauser to bring Henry Parker to justice.

Mauser banged open the office door. The younger agent, Leonard Denton, was already there. Clean shaven, smelled like a bottle of Drakkar Noir threw up all over him. Joe offered an imperceptible nod and sat down at the table. He sniffed, grimaced, the younger man's aftershave reeking like holy hell. Hygiene be damned, Joe didn't care much about anything at this point. Parker was still out there. Goddamn NYPD had the kid pinned like a rat and let him squirm away.

Leonard Denton had a squeaky clean rep in the department, squeaky to the point where people almost assumed he would flip out one day and go postal. He was efficient and by-the-book, admirable qualities. But being admired and having admirable qualities were two totally different animals. Denton requested this case for that very reason, to prove to the rank and file that he would take down a man who killed one of their own. When it came to tracking down a fugitive cop killer, you set the book on fire and laughed at it while it burned. And Mauser could tell from Denton's face that the man was completely prepared to do that.

Denton had requested that he partner with Mauser. Joe obliged. This would be their first time working together. And as much as a longtime partner could bring familiarity to a case, Joe wanted to be kept on his toes. Denton was six-one. A little too skinny. Probably drank too much coffee, didn't eat much, worked out like crazy. He didn't wear a wedding ring. Never talked about a girl, serious or just someone he was banging on the side. His life was streamlined for the job. The kind of guy you'd want to track down Henry Parker.

Joe had seen the body lying in the hallway like a sack of beef. He had to bite his lower lip and turn away, the tears of rage coming uninvited. Louis Carruthers had put his hand on Joe's shoulder, leaning in to console him, but got violently shoved away for his efforts. Louis knew, as did the other officers, that solace wouldn't come easily. The friendly arms retracted before Joe could brush them off. He would've taken a flamethrower to them if given the chance.

There was no way he'd let someone else—someone detached—be the primary on this case. It had to be his. It didn't just need closure, but the right kind of closure. Agent Joseph Mauser had to find Henry Parker himself. Since there was the chance Parker could cross state lines, the NYPD called in the Feds. Joe demanded the case. Nobody at the marshal's office offered any resistance. Agents with a personal stake in capturing a fugitive were dogged to the point of obsession.

Officer John Fredrickson. His brother-in-law. Dead. Shot

through the heart by some twenty-four-year-old walking disease. John had served the NYPD faithfully for twenty years. His wife, Linda, was Joe's younger sister. His death left behind two children, Nancy and Joel. Paying bills was hard enough in the Fredrickson household, Joe knew that, and now they'd lost their main source of income. Linda worked as a court stenographer—actually made a pretty decent living—but it wouldn't be nearly enough to feed three mouths. Joel was in college, and his tuition was already hard enough to foot.

His sister's husband, stolen from the earth by a demon with no soul.

Jesus.

Joe didn't know if he could go to the funeral. Seeing his dear friend in a box would be too much to bear. Standing over a convex piece of earth, saying meaningless farewells, what good did it do? What's done is done. That's what he told himself. No amount of tears could change anything, but they came anyway.

For years Joe Mauser had dipped his hands in death, and now death had hit home. The sad sacks who wept into lined hankies, the ones he was often forced to comfort, now he was one of them. His cheeks had gone flushed last night, and he'd felt warmth spread through him like a brush fire. He fought it off, stepped outside, claimed the heat was getting to him.

John Fredrickson. His brother-in-law. Dead.

And now, Len Denton. Short for Leonard. Christ, the guy even looked like a Leonard. With his wire-rimmed glasses and stiffly parted hair, thousand-dollar suit and Gillette shave gel, designer cologne and a goddamn name that almost rhymed. He bet Denton's parents were real proud of that.

As long as Mauser found Henry Parker, though…as long as he found Parker. Denton had something to gain, too. On some level, Mauser understood it. Respect could be as powerful a motivator as anger. Between the two of them, there was an awful lot of motivation.

"Agent Mauser?" Denton said. He extended his hand. Joe merely nodded. "I'm sorry for your loss. Truly, I am."

"Thanks." He shook his hand limply.

"I know you want this case closed quickly. That's what I'm here for. I know I don't have the personal attachment you do, but I can promise you that…"

"Save your breath. We're partners, fine. Don't expect small talk, chitchat, or bullshit. You want to be my friend? Help me skewer this fuck with a chainsaw."

Denton smiled. "I'm here to help you power it."

"Good." Joe pulled a manila folder from under his armpit, opened to the first page. A photocopy of Henry Parker's driver's license. Mauser leafed through several pages, flipping too fast for Denton to see.

"We got this from Henry Parker's landlord, guy named Manuel Vega. Shady asshole tried to rent me a ground-floor apartment for thirteen hundred a month after I questioned him." Mauser tried hard to mask the anger in his voice. Was it anger?

Suddenly he felt choked up, almost unable to speak. Joe coughed, wiped his eyes with the edge of his tie, showed Denton the file and flipped to the next page. "We've examined Parker's checking and savings accounts and frozen his funds. As soon as he deposits one paycheck it's gone to pay rent, phone, Internet porn, et cetera. Parker saves about a buck fifty a month." Mauser flipped to the next page.

"Phone bill?" Denton asked.

"Cellular. We couldn't find records for any landlines in his apartment."

"That's pretty common these days," Denton said. "Especially with the younger set. A lot of people use cells as their primary lines. Assuming you get service, it's cheaper than paying for a landline and a mobile."

Mauser nodded. He noticed several officers walk by the office, peering in through the windows. Rage on some faces, regret on others. All of the eyes desperate to find Henry Parker and cut his balls off. Mauser closed the blinds and watched the eyes disappear.

Ordinarily Mauser would have allowed the NYPD to remain primary in a cop slaying. Not this time. Joe had to find Parker before anyone. His was a personal anger, not professional. Not like the rest of them. He respected their anger, fed off it, but couldn't sate it. Refused to sate it.

Mauser pulled out Parker's most recent phone bill. He passed it to Denton, who scanned it, his finger tracing several numbers that were highlighted in yellow.

"What're these?"

"We marked any numbers that appeared on Parker's bill more than once a week. Not a whole lot, actually. His voice mail at the *Gazette*—he's a reporter there, just started a month ago. Doesn't call out of state much. His parents live in Bend, Oregon, but we've only found records of two calls made there in the past six weeks."

"That's good," Denton said. "Means he's not close to his parents. One less friendly face willing to take him in."

Mauser nodded. Denton pointed to one number that was highlighted numerous times on the list. "What's this one?"

"Girlfriend, Mya Loverne. Law student at Columbia. Father's David Loverne, the family's got money squirting out his asshole. She met Parker while they were undergrads at Cornell. You know the deal. Poor boy from the Northwest meets spoiled rich girl who's never been felt up by a guy without a trust fund. Rent any Molly Ringwald movie and you get the picture. Miss Mya graduated last May and decided to follow Daddy's footsteps into law school."

"At least he has good taste," Denton said. "There's a lot more money in law than in newspapers, unless you can figure a way to skim from Rupert Murdoch. Have you been in touch with Mya yet?"

"That's the next ride in the theme park."

Denton said, "I'm a Six Flags guy myself. Never got into Disney World."

Mauser eyed him contemptuously. "You gonna small talk me? Is that what you're gonna do?" Mauser stood up, turned to leave the room. "Fuck it. I don't need this shit right now."

"Joe, come on, man. I'm only…"

"You're only what?" Mauser said, spittle flying from his lips. "You wanna get cute with me? Six fucking Flags?"

Denton's eyes grew sorrowful and his head tilted down. He spoke solemnly and, Mauser could tell, honestly.

"I'm sorry about your brother-in-law," Denton said. "I swear I am. But Henry Parker's out there, and a thousand cops are walking the streets, hands on their holsters, looking for anyone under the age of thirty to pop. I'm here to help. You want me to stay quiet, fine. But I want to find Henry Parker, and I want to know why John Fredrickson died last night. Just like you."

Mauser stepped closer until he was breathing in Denton's face. "Not like me. Understand that."

Denton nodded. "Understood." He paused before asking his next question. Mauser knew he was doing it out of politeness. He wouldn't let his curiosity sit idle. "I don't mean to pry, but how's Mrs. Fredrickson? She's your sister, right?"

"A mess," Mauser said. He took a handkerchief out of his breast pocket and coughed loudly into it, then wiped his mouth.

"The kids?"

"About what you'd expect. Joel's in college, thank God the kid's already finished up the semester. Can't imagine going through finals with your father's murder hanging over you. You get older, somehow you're more prepared for this kind of thing."

"Have you seen Linda?"

"I went over to the house last night, after I left the crime scene."

Denton spoke softly. "You're the one broke the news to her, weren't you?"

Mauser felt a lump rise in his throat and nodded. Tears would come in an instant. His sister's husband. The man he'd shared so many laughs with, gotten stinking drunk with so many times. Watching ball games in front of the crappy Panasonic, cheering on their lovable loser Mets and hoping to God the Yankees got blown out of the water. One of his best friends. One of his only friends.

Mauser always considered it fortunate that Linda had married such a stand-up guy, not one of those louses who make a killing in the market and never see their families except during two-week vacations to the Poconos where they spend the entire time on their BlackBerries. If you married a cop, you did it for love. And so far, Mauser hadn't found any woman willing to give him what Linda had given John. He admired his sister for making that choice. He'd told her just that many times.

It's not a conscious decision, she'd told him. *It's not like I wake up every day and think "Should I or shouldn't I be with John?" I just am. He makes me happy.*

And now he was gone. Linda, alone with the kids. Joe knew he'd have to offer support. Moral. Financial. Becoming a surrogate father to his sister's children had as seductive a ring as a colonoscopy, but he had a responsibility to the family. And his first responsibility, one that would speed up the grieving process, was to find Henry Parker and gut him like a fish.

Mauser sat down, brushed his pants. Denton looked at him expectantly. Joe said, "Let's go talk to the girlfriend, Mya. See what the murderer's moll has to say."

Denton smiled. He stood up, tentatively reached out and squeezed Joe's shoulder.

"You sure you're up for this?"

Mauser nodded. "Let's go quick. I want to get into this thing before it all hits me at once."

"I'll drive."

"Yeah, better you do. I see someone on the street looks like the photo on that driver's license, I'll mow him down without giving it a second thought."

They left the precinct, Denton pulling the Crown Victoria onto the West Side Highway. Early morning sunlight filtered through the windshield. The cold leather on the seats prickled Mauser's skin. Soft rock was on the radio, the DJ sounding like he'd overdosed on Xanax.

"Mya Loverne's cell phone bill is forwarded to an apartment near the Columbia campus reserved for student housing," Joe said. "Keep your eyes open just in case our man decides he needs a morning pick-me-up."

"She live alone?" Denton asked.

"Yeah, why?"

Denton sniffed. "I couldn't afford my own place till I was thirty. Fucking unbelievable."

Mauser spoke, his voice apprehensive. "She's a pretty girl, I've seen pictures of Mya with her father, fund raisers at Cipriani, fancy dinners that cost more per plate than your mortgage. Heard rumors that Loverne is going to run for district attorney. It's kinda creepy, almost like he uses Mya as publicity t and a. She's always wearing these low-cut dresses and the cameras always get her good side. Both of them."

Denton said, "People almost always vote for whichever candidate's daughters are hotter. You see Bloomberg's daughter? Unbelievable that girl came from that guy." Denton took the 96th Street exit, forgoing his turn signal.

"You do the talking," Mauser said. Denton looked at Mauser, concern on his face.

"You sure you're up for this? I can get the case reassigned, no problem."

Joe waved his hand in dismissal. "Over my dead body. I'll be fine once we get there."

"Don't say that. Parker's body, that I can live with."

Joe smiled. "Deal." He lowered the window. Fresh air beat against his face. The trees shook gently, leaves rattling in the wind. He stared out the window, his eyes latching onto anything that moved.

Denton squeezed into a spot on 114th and Broadway, leaning over the headrest as he backed in. He didn't even use the side mirrors, Mauser noticed. Guy didn't trust anything but his own eyes. Mauser liked that.

Joe felt his knee joints groan as he climbed out of the car. Denton slid on a pair of designer sunglasses, his blond hair fitting in perfectly with the young men and women carrying thick valises who crowded the streets. Tanned and toned bodies looking healthy and vigorous in the bronzed sunlight. Ready to take their place among the proletariat of New York City.

"You're gonna ruin your part," Mauser said, pointing at Denton's hair. Denton ran a hand through it, combed it back into place with his fingers, laughed.

"You're a prick," he said with a grin. Mauser felt more relaxed. Maybe the rumors about Denton were bogus. The guy was rubbing off on him. "Come on, let's go talk to Ms. Loverne."

Mauser admired the building's facade, the clean red brick, like the vandals had too much respect to desecrate it with their "art." He watched as pedestrians strolled with their heads held high, too high to see the dirt at their feet. One thing Mauser had learned over the years was that students, almost to a one, viewed the world from the inside of a fishbowl. They had the bigger points covered—genocide in Kamchatka, illegal whale hunting in the Arctic Circle, shit like that. But if you asked about anything relevant to their lives they'd look at you with glazed eyes and go right back to sipping their double-mocha lattes.

Parker was just another in a growing line of young shit-heads who felt they put on their pants two legs at a time. They gain a little fame, a little notoriety, and suddenly they're Edward R. Murrow.

Mya Loverne's building had no doorman, only an antiquated buzzer system with a small camera for tenants to view their visitors from the comfort of their Jennifer Convertibles. Mauser found the directory on the wall, ran his finger down until it came to a stop at M. Loverne. Apartment 4A.

Denton pressed the gray nipple and waited. Mauser shuffled around, anxiety building inside him. Every moment they waited was more time for Parker to run. Denton pressed the buzzer again. Ten, fifteen, twenty seconds later, and still no answer.

"Screw this," Mauser said. He pushed Denton aside and jammed his thumb on the call button. He held it there for a full minute, then released for five seconds, then jammed it down again. Finally a tired female voice answered.

"Who is it? Henry?"

Denton tried to stifle a laugh. Mauser elbowed him in the kidney.

"Ms. Loverne?" Denton said.

"Who is this?"

"Ms. Loverne, my name is Leonard Denton, FBI."

"Excuse me? Why…what's the matter?" Denton waited a few seconds to let her heart rate build up. Get her good and fearful.

Then he pressed the intercom again and said, "We need to talk about your boyfriend, Henry Parker."

"Is there…do you have any identification or something?"

Denton held his government ID with the elegant blue FBI seal to the camera. After a moment of hesitation, the buzzer rang and Denton pulled the door open. He looked at Mauser, a blank stare on the older cop's face.

"And away we go."

11

I reread the story. Blood, thick like cement, swirled and pounded in my head. Misunderstandings. Errors of judgment. Callousness. Human frailty. Weakness. All of it was quantifiable, rectified by specific reactions. Errors could be fixed. Misunderstandings explained. Human frailty bolstered by gaining strength.

I'd dealt with all of these in my investigative journalism. But the emotions I felt when I read those words were completely foreign. There was no rational explanation as to how suddenly I was wanted for killing a police officer.

I'd always wanted to report about crime, corruption. Men and women convinced they'd get away with it, until I proved they couldn't. And now, with my picture splashed across thousands of newspapers all over the city, I'd become exactly who I'd hoped to expose. True reporters only want the story. They never want to be the story. And now here I was. The hero of the day.

I read the story again.

**Reporter, 24, Kills Police Officer
During Failed Drug Bust**

In what has been described by Police Commissioner Ray Kelly as a heinous act of violence against one of the city's most beloved peace officers, Detective Jonathan A. Fredrickson, 42, was shot and killed late last night while investigating a drug deal gone sour. The alleged shooter, Henry Parker, 24, a recent Cornell graduate and a junior reporter at the New York Gazette, fled the scene and has yet to be apprehended.

According to Commissioner Kelly, Fredrickson was responding to the site of an alleged heroin exchange in an apartment building at 2937 Broadway in Spanish Harlem. It remains unclear whether the tenants, Luis and Christine Guzman, were involved in the deal. The building's superintendent, Grady Larkin, 36, admitted to hearing strange noises coming from the Guzmans' apartment, which he relayed to Officer Fredrickson when he arrived at the scene. Fredrickson apparently discovered the Guzmans tied and beaten, and upon confronting the assailant, still present at the scene, was shot with his own gun in the ensuing struggle. Larkin claims to have seen Parker running from the crime scene, carrying a bag that may or may not have contained the alleged narcotics.

Luis Guzman, 34, on parole for armed robbery in 1994, and his wife were being treated at an undisclosed medical facility for wounds suffered in the attack.

Luis Guzman is listed in stable condition with a fractured jaw and three broken ribs and was unable to comment. Christine, 28, is suffering from a concussion and facial lacerations.

"He hit me," Christine said of Parker's brutalization. "He hit me a lot. I was screaming at him to stop, but he kept hitting my husband until he couldn't talk anymore."

She continued, "That policeman died to protect us from Henry Parker. We could both be dead. He sacrificed his life. We will never forget what he gave for us."

And, according to several sources within the NYPD and FBI, neither will New York's finest.

Said Kelly at an early morning press conference, "This city will not rest until Officer Fredrickson's killer is found. This investigation will be the very definition of swift justice."

The local branch of the FBI has been called in to aid in Parker's capture. The Assistant Director in Charge of the New York City FBI branch, Donald L. West, said his agents would receive special jurisdiction to cross state lines if found that Parker has fled the state.

Detective Fredrickson is survived by his wife, Linda, and two children.

The pounding blood in my head slowly came to a boil.
He hit me, she said.
Christine Guzman lied to the police. So did Grady Larkin, the superintendent, a man I'd never met. The world had collapsed onto itself, and I was caught in the middle.
It had to be a dream. I was a college graduate, had just started my dream job at a respected newspaper. I was sup-

posed to do great things, accomplish my goals, all the good stuff that would secure me respect and money, and give my reputation longevity. And now I was accused of killing a policeman. A husband. A father. A man who protected the world from criminals. Like me. How was this possible? John Fredrickson—a fucking cop—had nearly beaten two people to death, almost killed me in the process, and now I was facing the vengeance of an entire city.

Drugs. A heroin deal. That's what the paper said. That's what Fredrickson must have been looking for, and what the papers assumed I stole. But why would a cop go to such brutal lengths to retrieve drugs? And why did Christine claim they didn't have it, risking all three of our lives?

And why would a cop, with a family no less, risk everything by beating two unarmed people nearly to death?

I didn't have the answer.

And now thousands, maybe millions of people, thought I was a cop killer. John Fredrickson was a hero. I was a common thug, a young punk who thought he was above it all, whose vices led to a cop's death. I was part of the tainted blood I'd wanted to purify. And now they had to destroy me before I spread my disease.

I stepped outside the greasy deli where I'd been perched in a back booth with the newspaper folded in front of me. My stomach heaved every time the front door swung open, my muscles clenched and ready to run.

Ironic. I'd always wanted to be Bob Woodward. Pete Hamill. Jimmy Breslin. Recognized. Now, my only hope was that the world would see right through me.

I stopped at a thrift store and bought a pair of crappy

warm-up pants and a white T-shirt whose collar had already begun to fray. My sneakers I threw into a mailbox, replaced them with a worn pair of Sambas. A cheap pair of sunglasses hid my eyes. But these were only stopgap measures, using bubble gum to plug a ruptured dam.

There were few people in New York I could turn to for help, and if they came up empty… I tried not to think about it.

I walked quickly toward the subway, keeping an eye out for lurking transit officers. I felt light-headed, searching amongst unknown faces for any hint of danger. My hands could be shackled before I knew what happened, I could be beaten to death in my cell, either by cops who thought I'd killed one of their own or by criminals who'd consider it a feather in their cap to kill a man who'd taken a policeman's life.

Stepping onto the uptown 6 train, my legs felt weak, rubbery. It was all I could do to support my own weight.

The train chugged along, and at each stop I scanned the new passengers, watching intently for the royal blue dress of the NYPD. My life, it seemed, was now entirely up to chance.

I exited at 116th Street and found the nearest pay phone. It killed me to call him after this. I had to hope he'd believe the truth.

My fingers trembling, I inserted a quarter and dialed. The switchboard operator picked up, a woman's superficially perky voice on the other end.

"*New York Gazette,* how may I direct your call?"

"Wallace Langston, please."

"Just a moment." I heard a click, then ringing as my call was put through. I chewed on a fingernail, then stopped. Can't draw any attention. Must act normal. Just another guy on the phone.

A guy with a murder charge hanging over his head. A dead man haunting his thoughts. An entire city turned against him. A whole life…

"Wallace Langston's office."

Shit. It was Shirley, his secretary. She'd recognize my voice. And once she did, I'd never get through. She'd call the cops in the blink of an eye.

I raised my voice an octave and gave myself a slight lisp. Thank God my chosen profession wasn't acting.

"Yes, Wallace Langston. Is he in?"

"And who may I ask is calling?"

"Um…this is Paul Westington calling from Hillary Clinton's office. Mrs. Clinton is ready to give the *Gazette* an exclusive on her presidential aspirations."

Silence.

"Sure…just a moment." Another click, more ringing. Then Wallace picked up.

"Hello, Mr. Westington, is it?" He sounded rushed. Excited for the story. Sorry, Wally, Hillary couldn't make it, instead you're on the line with a wanted criminal.

"Wallace, it's me."

Beat. I held my breath, pulse quickening.

"Who is this?"

"It's Henry. Henry Parker."

There was a moment of silence as I waited for a response.

"Henry. Oh, Christ, Henry."

"Yeah."

"Henry, what have you done?" His voice was sad, ashamed.

I felt hot tears welling in my eyes. Wallace believed it, believed what they were saying.

"Wallace, please," I said, choking back a sob. "You have to believe me. I didn't do it. Nothing in the papers is true. I…"

"Henry, I can't speak to you. You need to go to the police. You need to turn yourself in."

"I can't turn myself in!" I cried. "I'll be dead before I make it to trial! I can't do it, Wallace. I need your help."

"I can't help you," he said softly. "The only advice I can offer is for you to turn yourself in. Please, Henry, that's what's best for everyone. If they find you before you do that, I don't know what will happen. God, Henry, how could you *do* this?"

The muscles in my jaw tensed. My outlets had just diminished by fifty percent.

"They won't find me," I said, and slammed down the receiver. Wallace. Jack. Could Jack have known about Luis Guzman? He was a lone beacon in the sea of journalistic turmoil, the man whose allegiances could never be bought, whose opinion never corrupted. But now I wasn't so sure.

Wincing, I glanced around. Nobody seemed to have noticed the outburst. Shaking, my throat dry, I took another quarter and slid it in. Dialing the next number, the last number, I said a silent prayer. After three rings, a voice answered the phone.

"Hello?"

"Oh, thank God. Mya."

"Henry."

"Mya, listen to me. I don't know what you've heard, but none of it's true. I need to see you. I need to talk to your father. He can help me."

"Henry, I…I saw the newspapers. It's all over the television. I don't think my father can speak to you unless you go to the police."

"I can't do that, Mya. I can't…"

"Wait one second, Henry." I heard a soft clap—her hand covering the receiver—then a shuffling sound in the background.

"Mya, are you there? What's going on?" Then she was back, her voice distracted.

"Oh, sorry, Hen. I'm just in the middle of breakfast." Her voice seemed remarkably calm. It unnerved me.

"Anyway, I need to come over. I need somewhere to stay for a bit until I figure things out. What the papers say, that's not what happened last night. Your father could…"

"I can't do that, Henry, I told you."

"Dammit, Mya," I said, starting to lose it. I didn't care if anyone was watching. "This is my life! You can't just shut me out."

"I don't want to, Henry. I don't have a choice."

"Oh? And why is that?"

Joe Mauser pinched his thumb and forefinger together and pulled them apart. He mouthed the words, "Keep stringing him along."

Mya nodded, her face grim. Denton was on his cell phone as he waited for the line to be traced. He held up three fingers. After a moment, two fingers.

"Twenty seconds," Denton mouthed.

Mya nodded. Mauser had to give the girl credit. Tears were flowing down her cheeks and she was biting her lip so hard he could see white where the blood was being forced out, but she was remarkably composed. Sitting next to her on the bed, hearing Parker's faint voice through the earpiece, it took all of Mauser's patience not to grab the phone and tear it to pieces.

Denton dropped one finger, then held up ten. Slowly counting down.

"Nine…eight…seven…six…" Denton mouthed. Mya watched him. She shut her eyes, squeezing out several drops that spattered onto the comforter.

Joe's heart fluttered. Just a few seconds and they'd have him.

"Four…three…two…"

Suddenly Mya yelled, "Henry, run!"

She bolted off the bed, the cell phone still in her hand. Denton lunged for her, catching the cuff of her jeans. She wriggled free and ran to the other end of the apartment. A door slammed shut and a latch clicked. She'd locked herself in the bathroom.

Mya screamed again, then Joe heard a beep as she severed the connection.

"God*damn* it!" Joe shouted. "Len, tell me we got something."

Denton ran for the door, signaling Mauser to follow.

"Parker's at a pay phone two goddamn blocks east from here. NYPD's on the way." Mauser thought he saw a disappointed look on Denton's face as he threw the door open and raced into the stairwell.

Denton said, "Joe, we gotta find this kid before anyone else does."

Mauser looked over his shoulder and smiled as he felt the reassuring weight of his Glock against his ribs. "Tell the NYPD to throw a fucking vise on this entire city. If anyone lays a goddamn finger on Parker before I fucking find him, I'll be bringing two bodies to the morgue today."

12

I shouted into the phone, "Mya? Mya? What happened?"

Run, she'd said.

Not a simple *Please go, Henry.* She was pleading with me, warning me.

I stepped away from the phone booth like it had contracted the plague. My cheeks felt hot. I looked left and right, saw nothing out of the ordinary, only the familiar sounds of traffic horns and pedestrian conversation.

Run.

It didn't make sense. What had made Mya so afraid? A rumbling in my gut said I needed to get out of there. I'd come uptown with the hope of seeing Mya, but I also had a backup plan in case she couldn't help. Now I'd have to scrap them both. I wasn't safe. Unease swept over me like a frigid wave.

Then I heard a sound that froze my blood. Footsteps. Not just the pitter-patter of feet stepping in tune to their bodies' rhythm, but the hard pounding of sprinting strides. I listened closer. There was more than one set of feet.

I spun around, and to my horror saw two men running toward me, less than a block away, their eyes deadlocked on mine. One of them held a gun. Light glinted off another object that I instinctively knew was a badge.

Run.

"Henry Parker!" the taller, thinner one yelled. "Don't you move a fucking muscle!"

My feet moved before I could think, and suddenly I was sprinting east down 116th Street, cutting between two lanes of traffic. The honking of horns filled my ears, drivers cursing at me in foreign languages. A car's bumper sideswiped my leg, knocking me off balance. I pulled myself together, saw a turbaned man in a taxi giving me the finger.

I darted to the other side of the street, rounded a corner, then wound my way through stunned pedestrians. Heads turned in unison as I sprinted past. My lungs felt ready to explode, the wind ripping at my face. I had no concept of how close the cops were, the pounding in my ears as loud as thunder.

Suddenly an arm shot out and grabbed me, tearing a large hole in the fabric below my armpit. I managed to spin away as a muscular man in a sweatshirt yelled, "That's Henry Parker! Stop, you fucking cop killer!"

My only salvation was the subway. No chance I could make it anywhere on foot. I had to get out of New York. People had begun to recognize me. Even if I could outrun the two cops, I couldn't outrun an entire city.

I dodged a line of garbage cans on the corner of 115th and Madison. Bracing myself, I shoved the cans one by one, sending them rolling down the street, littering the sidewalk with foul-smelling debris, creating a makeshift rolling barricade.

"Parker! Stop where you are!" a voice shouted. It was close; too close. I weaved in and out of traffic, my body a strange mixture of burning heat from the sweat and cold from the wind and fear. Every nerve in my body was on fire.

I beat the next traffic light, running as fast as I could, legs churning, my bruised ribs throbbing.

"Parker!"

"Henry!"

I made out two distinct voices. Both angry, vigilant. They weren't going to stop.

Between Lexington and Park, I finally reached the entrance to the downtown 6 train, my sides aching, ready to collapse.

Then a terrifying crash ruptured the air, like lightning on a clear day, and pedestrians around me ducked for cover. I felt something pinch my leg, like a bee sting.

Jesus...*what was that?*

I leapt down the stairs three at a time, knocking over a Hispanic woman who called me horrible names. No time for apologies.

I slowed down as I entered the station, reached for my wallet. Jumping the turnstile would draw unwanted attention. The station manager would see me, call the transit cops. Finally my slippery fingers ripped the MetroCard out and ran it through the scanner.

"Please swipe card again."

Oh, God. Not now.

I swiped it again, and a beep confirmed the fare was paid.

Breathing hard, I walked quickly to the end of the platform, trying to stay inconspicuous to strangers buried in newspapers and paperback books.

I went to the far end of the platform and ducked behind a column, my lungs heaving. I leaned over the yellow line and peered into the dark tunnel. Two bright lights were visible, and they were drawing closer. The train couldn't get here fast enough. I looked at my thigh, saw the hole in my jeans, my blood reddening the blue cloth. There was no pain, as though my nervous system had shut down. Oh, God…

Please let it get here before they do. Just give me more time.

Glancing at the turnstiles, my heart sank as I saw the two cops run onto the platform, their eyes darting back and forth. I plastered my body against a grimy pillar, trying to slow down my breathing. I couldn't hear any footsteps; the train was too close, the screeching of metal drowning out all other noise.

The first car of the giant metal snake rushed past, the air around me shattered in an instant, damp hair plastered against my forehead.

Come on!

Then the train began to slow down. Brakes grinding against the tracks, the wind subsiding.

When the train came to a halt and the doors slid open, I waited for the passengers to exit then slid inside the last car. I took a seat next to a young woman in a navy pinstripe suit wearing headphones, her head bobbing to a silent rhythm. A man across the aisle was reading a folded newspaper. Neither of them looked at me. I took slow breaths, my heart rate mercifully dropping.

I exhaled as the doors began to close. I knew exactly where to go next. It would only be a short few minutes before I got there.

Then right before the doors sealed shut, they sputtered open. Someone was trying to enter the train at the last second. Nobody in my car was holding the doors, so I stood up and peered through the windowpane into the adjacent car.

No.

Two pairs of arms were prying the door open like spiders caught in a Venus flytrap. I recognized the glint of a badge, then saw the faces through the window. The cops were coming inside.

Trying to act casual, I stood up and inched toward the opposite end of the car.

The conductor's scratchy voice came over the loudspeaker.

"Let's go, people! There's another train right behind us!"

I had no time to think. When the doors opened again, right as the cops entered the train, I bolted back out onto the platform. I sprinted toward the subway entrance, noticed a gun barrel jammed between another set of doors. The cops had seen me leave and were trying to pry their way back out into the station. The conductor's irritated voice echoed once more as the subway doors again flung open, the cops spilling back out onto the platform. Less than twenty feet away from me.

Run.

I followed the exodus of people who'd gotten off the train at 116th, ducking between two men, then sidestepping a woman lifting a baby carriage. I ran up a flight of steps to the upper platform. The musty smell of spilled coffee and extinguished cigarettes coated my nostrils with every sharp breath. The entrance to the street loomed just past the turnstiles, but I wouldn't make it outside. The cops had surely called for help. Any minute now they'd be circling the station like sharks aching for blood. In this situation, evasion was better than confrontation.

I ducked into a newspaper kiosk and grabbed the nearest magazine. *Penthouse.*

Whatever.

I splayed the pages open, standing just behind the soda cooler so I was out of sight. Peering over a picture of breasts the size of beach balls, I watched the cops scamper up to the platform. They spoke in staccato bursts, gesturing wildly around the station, then the younger one pointed to a mass of people walking up the stairs to the street. They ran toward the exit, shouting and elbowing past frightened commuters. When they disappeared from view, I collected myself and slowly walked back down to the lower platform. Another train was just pulling into the station.

I stepped behind a pillar—just in case—and waited.

The train stopped, the doors opened and I stepped inside. When the doors closed behind me and the car began to move, I knew I was alone. I took a deep breath and sat down.

An elderly woman seated across the aisle eyed me with contempt, shaking her head with disdain. Could she know?

Then I looked down and noticed the *Penthouse* still in my hands. I smiled, shrugged my shoulders and held the mag up for her to see.

"Sorry," I said. "Thought it was *Newsweek.*"

13

It took everything Blanket and Charlie had not to turn around, to simply stare at the man following them. Blanket looked to his right, saw Charlie biting his lower lip, and knew they were thinking the exact same thing. Mere steps behind them was the most brutal and cold-hearted killer they had ever known, and for men in their profession they'd known every cutthroat, backstabbing, soulless bastard to walk the earth. But *he* was different. He scared the life out of two men who'd grown up frightened of *nothing*.

The musty smell of the basement had grown all too familiar this morning. Blanket listened to the footsteps behind him, the enigma nearly silent. He'd only seen the man briefly—opening the front door to let him in—and was now doing his very best to hide his quickening heart rate and sweaty palms.

"Almost there," Charlie's voice rang out. A pointless statement, Blanket thought, said just to see if the man would respond.

"Watch your head," said Blanket, ducking under a swinging bulb. He eyed Charlie again. They shared a smile.

At the large door in the building's sub-basement, Blanket rapped the code. The metal slot opened. A pair of eyes looked out at Blanket and Charlie, unimpressed. Then they caught sight of the man behind them. The eyes widened. The man behind the door whispered.

"Is that…him?"

Blanket nodded solemnly.

The door swung inward. The three men entered. This ghost, whom powerful men like Michael DiForio called when they needed odds tipped in their favor, a man whom the shroud of death hovered over permanently, was mere inches behind them. That Michael had summoned him only underlined the severity of last night's incident.

As they entered the large conference room, a dozen men, none of whom had ever bowed to any man save Michael DiForio, stood, craning their necks for a better look. With no empty chairs available, Blanket and Charlie stood on either side of the door as it slammed shut. After a tense few moments, the men all sat down. Except Michael DiForio.

"Welcome," Michael said. "Glad you could make it on such short notice. Hope I didn't interrupt your morning tennis game."

The man said nothing. For the first time Blanket was able to see him clearly.

He stood a shade over six-four and looked slightly north of two hundred pounds. His brown hair was done in a Caesar cut, short bangs dripping over his forehead. He wore a black leather jacket—not frayed, but worn—and dark pants. Blanket estimated the man's age in the early thirties. But his dark eyes were reminiscent of policemen who'd been on the beat far too long, men who'd seen the depths of hell and had sunk too far to ever return.

"Michael," the Ringer said. He bowed his head slightly, more a formality than out of respect. "I don't imagine you called to talk trivialities."

DiForio grinned and said, "No, I didn't. So let's get right to business. You know, that's what I've always liked about you. No bullshit. Cut right to the chase."

Blanket noticed Charlie fidgeting, his fingers clenching and unclenching. They were in the presence of a ghost of the New York underworld, a man whose past was well-documented, revered like a disturbing bedtime story, and feared to the point of paralysis.

The Ringer had cut his teeth as a professional assassin at the tender age of fifteen. He worked as a contract man for low-level hoods, men who didn't care if the job was a little sloppy, a little too bloody to keep under wraps. The Ringer killed with a vicious disregard for cleanliness or subtlety. His targets were drug dealers who skimmed profits, middlemen who didn't deliver payments on time. Small-timers. Deaths the cops would pay little attention to. Lives that wouldn't be missed. Barely into manhood, the Ringer was a minor leaguer with all the ruthless tools to make the majors.

Once word spread of his brutal efficiency, the Ringer was given a healthy retainer to work exclusively for a single organization whose last mercenary for hire was found missing several vital organs and smeared across the Verrazano-Narrows Bridge. This new employer offered the Ringer his first meaningful assignment: the assassination of a rival organization's consigliere, a power play that would have citywide ramifications.

The Ringer ambushed the man at a trendy nightclub, killing three bodyguards in a spray of gunfire and smoke and blood. But somehow in the mayhem, the target survived. And for the first time, there was a living man who could identify the Ringer.

Two days later, four armed men broke into the Ringer's home, a fifth-floor brownstone on the lower east side. The shotgun blast that buckled the front door woke him and his wife, a struggling actress named Anne who was just a notch below gorgeous and talented enough to make the big-time.

The Ringer killed one man before the assailants fired a second shot. Realizing they had little chance of outfighting three armed men, the Ringer took his bride and ran for the fire escape. Then a bullet caught him in the lower back. The assassins grabbed him by his numb legs, pulled them back inside. One held them at gunpoint while the others doused the apartment with gasoline and ripped out the gas pipe from the stove.

The lead gunman leaned over the Ringer's limp body and said, "This is your first and last lesson, asshole." Then he put the barrel of the gun to Anne's head and pulled the trigger.

The Ringer took another bullet in the chest. One of the gunmen lit a cigarette, took a puff and offered it to the Ringer, who lay dying on the bedroom floor. Before leaving, the gunman tossed the lit cig into a puddle of gasoline.

Your first and last lesson.

As flames spread through the apartment, the Ringer managed to drag himself to the window, hurling his maimed body onto the fire escape. He tumbled down a flight of steps, then the apartment erupted in a massive fireball.

Four weeks later, all of the assassins were dead, their body parts strewn throughout the city with the precision of discarded cigarette butts. All save one man. One man who'd survived the Ringer's vengeance. One man who was never hunted down. And it was that man, the lone gunman who'd somehow escaped his rage, the man who'd sent a bullet crashing through his lover's head, who kept the Ringer's heart beating to this day.

The Ringer was dead to the world. Another statistic for the FBI. Another record closed. Two charred bodies were found in the smoldering wreckage. One was Anne, the other a failed assassin. The authorities assumed the Ringer had been caught in the blast. Now, years later, his name and face were a mystery to everyone but those he killed for.

But the Ringer's soul, his lost love, was the driving force behind every murder. The picture of Anne he kept in his breast pocket.

Right before climbing onto the fire escape, cradling his wife's body in his arms, the Ringer managed to grab an old photograph from the dresser. The photo was of Anne, sitting on a sandy beach wearing a beautiful yellow dress, an orange sun dipping over the horizon. It was taken the first night of their honeymoon. As blood leaked from his body, the Ringer put this photo into his right breast pocket. The photo was his final memory of the woman he'd loved so dearly, the only memory left of her. Anne's photo was his second heart, and it beat with the venomous blood of a man whose thirst for vengeance could never be quenched.

He would never love again, never care for another soul, living every day only to avenge his lover's death. And someday, everyone knew he would.

This was the man standing two feet from Blanket.

DiForio walked around the table. He held a newspaper in his hand. Blanket recognized the picture on the front. Nobody had to say a word. As soon as the Ringer accepted the job, if he accepted the job, Henry Parker's life was over.

DiForio held the front page up for the Ringer to see, then handed it to him. The man didn't even look at it.

"Henry Parker," DiForio said, "has something that belongs to me. A package with some important materials that I can't afford to lose. I need you to bring it to me. And when that's done, I want Parker to disappear."

The Ringer didn't move. DiForio looked him over.

"Don't you need a notepad or something? Jot all this down?" Michael asked. The Ringer stared straight at DiForio. His eyes showed nothing.

Michael continued. "We have one source rather close to the investigation. We know that the police haven't found Parker yet and that they expect him to try and flee the city. Most major departure points are guarded—Port Authority, JFK, LaGuardia. They think there's a possibility he got on the Path. You know, the train that goes to Jersey?"

"He didn't do that," the man said.

"Oh, no?" DiForio said, amused.

"No," the Ringer said, his voice monotone. "If Parker's going to run, it's not going to be across the Hudson. It's going to be far, far away from here."

"How do you know that?" Michael asked.

"Because that's what I would do." The Ringer thought for a moment. "Parker will need clothes and money. If he tries to use a credit card, the cops will be on him in no time. Get me his credit card numbers. There are too many variables the police can control that we can't. They have more manpower. They've already started looking. We're playing catch-up."

"What do you suggest?"

"Hopefully Parker is as smart as his pedigree suggests. He's not going to make stupid mistakes. With any luck, he's already fled and we're on even footing with the Department of Justice. Have the police started running taps yet?" DiForio looked at Blanket, who gulped, then spoke.

"They, uh, yeah. They've got taps up and running to, let's see…his girlfriend, this Mya Loverne broad who's a Columbia law student and…"

"Daughter of David Loverne. Where else?"

"His parents' house in Oregon."

"What else?"

"Cell phone, too. Police couldn't find one at his apartment, they assume he still has it. They're keeping a tap in case he's stupid enough to carry it around."

"He won't. If he's smart he'll lose the cell phone," the Ringer said. "Is that all?

"For now, yeah." The Ringer nodded.

"Now, your price," DiForio said. He fixed his tie and took a glass of water from the table. He put it to his lips but didn't drink. The room was silent, half the eyes on the Ringer, the other half on DiForio.

"I'm offering your usual fee," Michael said. He hesitated a moment, took a small sip of water, then added, "Times two."

The Ringer shook his head. "Ten," he said.

DiForio whistled. "A million bucks. That's a rich asking price to track down one hippie kid asshole."

"You wouldn't have contacted me if Parker wasn't threatening the sanctity of your organization," the Ringer said derisively. "I'd be working against the police and federal government to find a man wanted for the murder of a New York police officer. The price is one million. That or nothing."

DiForio looked at the ceiling, as though consulting the God of asbestos, then looked back and said, "Let's split the difference. Five hundred K."

Without warning, the Ringer turned, opened the door and left the room.

"Don't you walk out on me!" DiForio yelled. The Ringer ignored him and began to disappear down the corridor. "Hey, asshole, I didn't say you could leave!"

The Ringer turned around. His eyes held no interest in anything DiForio said.

"Your time is almost up, Michael. You won't find Henry Parker. At least not before the police do. And from the look in your eyes, I can tell you'd rather not have the police find this package." Blanket watched as DiForio's face reddened, his jaw muscles tightening.

The Ringer turned to leave. Then Michael spoke.

"I meant to ask you," DiForio said, the faintest glimmer of a smile on his lips. "How's your wife?"

Blanket gasped. A hush fell over the room.

The Ringer stopped dead in his tracks. Slowly the killer's head dipped into shadow. When he turned around, even in the darkly lit hallway, Blanket could see that his eyes were burning fire, hatred he never knew a mortal man was capable of.

Swiftly the Ringer stepped back into the meeting room. He whipped a pistol from his coat and pressed it to the base of Charlie's neck. He took a moment to look at DiForio, then squeezed the trigger and sent a bullet into Charlie's skull. The blast thundered around the small room as hands leapt to cover shattered eardrums. Charlie's eyes flickered, his brain and skull sprayed against the wall like a bloody Rorschach.

"Charlie!" Blanket yelled as his friend's lifeless body slumped to the floor. He looked at the Ringer with murder in his eyes. The man returned the glare, icy cold, and Blanket looked away. The Ringer turned his gaze to DiForio, the smoking pistol tracing a straight line to the powerful man's heart.

"This entire room can die before you open your mouth again," the Ringer said. "Now if you open your mouth and I don't like what I hear, not only will this package disappear but I'll hang the head of every miserable scum in this room from the tallest building in the city, and I'll watch the sun roast your ugly faces every single day until all that's left are your rotted, hollow skulls."

DiForio barely seemed to notice either this or the dead man slumped against the wall. Instead he smiled and tented his hands in front of him.

"One million it is," Michael said. "For that I want my package and Henry Parker. The package I want delivered without a scratch. Parker…his condition is entirely up to you."

The Ringer nodded slowly and stepped outside.

14

The Ringer slipped into his black Ford and closed the door. He could feel the warm sun on his face. He sank deep into the leather seat, closed his eyes and began the process.

His hand moved absently to his chest, stopping at the slim bulge in his shirt pocket. His fingers felt what lay beneath, pressed on it gently, making sure not to leave a mark or a dent. After so many years the photo was worn, faded around the edges, but the colors were still strong and vibrant. Just like his memory of Anne. The only woman he'd ever love in this lifetime.

In his mind's eye he could see her face, her stunning blue eyes. He could almost touch her, feeling the silky strands of her hair as she gazed at him with a happiness he never knew existed. Anne had accepted the life he'd chosen. A selfish life, but one he would have abandoned in a heartbeat if he knew its consequences.

Breathing in, he could smell a hint of her favorite perfume, the acrid scent of sweat as they made love. Her soft moans and touches on his back, fingers tickling his senses, knowing just how to make him shiver. She was his first and his last. His only.

Anne.

Then agony ripped across his face as he saw blood splashed over his hands. Her eyes contorted into shock and then glazed over as she fell, dead, into his arms. His wails shook the walls as flames began to lick the ceiling. Cries that God himself must have heard. Cries that made the devil smile.

He saw his wife's killer in the darkness, the knitted hood obscuring his features. Hands pale, skin soft. A young man. Only his eyes and mouth were visible. Eyes the Ringer would never forget.

His retribution was almost complete. There was only one man left.

The Ringer opened his eyes and picked up the newspaper. He looked at the photo of Henry Parker. Just twenty-four. Already a killer. Just like him.

In his mind's eye the images slowly merged and became one, Henry's face transposed as Anne's killer. When he was finished, the shrouded face of the man who'd killed his wife was replaced by Henry Parker.

And now Parker was responsible for Anne's death. A death waiting to be avenged. Hatred for this young man boiled up inside the Ringer. The tendons in his fingers tensed as he gripped the steering wheel, blood pounding in his temples.

The Ringer started the car and pulled onto Seventh Avenue, away from the old church where he'd been summoned, whose recesses currently housed some of the most remorseless men ever to walk the earth.

He cracked the window, let the breeze in.

Removing a cell phone from his pocket, the Ringer dialed the first number on his list. He had lots of calls to make.

He had a killer to find.

15

I rode the subway like a man about to go in for surgery: eyes wide open, fear coursing through my veins, waiting for someone to burst through the door bringing pain and suffering. Palms flat on my seat, I was ready to shove off and run at the first sign of a uniform. Paranoia was a trait I hadn't been exposed to often—aside from an ill-advised pot binge my sophomore year—and it seemed to enjoy taking over my body. My leg stung like hell, but the blood flow seemed to have stopped.

After a grueling sixteen-minute ride, I got off at the Union Square station and walked outside. The slight May breeze swirled around me. Demonstrators were chanting on bullhorns and holding well-made picket signs and L.L. Bean knapsacks, protesting corporate greed in style.

Ordinarily I'd stop and watch for a few minutes, but I was more concerned with the other people watching them. The cops. Standing by, hands on their hips, observing the docile demonstration. Making sure the crowd of neo-hippies didn't start tossing hemp bricks at the Virgin megastore.

Keeping my eyes fixed on a small contingent of officers by a coffee shop, I edged along the low brick wall surrounding Union Square Park, walked south and headed down Third Avenue.

Ironic, I thought. After living in New York for a month I'd finally started to feel like I belonged. I'd come here hoping to be embraced, but now I was being expelled like a diseased organ. Chasing a story, doing my job, led me into this nightmare.

The decision was obvious. I had to leave the city. I had to find out why that cop nearly killed me. My options were dwindling. I still had the reporter's notebook in my backpack, an unfriendly reminder of why I went to the Guzmans' apartment in the first place.

The cops had gotten to Mya, and I was no longer safe uptown. Was she cooperating with the authorities? No matter what happened, when this was over, Mya would no longer be part of my life. That was for certain. Three years disappearing as though they'd never happened. A road of memories that led straight off a cliff.

It was too much to process. I had to look at it objectively. What I needed to do, and how to do it.

I picked up a pay phone on East 12th Street and dialed the operator. Two rings and an automated voice answered.

"What city and state?"

"New York, New York. Manhattan."

"One moment while I connect you to an operator."

The phone rang, and I heard the typing of keys and a cheery male voice.

"Directory assistance, this is Lucas, how may I assist you?"

"I'd like the main directory listing for New York University."

"Thank you, sir, one moment."

The seconds ticked by, each moment agonizing. Then Lucas came back on. "Sir, I have two listings. One is an automated directory, and the other is for the campus switchboard."

"Is the switchboard manned by an actual human being?"

"I believe so, sir."

"I'll take that one."

"Yes, sir, and thank you for using…"

"Just connect me."

Another ring as he patched me through. This time a female voice picked up, sounding considerably less enthused about her job than Lucas.

"New York University. How may I direct your call?"

"Yes, hi. By any chance, do you have a student shuttle service?"

"Yes, we do," she said, and yawned audibly. "It's not officially sponsored by the university, but we do facilitate student-to-student commuting."

"Can you tell me which students have registered cars leaving today?"

"I'm sorry, we don't offer that information over the phone. The listings are posted on the bulletin board at the Office of Student Activities."

"And where is that located?"

"Sixty Washington Square South."

"Can you tell me the cross streets?"

"Just a moment." I heard the rustling of papers, then a

sharp curse, mumbling in the background, something about a paper cut. "Hello?"

"Still here," I said.

"The OSA is located on West 4th between LaGuardia and Thompson."

"Thanks." I hung up before she could say "You're welcome."

Heading west on 11th and then south on Broadway, I stopped at a bodega and bought an oversized Yankees T-shirt for five dollars. I ducked into a coffee shop that reeked of moldy gyros, went into the restroom and changed. My ripped clothes went in the trash can, buried under a pile of wet paper towels.

I winced and rolled up my pant leg to gauge the wound. My empty stomach lurched. An angry red gash ran across the side of my thigh, dried blood congealed around it.

Just yesterday I was sitting at my desk at the *Gazette,* and now here I was in a restaurant bathroom looking at a gunshot wound. Thankfully it looked like the bullet had just grazed the surface. I mopped the wound with wet towels, biting my lip at the pain.

This wasn't possible, I kept telling myself. Any moment I'd wake up in bed.

Please, just wake up.

I reached the OSA at five minutes of nine. Most self-respecting college students would still be asleep, tired from a night of post-finals partying or wasting time before the start of their summer jobs. Hopefully I'd find at least one that bucked the system.

I walked up the steps and opened the front door, but then stopped. What if they had newspapers inside? It was a safe bet that students—encapsulated in their own private bubbles—hadn't read today's front page, but a registrar or another administrative figure might care about current events.

I had to keep going. Standing motionless on the steps was suspicious. I didn't have a choice. My options were perilously few. This was my Plan B. There was no Plan C.

I took a deep breath, pressed the latch down and pulled the door open.

A cold blast of air-conditioning greeted me. Several students sat on a green couch held together by electrical tape, reading magazines they didn't seem very interested in. The room had the sterile vibe of a doctor's office combined with the comfort of the backseat of a New York taxicab.

I approached a portly guy pretending to read *Harper's Bazaar*, his eyes lingering on the well-endowed redhead across the room instead of last summer's fashion trends.

"'Scuse me," I said. He lowered the magazine and leered. "Do you know where they post the student shuttle listings?"

"No, sorry." He picked the mag back up and commenced fake reading.

"They're down the hall to your left. Right before the registrar's office." I turned to see the redhead smiling at me. She was reading a paperback with the cover torn off. The word *Desire* was visible on the spine. I pointed down the hall she was referring to, and she nodded.

"You can't miss it," she said. "The red tickets are for day trips, blue are for overnighters. Where you headed?"

"Uh, home," I said. "Thanks."

"No problem," she said, her eyes wide, as though expecting more conversation.

I grabbed a student newspaper and followed the hallway, hiding my face behind the pages as I passed a row of offices. Scraps and postings covered the light blue walls, hanging desperately on bent thumbtacks and staples. I casually glanced at a few. Table and chair sets for sale. One used rug, green. Three Siamese kittens looking for a home.

Then I found it. A wooden rack with about two dozen slips nestled inside, half red, half blue. A name was printed on each. Underneath the name was the student's destination. Underneath the destination was the date and time each student was departing campus, along with how much money they expected their passenger to contribute. Most asked for gas, but some expected meal money and/or room and board in case a hotel stopover was needed.

I started with the blue batch, which were apparently longer trips. Three were driving to California, two to Seattle, some miscellaneous trips to Idaho, Nevada and Oregon. I considered Oregon for a moment, debated taking a chance at going home. No way. The cops would be waiting for me to contact my parents. Luckily I had no intention of doing so.

Looking through the last of the blue slips, my heart sank. The next trip was leaving three days from now. No good. Time was running out.

I replaced the cards, smiling at a heavyset woman who lumbered past me with a stack of manila folders under her arm.

I took the batch of red slips, which were for shorter, day trips. If I didn't find what I was looking for here, the Path to New Jersey was a possibility. I really didn't want to be anywhere near New York, but getting out of the city was priority number one.

As I went through the red batch, my hopes began to sink. Nobody was leaving today. The phrase *Plan C* echoed in my head, but unlike Plans A and B the words rang hollow.

Kevin Logan
Leaves 5/28—12:00 p.m.
Montreal—gas, meals

Samantha Purvis
Leaves 5/30—10:00 a.m.
Amarillo, Texas—gas, E-Z Pass

Jacob Nye
Leaves 6/4—3:00 p.m.
Cape Cod—gas

Then, right as I was about to give up, I saw the second-to-last slip.

Amanda Davies
Leaves 5/26—9:00 a.m.
St. Louis—gas, tolls

At the bottom of the slip she'd left two phone numbers— apartment and cellular—for interested parties.

I checked my watch—8:57 a.m. Amanda Davies was leaving in three minutes.

I dashed outside, through the waiting room and past the

redhead, hurtling down the block where I stopped, breathless, at a pay phone. My leg was aching and my ribs throbbed.

Tune it out.

Sweat, once dried on my skin, was now oozing from my pores. I picked up the receiver—my watch read 8:58—and reached into my pocket for change.

In my palm lay a dime, two nickels, three pennies, and multicolored lint. I didn't have enough money for a goddamn phone call. I took a breath, debated for a moment, and dialed 1-800-COLLECT.

Last year, after my cell phone was stolen from my dorm room, I'd registered a calling card for emergency use. The fees were so astronomical I'd only used it once, drunk dialing Mya after a party where I accidentally dropped my new cell phone into a vat of spiked punch.

When prompted I punched in the calling card number, then Amanda Davies's cell phone number.

My watch read 8:59. I wasn't going to make it. A friendly voice came on the line.

"Thank you for using 1-800-COLLECT. May I discuss our new long distance plan with you?"

"No thanks, just connect me."

"Thank you, sir, have a good…"

"Just connect me!"

The automated voice of James Earl Jones thanked me for my patronage. Then the phone began to ring.

Two rings. Three. Four. I tried to match an image to *Plan C.* Still nothing.

Five rings.

I was about to hang up the phone. Then, with the receiver

a fraction of an inch from the hook, a female voice came over the earpiece.

"Hello?"

I brought it to my ear, and said, "Hello?"

"Yeah, who's this?"

"Amanda Davies?"

"Yes, who is this?"

"Amanda, thank God. I got your number from the student shuttle posting in the OSA. Are you still driving to St. Louis this morning?"

"I'm in my car right now."

"Shit. Listen, would you still be willing to take a passenger?"

"Depends. Where are you?"

"I'm on West 4th, somewhere on LaGuardia."

"What's your name?"

I hesitated.

"It's Carl. Carl Bernstein."

"Well, Carl, I'm in a red Toyota on 9th and 3rd, in front of the Duane Reade. I'm running into Starbucks to get a cup of coffee. If you're here by the time I get out, you're in. Otherwise, I'm gone."

"I'll be there."

"That's up to you." Click, then a dial tone.

I dropped the phone and sprinted east. The muscles in my side began to tighten, a cramp settling in. Pain lanced through the wound in my leg. Hopefully there would be a huge run on mochachinos. Maybe the espresso machine would explode. Anything to give me more time. I prayed, running as fast as I could, my leg feeling like an iron fork was being repeatedly jabbed into it.

I got to the Duane Reade at 9:06, doubled over to catch my breath, had to refrain from dry heaving. As I surveyed the cars parked on the street, my heart skipped a beat.

There was an empty spot directly in front of the drugstore. Big enough to fit a car.

Please, no.

I stepped into the space, frantically looking at the adjacent few cars, hoping to find Amanda's red Toyota.

"Fuck!" I shouted at the top of my lungs, all my frustrations escaping in a single, wretched outburst, all the pain and horror and shit that had suddenly fallen on me like a ton of bricks leaving me devastated. Amanda Davies had left. I was too late.

I collapsed on the curb, head in my hands, warmth spreading through my cheeks. My self-pity needed a minute to ferment. I had no other plans, nowhere else to go, nobody to turn to. My life was over. There was no salvation. Soon I'd be arrested, and if I got lucky I'd make it to trial.

Then a car horn blared, jolting the morbid thoughts from my head. I turned to see a humongous black SUV waiting to pull into the vacant spot where I was sitting. The driver was wearing designer shades and his hair looked like it could deflect small-arms fire. He lowered his window and said, "Hey, buddy, that spot's reserved for cars."

Nodding silently, I stepped onto the sidewalk and started walking. My fate, it seemed, was sealed.

"Carl? Hey, Carl!"

At first it didn't register. Then I heard it again and I remembered.

My name. The name I'd given to Amanda Davies.

I spun around, searching for the source. Then I saw it. A red Toyota idling at the intersection. A girl was hanging out the driver's side window. And she was staring right at me.

I jogged up to the passenger side, the pain in my leg and chest receding. The girl nodded at the empty seat. I opened the door, slid in and latched my seatbelt. She had a playful grin on her face.

"Carl?"

"Amanda, oh, God, thank you."

"Hey, it's just a ride, I don't think I'm worthy of deification just yet."

Then I noticed just how gorgeous Amanda Davies was. Her brown hair spilled over her beautifully tan shoulders, draping over lovely toned arms and smooth skin. She had on a green tank top and tight blue jeans, and there was a hint of faded sunburn on her neck, and a tiny mole by her right collarbone. Her skin had a brilliant luster to it and there was a slightly mischievous tint in Amanda's emerald eyes. If I had to be stuck in a car for hours with a complete stranger, I could have had it worse. Much worse.

"Sorry about that, Carl. I didn't mean to scare you, but I thought it'd be funny to play a joke, you know. Make you think I'd left." I forced out a laugh, and looked at my savior. Not only was Amanda Davies gorgeous, but she had a pretty sadistic sense of humor.

"You need to stop for anything before we get going?" she asked. "Coffee? Bathroom?"

"No," I said. To be honest I was starving, but there was no time to waste. "I'm good for now."

Amanda nodded, gunned the engine and merged into the

northbound lane. The car smelled faintly of grease and breath mints. An empty McDonald's wrapper lay crumpled on the floor, surrounded by a graveyard of Tic Tac containers. She saw me looking at them and smiled.

"What, girl can't go nuts on a McChicken every now and then? We need to eat tofu and broccoli every meal?"

"I didn't say anything."

"No, but you were thinking it."

"I wasn't thinking anything," I said defensively. She leered at me, a hurtful look on her face.

"You think I'm bulimic, don't you?"

My head snapped to attention. "What?"

"You think I chow down on burgers and fries all day then go puke it all up."

"I have no idea what you're talking about, I swear."

"I know your kind," she sniffed, slamming down the blinker and following the signs toward the Holland Tunnel. "You think you're hot shit cause you eat protein-enriched sprouts all day then spend eight hours on the elliptical machine. Well, let me tell you something, Carl. Some of us have natural metabolisms. We don't spend all day reading *Ladies Home Journal* and wishing we were Heidi or Gisele."

"Who's Heidi?"

"Oh, forget it," she said. "This obviously isn't working out. Maybe I should drop you off somewhere." My breath caught short. I stammered.

"You can't…you can't do that. No, I swear, I didn't think that at all. I just noticed the wrapper, that's it. You can eat whatever you want. I don't care if you have lard for breakfast. In fact I encourage it." Amanda looked devastated, her lips contorting into an ugly grimace.

"So you're saying I'm fat."

"No, Jesus H. Christ, I'm not saying that at all. You probably have the fastest metabolism on earth. If you want to eat McNuggets and candy all day…"

"Carl," Amanda said. Again, the name took a moment to process.

"Yeah?"

"I'm messing with you."

An awkward silence enveloped the car as her lips collapsed into a maniacal grin.

"You were screwing with me."

"Come on, you really think I care what a guy I just met thinks about my dietary habits? No offense, Carlito, but I don't. I give you credit for keeping your cool, though. I've been with other guys who've started calling me names and telling me to lay off the milk shakes."

"So you actually do this often. That's kind of scary."

"Saves me money on gas and tolls, can't blame a girl for wanting a little entertainment to go with it."

"Well then I'm happy to oblige," I said. "As long as we get to…St. Louis in one piece, I'll sing show tunes if it'll make you happy."

"If I hear one chorus from 'Dancing Queen,' you're walking to St. Louis."

We pulled into a line of cars waiting for the outbound Holland Tunnel. Traffic was agonizingly slow, but Amanda steered us into the E-Z pass lane. I lowered my head as we passed through the tollbooth, not wanting to offer an easy glimpse to an attendant who might be perusing the newspaper while bored on the job. Within minutes, we were heading west toward New Jersey.

Sodium lights whizzed by, my life now squeezed into a one-lane road. The speck of light at the end of the tunnel grew as we neared the exit. I felt nauseous. I was out of New York, away from my personal ground zero. Hopefully arriving in St. Louis by nightfall. But in the commotion to leave, I'd been so delirious that I didn't even consider the next step. All I knew is that an opportunity for survival had arisen and I'd taken it.

I didn't know what to do once we got to St. Louis, didn't know a soul in the whole state. I had no phone to use, forty dollars in my wallet and a gunshot wound in my leg. Mya was out of the picture, as was Wallace Langston. The police were probably circling them both like vultures. They were gangrenous appendages I had to cut off. Perhaps permanently. My life now existed in a parallel social universe, where I could trust only strangers, forced to alienate everyone who cared.

Guilt flushed through my system as I looked at the girl sitting next to me. Her eyes were stuck to the road, so delicate, innocent. I hadn't considered the implications of what this could do to her. Amanda Davies was there, and I'd blindly reached for her. And now she was at the mercy of chance. I wanted to apologize, to tell her what she'd gotten into. But if I offered the truth, she wouldn't be a stranger anymore. As long as my story was Carl's, as long as I remained a stranger, I was safe.

Amanda took a pair of aviator sunglasses from a pouch

above the rearview mirror. As we pulled onto US-1/9 south, the bright sunlight of morning shining golden on the horizon, she turned to me.

"You mind opening the glove compartment? Just pull the tab upwards. It might be stuck, so give a good tug."

I complied, and half a dozen maps spilled onto my lap. A tape measure. Three old movie tickets. Chewing gum that seemed to have petrified.

"Okay, now what?"

"Hand me that notebook," she said. "The spiral one in there."

Behind a mass of red-and-blue illustrated tributaries lay a tiny reporter's notebook, spiral bound at the top, with white lined pages. I'd seen many like it in various newsrooms, had a similar one in my backpack. Many reporters kept them on hand. Was Amanda a journalist? A writer? The odds were staggering, but who else kept a notebook in their glove compartment?

She took it from me and flipped to a clean page, then bit the cap off the pen while balancing the pad on the steering wheel. Then she began to write.

"Uh, hey," I said, watching the two-ton vehicles whizzing by in a blur on either side of us. "Isn't the first driving commandment 'keep thine eyes on the road?'"

She said, "I do this all the time."

I nodded, as though I'd seen this kind of motor vehicle behavior a thousand times. My hands, however, firmly gripped the armrest in the event she was lying.

"So how long's the drive to St. Louis?" I asked.

She stopped scribbling. "Depending on traffic, between twelve and fourteen hours."

"And you can make that in one sitting?" She looked at me as if I'd asked if her hair color was real.

"I've done it a hundred times. We might need a pit stop or two for coffee and bathroom breaks, but we should be there by midnight. You'll have to let me know ahead of time where I'm dropping you."

"Will do."

A moment later, she added, "So I'm guessing your clothes are all there."

"Huh?"

"Well, either all your clothes are wherever I'm dropping you off, or you don't run up much of a laundry bill."

"Yeah," I said, tugging at my brand-new shirt, the fabric stiff, chafing my armpits. "I have a whole wardrobe waiting for me."

"Gotcha." She scribbled some more in her notebook as I tried unsuccessfully to read over her shoulder.

Traffic began to thin out as we got farther from the tunnel. I didn't recognize where we were, but Amanda seemed confident in her bearings. The skyscrapers of New York were gone, replaced by high-tension power lines and smokestacks peppering the bluish-gray landscape. I'd never been to New Jersey. I'd never been to a lot of places. Funny that it took being wanted for murder to get me to see more of the country.

Amanda's notebook lay open on the armrest, and I decided to sneak a look. Her handwriting was cursive, flowing in decorative, effortless loops. Surprisingly I glimpsed my name—or rather the name of Carl Bernstein—at the top of the page.

"What are you writing?" I asked.

"Just taking notes," she said matter-of-factly.

"Notes on what?"

"You."

"What do you mean? You're taking notes on me?"

"Yup."

Just my luck, I thought. Probably hitched a ride with an FBI profiler's daughter.

"What kind of notes?"

"Just observations and stuff," she said, without a hint of annoyance. "Personality, clothes, speech patterns. Just things I notice."

Except for Carl's name in large lettering, her handwriting was too small for me to make out the rest of her notes.

"So tell me. What have you observed about me in the twenty minutes we've known each other?"

"That's none of your business, actually."

"If you're writing about me, it is my business. It's my business very much."

"That's where you're wrong," Amanda replied. "See, this is my car and my notebook. I'm writing this for my own eyes, nobody else's. What, you have a criminal record you don't want exposed? Should I drop you off somewhere on the turnpike?"

"That wouldn't be very appreciated."

"Well, when I'm in your car, you can take all the notes on me you want. I won't ask questions."

"I'll remember that." She nodded, reached down and flipped the notebook closed.

Time flew by as Amanda coasted down the highway. I wondered how many other passengers she had written drive-by profiles on. Despite the temptation, I refrained from asking. The less Amanda knew about me—and vice versa—the better. She could ruminate all she wanted about Carl Bernstein, but I couldn't let her know Henry Parker.

After an hour of complete silence, punctured only by the wailing strains of an all-girl rock band on the radio—something about "de-manning" their respective boyfriends—I decided to spark some friendly conversation.

"So, what's in St. Louis?"

"Home," Amanda said. "I have two months before the bar and my folks are on vacation in the Greek Isles. I have the entire place to myself to study in peace and quiet."

"You're in law school?"

"No," she replied, sarcasm dripping. "I'm taking the bar exam for veterinarians."

"Man," I said, rolling my eyes. "It must be exciting to be so funny. And *that's* my first observation about *you*."

"Touché," she said. Then her tone turned serious. "Actually, I want to be a child advocacy council. Custody cases, abandonment. Domestic issues, you know?"

"That's very noble of you."

Amanda shrugged. "I don't care if it's noble, it's just what I want to do. Applying for sainthood didn't really cross my mind." She waited a moment, then said, "What about you? What do you do?"

"I want to be a journalist," I said. She smiled at me, and I felt a swell of pride. "I want to be the next Bo…big investigative reporter."

"Noble," she said, and I laughed.

"I used to think so. Now every reporter ends up their own biggest story."

16

Mauser sipped a cup of scalding coffee. His calves burned from the chase that morning and the caffeine would quicken his blood flow. He wanted to retain a sense of urgency until he found Parker. If he invited a heart attack in the process, so be it. He was in decent shape for a man of years—as Linda often called him—but working out didn't prepare you for the exertion of real life. Full speed, no timeouts, no water breaks. What kept him going was catching John's killer. That made the pain subside.

He'd alternated hot and cold packs upon returning to Federal Plaza. Denton had phoned ahead to Louis Carruthers, who deployed NYPD uniformed officers to guard all potential subway exits for the 6 train between Harlem and Union Square.

Guarding the subway was near pointless, Mauser thought, adding more cream and sugar to his steaming brew. Parker would be long gone by the time the first cop arrived, and with so many exit points the chances that they'd catch him there were slim. All they could do was sit and wait. Wait for someone to recognize him. Wait for Parker to make a move, slip up. Expose himself.

Parker had all but run out of contacts in New York. Joe had any and all possibilities covered. A plainclothes was staking out Mya Loverne's apartment, instructed to tail her to and from work. Another two were stationed outside the *Gazette*. Chances were Parker had given up on both venues, but they had to be thorough. He'd already tapped the Parker residence in Bend, Oregon, but surprisingly Henry hadn't attempted to contact his parents. There had to be a reason for his silence. Perhaps there was an estrangement they didn't know about.

Twenty-goddamn-four years old, Joe thought. If he'd been caught up in a shit storm like Parker's at twenty-four, he would have thrown himself off the Brooklyn Bridge by now. Parker, though, didn't seem to be in that frame of mind. He wouldn't have run otherwise. Regardless, Mauser had to find the kid before some patrolman got lucky. He didn't want anybody else to administer punishment first.

Mauser closed the folder on his lap. A mound of paper saying nothing. They were playing this game as reactionaries, responding to Parker's movements rather than instigating their own. Just as he added a fourth packet of sugar to the coffee, Denton burst into the room. Mauser's eyes perked up.

"Well?" he said.

"We got a hit," Denton said. Mauser set the folder aside, looked at Denton expectantly.

"Whadda you got?"

"Parker made a phone call," Denton said, his eyes blazing. "We've been monitoring all credit cards linked to Parker and his family. Scary how few there are, actually. My nephew? Kid's thirteen, has eight credit cards. But the Parker clan, there's three of 'em and they have two credit cards between them."

"So let's go, what's with this phone call?"

"Phone company's records show that last year Parker bought a calling card, one of those cards where there's no spending limit, it's linked to your credit card. You call 1-800-COLLECT or an operator, plug in the number and they connect your call. Bill comes at the end of the month." Denton handed a printed record to Mauser, who scanned it.

"Only two charges on the card," Mauser noted.

"One of them this morning, 8:56 a.m."

"St. Louis," Mauser said. "The fuck's he know in St. Louis?"

"The number's a cell phone, registered to one Lawrence Stein. Married to Harriet Stein. They have a daughter named Amanda Davies."

"Wait," Mauser said. "Is it Davies or Stein?"

Denton handed Mauser another folder. Inside were scans of three driver's licenses, one from each of the parties.

"Amanda Davies is Harriet and Lawrence Stein's daughter. Adopted daughter, that is. Little Amanda spent eleven years being shuttled from home to home before kindly Mr. and Mrs. Stein took her in for good. It seems our Amanda declined to have her name legally changed to Stein, kept her birth name Davies instead."

Mauser asked, "Is she an old girlfriend?"

"Maybe a friend, but not from college. She's in law school at NYU, studying child advocacy, lives in the dorms down there."

"You checking her apartment's call log?"

"Already done," Denton said. "No matches to our man. Cross-checked Parker's residences at Cornell, so far we're coming up empty."

Mauser rubbed the stubble on his chin. He needed a shave badly, needed sleep and a hot shower. He'd hoped to have Parker by now. Every moment John Fredrickson's killer lived ate away at Joe from the inside. The hunt steeled his resolve while gnawing away at everything else.

"Davies…is it possible Parker was seeing her on the side? Taking a little extracurricular pokey without Mya Loverne knowing?"

"Doubtful," Denton said, pouring a cup from the pot. He took a sip and grimaced, leaving the cup for dead on the tabletop.

Denton continued. "Let's look at it from Parker's perspective. You're new to the city, looking for your career break. David Loverne's someone you want on your side, or at least not want to piss off. Would you cheat on his daughter? You might get your rocks off for a few minutes, but if Daddy found out about it you'd have trouble hailing a cab without getting a summons, and you can bet any public defender assigned to him will give him a defense worthy of the worst busstop ambulance chaser."

Mauser thought for a moment, then said, "Check Parker and Davies's phone records going back the last five years. Parker's desperate, grasping at straws. There's a chance he reached out to Davies because she was the only option."

"There's something else," Denton said.

"Yeah?"

"We ran a trace on all credit cards registered to Amanda Davies and Harriet and Lawrence Stein. New purchases, etc.—"

"And?" Mauser said, failing to keep the anxiousness out of his voice.

"We got a hit on an E-Z Pass going through the Holland Tunnel at nine twenty-seven this morning."

Mauser furrowed his brow, surprised. "They're going to Jersey?"

Denton seemed to change his mind about the coffee, picking it off the table and taking a deep swallow. He grimaced again.

"God, this is some terrible shit. It's doubtful Jersey's their final destination, but if you're headed to St. Louis to visit the lovely Stein family, the Holland Tunnel's how you leave the city. Right now all we can do is keep track of the E-Z Pass. If we get more hits or Amanda makes any credit card purchases we'll be on top of it. If it looks like she's heading to St. Louis, we'll be on the first flight out there."

"Sounds awfully sketchy," Mauser said.

"That's 'cause it is." Denton stood, picked up his nearly full cup and tossed it in the trash. "Fucking worst coffee I've ever had."

He sat back down and looked at Mauser. Denton's eyes seemed to be searching for truth without asking for it, as if waiting for Mauser to shed some light he hadn't been able to find on his own. Mauser stayed stone-cold, giving away nothing. Denton was in this for his career, nothing more. And while Joe could use that to his advantage, the case was personal to him and him alone.

"So," Denton said, breaking the silence. "We haven't talked about this, but how are you holdin' up?"

Mauser shook his head, ran his fingers through his hair. His eyes were bloodshot, clothes so heavy they weighed him down. Sleep was out of the question.

His brother-in-law. One of his best friends—one of his only friends—was cold on a slab in a basement. His heart punctured by a bullet, shot by a stranger. A man who didn't know his family, didn't know Linda. A goddamn junkie whose only use to society was as an organ donor.

Mauser could feel hatred coursing through his veins, lighting his nerve endings until he was ready to explode. But he held it in, let the rage out through his gnashed teeth and clenched fists. Mauser knew as well as anyone that you didn't work smarter when fueled by anger. Mistakes would get in the way. Precision over passion.

Let the pain boil just below the surface. Let it simmer awhile. You'll know when it's time to let it boil over.

Joe stood up, tucked Parker's file underneath his arm. "I want a plane on standby. If Davies gets within a hundred miles of St. Louis, I want to be in the air in half an hour."

"You got it," Denton said, a smile on his face. "Anything else?"

"The Steins' residence in St. Louis. I want phone taps."

"Done."

Mauser said, "As of right now, Amanda Davies is our number-one lead. Keep a lock on her E-Z Pass, it's accepted on every major highway in this country, if they used it once they'll use it the whole trip. But we can't assume anything. I don't want to end up in St. Louis, find out he was wishing her happy birthday and managed to catch a ferry to the Azores. Parker's got a limited supply of cash so keep his credit cards active in the event he tries to hit an ATM."

"What about that package the Guzmans mentioned? The drugs? Christine Guzman said he stole a bag of dope, carried it out in some sort of briefcase or knapsack. She said he left the crime scene with it last night."

"We don't even know if he still has it. Parker could have stashed it anywhere, a train station or bus terminal locker," Mauser said. "The dope is secondary. Once we have him, we'll find it."

Denton didn't seem relieved by this. "John was killed over that dope, Joe. Maybe if we find it we'll get a lead on Parker."

Mauser shook his head.

"Right now, we're looking for Henry Parker, not a fucking dime bag. We'll find the dope, the pot of gold at the end of the rainbow, Elvis, JFK and any other shit he stole once we get him. But right now Parker has precious few friends and seems smart enough not to give himself away. We're going to have to be creative."

Denton nodded, headed for the door. Mauser's arm lashed out, catching the younger man's shoulder. Denton whirled around, caught by surprise. Mauser's grip tightened, feeling Denton's bones shift beneath the skin. "But make no mistake. Right now, Amanda Davies is a possible accomplice to murder. If I think they're heading west, I want to be in the air before the next commercial break. If anyone gets to Henry Parker before we do…"

Denton's face paled. Mauser could tell he understood.

"They won't," he said. "We'll be there first."

When Denton left the room, Joe locked the door and picked up the phone. He took a long breath, felt a weight descending behind his eyelids. He dreaded this, dreaded every second speaking to her. Parker had done this to him. He'd made the simple activity of talking to his sister an event to be feared.

After a moment, when his breathing slowed, he dialed. Part of him hoped nobody would pick up. Out of sight, out of mind. His heart fluttered when he heard her voice answer with a tired, "Hello?"

"Linda. It's Joe."

"Joe," his sister said, her voice heavy. She sounded sedated. "How are you?"

"I'm okay, Lin."

"It's good to hear your voice, Joe. These people won't stop calling. Newspapers and reporters. Goddamn vultures."

"Maybe you should book a hotel for a few days," Mauser said. "The department will pick up the tab." He could almost hear her shaking her head on the other end.

"The kids need to be able to reach me. I don't want to hide. I don't want to upset their lives any more than they already have been."

"The kids'll be fine, Lin. You need to take care of yourself." He heard a wistful laugh on the other end. Then Linda began to sob. Joe felt his cheeks go flush as his sister wept for her lost husband.

"Linda?" he said, his chest contracting, hot tears filling up his eyes. "Lin, please talk to me." She blew her nose, a pitiful rattle.

"Funny," Linda said. "It was always John who said he'd take care of me. He never said anything about me taking care of myself. I guess I just believed he'd always be there, and I wouldn't have to worry. Why'd he have to leave me? Jesus, Joe. I loved him so much."

Mauser felt a tear slide down his cheek, sobs racking his throat.

"I know you did, Lin. I did, too. I know it's no consolation, but I'll be there for you. Now and always."

"Thanks, Joe. I know you will."

"You want me to come over?"

"No," she said with an air of finality. "I need to be alone right now. I know that sounds selfish since he was your family, too—but I need this. Do you understand? Please tell me you do." Mauser said he did.

"Can I do anything for you? Bring you anything?"

"You can do one thing for me," Linda said. Mauser felt a chill run down his spine.

"Name it."

"I want you to kill the man who killed my husband. I don't care what it takes, Joe. You find him and you fucking cut his head off."

"Lin…"

"I know, I know," she said. "Thanks for calling, Joe."

"I'll talk to you soon."

"I love you."

The words leaked from his mouth like a balloon's final gasp of air. "I love you, too."

Mauser put the receiver down. He dropped his head into his hands as convulsions of sadness and rage seized his body. When Joe looked up, his vision was streaked, his eyes burned.

For Linda, he thought.

For me.

17

The Ringer sat baking in his car, going over the conversation in his head. He'd just spoken with the Arab deli owner, confirming that the man had, in fact, seen and scared off Henry Parker that morning.

"Just picked up my bat," the man said, smacking the wooden mallet against his palm. The Ringer held his hands up in mock surrender. "And the cocksucker ran outta here lickety-split. You know one of the greatest things about this country is baseball. This Parker fellow probably saw it in my eyes. If I was born here I woulda made the majors. I would've thumped him a good one."

The Ringer placated the man for a minute, then returned to his car. He tuned the radio into 1010 WINS, where a rumor was circulating that the cops had found Parker—and lost him—in the area nearby Columbia's campus.

Mya Loverne. The cops were all over her by now. Why had Parker gone uptown and risked capture? There had to be a reason besides the girl. He was resourceful. There had to be another angle.

Parker was born with a pedigree that had been run over

by a Mack truck, but still managed to work himself into an Ivy League school, pulled good grades and landed a job at one of the country's most respected newspapers. He was a pull-yourself-up-by-the-bootstraps archetype. The Ringer hated them, hated chasing them. If forced into self-reliance early on in life, one's abilities in that regard would only mature with age. Knowing this, it was probable Parker had fled the city and the cops were searching for a needle in an empty haystack. That boded well. At least he was on equal footing with the cops.

He opened his notebook and wrote down every conceivable route out of New York he could think of. He crossed off the airports and bus terminals. It was impossible for Parker to get past security. Subways were a problem, but they could only take him within the five boroughs. From what DiForio and Blanket said, Parker had no reliable contacts in New York other than his employer and girlfriend.

His employer was Wallace Langston, editor in chief of the *New York Gazette*. The same paper that had, reluctantly, he was sure, run a front-page story about John Fredrickson's murder that morning. In a letter from the editor, Langston himself referred to Parker as a "young employee who'd met their hiring expectations with flying colors and had exhibited no hostile, let alone homicidal, tendencies," then adding, "The *Gazette* will do anything and everything possible to bring all the facts to light, without any bias or prejudice."

If Langston made any attempt to aid Parker, his paper would be in jeopardy. The Ringer knew these newsmen. Most of them considered themselves noble, even altruistic, but in truth they lusted for fame, the glory of the byline. Hungry writers were no doubt chomping at the bit to write the Henry Parker/John Fredrickson story. Betraying friendships for the sake of notoriety.

Columbia. It didn't add up.

The Ringer picked up the phone and dialed Information, asking to be connected to the Columbia University directory. A sweet lady, her voice young and slightly timid, answered the phone. The Ringer asked to be connected to whatever office handled student transportation.

This time, a gruff man, sounding like he hadn't trimmed his beard in several months, answered.

"Hi, my name is Peter Millington," the Ringer said. "And I'm thinking about coming to Columbia for grad school. I live in California and I was wondering if you could tell me what forms of transportation there are for students on campus."

"Well," the operator said, "you got JFK and LaGuardia a cab ride or subway trip away…."

"No good, my family won't pay for the airline tickets. What are the cheap ways if you need to go a long distance off campus?"

"There's plenty of buses, trains. You got Port Authority and Penn Station…"

"Anything else?"

"Well, if you're going cheap, there're the student shuttles."

"Student shuttles." A bell went off in the Ringer's head. "If I wanted to learn more, maybe talk to a student about these shuttles, how would I do that?"

"One moment, let me transfer you to someone who can help."

As he waited for the call to go through, the Ringer penciled three schools down on his list: Columbia, which was doubtful. Small chance Parker would hang around uptown, waiting to be snatched by a black-and-white. Hunter and NYU had higher probabilities. And both were right off the 6 train.

Finally he was connected to the Office of Student Services. Under the guise of Lennie Hardwick, sophomore and racked for time, he persuaded a very nice lady named Helen to check the student shuttle postings for him. One match came up, a junior named Wilbur Hewes who was driving home to Ontario at 11:00 a.m. this morning. No other rides were registered for today. Hitching a ride to Canada made sense—assuming Parker didn't get stopped at the border. The Ringer wrote down Hewes's name and asked for the phone number on the posting. Lennie figured he'd keep it in case he ever wanted to do some fishing up north.

The Ringer called Wilbur Hewes's cell phone, got a curt response on the third ring.

"Yeah?"

"Hello, is this Wilbur?"

"Yeah, what?" The Ringer could hear the rush of the highway, Wilbur's voice full of static. Horns blaring. Heavy metal music loud enough to make his eardrums throb. The Ringer smiled. Wilbur was stuck in traffic.

"Hi, Wilbur, my name is Oliver Parker. I'm calling from Montreal, and I was informed by the helpful operator at Columbia that my son Henry might have gotten a ride from you."

"No Henry here. Nobody responded to my posting."

"Really?" the Ringer said, crossing Columbia off the

list. "You sure he didn't tell you to keep it a secret? It's my birthday today, maybe he wanted to surprise me and show up unannounced?"

"Listen, man," Wilbur said. The Ringer could hear the agitation of bumper-to-bumper traffic getting to Wilbur. "Nobody called about a ride. Unless your son's hiding in my trunk, wedged between three big-ass suitcases, he's not with me. All right?"

"Absolutely. I'm sorry to bother you." Wilbur hung up.

After a quick call to Hunter, he learned the school did not offer such a service, at least not one that was officially sanctioned. In other words, without a contact at the school, he was out of luck. He crossed Hunter off the list.

He phoned NYU and was connected to the Office of Student Activities.

The OSA receptionist, a bitter-sounding battle-ax of a woman, said she wasn't allowed to offer the listings over the phone. He asked her for the address and hung up.

Traffic moved like oil through a funnel, slow and thick. He double-parked in front of the OSA and, inside, a helpful custodian directed him to the postings. Halfway down the light blue hallway, the Ringer found what he was looking for.

The portly woman seated behind a pane of glass was clearly the same person who'd refused to read him the listings over the phone. He offered a pleasant smile and picked up the listings. They were separated into two batches: red and blue. He licked his thumb and sifted through them. No dice. No cars were scheduled to leave until later in the week.

He was about to cross NYU off his list when, on a whim, he walked up to the receptionist and pulled out Henry

Parker's photo, cropped from the newspaper. He gently rapped on the glass. The woman, a glamorous mole poking from her left nostril like a burrowing hedgehog, was buried in a celebrity magazine.

"Sorry to bother you," the Ringer said. "I was supposed to drive my son home this morning, but I'm not sure he got the message and I'm worried he might have left without me. He's about six feet tall, brown hair. He might have had a backpack of some sort with him."

The woman squinted, crinkled her nose and leaned closer.

"Yeah, there was one kid in here like that. He was in some kind of big huff, too, not very patient." The Ringer's heart quickened. "You ask me, your kid needs some lessons in manners."

The Ringer nodded. "First thing I'll tell him. Do you know if he got a ride from a student?"

"He did take a slip from the board. I can't tell you what he did with it."

"Would you happen to know whose slip he removed?"

The woman looked less than eager to help.

"Please," the Ringer added, his eyes imploring. "His aunt is sick, emphysema. I really need to find him."

"Doesn't your boy have a cell phone?"

The Ringer offered a sheepish look. "No, his sister at George Washington has the only one in our family."

The woman sighed heavily, then punched some keys on the computer.

"We log in all registered student rides. I can check the ones that left this morning, if it's really that urgent. *If* it's that urgent."

"Believe me, it is."

The woman hit a few more keys, waited a moment, punched a few more, then came up with a name.

"Amanda Davies," she said. "Left at nine this morning to St. Louis."

"You know, I'd love to call Ms. Davies up, let my boy know everything's all right. Did Miss Davies leave a phone number?" The woman nodded, scribbled on a Post-it and handed it through the small slot at the bottom of the window.

"Anything else?" she said, her eyes darting back to pictures of a couple cavorting topless on a white beach.

The Ringer shook his head. "No, you've been extremely helpful. Thank you."

As he left the OSA, the Ringer dialed the operator.

"What city and state?"

"St. Louis, Missouri. I'd like the address and phone number for a Miss Amanda Davies."

Five minutes later the Ringer had reserved a plane ticket and called an associate in St. Louis who could get him an untraceable gun. Ten minutes later he was speeding to LaGuardia airport. Blood was in the water, and he would only be circling for so long before he was able to strike.

18

I was back in that hallway. The man was pointing his gun at me. His horrible, manic grin breaking through the darkness. His finger squeezed the trigger. There was a sharp report and I was blinded by the gun's muzzle. He squeezed again. And again. But with each successive blast, rather than the slug ripping through my body, tearing my flesh, John Fredrickson would stagger back. And another gaping wound would appear in his chest.

He looked at the pistol, as if wondering what went wrong, then fired again, his body jolting backward like a puppet yanked by a spiteful master. Every bullet meant for me instead struck him, blood spurting from his chest.

Once the clip was empty, Fredrickson stared at the gun, his jacket and shirt in gory tatters. He silently mouthed *what happened,* before collapsing onto the floor. When I looked down, the gun was gone from his hand. Then it appeared in mine.

Wake up, Henry.

Then I was back in the car with Amanda.

I blinked the sleep from my eyes. It was a dream. My neck had gone stiff. Apparently I'd fallen asleep against the window. My face felt sticky. The sky was dark. The dashboard clock read 8:52 p.m. Amanda was sipping a fresh cup of coffee. An unopened cup sat in the holder.

"I got you one, just in case," she said. "It's probably cold by now, but I didn't want to wake you."

"Thanks, I could use it." I pulled back the tab and took a sip. It was cold, and heavy on the milk and sugar. Amanda Davies clearly valued the little things in life.

She gestured toward the cup. "I wasn't sure how you liked it, but you seem like a light-and-sweet kind of guy."

"And you'd be right," I said. "So light and sweet…tell me, Sherlock, did you come to that conclusion based on the scientific evidence in your notebook?"

"No, but you look a little soggy around the tummy, I assumed you weren't one to skimp on the sweet stuff."

"Touché."

Amanda gave a wry smile and turned back to the road.

I stretched my arms out, feeling my muscles slowly loosen. Drinking the coffee only made me realize just how hungry I was. And how badly I had to pee.

A billboard appeared up ahead, and Amanda steered toward it. The sign read St. Louis/Terre Haute.

"How far are we?"

"Three hours, give or take. Traffic's not too bad, though some asshole cut me off a few miles back."

Then I noticed the spiral notebook sitting on her lap, a pen tucked into the binding.

"Taking notes while I was sleeping?"

Amanda nodded as though there was nothing strange about it.

"We're making good time," she said absently. "You need to let me know where to drop you. Give me some lead time, would you?"

"Sure," I said. My mind raced. At some point she'd realize I had nowhere to go, that nobody was waiting for me. An idea popped into my head. Feeble, but it just might work. Not like I had anything better.

"Actually," I said, "since I missed the last few bathroom breaks, it'd be swell if we could swing by a rest stop."

"No problem, Carl. First one I see."

The name still sounded odd, my lies building up like mud in an hourglass.

Ten minutes later, we pulled into a rest area filled with SUVs and minivans. People with all the time in the world, and no pressure to use it. The parking lot was surrounded by thick rows of trees, the smell of car exhaust and burger grease thick in the air.

"Ah," Amanda said, taking a deep breath. "I love the smell of lard in the evening." She looked at my frozen countenance. "You know, Robert Duvall? *Apocalypse Now?*"

"I got the joke, sorry. My mind's just somewhere else. Still waking up a bit."

"You're still tired? Must have had a hell of a night last night."

"You might say that."

"Well, I'm gonna grab some fries and a milk shake while you hit the little boys' room."

"I'll come with you. I could use a French fry transfusion. Besides, it's only fair that I pay."

"You're paying for half the gas, buddy. Better make sure

you can afford some Exxon Supreme along with my cholesterol burger." I laughed, quite forcibly, very aware that my cash supply was on life support.

As we walked toward the complex, anxiety began to tingle inside me, a sort of paranoid spider sense. I had forty dollars to my name and no immediate possibility of making more. I had no friends or family to turn to—or wanted to turn to. I looked at the girl walking beside me, wondering if she could sense any of this. Wondering what she'd do if she knew the truth.

Amanda went to the ladies' room, and I set the unofficial world record for the longest urination in history. Of course I still made it out of the restroom before she did and went straight for Mickey D's. I wasn't a big fast-food person, but the smell of beef-injected French fries may as well have been filet mignon. A minute later Amanda joined me on line.

"Thanks for getting a spot," she said. "You mind if we eat in the car?"

"Not at all. I actually need to talk to you."

"About what?" she said, scanning the menu. "I can't decide between a farmer's salad or a double cheeseburger."

"Let's wait till we get back in the car."

She shrugged. "Whatever."

I bought a value meal and an extra order of fries. Amanda bought some newfangled salad that, being McDonald's, probably still had the fat content of a jelly doughnut.

The first order of fries disappeared before we made it to the car, and by the time we pulled onto the highway all that remained of my meal were three lettuce molecules and a pile of dirty napkins.

"So are you gonna tell me where I'm dropping you? Or maybe I should just leave you at the first housing project I come to." She smiled, and I returned a weak one.

"Actually, that's what I wanted to talk to you about." Amanda looked at me, concerned. "I don't know how else to say this, but my aunt and uncle...I'm supposed to stay with them and, well, I called them while you were in the bathroom and they're not back in town yet. They're on vacation in Cancún and their flight got delayed until tomorrow."

A moment passed.

"And?" Amanda said.

"And I don't have a key to their house." She turned back to the road and sipped her vat-sized soda.

"Can't you book a hotel room for the night? Watch some free HBO or hotel porn or something?"

"I suppose I could," I answered hesitantly.

We were silent for several minutes. Amanda's knuckles were white from gripping the steering wheel. She'd been so obliging to this point, and what I had in mind went well beyond mere imposition.

Then Amanda spoke.

"I keep mace in my bedroom."

"What?"

"Mace," she said. "In my nightstand. I can reach it, aim and fire accurately in under two seconds. If you come anywhere near me while I'm sleeping, I'll burn your eyes out."

"Geez, and I thought we were getting along."

She smiled, but there was an edge to it. She was being polite, more than polite, but wanted to make sure I understood the generosity of the favor she was about to extend.

"Seriously," she said, taking her eyes off the road, the cold night sky. I felt a chill run through my body. What I owed Amanda could never fully be repaid. "We have a guest bedroom. You can stay one night, but just one. After that, if Auntie Bernstein isn't home yet, you're on your own. I'm all for charity, but I'm late on my dues to the ACLU."

"Amanda," I said, my gratitude sincere, "you have no idea how much I appreciate it. I swear I won't leave my room. I won't even sleep in the bed. I'll stay on the floor."

"You're just lucky my parents are out of town, otherwise you'd be in the honeymoon suite at Motel Rat."

"What are the nightly rates at Motel Rat?"

"Actually they charge by the hour, on account that most of the guests contract rabies and can't afford to pay their hospital bills."

"Then I'll be sure to wear disinfectant-coated pajamas." Amanda laughed, and I followed suit. "But seriously, this really is kind of you."

"Don't mention it. Besides, my house can get creepy when I'm alone. At least I know if anyone breaks in, they'll go after you first."

"And why is that?"

She looked at me like I'd missed the punch line to a really good joke.

"'Cause you're the guy, stupid. You're supposed to ward off evil with a baseball bat in your pajamas while I'm sleeping peacefully with a glass of warm milk by my side."

"I haven't played baseball since I was ten."

A flirtatious smirk appeared on her face. "Well then you'd better practice your swing."

19

"Joe, we got another hit."

Mauser strode over to the large roadmap Denton had hung in the conference room. Red pushpins had been stuck in at every checkpoint where Amanda Davies's E-Z Pass had registered. Mauser studied the chain of pins, in his mind extrapolating their path.

Jersey City, New Jersey.

Harrisburg, Pennsylvania.

Columbus, Ohio.

The line extended straight to St. Louis.

"Where's this new one?"

"I-70 West, heading toward Cincinnati. Assuming they're headed to St. Louis, Amanda Davies and Henry Parker should arrive by midnight."

Mauser felt a surge of adrenaline. The conversation with Linda was still fresh in his mind. Parker was running. The fucking guy was trying to get away with it.

"The hell with this," Mauser said. "I want to be in the air in half an hour. And another thing." He looked Denton right in the eye, lowered his voice. He checked the door;

it was closed. "I don't want St. Louis PD in the loop. Not yet."

"Joe?" Denton said, a hint of concern on his face. "What're you gonna do?"

Mauser's voice was granite, not a hint of indecisiveness.

"When we take Parker down, we take him down our way. Not one word about procedure or extradition. Henry Parker deserves to go down hard, and I don't want anyone there to soften his landing."

"Joe," Denton said, his voice imploring. "Remember there are other factors here. The drugs, number one. If Parker has info on Luis and Christine Guzman's supplier, maybe we take down two birds on this case. I say we find the package and milk that."

Again, Mauser thought, with the career aspirations. More cases for superstar FBI agent Leonard Denton to solve. Fuck it. If it meant Denton worked harder, saw more angles, his delusions of grandeur were acceptable.

"Fine," Mauser said, throwing on his overcoat and heading for the door. "Before we take Parker down, we'll bleed him dry."

Denton smiled and grabbed the car keys. "I hear 'death by a thousand cuts' is popular these days. I'll help you make the first incision."

20

We pulled up at Amanda's house on Teasdale Drive at 11:47 p.m., thirteen minutes before her self-imposed deadline. The air had an eerie quiet to it, as though the world was afraid to take a breath.

The Davies residence was a large, Tudor-style home, painted white with delicate gray trim, paved driveway, two-car garage and covered deck. Amanda circled the driveway and parked in front of the garage.

"Nice neighborhood," I said.

"We're only five minutes from the Wash-U campus," she replied, stretching her arms above her head and yawning. "I moved here when I was about twelve. Trust me, I was thrilled to get away from Midwest suburban hell."

She got out, knelt down in front of the garage door and yanked the metal handle upward. The garage rattled open. A silver Mercedes SUV was parked between cardboard boxes and rusty gardening equipment. She got back in the car and pulled inside.

"I could have done that," I said. "Opened the door for you."

"Why would you have?"

"I don't know. Feel like I should be helping out more."

"Please," she said. "How do you think I've put the car in the garage the last thousand times? All of a sudden I need you to do it for me?"

"I know, I know. You're empowered. You don't need any help."

"Damn right," she said, shutting off the engine. "You okay? Look a little, I dunno, more than tired."

She was right, but I played it off. "I'm fine. I didn't realize we'd bonded so much that you can judge my mental state."

"As long as you're sleeping under my roof I'll judge all I want, thank you very much."

"Well, at least let me help with your bags."

Amanda squinted at me.

"Deal."

She tossed over the car keys, which I thankfully caught.

"Front door's the little flat key. Go to town."

I stepped out of the car, a sharp pain lancing up my leg. I needed to clean the wound again before it got infected. But every step felt queasy, reminding me of just why my leg hurt in the first place.

"You okay there, spindly legs?"

"It fell asleep in the car," I said. "Just shaking it loose."

A soft wind blew, chilling the air. It was a challenge to open the front door while carrying two overstuffed duffel bags and my backpack, while simultaneously lugging a suitcase that exceeded the maximum weight limit of most airlines. While I lugged and pulled, Amanda tied her hair up in a ponytail and threw a baggy sweater over her tank top. She was effortlessly stunning, her natural beauty accentuated by the frumpy clothes. When she caught me staring, her lips curled into a demure smile. She had a look of fake pity.

"That's what you get for offering to help. Here, before you get a hernia." She took one of the duffels and carried it inside.

The house was cold and filled with stale air. Amanda fiddled with a thermostat as I set the bags down. Between the cold, my T-shirt, fatigue and my leg, I began to shiver. Amanda noticed this, looked concerned.

"Come on," she said. She led me through the foyer to a closet. Inside were dozens of sweaters, threaded with some of the most horrendous fashion designs and colors I'd ever seen. Ugly maroon cotton. Green wool with a bald eagle sewn into the chest. A smiling deer embroidered with purple stitching. And they smelled like they'd last been worn by Daniel Boone.

"Feel free to raid my dad's sweater closet," she said. "He hasn't worn this stuff in years. I never was good at giving Christmas presents. Somebody might as well get some use out of them."

I thanked her, and while normally I wouldn't be caught dead wearing sweaters so hideous they'd offend Bill Gates's fashion sense, beggars can't be choosers and all that. Besides, I didn't want to insult my host. And hey, bald eagles are patriotic.

I took a moment to take in the house's grandeur, the tall white walls and long mirrors like something out of a Raymond Chandler novel, and the full bar with smoky brown liquor that could warm me better than any sweater. The walls were lined with lithographs encased in crystal-clear glass, an oil painting of the famous arch framed in polished bronze.

"I'd offer you something to eat or drink," Amanda said. "But unless you're in the mood for instant oatmeal you're out of luck. I'll go shopping tomorrow, but I imagine you'll have your situation figured out by then, right?"

I nodded distractedly. We carried her bags up a narrow flight of stairs, Amanda flicking on a series of lights as we went. Down an off-white hallway, lined with deep blue carpeting, I lugged her bags into a dark room. I knew it was Amanda's bedroom before she even turned on the light.

Even with the moon's faint rays shielded by the drawn shades, I could sense a soft femininity in the dark. Half a dozen stuffed animals were perched on her bed, arranged with care. The room felt warm, inviting, different than the rest of the house.

Without thinking I said, "I like your room."

She turned to me with a big smile, the kind given when a genuine compliment comes from an unexpected source. Those always meant the most.

"Thanks," she said, a hint of girlishness sneaking into her voice for the first time since we'd met. I liked it, liked seeing that beneath the suit of armor was something delicate.

Right now Amanda felt safe, secure in her home. Perhaps a slight hint of adventure brought on by the stranger in her bedroom. She knew nothing about me other than the superficial notes in her journal, the truth as deep as her pen's ink.

Maybe this was a thrill for her. But I felt no such joy, no comfort, no adventure. Even in a moment like this, where I should at least feel a sort of vicarious comfort, the emotion was wasted. Because my life was in a state of purgatory, all the small joys I experienced now would add up to nothing more than faded memories, lost opportunities.

"Come on," she said, leading me out of the room. "I'll show you where you're sleeping."

She led me down the hall, past a bathroom and a linen closet, pointing out a closed door on the right.

"You can use that bathroom. Just make sure to put the seat down, okay? Otherwise we'll have problems." Smiling, I said I would.

There was a small guest room, the bed looking like it had never been slept in. "There's an extra blanket in the closet if you get cold," she said. "Just do me a favor and strip the bed in the morning so I can wash the sheets."

"No problem. That's the least I can do."

"Well, if I think of anything else involving manual labor I'll let you know."

I thanked Amanda. When she left I immediately collapsed on the bed. It was hard and uncaring. Running my hand under the comforter, I felt lumpy egg crates and a plywood board underneath. Thankfully the pillows were soft. I kicked off my shoes, my leg throbbing with every movement. Sitting back up, I closed the door, tentatively took down my pants and studied the bullet wound. The gash on my thigh was angry and red, and it hurt to put my full weight on it.

The pain was bearable, but suddenly I felt a dam burst in my head and all the frustration and hate and anger writhed inside me like demons trying to burst through my skin. I flailed against the mattress, my fists pounding, letting loose silent fury bottled up and shaken by the last twenty-four hours. Tears spilled down my cheeks as I cursed the events that had changed my life, that had made me a marked man. The hero of the day.

John Fredrickson's death. God*damn it,* why had I even knocked on the Guzmans' door? Barring some divine intervention, my life as I knew it was over. My pitiful thumps against the pillows meant nothing, only letting out the excess energy before it built right back up again. I pounded and punched until the blanket was covered in lumps and the stains of my tears, the first tangible evidence of my ever-growing sorrow. Alone in a strange girl's house, abandoned by the world. Kept company only by my alleged sins.

Once the anger subsided, I managed to stand up. My head was woozy, the adrenaline rush petering out.

I heard a shower start down the hall. Cracking open the door, I saw a fine mist leaking from the bathroom. Amanda was gutsy, trusting a stranger with the run of the house. Every girl I'd ever known took a minimum of thirty minutes to shower. No reason Amanda would be any different. There was a guest bathroom downstairs. Hopefully I could wash up and be back before she finished.

Gripping the banister tight, I eased down the stairs, toe to heel to hide any noise. The house was quiet save the shower, the wind outside building, whistling and whipping through the trees.

As long as I stayed in my own little world, looked at everything rationally, it seemed manageable. Cleaning my leg would be simple. Finding somewhere to go tomorrow would be hard. A few nights sleeping at bus stops would be a humbling experience, but one I'd have to stomach. But what then?

Two linen cabinets and one door to the basement later, I found the bathroom. The white tiles were freshly cleaned and I smiled at the quaint seashell-shaped hand soap. On a metal rack hung hand towels monogrammed with three letters—HSJ.

I opened the medicine cabinet, swore under my breath. Nothing. Not even a goddamn Band-Aid. What kind of people were Amanda's parents? What if a dinner guest accidentally swallowed a turkey baster? Shouldn't they at least own some Pepto-Bismol?

I closed the chest, ran a trickle of warm water from the faucet. I wiped away the dried blood with wet tissues. I gritted my teeth, tried to ignore the stabbing pain as my blood turned the water red. I threw the bloodied papers in the toilet and flushed.

Creeping back upstairs, I couldn't help but peek into Amanda's empty bedroom.

She was in the shower. What the hell.

I took an old yearbook off the shelf, flipped to Amanda's page. There was an aerial shot of her, the photographer standing on a roof or a ladder looking down. Amanda was cross-legged on a bed of grass, smiling. The picture was so happy, so serene, but there was sorrow behind Amanda's eyes, as though she wished that moment had perhaps occurred at a different time and place.

I noticed the covers on her bed had been pulled back a bit, revealing a small trunk underneath the mattress box.

The shower was still running. I knelt down and slid it out.

The top had plenty of dents and dings from years of being yanked from dark places. The Master Lock was undone. Without hesitation, I removed the lock and threw the cover back. When I looked inside, my breath caught in my throat.

Dozens, no, hundreds of small spiral notebooks filled the trunk nearly to the brim. They were all different shapes and sizes, some with pages torn and falling out, some looking like they'd been read a thousand times. I plucked one from the top of the pile, felt the small indents where her pen had pressed hard on the paper. When I flipped it open, I saw that every single page had been filled top to bottom. The same kind of notes she'd been writing in the car. Immediately I knew the other books were filled as well.

My fingers shaking, I read the first page:

July 14, 2003
Joseph Dennison.
Probably early 30s but dresses like he's 60, lots of beige sweaters and windbreakers, goofy grandpa hats. Kind of cute in a skinny, Tobey McGuire way, but older. Thin, but not a stick figure. Worked as a librarian for three years, says he wants to be a screenwriter. Helped me find that old V.C. Andrews book that the store in town didn't have. Wears too much cologne. I don't think he has a girlfriend and he's definitely not married. Says he's seen over a thousand movies and can remember the best lines from each one. I quizzed him once and he got them all right. It was kinda scary. Not attracted to him, but curious. Can't imagine there's

much room for advancement at the library, so why work there when you're 30? Some people's motivations are strange.

I read another entry.

August 29, 2003

Gas station attendant, likely late 40s, early 50s. Looks like he hasn't bothered to shave in four or five days. His workshirt is covered in oil and he looks miserable while he fills up my tank. There's no name tag, but someone who I assume is the manager calls him Ali. He says "thank you" when I tip him two bucks, then stuffs it in his shirt pocket. He gives the tip money to the guy behind the counter, who pockets it. I wonder how much Ali makes per year and if he has a family. I didn't remember to look for a wedding ring. I wonder if he's happy.

I put the notebook back, took another. Read six entries. Each one described a different person who'd crossed Amanda's path. Some were random, some familiar—an old boyfriend who dumped her the day after they exchanged I-love-you's for the first time. Some she'd only met for seconds and some she'd known for years. I'd never seen anything like it.

Then it hit me. Somewhere in the room was the notebook she'd used in the car with her first impressions of Carl Bernstein.

I dug to the very bottom of the trunk until I scraped bottom. I pulled out a notebook and flipped it open.

February 3, 1985
I miss Mommy. I don't know anyone else at school. The kids laugh when we sit in a circle and I don't know who to sit next to. Jimmy Peterson poured milk in my hair. I hate Jimmy. He's an ugly boy and his hair is too long. I pulled it once and Miss Williams sent me out of the room. Lacey and Kendra laughed when Jimmy poured milk on me. I hate them, too. Lacey has a pretty purple dress I wish was mine. Jimmy's house is two streets away from my new one and I see him some mornings. I don't like to look at him. Sometimes I hide behind trees. I wonder if his mother knows what a stupid boy he is. Maybe she's stupid, too. If Mommy and Daddy were here nobody would laugh at me.

I quickly closed the book and put it back in its place. The large, childlike handwriting, so heartfelt and pained, heralded a life that had been interrupted, deeply scarred.

What sort of insecurities did this young woman have, that every person she met needed to be catalogued?

I scanned the notebooks at the top of the trunk, found nothing about me.

Then I noticed Amanda's jacket thrown over her desk chair. I checked the pockets. Nothing. I gently opened her drawers. Nada. Sweat beaded down my neck. My leg ached.

The clothes she was wearing in the car. Maybe in her pockets.

I checked under the bed, only found dust balls and bent plastic combs. About twenty of those elastic ponytail holders.

Could Amanda have brought her clothes into the bathroom? It was possible she already put them in the wash. But then she wouldn't have left the notebook in her pocket. She'd been doing this for too long to be careless. It had to be somewhere.

I started rifling through her shelves, picking books off and searching behind them.

Then I noticed that the shower had stopped running.

I froze.

Panicking, I closed the trunk and slid it back under the bed. I straightened out the bookshelf, praying she hadn't caught me snooping.

Then I heard a noise by the door.

She'd seen me.

I held my breath, waited for a sound, afraid to look at her. How long had she been there? Had she seen me going through her notebooks?

I turned around slowly, fully expecting to see Amanda in the doorway, arms folded, ready to kick me out of her house and out of her life. I tried to sponge together an explanation. It was pointless. I had to come clean. I had to tell her the truth.

Yet when I turned around, the image that burned itself into my mind wasn't Amanda—who was standing in the doorway—but the man standing behind her with a gun to her head.

21

The look of absolute terror on Amanda's face froze me instantly. Her body was rigid, her mouth pursed shut. She was too scared to scream.

The man's countenance was calm, relaxed. He wore black jeans and a dark jacket, covering everything up to his lightly stubbled jaw. His eyes were cold, perfunctory. He was in his early thirties, with high cheekbones, short hair, sinewy forearms. His gun hand was firm, his posture steady, not rigid, ready to strike. He spoke in an even tone, but through gritted teeth. There was a faint trail of mist coming from the hallway. The shower. Jesus. He was in the bathroom with Amanda, using the shower as subterfuge. She was still wearing the same clothing. I even noticed a slight bulge in her pocket. The missing notebook.

"Amanda…" I said, the words spilling out of my mouth like water. "Who…"

"That's not important," he said, his voice like metal. The second time in a day a gun was pointed at my head. And just like the last one, the safety latch was off. I could tell he'd held people at gunpoint before. Many times. "The *what,* now Parker, that's what is of real importance."

"I don't understand," I said. Amanda trembled as involuntary sobs escaped her mouth.

The man nodded to me, flicked the gun. "I want the package you stole from Luis Guzman. That's the only thing you need to worry about. If you give it to me, you're the only one who will die here tonight."

The only one…

Amanda.

Oh, God.

"I don't have it, I swear."

"Parker, you're going to give me what you took or your female friend here will be breathing out the back of her skull. And I'm going to make you watch her die before I ask again."

"Carl," Amanda said, her voice shrill, pleading. Again the name took a moment to register. "Why is he calling you that name? What's happening?"

The man laughed softly, raised his eyebrows. "Carl? Is that what you told her? You really don't look much like a Carl."

"Amanda, I can explain."

The man shook his head. "No, Henry, you won't. There's no buying time, no explanations. You give me what I want and Miss Davies gets to wake up tomorrow morning."

Amanda twitched. He was too strong. She couldn't budge.

"Listen," I said, trying not to stammer, my body numb, "I swear I don't know anything about a package. The newspapers were wrong. The Guzmans were lying."

Amanda's head swung toward me. There was fear in her face, but a hint of anger as well. She knew I was hiding something. My deception had somehow led this man to her house. Had put a gun to her head. A cold lump rose in my throat. She could die because of me. And we both knew it. I mouthed the words *I'm sorry,* knowing how little consolation they must have offered.

"Carl, please," Amanda said. Tears streaked down her cheeks in wet rivers, tumbling toward her chin and falling softy to the floor. "Please, Carl."

The man laughed softly. Not to make a statement. He genuinely thought it was funny. "All right, Parker. I'll give you this one." He paused. "Tell her the truth."

I looked at Amanda, summoning sorrow to my face. I didn't need to try hard. The hollow feeling in my gut came on its own.

"My name isn't Carl," I said. "It's Henry. Henry Parker." Amanda's eyebrows furrowed. There was a hint of recognition, but no definitive response.

"And what did you do, Henry?" the man said. I looked at him, tried to glare, actually, but it was merely pitiful. "Go on, tell her."

Choking back tears that ran hot in my throat, I said, "They think I killed a cop."

"Who does?" Amanda's eyes were streaked with red. "I don't understand."

"The cops. The cops think I killed him."

"John Fredrickson," he said. "Pity. I heard his wife and kids really counted on him."

"Are you a cop?" I asked him, suddenly feeling stupid. Would a cop hold an innocent woman hostage?

"No, but I'm flattered you'd consider my judgment on par with theirs. I do know a lot of cops, though, and I can honestly say I'll be doing you a favor by killing you quick."

"Henry?" It was Amanda. She was staring at me as she said my real name for the first time. Her eyes were red, like they'd been singed.

"Yes?"

"Just give it to him."

What was she talking about? Amanda, more than anyone, knew I had nothing with me.

"Amanda, I don't know…"

"Henry, I don't want to die. Just get it. Get the package. Give him what he wants."

"Right, Henry," the man said. "Just get it."

Amanda said, "You had me put it in the nightstand when we came upstairs, remember? Just give it to him."

"Nightstand? Amanda, I don't know what you're talking about."

The man took a step toward me, pushing Amanda as he moved. He leaned closer. "Parker, I want you to go into that nightstand and give it to me. You have five seconds. If at the end of those five seconds I don't have it, Amanda's blood will be on your hands."

"Amanda, I…"

"One."

"But…"

"Two."

"Henry, get it," Amanda moaned.

"Three."

It hit me, just like that. I knew what was in the nightstand. Swallowing the thick saliva in my throat, I nodded. "Stop. I'll get it."

I took a step back, the man matching me by moving

closer. Amanda's nightstand was a small, knee-high balsawood table with a pullout drawer. Whatever he was looking for, it couldn't have been wider than a chessboard. Positioning my body so he couldn't see my hands, I cracked the drawer and stuck my hand in. I could feel paper scraps and loose change. A condom wrapper. Then I felt it. A thin cylinder, probably the size of a tube of lipstick. Mace. Amanda wasn't kidding when she said she kept it in her nightstand.

I curled my finger around the small tab. I could see their shadows just over my right shoulder. I had one chance, otherwise we were both dead.

"Amanda," I said, shifting slightly to my right. "Here it is."

I saw his grip loosen just barely.

At that moment, Amanda ducked down, grabbing hold of the gun as I whipped around and depressed the tab. A stream of clear liquid burst into the man's face. He cried out and took a step back, the smell making my stomach lurch. I grabbed Amanda's arm.

"Run."

We sprinted toward the door, my hand clenched firmly around Amanda's wrist. But suddenly I was jerked backward. Amanda screamed. The man was clenching Amanda's hair, holding it like a human leash.

Red lines streaked his eyes. Mucus dripped from his nose. He sniffled, but other than that he looked unaffected. He gently dabbed at his eyes with his sleeve, making sure not to rub any of the mace in too deep. *Jesus,* I whispered. Again he raised the gun. Amanda thrashed violently, trying to free herself.

"Parker," the man said, his face emotionless, eyes bloodshot. His complete lack of a reaction was terrifying. "I've been maced, I'd say thirty or forty times. It really doesn't sting so bad once you get used to it."

I tugged at Amanda's arm, but he held on tight.

"Please," she whimpered. He seemed to think about it for a second.

"Where was I? Oh, right. I'd just finished counting to four."

He aimed the gun at Amanda's head. I had no more tricks up my sleeve. Her body was between us, a barrier. I didn't know what was in this package, so I couldn't bullshit my way out. There were no more options. No more time.

Please don't let this happen. I'm sorry, Amanda, I didn't mean to get you involved. I don't know what to do. I don't...

Suddenly there was a loud crash downstairs, the sound of wood breaking. Amanda screamed. Confusion etched itself across the intruder's face. Then I heard footsteps downstairs, more than one set.

"Who the fuck is that?" the man said. "Who the *fuck* is here?"

People were coming upstairs. My eyes darted back and forth, looking for an escape. Suddenly two men burst into the room. One was heavyset, older. The other was slim, younger. It couldn't be. They were the same cops who'd chased me that morning. How could they have known where we were?

The older man's eyes glared at me with a burning hatred, my heart hammering. Then he saw Amanda. Then he looked at the man with the gun, its barrel still firmly pressed against Amanda's head.

"The hell's going on?" the older cop said.

"Jesus," the younger one said. He was staring at the man, his mouth flapping like a dying fish. He was looking at the man in black the way I was looking at them. Like he'd seen him before. "No fucking way."

"Amanda Davies?" the older man asked, his face trying to remain calm, his gun aimed at the space between me and the killer. Amanda nodded, whimpered.

"FBI. I'm Agent Mauser, this is Agent Denton. You're safe now." She didn't seem too convinced. The one who didn't introduce himself, Denton, stepped forward. He glared at me through gritted teeth, then turned to our assailant.

"Put the gun down. *Now.*" Denton's voice wavered, his hand trembling as he aimed his gun at the assassin, but looked no more convinced that the gun would do any more damage than a peashooter. Like the man was invincible.

Mauser continued. "Henry Parker, you're under arrest for the murder of John Fredrickson. Anything you say I don't give a fuck about. You make one move and I'll kill you."

My head spun. Three guns were drawn. All three of their owners wanted me dead.

"Drop it, asshole," Denton said, gesturing to the man in black. Mauser pointed his gun at me, but slowly it swung back to the stranger. I looked at Amanda. She twisted violently and managed to free herself. The man in black didn't seem to notice.

There was a quick flicker in Denton's eyes, then without warning he pulled the trigger and an explosion shattered the room. The man in black whipped around and howled, clutching his chest.

"Fucking Christ!" Mauser yelled, and then all hell broke loose. The stranger barreled forward, pushing Amanda and I out of the way and knocking over both agents. Mauser fell, his head slamming against the doorknob with a dull *thock.* Denton crashed into an armoire and hit the ground. A gun clattered to the floor as the man ran into the hallway and down the stairs, clutching his arm, blood smearing the wall. The two agents were dazed. This was our only chance. It was react or be killed. I grabbed Amanda's arm and pulled.

"Come on!"

We sprinted down the stairs, bolting through the front door and into the cold night.

No time to think. Just run.

There was no sign of the man in black. I could still smell faint traces of mace, the scent of something burning. Then I felt Amanda pulling my arm.

"This way."

She led me around the side of the house, past a shed and a locked storm cellar. We pushed our way through a row of trees in the backyard, branches ripping at my skin. Adrenaline flowed through my veins like a gas pump whose safety valve had been removed. I couldn't tell if I was dragging Amanda or she was dragging me, but soon we were running alongside a dimly lit road, the sky black above us, trees a misty green.

We slowed down as we approached a four-way intersection, my chest tight, blood thumping in my temples. There were few cars on the road. We were out in the open, our only cover the darkness of night. Somewhere in the gloom were three men who wanted me dead. It would only be moments before one of them found us.

"There, look," I said, pointing to a Ford crew cab paused at the red light. The truck's chassis bobbed up and down as if on hydraulics. I took Amanda's hand. We crouched down, slinking up alongside the flatbed. I peered into the side mirrors to see the driver, then stood up to get a better look. The driver wore a green trucker's cap, a mullet spilling out from underneath. Country music was blasting over his speakers, his head bobbing rhythmically. I cringed. The only thing worse than being chased by three men who wanted you dead was listening to country music while doing it.

Looking around, I made sure there were no other witnesses.

"Come on," I whispered to Amanda, gesturing to the flatbed. She looked at me incredulously.

"You can't be serious."

"They'll be here any second now. Please, you have to trust me. We need to get out of here."

Whether it was blind faith or the sheer terror of being caught, Amanda followed me around to the truck's rear. Just as mullet head's bobbing was at full force, I boosted Amanda up and over the bumper into the flatbed. The light turned green. I heard the tires squeal. The car started to move. Amanda's head popped up, a frightened look in her eyes.

Just before the truck peeled off into the night, I grabbed hold of the rim and hurled myself over the top and into the flatbed. A tarp lay crumpled in a heap. Staying low to avoid the rearview mirror, I grabbed it and pulled it over us. The warble of guitar music leaked out the windows as we gasped for air. The tarp smelled like dirt, tiny crumbs falling over our bodies as they were shaken loose from the road.

I looked at Amanda, the air between us hot and soiled. She glared at me and shook her head. I said nothing. There was no point. Soon I'd explain everything. I owed her that much.

Off in the distance, the Ringer watched the truck drive off into the night before it disappeared around a bend in the road. There were few lights to illuminate the street, but thankfully the faint glow of the traffic signals gave off enough so that he could read and memorize the license plate.

He gently touched his finger to the gunshot wound, sending shockwaves of pain through his body. He probed the torn skin, pain knifing through his body. He closed his eyes, squinting hard, trying to block it out. He pictured Anne's face in his mind and the pain subsided, warmth coating the wound like a soothing balm. He could feel her wet kisses on his cheek, their hands intertwined, her soft fingers, polished nails. The hurt was distant now, forgotten in the memories.

Pushing the wound again to the forefront and keeping Anne in the back as an anesthetic, the Ringer ran a finger along his chest and shoulder. There was no exit wound and the bullet hadn't lodged in his flesh. The slug had likely just shattered a rib or two and ricocheted away.

He could feel blood soaking his clothes. There was nothing he could do but ignore it. Cold night air ripped through the hole in his jacket. The hole by his right breast pocket. The blood on his clothes. Soaking everything…

Then the Ringer froze.

No. Please, *no*.

His fingers trembling, the pain burning, the Ringer found the small pocket at his breast where he kept Anne's photo.

The only memory of his long-lost beloved Anne. The only remnant of her life. The only attachment he had to her except the memories that faded more and more every day.

Please, let it be safe.

He fumbled with the fabric, the pain worming its way through his mental roadblocks. Holding his breath he removed the picture, the traffic lights providing just enough illumination. What he saw shattered his heart and sealed Henry Parker's fate.

His deal with Michael DiForio was forgotten. Henry Parker's death was the only thing that mattered now.

Coating the fragile picture was a layer of slick blood. His blood. Anne's face had disappeared somewhere beneath the congealed mass of red, her face punctured by a bullet hole. Delicately he tried to cleanse the picture, but the material merely crumbled in his fingers. And once again, the Ringer's life had contributed to Anne's death. From this point on, her face would remain intact only in his mind. But memory was far more fallible than a photo.

A guttural scream of rage escaped the Ringer's lips as he pressed the remnants of the photo to his chest, his heart beating beneath it, blood seeping from his wound.

Anne left his world years ago. But to the Ringer, Henry Parker had just killed her all over again.

22

I don't know how long we were in the back of the truck. Every second was gut-wrenching, the tension a suffocating blanket. Add to that potent mix the girl whose life I'd endangered, who would no doubt beat the living shit out of me as soon as we were safe, and the ride in the back of the flatbed felt similar to bodysurfing the seventh circle of hell. Country music notwithstanding, it was the worst two—or was it three, or four, or five?—hours of my life.

We made a few brief stops—traffic lights I assumed, since we always were moving within minutes. I thought about my backpack, still containing the tape recording from the Luis Guzman interview, that I'd left at Amanda's house. When the driver, David Morris, according to the sloppily scrawled name on his toolbox, finally came to a complete stop, we waited what seemed like eons before daring to poke our heads out.

I eased the tarp up and saw a white neon sign hovering above us that read *Ken's Coffee Den*. The *C* in *Coffee* had blown its bulb. Ken's offee Den was good enough for me.

We had stopped at a rest area—who really knew where—

but we were out of St. Louis. There was a small diner and a Mobil station. A busy highway ran parallel. The black night was slowly easing into the gray of early morning. Where were we?

"We're clear," I said to Amanda. "Let's go."

They were the first words I'd said to her in hours. She barely acknowledged me, but before I could move she'd leapt out of the truck and started walking across the parking lot. I jogged up to Amanda, praying she wouldn't scream bloody murder before I could explain.

The first rays of sun began to peek out of the horizon, streaks of beautiful orange and gold melting the gray. I checked my watch. Another day had passed. It had been almost thirty-six hours since John Fredrickson had died. Thirty-six hours since my life had irrevocably changed. For a moment, I forgot everything. Forgot John Fredrickson, forgot that three people wanted me dead, forgot that I once had a life, a good life, which I might never see again. The beauty of the morning sky, the whispers of cool air, they took me far away. All I could think about was Amanda, the look in her eyes when I told her my real name and revealed my betrayal. This was my life now. And there was no turning back.

"Amanda, please." I tried to grab her sleeve. She pulled away and kept walking. "Just let me explain."

Suddenly she whipped around, her gaze cold as stone.

"Who are you?" she said. "Right now, tell me the truth. And if I even *think* you're lying, I'm marching right into that restaurant and calling the cops."

I closed my eyes. It was time to come clean.

"I'm wanted for the murder of a New York City police officer named John Fredrickson." The breath seemed to be forced from Amanda's lungs as she took a step back.

"Did you…" She took a deep breath. "Did you actually kill a cop?"

"No, I didn't. There's something fucked up going on, but I don't know what it is yet. Just give me a minute, and I'll tell you everything I know."

Amanda stood and listened as I told her how I'd come to New York and taken a job at the *Gazette*. About Luis Guzman, how I had interviewed him for Jack's story, how I'd tried to help them that night when I heard the screams. How John Fredrickson could have killed all of us. And how he'd died. How there was a package that went missing, and everyone assumed I stole it. Lastly I told Amanda how I found her, how I lied to her in order to flee the state. How I would be dead if it wasn't for her.

When I finished, it was like a two-ton weight had been lifted from my shoulders. Finally somebody else knew as much as I did. Amanda's eyes stayed even. Listening, not judging. I told her the truth, that I didn't know the man who'd held the gun to her head. That I'd recognized the two cops who'd followed me from New York, and that I didn't know how they found me. When all had been said, Amanda looked at me and spoke.

"I believe you," she said, her voice earnest. A lead ball dropped into my stomach.

"Why?"

"Let's just say that of the four people in the room last night, you were the only one I honestly knew wouldn't hurt me."

"I guess that's as good a reason as any to trust someone."

"That's not the only reason. I look at you and I know you're not an evil person. You're not someone who would do such horrible things."

I couldn't help but say, "I lied to you before, you couldn't tell then, you bought it. How do you know I'm not lying now?"

Amanda considered this. "Because you just said that. I know you weren't lying to me before for the sake of lying. You were lying to save your life. Shit, I'd claim to be Lindsay Lohan—retch—if I thought it would save my life.

"There is one thing, though," she said, "that you haven't been totally honest about."

I shook my head. "No, everything that's happened I've…"

"Your name," she said. "You still haven't told me your real name without someone holding a gun to my head. I want you to say it on your own." I smiled and looked at her.

"It's Henry. Henry Parker. It's really nice to meet you, Amanda."

Amanda took this in, tasting my name on her tongue.

"Henry." She squinted a bit, like she'd just tried on a pretty shirt that didn't fit. "I've never met anyone named Henry before."

"And I'm happy to be the first."

"And what was that name you used on me? Carl?"

"Carl Bernstein."

"Where'd you come up with that?"

"Carl Bernstein?" I waited for a sign of recognition. She looked at me as if to say *and?* "You know, of Woodward and Bernstein? *All the President's Men?*"

Amanda slapped her forehead. "Ugh, you cheesy asshole. I can't believe I didn't catch that." She still looked confused. "But of all people, why Carl Bernstein?"

"Woodward's kind of my hero. He's one of the reasons I wanted to be a journalist in the first place. But I figured you'd recognize Woodward. Bernstein hasn't really been on the radar."

"Well, I give you points for originality."

"I try."

"Come on, Mr. Bernstein, I could eat my body weight right now. We need to figure out what to do next." She started walking toward the Coffee, er, offee Den.

"What do you mean, next?"

Amanda stopped and put her hands on her hips, lecture-style. "Well, unless you plan on running for the rest of your life, we need to figure out why this cop tried to kill you and what that man tonight was looking for. You're a reporter, right? Got any theories?"

"I haven't really had time to do a lot of thinking the last few days. Kind of been spending too much time trying to save my ass."

Amanda checked her pocket, pulled out a crinkled wallet with a few bills inside. "Come on, first cup's on me."

We walked inside the diner, passed David Morris, who was gorging himself on an order of eggs sunny-side up, and took a booth in the back. I buried myself in the menu, which, like all roadside diner menus was like the Yellow Pages, only thicker.

A woman whose name tag read *Joyce* and who smelled like David's truck asked for our order. Amanda ordered a bagel and cream cheese. I got a side order of toast. Two bottomless coffees.

"Not hungry?" Amanda asked.

"Starving."

"So why don't you get something a little more, you know, filling than toast? There's enough choices here they should rename this place the indecisive diner."

"Money," I said. "I'm guessing we have a few hours max before they cancel or trace your credit card. We'll have to make due on whatever cash we have on hand. Let's just say the value of a dollar just appreciated." Amanda immediately thrust her hand in the air.

"'Scuse me, Joyce? Can you change my order to just toast, too? Thanks."

When Joyce stalked back to the kitchen, Amanda said, "Now the big question. What was that man talking about, that package? What was he looking for?"

I shook my head and took a sip of ice water.

"I honestly have no idea. The New York papers said Fredrickson was killed over a drug deal gone bad, but I didn't see any sort of drugs or paraphernalia in the Guzmans' apartment. Luis was arrested for armed robbery, not drugs. Fredrickson was there to pick up some sort of package from the Guzmans, but I don't think it was drug related."

"Maybe they kept it under the couch or something. Could you have just missed it?"

I shook my head. "No way. I've been around people who've done drugs, even dealt, and they all have this tension about them. Not really paranoia, but like they've permanently conceded that they're doing something wrong. It's a little bit of shame, I think, a slouch in their shoulders, fidgeting constantly. I didn't see any of that in Luis or Christine."

"So, what then, if not drugs? You said Fredrickson was looking for a package, and now this guy with a gun is looking for it, too. There are two common threads here involving that package—you and violence. People think you have it, and they're willing to do terrible things to get it."

"The five questions," I said.

"What?" Amanda asked.

"Every story has to answer five basic questions. Who, what, when, where and why. Unless every one of those questions is answered, you don't have a full story. You can observe everything about anything and anyone, but unless you hit all five *W*'s you're missing the whole story. You're getting a superficial imprint that carries no weight."

Something flickered across Amanda's face. The notebooks. I knew I'd touched a nerve. And I'd done it on purpose.

I cleared my throat. She did the same.

"So let's go through the list," she said. "Who?" Thankfully, amidst all the chaos I'd managed to hold on to my notebook, now crumpled and wrinkled after hours in Amanda's car and David Morris's truck. "What do you know," she said, grinning. "You keep one, too?"

"I always keep a log when I'm on a story. Only shitty and lazy reporters go on memory." I paused. "What happened to yours?"

Amanda blinked, looked down. "I left it at home."

"I'm sorry to hear that." Amanda nodded remorsefully. I raised my hand and signaled Joyce. "Excuse me, but could we borrow a pen?" Joyce looked at me like I'd asked for her firstborn child, then took a pen from behind her ear and handed it over. I looked at the pen, took a napkin and wiped it down. Who knew where her ears had been?

Flipping open the notebook, I uncapped the pen and prepared to write. "Okay," Amanda said. "Who?"

"Kind of a multipart question. The Guzmans. Luis and Christine. Christine knew what Fredrickson was talking about, so he went there for a reason. Fredrickson, of course. The man in black. The cops."

"Hold off on the cops," Amanda said.

"Why?"

"Think about their motivations. Right now, they're in it for you and you alone. We're trying to figure out what was going on before they got involved. What were the Guzmans hiding? What was Fredrickson looking for? And this guy in my house, how exactly is he involved?"

"I'm not sure, but he's definitely not a cop. Maybe he knew Fredrickson somehow or knew about the missing package. Then he somehow connected me to you, and found us in St. Louis."

Amanda was chewing her nail.

"Everything okay?"

"I'll let you answer that. But you know what's scary? That this guy found us. I didn't tell anyone about you, and I'm pretty sure you weren't stupid enough to tell anyone about me."

"Pretty scary," I said. She nodded.

I wrote these names down, drew an arrow connecting Fredrickson to the Guzmans. Another one connecting the man in black to both of them. Looking up from the paper, I caught Amanda staring at me.

"What?"

"Nothing," she said. "But I've seen better handwriting from animals without opposable thumbs."

"Lay off. As long as I can read it."

"Suit yourself." She leaned back, folded her hands above her head and yawned. "So is that it for the 'who'?"

I fiddled with the pen, tried to think of who else might be involved. Then it hit me. I flipped through my notebook, and found the name I'd written down two days ago. The Guzmans' landlord. Grady Larkin.

Amanda looked surprised. "Why do you think he's involved?"

"Grady Larkin was quoted in the newspaper article as saying he heard a strange noise, then saw me fleeing the scene. Something just seems a bit off. Like he preferred to give an ex-convict the benefit of the doubt." I put Larkin's name down with a question mark next to it, drew a dotted line from him to the Guzmans.

"Anyone else?"

"I think that's it. For now."

"Okay, now the 'what.'"

"Big question," I said. "Drugs, maybe, but doubtful. Something valuable. That man at your house was ready to kill us both for it. You don't attempt murder for a package of Twinkies."

"Now that depends how old the Twinkies are. Maybe if they're antiques you could get a good price on eBay."

"Point taken. But the 'what' is pure speculation. All we know is that to the right person, the package is worth killing for." My statement sunk in like a hypodermic needle. Worth killing for. We stared at each other for a moment, the gravity of the situation hitting home. Amanda broke the silence, thankfully, because I was ready to break down and cry.

"Okay, where?"

"New York," I said. "Harlem, specifically. The apartment building at 2937 Broadway. Fredrickson was a New York cop, so it's probably New York specific."

"You don't think St. Louis is involved?" I shook my head.

"St. Louis was circumstantial. The cops and the other man somehow tracked me there. It was blind luck that we ended up at your house."

"Okay, another question," Amanda said. "How exactly did they track you? How'd they figure out you were with me?"

"I really don't know. Maybe someone saw me at NYU and reported it. The receptionist saw me checking out the student shuttles, she could have done something, said something. Maybe there was a camera set up at a tollbooth. There are a hundred possibilities." Amanda hardly seemed satisfied by my response.

Joyce returned with our toast. Amanda's looked crisp, light. Mine was burnt. Amanda sighed and handed me a slice of hers. I thanked her and spread a generous dollop of strawberry jam on it.

"Okay, when?" she said.

"My involvement began the day before yesterday, but the meeting between the Guzmans and John Fredrickson was likely set up earlier."

"Why do you think so?" Amanda asked.

"When I arrived for the interview, Luis was decked out

like he was going on a date with Hillary Clinton. But my question is this—if the Guzmans didn't have this package, why did Luis bother getting dressed up?" Amanda thought about this, took a sip of coffee.

"Sympathy," she said matter-of-factly.

"Come again?"

"Obviously Luis knew Fredrickson wanted something he didn't have." She took a bite of toast, smeared the rest with butter. "You ever get called to the principal's office in high school?"

"Why?"

"Just humor me."

I laughed. "Yeah, once or twice."

"Well, what'd you wear?"

"I don't know. Khakis, a sweater."

"But you showered and shaved right? You looked presentable, didn't you?"

"Of course."

"The same reasoning applies. When you know you're in trouble, you want to look like you're really sorry, dress your best, yada yada yada. Luis knew Fredrickson would be pissed, and he wanted to soften the blow."

"Lot of good it did him. Which means they were probably protecting themselves by lying to the newspapers. They figured it was better to pin the package's disappearance on me." We both nodded, a joint sense of satisfaction that brought levity to the situation. This was what we were both born to do.

"Now the big one," Amanda said. "Why?"

"Why," I said, then repeated it softly, looked at Amanda,

ran my palm over my two days of beard stubble, and said, "I have no idea. But those three men after me, I don't think they're going to just stop. If I can't figure it out, in the next few days I'll either be in prison or dead."

23

Mauser took two Advil and popped them in his mouth. Then he thought twice and popped two more. He thanked the young kid who stood over him with the medicine bottle, grinning like a dog who'd just won first prize. Joe's head throbbed, blood pounding in the knot over his left temple. The Advil couldn't work fast enough. The kid in the light brown St. Louis County Police Department uniform looked thrilled just to be at the scene. Mauser thanked him again, slowly pushing off the bed where he'd been sitting for the last half hour, trying to shake away the cobwebs.

Denton was out in the hallway. The head of the Bureau of Fugitive Affairs, some guy named Wendell whose face didn't look a day over thirty, yet whose hair was already going salt-and-pepper, was scolding him, cursing like his schoolmates had just taught him some brand-new four-letter words. Mauser had gotten the first half of Wendell's riot act before shooing the man away, claiming his headache might trigger involuntary violent reactions to "assholes who think that their mouths are bullhorns."

Denton had a blueberry-colored bruise on the side of his

neck where he'd hit the armoire. He'd been absolutely livid, but Mauser was able to calm the man down, told him the department would give hazard pay for hickeys attained in the line of duty.

They found a knapsack that belonged to Parker. Denton tore it open, had a dismayed look on his face when all they pulled out was a tape recorder and a reporter's notebook. Nothing on the tape except an interview with Luis Guzman, the man Parker later attacked. A perfect cover, really. Parker interviewed him, pretended to do his job, to make it look like he had a legitimate reason to be there.

Mauser eyed Len Denton. It wasn't just anger that had gotten to him, but something had struck fear into the young agent. He was surprised Denton had pulled the trigger so easily, hadn't even bothered to negotiate, had taken a huge chance that the bullet wouldn't strike Amanda Davies. He wondered if the younger agent's nervous system had hit its breaking point, like so many agents who weren't cut out for fieldwork.

He watched them argue in Amanda Davies's hallway, Denton absently scratching his bruised neck. Wendell turning purple, then blue, then a shade of gray that couldn't have been healthy. The bedroom still smelled heavily of cordite and mace residue. The shell casing from Denton's gun had already been removed by forensics, along with blood samples and fingerprints from the black-clad assassin. Despite his hesitations, Mauser would support Denton's decision to open fire.

He'd seen the look in the man's eyes, knew it was almost blind luck they'd shown up when they did. The man would have killed both Parker and Davies, without question.

He watched Denton, their eyes connecting and rolling in unison. Wendell was really going to town, enjoying it, too. Finally the bureau chief stopped shouting, more like he'd run out of gas than colorful vocabulary.

A quick search of the surrounding area had turned up nothing but some broken branches and footprints that led to the highway. Blood droplets would be almost undetectable in the mud, so they couldn't tell if Parker or Davies were wounded. There were no bodies, no sign of Parker, Davies, or the man Denton had shot.

Anger rose inside Joe Mauser as he realized they'd lost their only lead.

Wendell walked into Amanda Davies's room, his eyebrows quivering as he stopped in front of Mauser. Joe sighed. For his own sake, he hoped Wendell realized how short his fuse was.

"What you and your partner did tonight was thoroughly unprofessional," Wendell said. "Not informing my department about this fugitive was a breach of protocol that just boggles my mind. And not only did you fail to arrest this man, you put other lives in danger. What if he'd broken into another home? What if he'd—"

"But he didn't," Mauser interrupted.

"That's not the point," Wendell continued unabated. "This is my county, not yours, agent."

Spittle hit Mauser in the face. He calmly wiped it off, but felt warmth begin to spread under his collar. Looking for his partner, Mauser saw Denton out in the hall chatting with a pretty blond officer. Figured.

"Chief," Mauser said. "With all due respect, please shut the fuck up. Right now."

Wendell folded his arms across his chest, waiting to hear what this brute had to say. Mauser continued.

"The reason we didn't inform you is because we couldn't confirm Parker's location. If we'd put out a statewide APB, he'd have disappeared faster than you can stick your tongue up your supervisor's ass. We had Parker, in this house, done deal."

Wendell snorted, gestured to the doorway. "Done deal. Well, where is he then if you don't mind me asking? Maybe hiding under the bed? That's a good hiding spot, perhaps we should check there. You and your partner had him cornered, in a house, alone and unarmed. You had weapons, he didn't. You had the drop on him. Maybe you should have asked Parker to tie himself up, stand out on the porch wrapped in a pretty pink bow."

"Again, all due respect, chief," Mauser said. "But you know full well what happened. There's no way we could have predicted this other man to show up."

"Yeah, your boy Denton there put a bullet in him and you still managed to lose all three of them."

"Matter of time," Mauser said. "The grass is wet outside. You have two trails of footprints. I'll let you guess which ones belong to Parker and the girl. If you'll notice, they both lead to the highway. You've got roadblocks in place?"

"Being set up as we speak," Wendell said. Mauser nodded.

"Good. Now there are precious few places they could have gone. You want my advice, chief? Check rest stops, motels, fast-food joints on all interstate roads into Illinois. That's your best bet."

Wendell nodded absently, as if unwilling to concede anything. Denton entered, slipping a scrap of paper into his pocket. Mauser immediately knew he'd snagged the blonde's phone number. Always on the hunt. Denton put his hand on Joe's shoulder, spoke in a low voice.

"How you holding up, hoss?"

"Don't call me 'hoss.'" Denton held up his hands in mock surrender. Mauser rubbed his temple. "Fucking head feels like a bear sat on it."

"Maybe you should go in for an MRI," Denton said. "If you have a concussion you might need to sit out a few plays."

"Fuck that," Mauser said. "Get me some aspirin and I'll be fine. Parker has two hours on us. The longer we sit here, the greater chance he and the Davies girl have of getting picked off by that black-clad S and M freak you plugged."

Denton nodded. Mauser detected a slight twinge in the man's neck. He couldn't tell if it was remorse, or something else. "Quick shot you took back there, too," Mauser said, his eyes softening a bit.

"Yeah, suppose it was."

"Girl was in the way. You didn't have a clean line of sight."

"Cleaner than most. Cleaner than the one you took yesterday up in Harlem." Joe had to concede that, but for some reason his firing felt justified. "You saw the man's eyes as well as I did. If we'd gotten here five minutes later Davies would be dead. Besides, I've made that shot a dozen times. I aimed for the suprascapular nerve in the shoulder. You hit that, he drops the gun. Worked out pretty well, all things considered."

"You didn't come anywhere near to hitting his shoulder.

You were aiming to kill, Leonard, don't play stupid. Now Parker's still out there. We need to bring him in or that Davies girl won't stand a chance."

Denton nodded absently. Hostage or not, Amanda Davies was now part of the equation. And add to that this new, violent wild card.

Loud voices rang in the hall outside, a commotion brewing. He heard Wendell's edgy voice. *Are you sure? Are you positive? Is that even possible?*

Mauser cocked his head, tried to eavesdrop. He caught sporadic words, then turned to Denton, who was doing the same. After a few moments, Wendell marched back into the room, hands firmly on his hips. A balding techie stood next to him, eager, jittery. Wendell looked like a parent ready— and perversely thrilled—to deliver a scolding.

"Well, agents, you've officially hit the fucked-up jackpot," Wendell said, a slight grin on his face. That grin, Mauser recognized, was pure schadenfreude. "Tony? Show 'em."

Tony the techie handed a few pieces of fax paper to Denton and Mauser. It was a criminal profile, faxed over from the Department of Justice. Without reading it, Mauser said, "What is this?"

"We've got an ID on your mysterious assassin, the one with a fresh new bullet hole thanks to Jesse James here and his itchy trigger finger. We lifted full prints from the Davies girl's desk. Frankly, it's the only part of the night that's not a complete disaster. No coincidence it's my men who saved it from being just that."

Tony said, "We pulled fresh latents and ran them through IAFIS."

Joe nodded. IAFIS was short for the FBI's Integrated Automated Fingerprint Identification System, a searchable database that contained records on over fifty-one million subjects. Until IAFIS became operational in 1999, it could take months to check fingerprints. Nowadays two hours was considered slow.

"They sent back a perfect match. Guy's got a pretty impressive record. Not, you know, in a good way. No convictions, but he's been questioned in a laundry list of crimes ranging from 'sorry officer, won't happen again' to 'I have a special spot reserved in hell.' Our mysterious friend did time in juvenile hall for grand theft auto, but allegedly graduated to homicide by the ripe age of eighteen."

"Allegedly," Denton said. Wendell snorted.

"Yeah, right. Allegedly. Not just one, but four homicides to be exact. Every time he either had an alibi that held up, or the lead witness was found at the bottom of an elevator shaft. You get the idea."

Mauser looked at the first page. A mug photo. He recognized it as the man Denton had shot, only this photo looked at least ten years old. The man's hair was a little longer then, features softer. He was smiling, a big toothy grin. Confidence up the ass, like he didn't have a care in the world, knew he was going to get off with a pat on the ass and a lollipop in his mouth.

The man they fought tonight had the same skin color, eye color, the same bone structure, but Joe could tell the man's soul had been ravaged in the years since the mug shot was taken. This man was cold, unforgiving, devoid of confidence because confidence didn't exist in his world. Someone had stuck a steel blade deep into the man's heart and twisted it.

Mauser read the name on the profile.

Shelton Barnes.

Joe heard Denton emit a small gasp, his head shaking slightly. Wendell continued. "There's an outstanding warrant for the arrest of Shelton Barnes from the murder of a teamster in Williamsburg. Guy was shot twice in the back of the head, then his eyes and teeth were removed. Fingers chopped off, never found. Poor bastard's wife identified him from a scar on the inside of his thigh he got from scaling a chain-link fence as a kid."

Mauser scanned the profile. How was Shelton Barnes connected to Henry Parker? And how did Barnes end up in St. Louis? The man was wanted for murder in an entirely different state, had evaded capture for ten years, then he suddenly turns up in the middle of their manhunt? It didn't make sense.

"You're missing the best part." Wendell handed over another page with a grainy, poorly lit photo. Mauser looked at the gruesome picture, felt his body shiver, his stomach turn over. He took a deep breath. He looked at the photo of the charred, mutilated thing that used to be a man. The body was beyond unrecognizable, the skin having sloughed off, the bones chipped and brittle. It looked less like a skeleton than a piece of meat left too long on a grill. He heard Denton swallow. Mauser looked up, his mouth dry.

"I thought you said the guy Barnes killed in Williamsburg was shot to death," Mauser said. "This guy looks like he got stuck in a deep fryer."

Wendell shook his head, and suddenly Mauser understood.

"That's not the man Shelton Barnes killed," Wendell said, his voice even. "That *is* Shelton Barnes. According to the Department of Justice, Shelton Barnes and his pregnant wife died in a fire ten years ago. Looks like the only thing you two turned up tonight is a goddamn walking corpse."

24

Paulina threw the copy down and eyed Wallace Langston. He picked it up, scanned it quickly and handed it back.

"I'm not going to run this."

Paulina pursed her lips, that scowl she'd perfected over the years. The one that wordlessly said *What's the matter with you?*

"Wally, forgive my insolence, but that's bullshit. Every paper in this town is having a field day with us. Henry Parker is getting more ink than Blair and Frey combined. We're talking *murder,* Wally. This isn't some stupid plagiarism case we can ignore."

"I know that." Wallace looked and felt like hell. The last two days had been the longest of his professional life. He still couldn't believe it, didn't want to. Parker had such terrific potential. He was a reporter the *Gazette* could hang its hat on for decades. The talent and work ethic of a lion, the integrity of the very man he'd idolized. At least that's what Wallace had thought. "But that editorial you wrote is pretty darn vicious. I know we need to report on the Parker search, but we don't need to drive a stake in our own heart."

"Our heart?" Paulina said, anger rising. "What heart? The kid is twenty-four years old. You know how many burnouts we've seen over the years? If Parker had never worked here, who would have known?"

"I would have," Wallace said. "Jack would have."

"Right…Jack." Paulina's voice quieted. "Funny, this whole thing started because of a story on Jack's plate."

"Don't start, Paulina."

"I'm just saying, guy's old. Doesn't have it all together. Who knows what his motives were for sending Henry into the field?"

"Right now I don't know and I don't care. But we're going to handle this scandal like professionals. Period."

She placed the editorial on Wallace's desk again. "Then run my column. Be professional. Don't avoid this. You talk about integrity? My article is the truth a lot of people are feeling. You can bury it, and admit that the *Gazette* takes shortcuts. Or you can print it. Let everyone know this paper isn't afraid to hit hard."

Wallace sighed. He read the piece again. Paulina had torn Henry Parker to pieces, and was now asking him to publicly scatter the ashes.

"Run it," he said. "Tighten up the first graph. But it'll be in the morning edition."

Paulina smiled, thanked Wallace and left his office with an extra hop in her step.

25

When we'd reached the bottom of our bottomless cups of coffee and licked the last toast crumbs off the plate, Amanda and I left Ken's offee Den and headed into the morning sunlight. David Morris's Tundra was nowhere to be seen. After four hours of "Achy Breaky Heart," I wasn't too sad to see him go.

Studying the cars in the rest stop parking lot, I noticed that most had Illinois license plates. A few Missouris, one or two from Wisconsin. Before we went anywhere, I went back into the diner and grabbed a road map from a kiosk. On the back cover was an advertisement for a walking tour of the state's capitol, Springfield. Inside were coupons for an upcoming Cubs game. Somehow, we'd ended up in Illinois.

I unfolded the map, trying to pinpoint our location, then gave up. Beyond the rest stop on the southbound side of the highway was a blue sign indicating we were at the Coalfield exit on Interstate 55. Another green sign beyond that read "Springfield—10 Miles." My legs felt rubbery just thinking about it.

Amanda appeared beside me, her shoulder brushing against my arm. The first real human contact I'd felt in hours.

Her eyes were striking in the morning light. From the first moment on that street corner in New York, I knew Amanda Davies was stunning. But thinking about how much she'd done for me, how much she'd risked, she was that much more beautiful.

She must have caught me staring, because a bashful smile crept over her lips.

"What?" she said. I smiled, shook my head.

"Nothing. Thank you."

"For what?"

"For believing me. You could have hitched a ride or called the cops, done any number of things. And I'd be lost. Completely."

"You don't need to thank me. I'm doing this because I want to."

"I know you are. But thanks anyway."

Again I thought about her notebooks, and it occurred to me that for the first time Amanda had been forced to see past the surface of her subjects. Before last night I was Carl Bernstein. Merely an entry, one of hundreds. But now I was three-dimensional. Flesh and blood. Someone to touch rather than just see.

"So what do we do now?" she asked.

"Now," I said, "we contact our primary sources. The 'who' list." I pulled the notebook from my pocket and looked over the list of names. Three in particular stood out.

Grady Larkin.

Luis and Christine Guzman.

For the first time, I found myself thinking about John Fredrickson's family. The newspaper said he left behind a wife, two children. A family had been shattered. My heart felt weak, knowing these lives were damaged forever because of me. Despite my innocence, nothing could fill that family's void.

Everything hit me like a punch to the gut and suddenly I felt nauseous. I bent over, hands on my knees, heaving. Amanda, ever courageous, rubbed my back.

"Henry? Henry? You okay?"

I shooed her away with a wave and resumed heaving. When my stomach's spin cycle stopped, I stood up and wiped my mouth with the back of my hand.

I gathered myself, still panting, hands trembling. Amanda looked me over as I clenched and unclenched my fists. She seemed to know what I was thinking.

"Yeah, I just…" My voice trailed off. I looked into her eyes, warm and sorrowful, as if sharing my misery would help lighten the load. "It just doesn't seem real."

She nodded. "I know."

"I mean, I have a home and a family I haven't even spoken to since everything happened. My mother, she'd be devastated."

"What about your father?"

I shook my head.

"He won't care. This would just confirm his assumption that I was born to fail."

"Well, then it's up to you to prove him wrong." I nodded. Years ago I'd made the choice to distance myself from my parents. Accomplishing that goal brought a sense of both pride and regret. And now I couldn't turn to them even if I wanted to.

"Now come on," Amanda said. "We have work to do."

She took my arm and we headed toward the highway. I'd walked ten miles before, but never with a definite purpose or destination. Cold nights, breath streaming in front of me, nowhere to go but to be lost in the woods of my own thoughts. Back home, when I couldn't take things anymore, when the rotten stench of beer and sweat literally forced me out of the house, walking was a cure from my father's passive aggressive anger. I waited years for him to explode, to release all his hatred in a viscous torrent, but instead it wafted out like a leaky gas main, making me woozy and sick for years, poisoning me slowly.

One of my favorite analogies is the frog and the pot of water. I used it on sources that were reluctant to speak. It helped them understand the severity of their situation.

If you put a frog in a boiling pot of water, he'll sense the heat and immediately jump out of the scalding liquid. But if you put a frog in a cold pot of water then slowly raise the temperature, the frog will boil alive. He becomes accustomed to the gradual temperature change, right until it kills him.

The lesson is that people stay in terrible situations simply because they've gotten used to them. The water around them is so scalding and hurtful but they don't know any better because it's happened in such small increments. Thankfully I was able to leave my own pot before it was too late.

We started off down the interstate, walking side by side, halfway between the surge of speeding vehicles and the protection of the tree line. I didn't realize it until the third or fourth mile, but my leg was really starting to hurt. Not the kind of ache from a cramped muscle or even a deep bruise. No, this was beneath the skin. Nausea swept through me, but I fought it off.

Soon buildings began to appear on the horizon, rising above the endless span of highway. The humidity dried up, the sweat once pouring from my body now drying, causing my shirt to stick to my skin. Peeling it off caused an icky sensation, like hearing the wet sound of a bandage ripped from a fresh cut. Amanda seemed to notice this, and leered at me whenever I pried the sleeves loose from my biceps.

"This is the first time I've ever said this," I said, "but I could really go for a good shopping spree right about now."

Amanda laughed, but there was weariness in it. Still, I had to admire her being able to keep a sense of humor under the circumstances.

"If we get out of this, I'll take you to Barneys. You'll fall in love with their suits." She playfully tugged at the waistband of my pants.

"Forget suits, I'd drop twenty on a crappy Fruit of the Loom right about now."

"I bet Mr. Fruit of the Loom would be flattered to hear that."

As we walked, time seemed to go into a strange sort of wind tunnel, everyone speeding past us. We were running on fumes, the colors all blurring together, like life was a record going at 33 1/3. Amanda was beginning to walk sluggishly, dragging her heels, her shoulders slouching.

"You okay?" I asked.

"Just a little tired," she said. "Haven't slept in like thirty-six hours."

Same as me, I thought. But I had reasons to keep going.

Amanda wasn't fighting for her survival, she was fighting for a man she'd met a day and a half ago. We needed a place to rest, even if it was just for a little while.

One hour and three more miles later, according to my body's—likely faulty—pedometer, we saw a sign for gas, food and lodging, and an arrow veering off the freeway. I looked at Amanda, who shrugged, as if to leave the decision to stop entirely up to me.

"We should rest," I said. She slowed down, seemingly mulling over this idea.

"If you insist."

We followed exit 42 until we reached an intersection. Half a dozen fast-food joints populated either side of the highway, competing for layover dollars from families on the go. A Motel 3 lay about a half mile down the road, the roof a muddy red. A large neon light proclaimed that, yes, they did have vacancies and at least the *V* in TV. If the laws of division were correct, a Motel 3 would be half as good as Motel 6. And right they were. It resembled a two-story slab of pancake-colored timeshares, the paint looking like it hadn't received a second coat since before Sherwin married Williams.

We entered the motel, where an elderly man with a crescent moon of gray hair was resting his eyes at the reception desk. I rang the bell. The man stirred, picked his head up and wiped the drool from his mouth.

"What?" he said, his voice irritated, like a cranky teenager woken from a nap.

"Hi, uh, we'd like a room."

He grimaced, then reached beneath the counter for a water bottle with an inch of viscous black liquid at the bottom. He raised it to his mouth and spit chewing tobacco into the lip. Whatever missed the bottle dripped down the side like an insect's number two.

"Minimum's one night. None of that 'we need fifteen minutes for a quickie' bullcrap. You want that you best go a mile down the road to the Sleep 'N' Snuggle Inn, fifteen bucks an hour at that slop house."

"Then we'll take a room for one night," I said.

"Don't you be bull crappin' me," he spat. "If you plan on stayin' more than three nights I need a down payment. Too many peoples coming in here staying and don't paying."

"Just one night," I repeated. "Honest. And we'll even pay that up front."

"Well, all right then."

He reached under the counter and pulled up a gigantic logbook, its yellowed pages more like remnants of Talmudic scripture than loose-leaf. He turned it around to face us, and motioned to a pen attached to a chain. Not a dinky chain of metal balls like they have at banks, but a full damn chain. If this is how he protected writing implements, I wondered how he tethered his pets.

"Need your name—both of 'em—and John Hancocks."

"No problem. Can we pay in cash?"

"This is still America, right? Haven't gone all to plastic yet."

"Far as I know," Amanda said.

I took the pen and logbook and began to scrawl. *B-O-B W-O-O-D.*

Before I could finish, Amanda jabbed me in the ribs.

S-O-N, I wrote. Bob Woodson. Stupid name.

Amanda took the pen. With delicate penmanship, she wrote in *Marion Crane*. When I looked at her, she was blushing.

Marion Crane. Janet Leigh's character in *Psycho*. The woman who ran from her lover and the police with $40,000 of embezzled cash, before becoming Norman Bates's carving block.

Marion Crane. The girl who just wanted a better life.

He said, "Now I've blocked the rooms from dialing those 900 numbers. You want me to unblock it, I'll need a credit card imprint. Seen some people run up ungodly charges on those things."

"No thanks, that won't be necessary," I said.

He gave me a creepy smile, smiled at Amanda. "I'm sure it won't."

He handed us a small key attached to a palm-sized block of wood. "So you don't be stealin' it," he reprimanded us. The key was stamped *4*. He pointed us down the hall and told us to hook a right. All the doors were a faded red, the paint cracked and dirty. We passed by a soda machine. I was thirsty, but the machine was sold out except for the Diet Shasta Orange. Yum.

After we turned the key, room 4 took several hard kicks to open. Just like home.

The bed was concave, as if it had recently been vacated by a particularly obese buffalo and hadn't yet taken back its normal shape. Thankfully the bathroom was clean. The shower stall was cramped, but at least the water ran.

Amanda collapsed onto the bed. Her legs hung off the end as she took long breaths. I sat down at a small desk in the corner and pulled up my pant leg, pain shooting again as the fabric grazed my wound. Dried blood the color of charred wood had congealed around the yellowed gash. I gently pressed my finger against it, winced.

I stood up and went over to the scratched oak dresser, throwing open the drawers one by one. All I found was a Gideon's bible and a wadded-up tissue. Ew.

"What're you looking for?" Amanda asked, her voice sluggish.

"Just checking to see if anyone might have left some spare clothes, socks maybe."

"Sure, I bet the Salvation Army figured they didn't need little Johnny's socks anymore and tossed 'em in the drawer."

"Whatever," I said, easing back into the chair. "I need to get out of these clothes, take a shower."

"Be my guest."

I removed my socks and shoes and lay them neatly by the radiator. Stepping into the bathroom, I hung my shirt and pants on the shower stall, hoping the steam might rinse away some of the sweat and dirt.

Steam wrapped my body like a glove and I closed my eyes, the world seeming ever so far away. Just a few minutes, and I forgot all about John Fredrickson. The last two days never happened. The weight of the world disappearing down the drain.

I was back in the Guzmans' apartment. Luis was reciting lines from *The Glass Menagerie* while Christine showed off booties for their unborn child.

I was back at the *Gazette,* writing obituaries while Wallace and Jack observed from across the newsroom. Everything was right with the world.

Then it all came rushing back like a busted dam. The gunshots. John Fredrickson's body prone on the ground, blood everywhere. The pistol pointed at Amanda's head. The cold glare from the man in black. The cops who wanted me dead. Hours cramped in the back of a truck, knowing every breath might be my last. Death and destruction, all following me like my own shadow.

Suddenly I was awake. I looked at my watch. Half an hour had gone by in a blink.

I shut the water off and grabbed a crinkled towel. My clothes were still damp, so I wrapped the towel around my waist and rejoined Amanda. Modesty damned to hell, I wasn't going to put those nasty clothes back on until they'd been boiled and disinfected.

To my surprise not only was Amanda awake, but she was wearing a different shirt. A large plastic bag lay at her feet.

"Is that new?" I asked, incredulous. When we arrived, Amanda was still wearing her fleece. Now she had on a blue T-shirt with the letters CPD embroidered on it. Chicago Police Department. What a sense of humor. "What's in the bag?"

She threw it at me, and I thankfully managed to catch it while keeping my dignity around my waist. Inside was a shrink-wrapped package containing a fresh T-shirt, a package of underwear, size XXL, and a pair of cargo shorts that looked like a stiff breeze could undo the lining. I looked at Amanda, her eyes sparkling, anxious for my reaction. Had she gone shopping?

"Sorry about the underwear," she said. "They were out of large and XL, and you don't look like a medium kind of guy."

"Large usually, but I'm not going to complain." I paused, looked into her gorgeous eyes. "Thank you."

She nodded. "So what do you think of the T-shirt? I felt it was appropriate."

I shook my head. "Maybe I should get one that says 'Fugitive' on it. We can wear them at Halloween, maybe accessorize with a ball and chain. I'll carry the pickax."

"You can be Harrison Ford. I've always had a crush on Tommy Lee Jones."

"I'm not sure I needed to know that. Besides, you're much prettier than Tommy Lee Jones. And a lot less leathery."

"I'll take that as a compliment."

"Well, he is an attractive man," I said with a grin. "Amanda, really, you didn't have to do this."

"I know, but I did it anyway."

My smile came easily. I emerged from the bathroom a minute later feeling like I'd just taken a dozen hot showers after being stuck in a mudslide. New clothes never felt so good.

"Jesus, your leg," she said. I glanced down. The wound was angry and yellow and deeper than I'd thought. "What happened to you?"

"A bullet…when I was running from those cops." I made a slicing motion through the air to drive the image home. Amanda shuddered.

"We need to take care of it," she said.

"We don't need to do anything," I replied, stern.

"Hold on," she interrupted, bolting for the door. "I'll be right back."

Before I could stop her, Amanda was gone. I sighed, in no

position to chase after her, and turned the television on, flipped to CNN. Then I turned it off. I didn't want to see the news. Everything was already too real.

What if I had just turned myself in? Surely things could have been worked out. Surely the truth would have been revealed.

Surely...surely bullshit.

The only witnesses had publicly testified to my guilt. If my case ever went to court, it was the word of a man accused of killing a cop against three people plus the entire NYPD. Hell, if I was a cop I'd want me dead, too. But my survival depended on smoking the truth out from its hiding place. The mystery package, the one both Fredrickson and the man in black wanted, held the answer.

Five minutes later the door swung open. Amanda was holding another bag. She took out a bottle of alcohol and some cotton swabs, several gauze pads and an Ace bandage. Her face had the confidence of a doctor ready to perform her very first surgery while drunk and high on methamphetamines.

She sat me down, gently biting her lip as she poured alcohol onto a cotton ball. I closed my eyes, then felt a hot, searing pain rip into my leg. I gritted my teeth, a sharp yelp escaping my lips as she increased the pressure.

"Let me know if this hurts."

I nodded, said I would. If she hadn't picked up that it hurt like a motherfucker, I wasn't about to tell her.

Eventually the pain died down to a dull throbbing sensation. Her hands were fluid, swapping pads caked with dried blood for clean ones, no hesitancy about touching my wound or cleaning it. Her fingers seemed hungry, kneading my skin as though it contained some hidden antidote for her as well. As much as she was helping me, fixing me, I knew I was helping her, too.

When she finished, Amanda placed a clean gauze pad over the wound and fixed it in place with the bandage. She fastened the end with small metal clasps and gave my leg a quick pat.

"How's it feel?"

"Hurts like hell," I said. "Are you sure it needs to be so tight? I think you cut off circulation to my leg."

"Better than it getting infected. If the wound gets gangrenous, an amputation might be necessary." She winked at me.

"Maybe it needs to be a little tighter."

Amanda washed her hands, collapsed back into bed and sighed. Her eyes closed, her chest rhythmically rising and falling. My eyes traced her delicate curves, the brown silky hair spilling over her neck. Why now, in the middle of everything going wrong, did something feel so right?

"Why are you helping me?" I asked before I could think not to. Amanda didn't move, simply laid there, breathing.

"It's the right thing to do," she said drowsily.

"How do you know it's the right thing? You just met me. You don't know anything about me."

"I know enough about you," she said softly. "Believe it or not I'm a good judge of character. I trust my instincts more than any person's word. Those men in my house tonight, you're not like them."

"That still doesn't explain why you're helping me. You could go home right now, call the cops and tell them where I am. Why don't you?"

"Don't you get it?" she said, rising to rest on her elbows, her voice plaintive. "I'm in danger, too. And if I turn you in, no justice will have been done. We'll never know what Fredrickson was looking for, or why the Guzmans and Grady Larkin lied, what they were protecting themselves from. I'm with you, Henry, to the end of this. No matter what."

"Thank you," I whispered, knowing the enormity and truth in those two syllables.

Amanda nodded. Soon her breathing steadied, her eyes closed and she fell into a deep sleep.

Watching her sleeping peacefully only made me more aware of my own body. My bones felt like they'd been rubbed against a cheese grater. I needed a long, peaceful sleep, if only to remind me of the life I used to have. But sleep never came. I just watched Amanda, hoping her dreams were peaceful. Soon, I hoped, our reality would mirror those dreams.

26

David Morris was combing his hair—the thick, long hair that Evelyn fucking hated, god*damn* her—when the doorbell rang. Slamming down his plastic comb, David yelled at her to answer it. She didn't respond. He heard the muffled sound of the television. Some sort of damn daytime talk show. Fuck. Couldn't she get off her ass *once* a day?

David insisted she get a job months ago, and what did Evelyn do? Watched more television. Now that he was working full-time again, coming home late at night and sleeping until early afternoon, she had all day to be productive. Twice a week he had to make the three-hundred-mile drive from St. Louis to Chicago, arriving home long after the midnight hour, dropping into bed like a sack of bricks. And yet he still made time to get the kids ready for school, pack their lunches and drive them to soccer practice. Years ago he would wake Evelyn up for a quickie, gently tickle her neck and bite her earlobe. These days the thought of munching her ear made him sick.

Ever since they'd moved to Chicago, Evelyn had made David's life a living hell. His salary was off the charts, but his home life sucked worse than an Eagles reunion. At least twice this month, David had seriously considered grabbing the kids from under her nose and getting out of the hellhole he called home. Throw some Hank Williams on the radio, throw his arm around David Jr. and little Cassie, and he'd be home free.

David pulled on an AC/DC shirt and trudged downstairs, leering in the direction of Evelyn's talk show, silently cursing whichever red-faced evangelist had her attention this morning. He peeked out the side windows before opening the front door. Force of habit.

The man outside was wearing black pants and a black shirt, sunglasses shielding his eyes. He held his arm at an awkward angle, like he'd recently injured it. David was no stranger to the law—hell, his band had torn up the southwest in his younger days and he'd spent a few nights in county lockup—so he immediately knew the visitor was a cop. Sighing, he opened the door.

"Can I do for you, Officer?" The cop laughed, showed his white teeth, then removed his sunglasses, wincing as he bent his arm.

"Is it that obvious?"

"Can practically smell the gun oil through the front door." David looked around for the squad car, saw only a beat-up rental. "Where's your vehicle, Officer?"

"Federal Marshal, actually."

"Fibbies drive rent-a-cars? Lemme see some ID." The man pulled out his wallet—a handsome leather model—and flipped it open. Inside lay a government-issued ID stamped with one of those five-pointed stars sheriffs in western movies wore on their vests. The agent's name was Spencer Bates.

"So what can I do for you, Agent Bates?"

Bates pointed to David's truck. "That your Tundra?"

"Be a mighty coincidence if it were someone else's."

"Mind if I have a look?"

"Mind if I ask what this is all about?" Bates smiled and apologized.

"Mr. Morris, we're tracking two fugitives by the names of Henry Parker and Amanda Davies. We have reason to suspect they hitched a ride out of St. Louis last night, and we're doing a search of all vehicles we have reason to suspect may have aided in their escape."

"I was in St. Louis all day yesterday for a meeting. What's my truck got to do with this? I didn't aid nobody."

"We have a record of your E-Z Pass being charged at a tollbooth in downtown St. Louis late last night, around the same time the suspects were seen fleeing Ms. Davies's house in that neighborhood. We're just being thorough and following procedure. There's a possibility they could have climbed in the back while you weren't paying attention."

"No way," David said, stroking the hair flowing down the back of his neck. "I woulda seen something."

"Maybe," the agent said. "Maybe not."

"Well, suit yourself, I got nothing to hide. Let's go examine my vee-hi-cle."

Better to get the cop off his back than give him a reason to get suspicious. Bates walked over to the truck and lifted the tarp covering the bed. He ran his finger along the metal, looked at it, nodded.

"Whaddaya got there?" David asked, squinting. He joined Bates at the car.

"If you look at the dust patterns in the flatbed…" Bates said.

"Ain't no dust patterns in Betty. I keep her good and clean."

Bates rolled his eyes. "If you look at the dust patterns, Mr. Morris, they're uneven, like someone was wriggling around. You can even make out where a derriere might have lain for several hours."

"A derriere?"

"Someone's ass, Mr. Morris. Now let me ask you, did you examine your flatbed when you got home? Was it empty?"

Morris nodded enthusiastically. "Of course. I keep my toolbox there. Wouldn't leave it sitting around overnight. Goddamn vagrants here'd steal it in half a minute."

"Did you stop anywhere else last night on your way home? For gas? Food perhaps?"

David thought, put his hand to his lips. "One stop," he said. "Gas and coffee. Some place on I-55. Ken's something. Ken's Coffee Den."

David felt a surge of pride. He was assisting in a federal investigation. This shit ever made the news programs, maybe he'd get interviewed. Maybe write a book, be like that Mark Fuhrman guy, get as much money as that blond chick who screwed Scott Peterson. Plus those anchorwomen were hot. He'd ditch Evelyn for one of them in a heartbeat.

Bates took out a notepad and wrote the information down. "Ken's Coffee Den, you said? On Route 55?"

"Interstate 55," David said. Bates nodded.

"Can you think of anything else? Any other stops you might have made?"

"No, nothing."

"Any strange movements you may have noticed during the ride? Maybe a bump or a pothole, something unexpected jostle you?"

"Nope, nothing." Bates folded the notebook up and slid it into his pocket. "Can I help with anything else, Officer?"

"Agent, actually." Bates walked him back to the front door. David opened it and stood just inside.

"So, Agent Bates," David said. "Let me ask you something. You find this Parker guy, people start asking who helped out with the, you know, the investigation…any chance you could drop my name? Tell 'em I might be interested in working for the, you know, federal government?"

Bates laughed. "I'd be happy to."

"The government, they pay well?"

"Not well enough," Bates replied with a grin.

"Doesn't matter," David said. "Anything to get out of this shithole. Listen, I hope you catch those fuckers. I mean that. You need anything else, give me a ring. Maybe I can help with, you know, the investigation."

"I surely will, Mr. Morris. I surely will."

David nodded, suddenly felt good. Really good. He'd done a good deed, and the FBI of all things owed him one. Wait'll Evelyn heard about this.

"Just in case you think of anything else, here's my card." Bates reached into his pocket, fumbled around.

David heard the blade before he felt it, the thin whistle in the air right before it plunged hilt-deep into his chest. David felt his insides tearing, like a balloon was being ripped apart inside of him. Then there was a horrible burning sensation, then he felt cold, then another sharp pain as the knife was pulled from his heart. David Morris was dead before he hit the ground.

Shelton Barnes stepped over David Morris's body and dragged it inside the house, closing the door gently.

A television was playing somewhere on the second floor. Barnes looked at Morris, blood still pumping from the three-inch gash in his chest, then slowly made his way upstairs.

27

"Columbia Presbyterian, this is Lisa speaking," said the cheery voice. Not that I advocated people being morose, but you'd think a hospital operator would have a greater sense of gravity.

"Luis Guzman's room, please," I said. She put me on hold, my breath following suit. Amanda had paid for the motel room, a reasonable $39.99, in cash. We were standing on a Chicago street corner, crammed into a dingy phone booth, the afternoon sun fading away. Columbia Presbyterian was the fourth New York hospital we'd called. The first three had no record of a Luis or Christine Guzman. The newspapers hadn't disclosed their location, so finding them came down to trial and error. Only in most trials, you didn't have freaky men with guns breaking into your house and cops shooting you in the leg.

"Please hold," Lisa said. Muzak pumped through the earpiece. I held it out for Amanda to listen.

"Couldn't they play something a little more, I don't know, uplifting?" she said. "I mean, Yanni and John Tesh, it's almost like they want you to hang up."

After a minute, Lisa clicked back on. "Thank you, sir, I'll transfer you now. Have a pleasant day."

I tapped Amanda on the arm. She mouthed *that's it?*

I nodded, put my finger to my lips.

Two rings later, a husky voice picked up. It wasn't Luis Guzman.

"Yeah?"

"Um, hi, I'd like to speak with Luis Guzman."

"Who is this?"

I cleared my throat.

"This is Jack O'Donnell, *New York Gazette.* Luis and I spoke briefly last week in regards to an article I'm writing based on his prison experience. He knows the name, it's part of his parole package."

There was muffled speaking, like someone was pressing their hand to the receiver. I heard the words *O'Donnell* and *reporter.* Amanda gripped my sleeve with one hand and crossed her fingers on the other.

"One second, Mr. O'Donnell." I wiped my brow. After a few seconds a different voice came on the line. It sounded sickly, weak. Like the person on the other end had just run a marathon and couldn't get a water break.

"Hullo?"

I recognized the voice instantly. "Luis Guzman?"

"Yes, that's me."

"Mr. Guzman, are you alone in your room?"

"Excuse me?"

"I'd like to ask you a few questions, but it's imperative I know the police aren't present." I waited a moment. "If they are, I won't speak to you. Do you remember me, Mr. Guzman?"

"Of course," he said. "You're the one who sent Henry Parker to my house. You said if I didn't cooperate you'd call my parole officer. Thanks a lot."

"That's right, Mr. Guzman. But this isn't about that. Right now, all I want is your story—your story—to be read by millions of New Yorkers. I want them to know the real Luis Guzman and I want them to know the truth about what happened with Henry Parker. I want you to be a celebrity, Luis, a star."

"You still want my story?"

"Absolutely. But I'm afraid I can't promise any of that if my security is compromised. Now, Luis, are the police present?"

"They stand outside my door, man. For protection, you know? They don't come inside unless I buzz them in or someone calls."

"Okay then, let me get to the point." I was growing more confident with the charade. "As you know, Luis, I have a co-lumn that's read by hundreds of thousands of people every day, syndicated in forty-three states and twenty foreign countries. And I can make sure that every one of those people hear, from you, what *really* happened two days ago."

A few moments passed. My heart beat faster. Luis could hang up at any moment, call the police who were just out-side his door. The line could be traced instantly, my search could end before I knew it.

"All right, Mr. O'Donnell. What do you need to know?" I cleared my throat. Amanda smiled, rubbed my elbow. For the first time in days I felt that rush again.

"Luis, first off, what is your relationship to Henry Parker?"

"I never met the kid until that night."

"That a fact?"

"Yes, that's a fact, *amigo.*"

"Right, *amigo.* Now, the other day you went on record stating that Parker was looking for drugs, that he tried to steal them from you, and in the process beat you and your wife. Terrible, terrible thing. Just so we're clear, how large was this stash Parker attempted to steal? And what kind of drugs were in it?"

"Hey, Mr. O'Donnell...I tell you the truth...am I going to get in trouble?"

"What do you mean?"

"I mean, I can tell you this now, but you can promise you won't tell anyone until the story comes out, right? Until I'm out of this stinking bed?"

"Absolutely, Luis. You have my word." *And tough shit if I don't stick to it, you lying prick.*

"There was no stash," Luis said. "We didn't have nothing."

I waited a moment, let Luis think I was considering this. "So, Luis, why did Henry Parker come to you for drugs if you didn't have any?"

Luis paused. "When I was younger, you know, a stupid kid, I dealt a bit. I'm not proud of that shit, but it's all public knowledge. My PO says it helps to come clean. Anyway this Parker kid was probably a junkie, figured I was still into the stuff and just went nuts. You had my record, you saw my priors."

"So you think Parker was a junkie?" I asked, my blood starting to boil.

"In my opinion, yeah."

"So are you still dealing?"

"Hell, no," Luis said irritably. "I haven't touched that shit since I was a teenager. Parker was high, that's all. Guy was looking for a rush. That's what I told the papers and that's what I'm telling you now."

Wonderful, I thought. I'd spent most of college trying to avoid becoming a pothead and now the entire world thought I was a dope fiend.

"So, Luis, you're saying an unarmed twenty-four-year old newspaper reporter, who was high on drugs, was able to subdue an ex-convict and his wife single-handedly?"

Luis hesitated. Amanda pinched my arm. I needed to step back. I was on the offensive. Any more pushing and I could scare him away. Backtracking, I posed a new line of questioning.

"Sounds like this Parker was one messed-up kid."

"Got that right, man."

"All right, Luis, answer me this. Officer Fredrickson. How did he find you?" Fifteen seconds passed while I waited for a response. "Mr. Guzman, are you there?"

"Yeah, yeah. Just thinking, picturing it in my head. How it happened exactly, you know? Still a little woozy."

"Take your time," I said, trying hard to disguise the disgust in my voice.

"See, what happened was," Luis said, "Parker hurt my wife, Christine, and that's when Officer Fredrickson found us. He must have heard the commotion, you know. He wanted to protect us."

"I was under the impression your superintendent, Grady Larkin, first reported hearing these noises."

"Yeah, that sounds right. Everything just happened so fast, you know? Hard to remember the details."

"Sure," I said, gritting my teeth. "So how much time would you say elapsed between the beginning of the struggle and Officer Fredrickson's arrival?"

"Elapsed? I don't know. A minute. Two minutes."

"You're pretty lucky Officer Fredrickson was in the neighborhood."

"Yeah, guess so."

"How long have you lived at 2937 Broadway, Luis?"

"Seven years."

"And when did you get out of prison?"

"Seven years."

"So you moved in right after you got out of jail?"

"That's right."

"Lucky that apartment was available, real estate in New York is a bitch."

"Don't have to tell me, man."

"So what's your monthly rent?"

"'Scuse me?"

"Rent, Luis. What do you pay per month?"

"Rent? I, uh, we pay I think sixteen hundred a month."

"You think sixteen hundred or you know sixteen hundred?"

"I'm pretty sure it's sixteen hundred."

"Would Christine know for sure?"

Luis laughed. "Christine? No, man, she never looks at the bills. She doesn't work, either, just takes care of the preparations for our baby. Me, I pay the bills. I work hard. I don't need drugs to do that."

Amanda mouthed the word *what?* She saw the anger in my face, but knew we were getting somewhere. I held up one finger, mouthed *wait*.

"Would Grady Larkin know how much you pay in rent, Luis?" He seemed taken aback.

"Grady? No, I don't think so. He don't know much." The door was left tantalizingly open, but I could tell from his voice I couldn't press further.

"Now just to clarify, you believe Henry Parker's motivation for assaulting your family was stealing a stash of drugs that you never had."

"That's right."

I paused. "Mr. Guzman, I'm through for now. If I have any more questions, I might call back."

"What, that's it? You got nothing else?"

"For now, no. However I urge you not to divulge details of our conversation to anyone, including the police. If anything we've discussed should leak, say to another newspaper, or if I get one phone call from the NYPD, your story doesn't get printed."

"My lips are sealed."

"Glad to hear that, Luis. Glad to hear that."

"One thing, Mr. McDonnell."

"O'Donnell."

"O'Donnell. Mr. O'Donnell, that Parker kid, he…" Luis's voice trailed off.

"Yes, Luis?"

"Henry seemed like a good kid. He didn't know what he was doing. In your story, when you write it, can you make sure to print that? That I don't hate the kid or nothing?"

"Sure thing, Luis. Consider it done."

"Thank you, Mr. O'Donnell."

"Call me Jack. Goodbye, Luis. Give Christine my best for a speedy recovery."

I hung up. Amanda clasped her hands together and comically batted her eyes. "My smart reporter, so professional," she cooed.

I bit my lip, thoughts running through my head like a slot machine gone haywire. "It doesn't make sense," I said.

"What doesn't?"

"The money. When I asked Luis what his rent payments are, he couldn't give a straight answer. And he got real apprehensive when I mentioned the super, Grady Larkin."

"So?"

"Luis said he was paying sixteen hundred in rent per month for that apartment. That's a little pricey for a security guard."

"You think he's lying?"

"Sixteen hundred a month over twelve months is—" I did the math in my head "—nineteen thousand, two hundred a year. Luis pulls in twenty-three grand, his wife doesn't work and they're trying for a child. It doesn't make sense." I paused. "Unless…"

"Unless what?" Amanda asked.

"Unless he really doesn't know what they're paying."

Amanda looked confused. "How could he not know?"

"Maybe they're being subsidized, somebody else paying a portion of the rent."

"You think that's possible?" she asked.

"Maybe," I said. "Maybe not." I picked the phone back up and dialed the operator.

"City and state?"

"New York, New York. Manhattan."

"What listing?"

"I need the number for a Grady Larkin at 2937 Broadway."

"Is this a residence or business?"

"Residence."

"One moment, please." Ten seconds passed. Twenty. Amanda bit her nails, then smiled shyly and tucked her hand back into her pocket. Finally the operator returned. "Sir, I have no listing for a Grady Larkin at that address."

"Can you run just the name then? Leave the address blank. And extend the search to businesses."

"One moment." More time passed. I started biting my nails, my pulse quickening. Amanda smacked my arm and I tucked my hand into my pocket.

"Sir? I still have no such listing in Manhattan. Shall I try a different borough?"

"Are you positive?" I asked. "How did you spell the name?" She relayed it back to me, her spelling correct. Impossible. Grady Larkin lived in that building. I'd seen his name on the directory. He'd been quoted in the newspaper. Hanging up the phone, I turned to Amanda.

"What? What's wrong?" she asked.

"The superintendent. There's no record of him at that address." I knew what had to be done. I said, "We need to find Grady Larkin."

Amanda looked skeptical. "You think this rent thing has something to do with John Fredrickson?"

"Not directly, but I think it's a thread that might tie into a larger spool. Something's not right. Between the Guzmans lying about the drugs and this, Grady Larkin has to know something. He'd have records of payments, security deposits."

"So tell me, Mr. Bernstein," Amanda said. "How do we find Grady Larkin?"

There was only one thing we could do. One way to find out what was going on. One way to try and clear my name before the shadows caught up with us.

"New York," I said solemnly. "I need to get back to New York."

Amanda waited for the punch line, then realized there was none.

"Henry, that's insane. You know how many cops are looking for you? All the train stations and bus terminals with your picture plastered everywhere, it'd be like dipping yourself in cow's blood and hiding in the middle of a shark tank."

"I don't have a choice. It's either that, jail or a grave."

"You mean *we* don't have a choice."

"I don't want you coming with me. You saved my life. I can't ask anything else."

"You don't have to ask," she said. "And I'm not even going to let you. I'm coming with you."

Amanda said it with the kind of finality that let me know there was no changing her mind.

"Right now we have a slim advantage. Nobody knows where we are. The sharks are swimming in a completely different tank than us. But that won't last long." I took out the map. "Union Station. It's a cab ride from here. If we can get on a train, we'll be on our way back to New York before they even know we're not in St. Louis. But the question is, once we get to New York, how do we keep from walking right into a phalanx of New York's finest?"

Amanda put her arm around me and winked. "Henry, you clearly haven't lived in the Big Apple very long. The whole trick to going unnoticed is by being even more noticeable."

"I don't follow."

She took my arm, led me away from the pay phone. "Come on," she said. "Let's go for a walk. I have seventy dollars, it should be enough for two one-way train tickets, with just a little left over for something special."

28

Six hours and still nothing. There was no trace of Henry Parker. No sign of the Davies girl. It was like they'd vanished into thin air. The roadblocks had gone up, but not fast enough. They had no way of telling if Parker was still in St. Louis, had crossed state lines, or if he was hiding in a fucking shrubbery outside this very house.

His head was wracked with pain and guilt, and through it all agent Joseph Mauser could hear Linda's voice.

You're letting him go. The man who killed my husband. How does that feel, agent? How does it feel to know my family is smaller by one and you can't do anything?

He and Len sat at a table in the Davies kitchen. They'd managed to reach Lawrence and Harriet Stein on their vacation in Santorini. Told them their daughter had been kidnapped. The Steins would be on the first flight back to the States, but had no idea where their daughter might be.

"Who are her friends?" Mauser had asked.

"Um…we're really not sure."

"Old classmates, boyfriends, someone she might contact for help?"

"Maybe my sister?" Lawrence Stein had suggested. "Or Harriet's ex-husband maybe, I always thought Barry and Amanda were close."

Clearly these two didn't know their daughter very well. They couldn't offer any names. They couldn't name any friends she'd seen in the past year. They were about as helpful as asking a stranger on the street if he knew where Amanda Davies was. Linda would have been appalled. She took such pride in being a good mother, never understanding how awful some parents could be.

They'd discovered a trunk full of old notebooks in Amanda's room, one of the strangest things Mauser had ever seen. Every one was filled with descriptions of people Amanda had met. They were being combed through for leads, but there were literally thousands of names to follow up on, and most of the entries were hopelessly dated.

Denton was drinking a bottle of water, tapping his finger against the dining room table. St. Louis PD had been coming in and out of the Stein house all night, still looking for forensic evidence that could provide a clue. Everything in Amanda's room had been bagged and tagged. Joe only hoped the poor girl would live to sleep in her own bed again.

"What if Parker somehow crossed state lines?" Joe said, half to himself. "As much as I hate to do this, we might need to expand the search to adjacent cities."

Denton looked at Joe. He seemed to know that Mauser had resigned himself to this. The last thing he wanted to do was allow local authorities to collar Parker before he could wrap his hands around that young neck, and squeeze. But the longer they waited, the greater chance he would be picked up on someone else's terms. Or not at all.

"I know how bad you want him, Joe. We all do," Denton said. Mauser nodded. He'd been awake for nearly forty-eight straight hours. His eyes were heavy. And he'd probably built up such a tolerance for caffeine that coffee had been rendered useless.

Joe reached into his pocket, took out his cell phone. With a heavy heart, he dialed the Department of Justice.

When the operator answered, Mauser asked to be connected to the DOJ's Criminal Division. Ray Hernandez was an old friend. Guy worked around the clock. No family, no children, no life. Maybe that's why they'd bonded.

"Department of Justice, Criminal Division. This is Hernandez."

"Hey, Ray, how's my favorite burrito bandit?"

A hearty laugh came from the other end.

"Joe, you alky fuck, how's it going? Hey, I heard about your sister. Man, I'm so sorry, please give Lin my best. Are you close to catching this Parker dick?"

"We almost had him last night, but there was a pretty big snafu I won't bore you with. Anyway, Ray, I need your help. I need you to run a search of all violent crimes in states including and adjacent to Missouri in the last six hours."

"That's a lot of crimes, my friend. Any chance you can narrow it down?"

Joe thought for a moment.

"Okay, limit the search to grand theft auto and armed robbery."

"Gotcha. I'll run a check in Missouri, Iowa, Nebraska,

Kansas, Oklahoma, Arkansas, Tennessee, Kentucky and Illinois."

"And cross-check the victims and criminals to see if they have homes or businesses in St. Louis or neighboring counties."

"Will do. I'll call you back."

"Oh, and Ray?"

"Yeah?"

"Check on homicides, too."

"You got it."

Half an hour later, Mauser's phone rang. It was Hernandez.

"Okay, here we go. In those nine states, in the last six hours, there've been three grand theft autos reported, seven armed robberies and three homicides. All of the GTAs and robberies have suspects that don't match your Parker fugitive."

"What about the homicides?"

"First 189 was last night in Little Rock, four hours ago. A burglar broke into the home of Bernita and Florence Block, strangled Mr. Block with a garden hose, stole his antique coin collection and her costume jewelry. The perp was apprehended a mile away, still had the garden hose tubing on him."

"America's dumbest criminals. Go on."

"The other two 189's were a pair of stabbing deaths in Chicago, David and Evelyn Morris. Perp wasn't apprehended. But get this," Ray said. "According to David Morris's tax statements, our man works construction in St. Louis, also does some side work for neighbors in the area. Repairing decks and fences, seems to report all his income, amazingly.

I cross-checked Morris's credit card charges, and we got a hit within your time frame."

"Where?"

"Morris bought a pack of cigarettes from a grocery store less than a mile from the address you're at right now."

"Jesus Christ," Joe said. "You said Morris lives in Chi-cago?"

"Lived in Chicago until last night. Guy's got two kids. Messed up world."

Two more children left without hope.

Mauser bolted out of his chair and threw on his coat. Denton followed, confused. "Thanks, Ray, I'll buy you a beer next time I'm in town." He hung up.

"What is it?" Denton asked. Mauser sprinted to their car, Denton chugging behind him. "Joe, what happened?"

"Call the Chicago PD. Get them to halt all transportation that's left the city in the past six hours. I want any buses or trains searched. Have them station cops at O'Hare as well as all bus and train terminals. I'll call Lambert International and get a plane on standby."

"You want to clue me in to what the hell's going on?"

"We found Parker," Joe said, gunning the engine. "And now he's wanted for three murders."

29

The Amtrak train hurtled along on tender rails. My stomach churned, every muscle in my body thanking me for this brief respite. Then I caught sight of my reflection in the train's window.

Jesus H. Christ. Amanda sure had a vivid imagination.

I admired the fake gold running from my right nostril to my right ear, the long, blond wig covering all but a sliver of my brown sideburns. All kidding aside, I looked like the love child of Joey Ramone and a rodeo clown. Completing my getup was a pair of tattered black jeans covered with glitter pen scribblings, written to the gods of whatever '80s hair bands Amanda worshipped. I wore a black T-shirt with a red *A* in the center. The word below it read *anarchy*.

Amanda wore black lipstick, dark enough to make people think she'd been seriously making out with a chocolate bar, and her mohawked hair had enough gel to sate the cast of *Friends* for another ten seasons.

Right.

On a train that was otherwise packed, nobody was sitting within ten feet of us. Amanda was scribbling in a familiar notebook.

"You said you left that at home," I said.

She shrugged. "I lied."

She closed the pad and stuffed it into the nylon fanny pack we'd bought at Union Station for $1.99. Nothing said "you don't want to talk to us" more than a fanny pack. I shook my head at the wad of twenties inside.

"I still can't believe you stole that guy's wallet."

"I didn't steal his wallet," she said defensively. "I borrowed it. Besides, did you see that Rolex? Trust me, Henry, we need the money a whole lot more than he does."

I hoped Mr. Rolex would understand that logic.

I looked past Amanda, saw a conductor collecting tickets. He was overweight, blue hat sitting awkwardly on his head, midsection resembling a stuffed mushroom. Smiling as he clipped tickets.

Then I looked at Amanda, her silly makeup unable to obscure her natural beauty, the softness of her eyes. She knew the truth about me, about Henry Parker, and deep down I knew I'd never lie to her again.

On an adjacent seat I noticed a discarded *Chicago Sun-Times*. I picked it up, figured it would keep my mind off the mound of shit that was suddenly my life. Most of the news was local: a three-alarm fire at a nursing home in the North Shore, a Cook County bowling alley under investigation for ties to organized crime. Then, on page three, I saw a column that would have made me lose my lunch if I'd eaten any.

The author was Paulina Cole. Her byline read *Special to the New York Gazette*.

The headline was The Art Of Deception.
The subtitle read The Truth About Henry Parker.
I read on.

Henry Parker came to New York with a journalistic pedigree any young reporter would kill for and an eye most people would die for. And suddenly, two days ago, somebody did. And now one of the most-watched manhunts in New York City history is still in progress. And the questions remain.

The noble profession of journalism has taken its lumps in recent years, mainly from rampant plagiarism scandals that have tried in vain to discredit the rest of us, who are hardworking and honest, who make our livings with a clean conscience and have weathered this ship through the turbulence of the past few years.

But at the same time, the media glorifies these alleged villains, giving them even more access to the fame and fortune they so desired, despite working in a vocation where the noblest of writers desire none. Several of these literary desperados inked book deals worth hundreds of thousands of dollars within weeks of their scandals, had movies made about their transgressions and had more ink spilled on their scandals than most wartime atrocities.

You might say we don't have our priorities straight. That we foster this culture. But hopefully once the dirt is uncovered in this sordid mess, we can go back to healing that rift.

Those of us who knew Henry Parker can scarcely

believe this shocking turn of events. Yet it should come as no great surprise that the evolutionary leap in journalistic crime has finally reached a fatal precedent. We can only hope this tragedy, which has an entire city— nay, a country—up in arms, reaches a swift resolution. We can only blame Henry so much.

As the media and the ever-adoring public deifies its journalists, crowning them with the same mantle of celebrity bestowed upon those in other forms of entertainment, it should come as no shock that the crimes inherent in those mediums have cross-pollinated this world.

And so I've been forced to ask myself this question, a question that strikes at the very heart and soul of this nation, and the news which serves as its soul: Was this violent, uncaring gene embedded in Henry Parker's DNA from the moment he was born, or was it this world that drove a good man bad?

I let the paper fall from my hand. Suddenly I felt cold, dizzy. Amanda picked up the paper and read Paulina's column. Then she crumpled it up and threw it into the aisle. My head pounded. It took all my strength to hold in the wretched sorrow that filled my chest like a lead balloon.

"Don't listen to a word of it," she said. "You know the truth. I know the truth. And soon everyone will."

"It's not that," I said, my voice weak. "Things like this don't go away. I worked with Paulina. I don't buy this 'me against the world' b.s. She's trying to make a name for herself off this mess, and pretending she's doing something noble."

"And there's nothing you can do about it right now. So don't waste your energy."

"I know," I said. "It's just…this is my life. How can I ever go back there after this?"

"We'll find a way," Amanda said. "People need heroes right now. They don't realize that when all this is over, it'll be you, not Paulina."

I couldn't help but smile at Amanda.

"You have no idea how ridiculous you look," I whispered.

"Look who's talking. You know punk went out of style when we were in high school," she said.

"I'd be hurt if I didn't know you picked this stuff out." I looked at the spiral notebook peeking out of the fanny pack. "Hey, can I ask you a kind of personal question?"

"Of course," she said. Her eyes were dubious.

"Why do you write what you do in those notebooks?"

Amanda looked at me for a moment, our eyes locking, then she turned away.

"Why do you want to know that?"

I paused as an elderly couple inched past, watching us like we were disrupting their peaceful earth just by existing.

"When we were at your house," I said, "I went into your room when I thought you were in the shower. I noticed the trunk under your bed, and…I don't know. I just couldn't help myself. I read them. I read about all those people you'd met, everything you wrote about them."

"You read them," she said, more a statement than a question. I nodded, guilt burning through me like hot coal.

I said, "Take curiosity and turn the volume to eleven, and that's what's inside me. So I'm sorry. But I need to know."

She said nothing, her mind somewhere else. I paused, trying to find the words.

"I've been around every kind of journalist imaginable,
from people who take the most detailed records to people
who claim they have a dictaphone in their head. But I've
never seen anything like that. Why do you keep records of
everyone you meet?"

Amanda shifted her body, staring out the window. Roads
passing by so fast. So many miles traveled, none really observed. A single tear escaped her eye. She quickly wiped it
away.

"My parents died in a car accident when I was five. One
second you have the whole world, the next second the world
the way you know it just ceases to exist.

"Social services moved me from orphanage to orphanage.
I was still in shock. You can't really explain death to a five-
year-old, so for years I thought my parents were just on a long
vacation. I don't know how many orphanages I bounced
around, I lost count after the first four or five. Then when I
turned eleven, Larry and Harriet Stein adopted me."

My mouth opened, but no words came out. Amanda stared
out the window.

"Most orphans are so happy when they finally find a
home. But when I was adopted, it just crushed everything. It
was like somebody slapped me in the face and said, hey, your
parents aren't coming back."

"I'm sorry." She didn't seem to hear me.

"The whole time I was in those awful places, I watched
couples take child after child home with them. My friends
disappeared like I'd never even known them. My parents

died and nobody wanted me. I was like a girl somebody lost at the bus stop and didn't bother to look for. I couldn't make any friends because in time, they all left me."

"I don't understand," I said softly. "Why the notebooks?"

Amanda sat back, resting her head against the seat. She closed her eyes and I could almost see the pain rush through her as she conjured up these painful memories.

"Nobody wanted me, nobody stayed in my life." A fat tear streaked down Amanda's cheek. She went to wipe it away, but I gently took her hand, letting the droplet fall. Her eyes were so wide and open, I just wanted to jump in, see everything from the inside.

"I figured that if eventually everyone left me, I had to do something to make them stay. And since I couldn't physically make them stay, I wanted to remember them. So everywhere I went I brought along a notebook. Whenever I met anyone, even if it was only for a few seconds, I wrote about them. When my friends left me, I would open a notebook and read about my memories. But the worst part was that over time, I started to judge people based on the littlest things. The way a couple held hands. The way a parent spoke to their child. The way someone held a soup spoon. Every detail was symbolic of an entire life. And for me, that was much easier to understand."

Amanda turned in her seat until she was facing me fully. "We're pretty similar, me and you," she said. "We both try to see what's beneath the surface based on what little we can discern from it. Only you, you dig deeper. Me, I let it go. It's always been easier that way for me. But you cut through the skin."

I gripped the armrest as the train shook. Amanda turned back to the window. She had nothing else to say.

Underneath the makeup, her eyes remained the same. I didn't know it at the time, but as I searched through Amanda's hidden notebooks, I knew her heart beat to the same rhythm as mine.

Perhaps meeting Amanda under different circumstances could have led to something beautiful, sincere.

Amanda. Studying to become a child advocacy lawyer. She worked to help those who couldn't help themselves, because help wasn't there when she'd needed it. Like I wasn't there for Mya. And now Amanda was here for me.

I placed my palm in hers, her skin cool to the touch. Her fingers closed around mine. Tighter, then tighter still, until our hands were knotted like twine, the bond unbreakable. Her head fell onto my shoulder as I listened to her breathe. Steady. I could almost feel the life coursing through her.

"Where are we?" Amanda asked wearily. I checked my watch.

"We should be at Penn Station in less than two hours," I said.

"Thank God," Amanda said, letting out a deep breath. "I need a massage and a painkiller, stat. And we need to get that leg of yours to a doctor."

"I think I saw an unwrapped Tylenol under my seat cushion. You're on your own with the massage."

"Thanks. You're quite the gentleman."

Suddenly there was a horrible screaming of metal, and I was thrown forward in my seat. Dozens of suitcases toppled onto the floor around us. I heard the squeal of grinding gears.

My soda can fell onto the floor, spilling fizzy brown liquid everywhere. People standing in the aisles flailed for balance as the train jerked back and forth. The high-pitched shriek of metal on metal rang out like fingernails on a blackboard, then filtered through the world's loudest bullhorn. I jammed my hands over my ears and pressed my body against Amanda's, holding her. Then the realization hit me like a hammer to the gut.

The train was slowing down.

When we finally ground to a halt, I looked out the window. My heart pumped like mad, my mouth dried up. There was no station outside, no platform to exit onto, no passengers waiting to embark. All I could see was a dusty road alongside the train tracks and a highway off in the distance.

We were trapped.

A static-filled crackle broke through the passengers' groans, and then a voice came over the loudspeaker.

"Ladies and gentlemen, please remain in your seats. We've just been informed by the Manhattan Transit Authority that they've received notice of a possible disturbance on this train. Amtrak staff will be coming through the aisles. Please have both your ticket stubs ready as well as picture identification. We apologize for the inconvenience, and we'll be underway as soon as this issue is resolved. Thank you for your patience and understanding."

The microphone clicked off. Cold sweat trickled down my back. In layman terms, there was a situation on the train. In real-life terms, we were in huge fucking trouble if we didn't get the hell off of it.

I stood up, located the exits at either end of the car.

I took Amanda's hand and we headed for the nearest exit. Just as we approached the door, a conductor appeared through the window. He was in the adjoining car checking tickets and identification. He looked none too pleased to be doing it.

Amanda tugged my arm.

"Henry, what do we do?"

I turned around. The other exit looked clear. I looked out the window, saw that the train tracks ran parallel to a line of trees fifty yards away. Through the treeline, I could see cars speeding down a highway.

"There," I whispered. "The highway." Amanda looked at me like I'd just given birth.

"How the hell…"

"Come on," I said, pulling her to her feet. "Just act sick."

When the conductor entered our car, I ran toward him, my arms and nose chain flapping wildly. Passengers stared at us as they waited with tickets and IDs in hand. I snapped my fingers and yelled.

"Hey, you, Mr. Ticket-Taker person. My girlfriend's sick and she's gonna puke all over your crappy blue leather seats if you don't do something right quick."

"Henry," Amanda breathed. "What are you…"

"Start retching," I said from the corner of my mouth. No sooner had I said it than a low guttural moan came from her lips, followed by a thick hacking cough. I felt warm spittle hit my cheek. The girl was good.

The conductor apologized to the passengers as he wedged his way down the aisle. Amanda—who I was now convinced should have studied at Juilliard—threw her arm over my shoulder and feigned collapsing. I held her up, with visible difficulty.

"What's going on?" the conductor asked, his face a mixture of disgust and concern. Disgust, I imagined, with our appearance. Concern, because Amanda genuinely looked like she was ready to vomit all over the old lady in the next seat.

"Girlfriend's gonna puke, stupid. You want it to get all over your nice train?"

"Goddamn it," he said, wiping his brow with a fleshy hand. "Can't you just take her to the restroom?"

"Toilet's clogged. There's shit all over the seat."

"There's another bathroom two cars down."

On cue, Amanda covered her mouth and burped.

"Don't think she's gonna make it, my man."

The conductor took off his cap, ran a hand through his thinning hair. A woman seated a few rows down yelled, "Hey, let's get a move on."

"What do you suggest I do?" the conductor asked, his patience wearing thin.

I replied, "Just give us a minute for some fresh air, to let her clear out the mucous and phlegm and bile, you know. We'll be back in no time, I promise. And Mrs. Crabapple here won't have to worry about her getting her hair mussed."

"I'm not supposed to let passengers off unless we're stopped at a station." Again, like the world's finest clairvoyant, Amanda leaned over and let a thin string of saliva drip from her mouth to the floor. The conductor watched in horror.

"That's just revolting," said the old woman in the next row. "Please get this creature away from my seat." The conductor cursed under his breath.

"Come on."

He gestured for us to follow him. Amanda limped like she'd been shot in both kneecaps. He led us to the entryway. The conductor, perhaps having one final doubt, looked back at us. Fortunately Amanda's trail of saliva was now several feet long. That was all the convincing he needed.

He grabbed a small black handle and pulled it down. There was a loud fizz, like a freshly popped soda can, and the doors retracted.

Amanda sighed. "Air, sweet air."

"You have five minutes," the conductor said. "After that I'm not making any promises."

"Gotcha, chief. Let's go, honey. I knew you shouldn't have eaten all that bacon before going to the rave."

We stumbled down the steps, and I led Amanda to a patch of dry grass twenty yards from the train. As she leaned over, I caught the conductor going back inside. I waited until he was out of sight, and said, "Now."

We bolted toward the cover of the tree line and the expansive stretch of gray highway behind it. A bolt of pain shot down my leg with each step, but there was no time to look back, no time to make sure we hadn't been seen.

Then we were in the trees, ripping past branches, hiding behind a pair of large oaks. A soft wind poured down on us as we caught our breath. I peeked out from behind the tree, saw the blue brim of a conductor's hat scanning the area. Then the conductor retreated inside and the door closed behind him.

As we began walking toward the highway, I heard the screeching of metal behind us, then an air-shattering horn. When I turned back, the train was pulling away.

I looked at Amanda, sweat dotting her forehead.

"You did real good, kid." I brushed a strand of brown hair from her face, feeling her soft skin beneath my finger. She smiled, and I knew she felt it, too. "You did real good."

"Thanks." She was flushed a deep red from the exertion and, maybe, because she was blushing. "So how far are we from the city?"

"My guess? Nine or ten hours by foot, three or less by car." Amanda furrowed her brow.

"I've never hitchhiked before."

"Well, I'd never been shot before, but I guess there are some things you don't have much say in."

She took my hand as we approached the highway, the sun beating down on us, relentless. New York lay somewhere beyond the horizon. We were so close to the lion's den, and somewhere within lay the truth. Somehow, I had to pry it loose before the jaws collapsed on me. Heading toward the highway, I wondered if I was walking toward absolution, or some terrible destiny.

30

The cell phone woke Mauser up. He'd been dreaming. Barbecues and beer. Baseball and bratwurst. Summers with John and Linda, their beautiful kids. Joel just learning to throw a football. Nancy playing in a new sundress.

And then the dream shattered just as quickly as their lives had been.

Denton was speeding down the highway. Lambert International was close. The plane was on standby, waiting for instructions on where to fly the two agents. The sky was growing dark, just a hint of red as the sun dipped below the horizon.

He clicked the answer button.

"This is Mauser."

"Agent Mauser, Bill Lundquist over at the Chicago Transit Authority."

"Mr. Lundquist."

"Agent Mauser, I've been alerted by Amtrak security that on a commuter train that left Union Station this morning, a conductor reported a couple leaving the train during one of the security checks you advised."

"What do you mean they left the train?"

"Well, sir, he said the couple didn't fit the description given, he said they looked like they were coming from a rock concert or something, that they didn't look threatening. The train stopped right outside of Bethlehem, Pennsylvania."

"Go on." He could feel his blood steaming.

"The girl feigned illness, and they persuaded the conductor to let them off the train for air. When he went to check on them, they were gone. He assumed they came back inside while he wasn't looking."

"Jesus Christ, that was Parker and Amanda Davies."

"Yes, sir, we're pretty sure it was. I'm so sorry for this."

"Stop with that. It's over. But fire that fucking conductor."

"He's already been removed from duty."

"Good. And Mr. Lundquist, what was that train's final destination point?"

"Penn Station, sir. New York City. Also, they found the couple's ticket stubs at their abandoned seats. They were paid in the full amount."

"God*damn it*," Mauser spat. He closed the phone, dialed the supervisor at the Manhattan Transit Authority's security division. "I want officers choking Penn Station to death, as well as all bus terminals. They're headed right for you, be on guard, we'll be there in a few hours."

"We can make it," Denton said. "We'll be at Lambert in less than ten minutes, I've already cleared a hangar at La-Guardia's Marine Terminal."

"If we're not there in under ten minutes, I'm opening this door and kicking you onto the highway." Denton nodded.

"Fair deal."

New York. Why would Parker go *back* to New York? There was barely a soul in the city who wouldn't recognize him, and they were all out for blood. Hundreds of cops with itchy trigger fingers. He needed them to wait. Joe needed to find Henry first.

And then his phone rang again.

"Jesus Christ, what?"

"Joe? It's me."

Mauser went cold. His eyes closed.

"Linda." Silence while he gathered up the strength to speak. "I'm sorry, it's just…things are stressful right now. How're you holding up?"

"Fuck the pleasantries, Joe. Have you found him yet?" Mauser sank into his seat, felt that dull ache again.

"Lin, I really can't talk right now. I'll call you when we know more." The lump in his throat rose and he blinked back hot tears.

"Just tell me, Joe. Have you found the man who killed John? Who killed your brother-in-law? The father of my fucking children?"

Mauser could barely choke out a whisper.

"No."

"I didn't hear you, Joe."

"No. We haven't caught him yet. But I swear to you we're close."

The line went dead. Linda had hung up. Joe's fingers shook as he snapped the phone shut. He took a breath and regained his balance.

31

The Ringer's shoulder throbbed as if rubber pellets were being bounced off it at 100 miles an hour. His only anesthetic had been damaged beyond recognition. He was just about to enter Ken's Coffee Den on Interstate 55 when his cell phone rang.

"Yes?"

"This is Blanket. From Mr. DiForio's."

"I know who you are."

"Right. Anyway, Mr. DiForio just received word from our contact at the Manhattan Transit Authority. Apparently they're very interested in a certain train that left from Union Station in Chicago yesterday, heading to Penn Station."

Chicago. Not far from here…

Blanket continued. "Mr. DiForio would like to remind you how important it is that we find whatever carry-on luggage these commuters had on them. He wants to remind you not to get overzealous in finding these commuters, and that you're not to damage whatever carry-on luggage you find."

The Ringer remained silent. He clenched the phone until he felt the plastic bend beneath his fingers.

Anne. I'm so close. I can see your face, your beautiful face. And I see his face crushed in my hands as he begs for his life. I want you to see it, too, baby. I want you to see what I will do for you. I'll be with you soon. But I have one more mission to accomplish.

"Do you understand what Mr. DiForio wishes of you?"

Shelton Barnes hung up. He was no longer the Ringer. The facade had been lifted. The man underneath the mask revealed. Once again, he was nobody's servant but Anne's, and Shelton Barnes was the name she'd always known him by. The name he'd discarded years ago when his life exploded in a fiery ball. The name he was finally ready to reclaim.

Barnes took Anne's photo from the flap in his breast pocket. A gasp escaped his lips. The pain would never die. Her delicate features obliterated. Now, the only true memory of her was in his mind.

A tear streaked down Barnes's face as he gently placed the photo back in his pocket. The sky was darkening, a harsh wind blowing through the air, chilling him to the bone. A dark storm of vengeance was coming for Henry Parker, and the chase was drawing to an end.

Anne. I miss you so much. Soon the day will come when I can join you. I wait for that day with open arms, open lips. To feel your kiss, your touch. We'll be together soon.

But not yet.

Not yet.

Barnes started his car and pulled onto the Interstate, following the signs toward I-90 East. Toward New York. Toward Henry Parker. Toward the man he had to kill.

32

I woke up as we were passing through a tollbooth, following a sign to the Harlem River Drive. I blinked the sleep from my eyes.

"Jesus, talk about the worst company in the world." The driver shot me a glare, then returned his eyes to the road. "I mean you didn't both have to fall asleep, did you?"

Mitchell Lemansky. He'd picked us up on the side of the road. Amanda spent half an hour showing off some leg on the highway, despite my protests. Mitchell wasn't too happy when I climbed into the front seat, Amanda in the back. And we both feel asleep in approximately four milliseconds.

I turned around to see Amanda sprawled across the back seat, legs curled up beneath her, arms folded under her head like a makeshift pillow. She looked like she was catching up on a month's worth of sleep. I only wished I could join her.

The sun had slipped beneath the clouds, a blue-black dusk settling over the city. I'd wanted so badly to be accepted by this town, to become a part of it, and now I was returning as an unwanted guest to a city that would love to dispatch me with extreme prejudice. I gently rubbed Amanda's exposed ankle. She stirred, her eyes fluttering open.

"Wha…where are we?"

"We're almost there," I said. She nodded, yawned.

"I was dreaming," Amanda said softly. "I was dreaming that something terrible happened to you and there was nothing I could do about it."

"It was just a dream," I said. "Nothing's happened."

My heart wasn't in it. We both knew something terrible had already happened, and that rectifying it would be just as difficult.

"Are you two done? Christ, I've had better conversation from rocks. Now where you headed? 105th and Broadway, right?"

"That's right," I said. "Listen, sorry about all this. We're just totally burnt out and…"

"Save it," he said. "We're almost there."

We went crosstown on 114th Street, then made a right onto Broadway. I checked my watch. We'd apparently made good time, but I took no solace in that.

It had to end. There had to be a resolution. I knew Grady Larkin held some answers. The only problem was, I didn't want him to know the questions.

Dread filled me as the apartment building came into view, memories of that night flashing in my head. Acid running through my veins like a psychosomatic warning sign. Mitch parked across the street, turning to me with a slightly annoyed look on his face.

"Well, 105th and Broadway, just like you asked. Now,

would it be too much trouble to ask for some cash? Or would you rather just fall asleep again?"

I fished in my wallet and pulled out a crinkled ten. Amanda added a five.

"I'm sorry," I said, the emotion genuine. "Really, you're a lifesaver. It's been a hell of a week." Mitch nodded, picked at a hangnail.

"Right, sure. Well, listen, take care, guys. It was nice to meet you both in the eight seconds before you started drooling." He extended his hand. I shook it. So did Amanda.

"Take care, Mitch."

"Will do," he said. "Be careful up here. I don't like this neighborhood much. Always feels like something bad is about to happen."

"I know what you mean."

We waved as he drove off, flashing his blinker and disappearing into the night. Then we were alone.

The building stood in front of us like some vast gothic tenement. The last time I was here, nearly three days ago, I was almost killed. My life changed forever. What was once a run-of-the-mill apartment complex had taken over my nightmares.

Welcome home, Henry.

There didn't seem to be any police activity, just a homeless man staggering around by the building's entrance. He looked drunk, uninterested in us. I hoped looks weren't deceiving, and he wasn't an undercover cop. Paranoia came pretty easy when you'd been shot and hunted.

Moonlight bathed the street, and a chilled wind blew through the city.

"So what now?" Amanda asked.

"Now," I said, "we see what Grady Larkin knows. It's a good thing you're in the market for a new apartment." I explained what I had in mind.

I squeezed Amanda's hand as we approached the front door, then pressed the buzzer for Grady Larkin's apartment. A scratchy voice answered.

"Yeah?"

Amanda said, "Hello? I'm trying to reach the super? I need to lease an apartment and, well, I hope it's not too late, but I'm getting desperate and I heard from a friend that you have some vacancies."

"Are you shittin' me, lady? You know what time it is? Office closed like four hours ago."

"No, I'm not shitting anyone. Please?" She ad-libbed, "My boyfriend just dumped me and I have nowhere to stay."

There was an exasperated sigh on the other end, then the buzzer rang and the door unlocked.

The lobby was cold, quiet. Not the quiet of mourning, the quiet of fear. Our steps echoed through the hallway. We were trespassing on dangerous ground, and the building seemed anxious to protest.

We took the stairs down to the basement. The tiling looked bright, fresh-scrubbed. Larkin must have cleaned up after the police had left the crime scene. A complete one-eighty from the grimy textures last time I was here.

We arrived at apartment B1. I looked at Amanda, mouthed the words *thank you*.

You're welcome, she returned.

I took the thick black marker out of my pocket, purchased

at Union Station for ninety-nine cents, and placed it on the floor by the doorjamb.

I stepped around the corner, out of view of Larkin's apartment. I felt steam on the back of my neck from the nearby boiler room. Wiping sweat from my eyes, I heard Amanda knock on the door.

I heard the creak of hinges that hadn't seen WD-40 in many moons, then a throaty voice said, "So you need an apartment?"

"Yeah, um, my friend said he heard about a few vacancies here, and I was hoping I could look at whatever's available. I'm in the market to lease, like, ASAP." Her voice was girlish and naive, like a child asking for a cookie and expecting a slap on the wrist. Grady Larkin cleared what sounded like a pint of phlegm from his throat.

"You say your boyfriend dumped you?" I could almost picture Larkin leaning against the doorframe trying to sound seductive, arms folded as he pushed out his biceps. Amanda must have been trying pretty hard not to laugh.

"Yeah. Can you believe it?"

"No, I definitely can't. Stupid prick." I could almost sense his eyes feeling her up, and it made my skin crawl.

"I got a few openings, maybe a few more'll open up soon. Had a few, how you say, incidents here recently."

"Oh, yeah?" Amanda said. "What kind of incidents?"

"S'not important," Larkin replied. "But I think I can fix you up."

During our journey I'd grown protective over Amanda, despite the inherent irony. Since we'd met, she'd done nothing but help me survive, risking her life and future in the process.

She believed in me. I only hoped I deserved it. And it hurt like hell to stand in the shadows while a creep like Larkin tried to play the young Marlon Brando.

"So let me see here," Larkin said. I heard the rustling of papers. "I got an apartment just opened up on the fourth floor and another one on the first that'll be available at the end of the month."

"Do they have cable and Internet access?"

"They have anything you want," he said, a sly tone to his voice. "Come, let's have a look-see."

I heard the stairwell door open, footsteps ringing on the steps, voices fading away. I waited, praying the trick would work. After a moment I heard a soft thud. That was my cue.

I held my breath as I stepped around the corner. I exhaled when I saw the plan had worked. As Larkin opened the door, Amanda had subtly wedged the marker between the door and the doorframe, preventing the lock from catching. They were in the stairwell before Larkin had a chance to notice. I pocketed the marker and slipped inside Grady Larkin's apartment.

The home was dark, stale, and smelled like I was trapped inside a filthy ashtray. There was a small bedroom in the back, brown sheets thrown haphazardly across the bed. A worn paperback book lay on the floor. A picture of a heavy-set woman holding two small children stood on a nightstand. The woman's smile looked authentic, joyous. Larkin's mother, no doubt. I bet she was *really* proud of her son.

A dirty old computer sat on the desk. Above it hung a calendar of half-naked women posed on a motorcycle next to—were my eyes deceiving me?—G. Gordon Liddy. Something told me Larkin didn't throw many parties.

A steady hum came from a large copier in the corner. A rusty gray filing cabinet caught my eye, each drawer with dates in chronological order.

I pulled out the top drawer and found a shockingly neat collection of files, organized by tenant and month, dating back to 1999. Opening this year's "May" file, I found a copy of Luis Guzman's most recent rent check, made out to Grady Larkin. Sixteen hundred dollars my ass, that fucking liar.

Luis Guzman's most recent rent check was for a measly three hundred dollars. Either someone else was subsidizing his rent, or Luis Guzman would never find a career as an accountant.

Three hundred dollars for a month's rent in Manhattan for a two-bedroom apartment. Not only was that uncommonly low, it was impossible.

My fingers flew through the entire file. I found twenty more checks written by Luis Guzman, all addressed to Grady Larkin. As I went farther and farther back in the file, I realized this was more than an anomaly, but it actually had a precedent.

Contrary to everyone else who'd ever lived in New York, Luis and Christine Guzman's rent had actually decreased over the years. The oldest check was dated January 1999. It was for six hundred dollars. Double what they were paying now, but still extraordinarily cheap by Manhattan standards. In January 2002, their rent dropped to $525, and then again to $450 in May 2003. Since January of 2004, they'd been paying just $300 per month. Thirty-six hundred dollars a year.

I should have looked harder before signing my lease.

I made a copy of the first check of each payment period and stuffed them in my pocket. I searched other tenant files to see if the theme held. Unsurprisingly, it did. I pulled out a check signed by one Alex Reed, dated February 2001 for four hundred dollars. In the memo area, it read *Rent: Apt. 3B*. One from October 2005 was for three-fifty. Alex Reed's rent had steadily decreased the longer he lived in the building. Just like the Guzmans'.

It didn't make sense. Lots of New York apartments were rent-stabilized, but I'd never heard of rent-descending. There had to be a reason for it.

I pulled out every file I could, and in the next five minutes I discovered that there were no fewer than ten residents of 2937 Broadway whose rent had declined sharply the longer they remained under contract. Even more surprising, though, was that there were many tenants whose payments increased over the same period.

Something was definitely wrong.

Half the building was paying less than when they moved in, and the other half was paying more. I separated the checks where the rent had gone down and made copies. Soon my pockets were bulging, the copier's hiss steady and unceasing.

As I went to close the filing cabinet, one more folder caught my eye. It was labeled *Payments—outgoing*.

I opened it.

Inside I found checks written by Grady Larkin made out to various contractors. Exterminators. Electricians. Plumbers. Dozens to Domino's Pizza. And each month, like clockwork, one large check was made out to a man named Angelo Pineiro for between twenty and thirty thousand dollars. For some reason, Angelo Pineiro's name stuck in my head. I'd heard it before.

Then I heard a sound that made my heart skip a beat.

A steady pounding coming from the hallway. Footsteps. Voices growing louder.

Amanda. Grady. They were coming downstairs.

I thrust the last few checks into the copier, listening to the hum as it churned out carbons. When each one was ejected, I placed it neatly back in the filing cabinet. Sweat poured down my face. Their voices grew louder, as did the sound of feet echoing on metal.

I put one last check in the copier and pressed Start. The machine sucked the paper in, but instead of shooting out the original, all that came out was a sharp beeping noise. I looked at the LCD display.

In bold, blinking letters, it read Paper Jam.

Oh, God. Not now…

Frantically I opened the copier's lid, hoping the original would be there. No dice. It was stuck somewhere inside the machine. I'd never been particularly savvy when it came to heavy machinery, and had no desire to go rooting around in the belly of some demonic steel beast, but I couldn't leave any trace that someone had been in Larkin's office. The LCD display instructed me to remove the middle portion from the copier to facilitate paper removal. Whatever the hell that meant.

The voices grew louder.

I pulled at a plastic tab that resembled the one blinking on the display. To my surprise, a shelf slid out effortlessly. Turning a mysterious green dial counterclockwise, I heard the sound of paper crinkling. Hopefully it wasn't the original.

I kept turning the dial, and the tattered edge of a piece of paper peeked out of a thin slit. Turning the dial faster, I pulled at the page. It was a copy of the check. The original was still somewhere inside.

I pulled harder, horror sweeping through me as half the page tore off in my hand. I spun the dial faster, and the rest of the page came out. I pushed the compartment back in and heard a faint whirring noise. The original check, flat and perfectly preserved, came spitting out of the feeder. I thrust it back into the cabinet, shut the file and bolted out of Larkin's apartment, the torn page crumpled in my hand.

Just as I rounded the corner, the stairwell door banged open and footsteps came to a halt in front of Larkin's apartment.

"So you'll let me know about 4A, right? I got three other buyers. Maybe if you give me a deposit tonight I'll be able to hold it for you."

"Actually, I'd like to talk it over with my husband before I commit."

"Your husband? I thought you said your boyfriend just dumped you. I don't see no ring." Amanda gave a high, airy laugh. I took slow, deep breaths, oxygen flowing through my parched lungs.

"I don't wear my ring. And my boyfriend did dump me," Amanda said. "Our love is based on the spiritual, not the material. And who are you to judge my personal choices?"

"Right, whatever," Larkin said. "So listen, I'll hold it for you till tomorrow. After that, I'm not making any promises."

"So then I'll call you tomorrow. I can let myself out."

"You do that."

There was a loud squeak as Larkin's door opened, a satisfying clunk as the lock hit home. I waited a moment, then stepped around the corner. Amanda was smiling. A quick nod and we headed up the stairs and out of the building. My pulse was racing, my neck, my wrists, my hands, my whole body tense with this new information.

We crossed the street and stood in the safety of a nearby bus shelter.

"So, what'd you get?" she asked.

I pulled the copied pages out and showed her, explaining the payment inconsistencies over the years. She looked puzzled, shuffling through the various checks like a student who couldn't understand why she only received an A minus.

"So what does all this mean? What do we do with these checks?" Her eyes were expectant. Fortunately I'd thought about our next move while still inside Larkin's apartment. I knew exactly what to do.

"We need to find out who these tenants are, what they all have in common and why Grady Larkin is the greatest landlord in Manhattan. Somebody is subsidizing the rent, but for only select tenants," I said. "We need someone who can get some dirt fast, and get it without making any noise. And I know the perfect guy to do it."

33

Dusk had settled over New York, a dim blue-black that seemed to mirror everything I felt on the inside. Weariness had crept over me like a cold front, and there was no shelter in sight. The man who'd wanted to kill me back in St. Louis, he wasn't a cop. The cops wanted me dead for killing one of their own. But this man was a deadly mystery. I still didn't know what he was looking for or what was in that package, but unless he was dead he likely hadn't abandoned his quest. And a man like that didn't die easy.

I'd been lucky to escape New York the first time. Lightning wouldn't strike twice. The truth was buried here, and it would have to be uncovered soon.

I changed a dollar at a local grocery store, trying not to stare at the newspapers stacked up like tinder on the metal rack. On the cover of the early bird edition of the *Gazette* was another column by Paulina Cole. The headline read Henry Parker: A Villain For Our Times, Or Of Our Times?

Incredible. Somehow I'd managed to buck the trend. In this city, unless you were a celebrity with visible cellulite or a politician having a homosexual affair with the pool boy, you didn't get hero-of-the-day treatment for more than twenty-four hours.

Not exactly the kind of story I hoped to hinge my reputation on. For years I'd dreamt about being featured on the front page of the New York papers. And now here was my dream, in full black and white.

"You okay?" Amanda asked, as a kindly man with a brown turban handed me two quarters, two dimes and six nickels.

"Yeah, it's just…" I stopped, my head falling to my chest. "I want this to be over. I want my life back. I want you to have *your* life back."

"We will," Amanda said, gently placing her hand on my arm. She was trying to comfort me, but unease soiled her voice. She knew how perilous the situation was, that at any moment I could be cuffed and thrown in prison. Or worse.

We stepped into a phone booth a few blocks down. An elderly man sat on a stoop sucking on a pipe, watching me. He took in a lungful and exhaled a plume of white smoke. His eyes refused to let go of mine.

I took the bundle of papers from my pocket and dialed the number I knew by heart. This is what it came down to. This one phone call.

It could reaffirm everything I believed in, or dash my hopes in one fell swoop. If he was true to his word, if he really did believe in me that day, this was when he'd show it. He had to. Or everything I'd ever believed in was dead.

The line picked up after just one ring. The familiar greeting sent a chill down my spine.

"*New York Gazette,* how may I direct your call?" Amanda looked at me, her grip on my arm tightening.

I took a deep breath.

"Jack O'Donnell, please."

"May I tell him who's calling?"

"His husband."

"His…what?"

"Just connect me."

O'Donnell picked up the phone before the first ring had ended.

The last time I heard that voice, it was giving me a chance to prove myself. But I'd thrown it away, burned it and pissed on its ashes. I only hoped he was really on the level.

"This is O'Donnell."

"Jack?"

"Speaking."

"Jack," I said, my voice trembling, my throat choking up. "It's Henry Parker."

A few seconds passed.

"No, I'm sorry. Henry Parker doesn't work here anymore."

My stomach lurched and suddenly I felt queasy. Jack had confirmed my fears. The *Gazette* had officially fired me.

It was all gone. My career was over. Even if I made it through this alive, I had nowhere to go.

"No, Jack. This *is* Henry Parker."

There was silence on the other end.

Right when I thought he'd hung up, O'Donnell said, "So let me guess, Mr. Parker. You're calling to confess your sins, right? And you'd also like a front-page column, a nice book deal and the chance to direct the movie based on your life. The whole Unabomber deal, right?"

"No, Jack, I…"

"Save it. You're the fourth Henry Parker to call today. You guys really don't have an original thought in your head, do you?"

My brain raced at warp speed. I had to convince him. Suddenly everything came pouring out in a geyser.

"You gave me the assignment to interview Luis Guzman. Wallace had me writing obituaries, but you took it upon yourself to give me a chance. I pass by your desk every day. I sit next to Paulina. Wallace has a miniature American flag on his desk, next to a photo of his wife. The office smells like roasted peanuts during the day and like deodorant at night. I know that you're always the first one in and last one to leave and your chair has a pink bubblegum stain on the right arm."

My pulse drummed louder. I heard a tiny gasp on the other end, like someone about to take a breath then deciding better of it.

"If this is really Henry Parker…"

"It is, Jack." I gave him my social security number and my dorm room number from my freshman year in college. "You can look those up if you want to. But you don't need to."

"Parker, Jesus. What…where are you?"

"That doesn't matter right now. What I need, Jack, please, is information."

"Information? Are you kidding me? Christ, Parker, I shouldn't even be talking to you. I could lose my job."

"That's not true and you know it."

"Regardless, Henry, you've got some goddamn nerve asking me for a favor. You don't know what it's been like around here. Wallace practically had to hire a PR army to take care of the absolutely inordinate number of calls about you. Not to mention that half the staff thinks you're guilty as sin."

"What do you think?"

I heard a sigh on the other end.

"Honestly, I don't know. I'd prefer to reserve judgment." He paused. "Are you guilty, Henry?"

"No, I'm not."

"If that's true, it'll be proven in a court of law." *Why was he saying this?* Could Jack have known all along?

"We both know I won't make it that far. At least one person wants me dead, and that's not counting the cops."

I heard the interest in his voice pick up.

"Who wants you dead, Henry?"

"I'm hoping you can help me figure that out."

Another sigh.

"You know Paulina just agreed to write a book about you, tie it into the larger picture about the lack of ethics in journalism," he said. "Pretty good money, from what I hear. She asked Wallace for a sabbatical."

"You're shitting me."

"They want to have it in stores by the fall."

"I didn't think I was important enough for anything like that."

"A week ago, you weren't. Now, things have changed. Those columns she wrote got a lot of attention, syndicated everywhere. And ever since that husband who killed his wife's blond bimbo mistress wrote a huge bestseller, they're hungry for the next big scandal for America to sink its claws into. And you've been chosen, my friend. Apparently it's going to have something to do with the dichotomy between good and evil and how the media portrays their heroes and villains. Some bullshit like that."

"Trust me when I say this story I'm working on could blow Paulina's out of the water. There's more to it than just Luis Guzman and John Fredrickson."

"All right, Henry, you have my attention. What have you learned?"

I pulled out the list of names from Larkin's office.

"I need you to run background checks on ten people for me."

There was a pause. "Who are these people? Where did you find their names?"

"I can't say," I said. I didn't want to give him any leads. Just in case. "You have a pen and paper, Jack?"

"You have a death wish, Henry?"

"Not until this week. Here you go." I read off the ten names, spelling out each one, along with the bank account numbers the checks were cut from. But there was one name I didn't tell. I needed to keep that one for later.

"Now what exactly am I looking for?"

"Anything. Everything."

"And what if I decide to go to the cops right now? I'm sure they could trace this call and have you pinned down in minutes."

I was expecting that.

"If you do, I'll see that the *Gazette* is the very last newspaper to get the full story. I'll make sure the *Times,* and maybe the *Dispatch* depending on the mood I'm in, get the full, uncensored exclusive. They'll sell out their stock while the *Gazette* covers a hot dog vendor strike," I said. "But if you do this for me, you'll get first crack. No holds barred. I'll tell you the whole story, warts and all. And trust me, Jack, it's a hell of a story." I clenched Amanda's arm, feeling the warmth of her skin. She put her hand on mine, gave it a light squeeze. I waited as O'Donnell considered. Finally, he spoke.

"Call me back in an hour," Jack said.

"Done." I paused. "Hey, Jack?"

"Yeah, Henry?"

"I need to know…not because I really believe it, but…I don't know anything anymore. I need to know…did you know about this? Did you know about Luis Guzman? Did you purposefully send me to him?"

"Are you asking me if I set you up?"

"Yes. That's what I'm asking."

"Absolutely not," he said. "So you'll call me back in one hour."

"Sure, Jack."

"And, Henry?"

"What?"

"Don't get killed before then."

I hung up the phone. My hands were shaking.

"What's wrong?" Amanda asked.

"Jack. We need him to come through." Then I looked at her. "But I don't believe him."

34

We sat down in a coffee shop on the corner of 104th and Amsterdam. The hour couldn't pass fast enough. The diner was empty, save a hefty black chef and an older couple who looked like they'd spent the last twenty years sitting motionless in the same booth.

We hid ourselves behind two oversized menus. I ordered a bagel with cream cheese and a cup of coffee and Amanda did the same. We tore into the food when it arrived and quickly raised our cups for refills. The caffeine was all I could hope for to keep me awake, keep my nerves sharp.

"So if you don't believe him," she said, "how do you know Jack isn't going right to the cops?"

"Because if he's involved in this, he needs to find out what I know. He wouldn't want anyone digging any deeper."

"Jesus, you think..." she said, her body going rigid "...you think he might have something to do with that man at my house?"

That hadn't crossed my mind.

"It's possible." Amanda took a long drink of water.

"So what do you think Jack's going to find out from those

names?" Amanda asked, chewing her bagel, brushing crumbs from her lap.

"I really don't know. Maybe nothing. Maybe those people were all related to Larkin somehow, like his third cousins, and he just decided to give them a break on rent."

"You really think that's what happened?"

I shook my head.

"No. I don't." I took another bite and kept chewing until I felt Amanda's eyes burning a hole through me. "You okay?"

"No, Henry, I'm not."

"What's the matter?"

She paused, cocked an eyebrow. "Honestly?"

"Yeah. Honestly." I felt a hole gnawing in my stomach. All I wanted to do was reach out, comfort her.

"I'm scared, Henry."

"I am, too."

"No," she said, her eyes vigorous. "Not like I am. You know why I want to work in child advocacy? Because growing up I was sick of nobody standing up for me. I spent every day hoping someone would give me a better life, and now I'm at the point where I really feel I can help people who need it. But here you are, trying to help yourself, me trying to help you, and not only am I scared that something terrible's going to happen, but no matter what, I can't control it. I can't help anything."

The cold hole in my stomach spilled open, the guilt pouring out. My hand went to Amanda's cheek. The warmth in her face made me shiver. I gently stroked her smooth skin and watched her eyes close. She closed her eyes, nuzzled her cheek into my palm.

"I wouldn't be here if it wasn't for you," I said, making no effort to fight my trembling voice. My eyes watered up. I didn't care. "Without you I'd either be dead or in jail. I'm going to fight this until I can't fight anymore, and it's only because of you I can do that. You didn't leave when you could have. I'd like to think I would have done the same for you, but truthfully I don't know. Saying thank-you doesn't even begin to say a thing. But thank you, Amanda."

Amanda's laughter was intermittent with sobs. She wiped her face with a napkin and took a sip of water.

"When this is over," she said, "then we can be thankful."

I said, "We'll have a weeklong celebration, just for you. I'll call it 'Daviesfest.' We'll get all the big bands, have an outdoor concert, fire up the grill and invite some grungy roadies. It'll be a ball."

"Can we get Phish? I've never seen them live."

"I think they broke up, but hell. Sure. We'll get Phish." She smiled.

"That sounds really nice. Promise me it'll happen, Henry." I hesitated, trying to muster up those two words. She saw my mouth open and close, seemed to know what I was thinking. "Better yet, don't promise me now. Promise later." I nodded.

Then from the corner of my eye, I noticed the elderly couple shifting in their seats. I tried to stay calm, but something about their demeanor bothered me.

When we came in, they were sitting silently, sipping teas, comfortable as a girl wearing her boyfriend's sweatshirt. Now they seemed nervous, eyes twitching back and forth. They were huddled together, mumbling. Then the man caught my eye, held it for a second, and that's when I saw it.

A split second of fear flashed across his face, then it was gone.

He stood up, leaned over to his companion, and they got up and left the diner.

The counterman shouted, "Later, Frank, Ethel. Good night, you two crazy kids!"

They didn't return the sentiment.

I grabbed Amanda's arm and said, "We have to go."

"Why? What's wrong?"

"I think they recognized me."

"You're kidding." She bolted from her chair as I shook my head.

"Come on."

We left the coffee shop and started walking west. Then uptown. Then east. Then downtown. We must have walked thirty blocks without saying a word. With every step my leg felt like someone was lashing it with a whip. Finally I checked my watch. An hour and a half had passed since I'd spoken to Jack O'Donnell.

We found another pay phone and I rang the *Gazette*. Once again, Jack picked up on the first ring.

"O'Donnell."

"Jack, it's Henry."

"Christ almighty. The hell've you been, Parker?"

"Sorry, I'm not really in charge of my schedule right now."

"Whatever. Anyway, I've got some information on your mystery people."

"And?"

"And before I say a word, I want to know where you got these names."

"No way, Jack. The deal is you give me the info and I talk later. Otherwise I'm at the *Dispatch* and I'll spill faster than Jeffrey Wigand."

"You're bluffing."

"Try me."

Somewhere, sometime, I'd always wanted to say that. I felt I pulled it off rather well. O'Donnell must have agreed.

"That's the way it's gonna be?"

"That's the way."

"All right then, Harry Truman, I found three very interesting connections between your friends. Do you want door number one, door number two, or door number three?"

"All of them. What's the first connection?"

"First? Okay, well, every single one of these folks has done time. And I'm not talking a week in the joint for taking a hit on your mother's bong. I'm talking serious, get-comfy-in-solitary-confinement time. Every one of these winning personalities has served between two and twelve years in prison."

I looked at Amanda, the blood draining from my face. I couldn't tell how much she could hear, but she sensed something was wrong. Cold sweat spread over my body, inking its way down my spine.

"What's the second?"

"The second is that seven of these men were arrested again within five years of their initial release. Four went down for drug trafficking, two for transporting stolen goods across state lines and one for assault and battery while in possession of narcotics."

"Jesus." The words escaped my lips without thought. So

far this information was like two successive uppercuts to the jaw, leaving me shaken. All these men lived in *one* building?

"You want to hear the third, or should we call it a night?"

"No," I said, numb. "What's the third?"

"Okay, well, five of these guys are currently deceased."

I felt bile rise in my throat.

"Did you say five of them are dead?"

"Yes, deceased is a fancy word for dead. Three were shot by the police, one committed suicide, the other was murdered by his partner while robbing a bank."

"Five of them are dead?"

"You're a quick one. One more of these fellows was shot during a robbery, but he healed quite nicely, currently lives in Dover. Nice place to convalesce, I hear."

"Which one lives in Dover?"

"Guy named Alex Reed. He moved after taking a bullet in the gut from a .357. Blew out half his lower intestine. Ironically, he was the one being robbed."

The information was being processed way too fast. My head hurt. At least ten men in that building had served time, same as Luis Guzman, and five of those ten were dead. If I hadn't gone back that night, Luis and Christine would have been numbers six and seven.

But there was still one name to give O'Donnell. The one name I'd held back.

"Jack?"

"Yeah, Henry?"

"I need you to run one more name for me."

"Henry, I'm sticking my neck out as it is. I can't keep doing this or someone's gonna lop it off."

"Please, Jack. Just one more, I promise."

O'Donnell sighed. "All right. You'd better give me one hell of a story once this is over."

"I will, you have my word."

"Okay. So who's the guy?"

"His name is Angelo Pineiro. I think he might have some sort of connection to the other men on the list."

Another noise came over the line. Jack wasn't sighing this time. He was laughing.

"Angelo Pineiro?" O'Donnell said derisively. "That's who you're asking about?"

"Yeah," I said. "Why?"

"Well, do you want the long or the short version?"

"You know him?" I asked. "You recognize the name?"

"Recognize the name? Hell, I've written about the guy. Angelo Pineiro. His nickname is Blanket. Affectionately known amongst the law enforcement community as Lucifer's Right Hand. In short, Angelo Pineiro is the guy who holds Michael DiForio's dick every time he takes a piss."

35

Joe Mauser dug his nails into the armrest as he felt the landing gear shift below the plane. The pilot announced the landing preparation, so Joe took another sip of scotch from his flask, held on so tight his knuckles turned white. Why couldn't Parker have just hid at the Marriott?

Denton sat next to him, chirping into an Airfone and scribbling away on a cocktail napkin. The call sounded important. Maybe there was some good news. Joe was praying for that. Parker had fucked with them long enough. And Joe couldn't bear another call from Linda until justice had been served. John's killer had been on the loose for long enough. It was time for retribution.

Denton hung up the phone, nodding toward Mauser's silver flask, engraved with the letters JLM.

Joseph Louis Mauser.

Joe always told people he'd been named after the boxer Joe Louis. It was bullshit, of course. His grandfather had been named Louis and his godmother Josephine. Didn't matter. Everyone who knew the truth had passed away a long time ago.

"Grab a nip?" Denton asked. Mauser handed him the flask without saying a word. He peered out the window, watching the thousands of tiny lights dotting the New York landscape. Everyone going on with their lives, blissfully ignorant to the soulless murderer in their midst. A slight shudder ran through Joe's body as the liquor took hold. When Denton finished his plug Mauser downed another take.

"Take it easy there, chief," Denton said. "I got some news that'll warm you up better than any drink."

"This is Glenlivet, aged twelve years," Mauser said. "You better have some pretty fucking incredible news."

"Don't worry." Then he said, "NYPD has a beat on Parker and the Davies girl."

"No shit?"

"Nope. Some old man claims he saw Parker and the Davies girl sitting in a coffee shop up in Harlem. The uniform who took the report was skeptical as hell, said the witness looked like he was a heartbeat away from death itself, but both descriptions fit. The diner's chef corroborated his story, saying he'd seen Parker's picture in the newspaper that morning."

"So Amanda Davies is alive."

"Guess so," Denton said. "But why would he kill Evelyn and David Morris, and not kill Amanda? Could he be keeping her as a hostage?"

"You know how hard it is to carry a hostage a city block, let alone cross country? Personally, I think she's in it with him." Then something clicked in Mauser's head. "You said they spotted Parker up in Harlem. Where in Harlem?"

Denton looked at the soiled napkin.

"Says here the place is called Three Eggs and Ham. Cute. It's on 104th and Amsterdam."

"104th and Amsterdam. That's right by…"

"The building where Fredrickson got whacked." Mauser glared at Denton, who seemed to realize his poor choice of words. "Sorry, Joe, where he was murdered. Anyway, NYPD's combing the neighborhood. It took the witness a good fifteen minutes to call 911—had to change his Depends, I guess—so Parker could be anywhere, but they're giving it due diligence."

"I don't want due diligence," Mauser said, seething. "I want them to pin Henry Parker to a wall. I want to look into his eyes as I put my gun under his chin. I want to see the fear in his eyes right before I blow due diligence out the back of his head."

Mauser felt the plane shake and tilt starboard. He gripped the seat tighter and closed his eyes, wishing the liquor would just let them stay closed until landing.

"I want that as much as you do, Joe, trust me on that."

Mauser, his eyes still closed, said, "I don't think you do, Len."

He opened his lids, looked at the younger man next to him. He could sense an anger boiling within Leonard Denton, but a quiet one. This anger lived within his blood, didn't depend on heated circumstances to boil. That was the most dangerous kind.

"So why do you think Parker came back?" Denton asked. "Why risk returning to the scene of the crime? You think it might be the drugs, the package he stole from the Guzmans? Maybe he went back for it?"

"Honestly, Len?" Mauser said. "I don't give a shit. I'm not gonna waste my breath on theories about why Parker did this or why Parker did that. That's up to the courts, if he ever sees the inside of one. If we find the drugs, hoo-rah."

"What about Shelton Barnes?"

Mauser detected a hint of fear in Denton's voice. Was it possible the man was still alive? Joe was still in the dark as to how and why this dead man had ended up armed at the Davies residence in St. Louis.

Fuck it.

It didn't matter. Nothing did. As long as he found Henry before the NYPD or Shelton Barnes. There were so many wild cards in the deck it was getting difficult to juggle. But it would all be worth it if he was granted just one second alone with Henry Parker.

"So what's the plan then?" Denton asked.

"I'm willing to bet Parker's still on the island. He wouldn't have come back without a damn good reason. Maybe it was the drugs. I want the NYPD to question every doorman, tourist, subway station attendant and dog walker within a one-mile radius of that diner. But I don't want Henry taken into custody before we get there. I have my agenda and it's not changing."

"We have the same agenda, Joe. Don't forget that." Mauser looked at Denton, the man's eyes bright, a small spark behind the pupils. There was a tangible anger there, bolstered by fear, and it would have to be dealt with when this was over.

Joe lowered his voice, allowing the alcohol to temper his emotions.

"Len, I know you're pissed you haven't moved up in the department faster. But believe me when I say that half this job is luck. You get a good lead, a case breaks, and that's your career right there. And as soon as we catch this soulless prick, everyone at the bureau will know I couldn't have done it without you."

"I appreciate that, Joe, I really do," Denton said, a faraway look in his eye. "But sometimes you need to make your own luck."

"Yeah," Mauser said, relaxing into his seat as the plane righted itself. "Sometimes you do."

36

I couldn't stop shivering. I was pretty sure my leg was going numb. I wrapped my arm around Amanda's waist as we walked downtown. Just another couple strolling at night on the clean-swept streets of Manhattan. Nothing to see here.

Jack O'Donnell's voice sounded in my head like a church bell gone haywire. Those two words were beyond frightening, beyond rational thought, terrifying and inconceivable.

What had I gotten myself into?

Michael DiForio.

I knew that name, heard it bandied about the newsroom like an acid-coated breath mint. People stopped and stared when you said it, raised their eyebrows and listened closely for what they expected to be a gruesome tale. Only people like Jack O'Donnell stayed quiet. They were the ones who knew the most. Who knew the reality of the man's savagery.

We'd all heard stories that could keep you up at night, make you tuck your children in a little more snugly, double-check the windows and bolt the doors. The breathless rumors of an army silently brewing beneath the city's surface.

Now I knew why Luis Guzman was dressed up that night,

why he looked like a man waiting for the executioner's song. Luis Guzman was supposed to deliver something—drugs, arms, who knows—to John Fredrickson. This was the mysterious package everyone assumed I'd stolen. And somehow it was linked to the most dangerous man in the city.

Ten ex-convicts, all paying meager rent to live at 2937 Broadway, payments decreasing through the years. I tried to piece it together. It seemed like car insurance: if drivers stay accident-free, their rates decrease. These ex-convicts had done something to justify the decreases. And one option made perfect sense.

These men all worked as couriers for Michael DiForio. They'd all done time, and within weeks of their release were living at 2937 Broadway, paying well below market value in a building owned by a ruthless criminal. My guess was that after leaving prison, Michael DiForio contacted each of these men, offering them a sweet deal. In exchange for running errands, they would receive a large subsidy to live in his building. And to a man just paroled and making minimum wages, saying no wasn't an option.

The offer was this: Live in our building. You'll pay very little rent. You'll have a chance to save money. You'll have a chance to restart your life. But you must work for us. Don't ask questions. If you're caught, you don't know us. You've seen *Mission: Impossible*, right? Disavow all knowledge. Otherwise we disavow you.

And in exchange for loyal service, their rent steadily dropped. Until, that is, they were caught or killed. Like the Guzmans would have been if I hadn't knocked on their door.

I still didn't know what John Fredrickson had come to collect that night, or what the man in black had followed me across the country for. That mysterious package held the key. And now I had to find it.

Sirens wailed in the distance, cutting through the humid air. The noise seemed to permeate my whole body, every molecule racked with pain and weariness. The last three days had taken their toll. My body ached, my eyelids drooped. Sleep would come in an instant if I let it. But if I welcomed sleep, I'd wake up in irons. Or a box.

I had one more phone call to make. This time, though, we couldn't take the chance of being seen. The sirens were too close, and I had no more energy to run.

We entered the subway at 81st and Central Park West, right outside the Museum of Natural History, its oversized flags whipping in the wind.

I purchased a four-dollar MetroCard, led Amanda through the turnstiles and headed down to the grimy platform. Rats scuttled between the tracks, squirming in and out of the metal rails, sniffing crushed soda cans and bone-colored cigarette butts. Discarded on the platform was the latest issue of *New York,* sporting a headline which read Organized Crime: New York's Comeback Kid.

I found a pay phone, dialed the main line at Columbia Presbyterian and asked for Luis Guzman's room. A cop answered. I identified myself as a reporter for the *Daily Bugle.*

After a moment, Luis Guzman came on the line. His voice sounded stronger than the last time we'd spoken.

"Yeah, hello?"

"Luis?" I said, this time making no effort to disguise my voice.

"Yeah, hello? Who's this?"

"Luis. It's Henry Parker."

"I'm sorry I don't know no…holy shit." He remembered. "What…how could you…"

"Listen, I don't have much time. I know about Michael DiForio. I know about the deal he cut you. I know John Fredrickson was supposed to pick up a package from you the night he died and I know you didn't have it. What I need to know, Luis, is what was in that package and where I can find it."

"I…I never got it, I swear to God."

"I believe you," I said. "But I still need to know what was in it and where it is."

"I swear I don't know," Luis said. "It was supposed to be delivered that day, at one o'clock. But it never showed. I don't know what was in it. I just know it was important."

"How important?"

"Michael, he had this man. A guy named Angelo Pineiro. Angelo called me every now and then. He said he trusted me, that he'd only call when Michael really needed it. He said unlike the other guys I wasn't no junkie. I wasn't going to wig out, go nuts. He said there was an important package coming and I had to protect it or I'd die. That's what he said. Said it was the kind of package that if you fucked up the delivery you'd just disappear. He said I had to hold on to it and Officer Fredrickson would pick it up later."

"Why didn't you tell Fredrickson the package never arrived? He would have understood, right?"

"I did tell him," Luis pleaded. "I swore to him I never got the package, but he didn't believe me. And now they think you got it, Henry. They think you stole it. And Michael will do anything to get it back."

Then it hit me. That's where the man in black came in. He was sent by Michael DiForio to retrieve the package. The package Michael DiForio thought I'd stolen. And he'd kill me, if necessary. Everything was getting so deep, so dark. Michael DiForio was deadly enough, but bringing in a mercenary meant he needed someone even more vicious.

"Who was it, Luis? Who was supposed to deliver the package to you?"

"This photographer guy named Hans Gustofson. I only met him once. Kind of a jittery fuck, like he thought someone was always watching him. He lived in Europe, but this guy Angelo say he kept a Pied-a-something in New York. Big-ass motherfucker, too. Used to be a bodybuilder."

"Hans Gustofson," I said. There was a glimmer of recognition.

"Told me he was working on something big. That he'd either finish it or die trying."

"Do you know where Gustofson lives?"

"I don't know, somewhere around…" Luis stopped talking. I heard the sound of scuffling on the other end, footsteps on linoleum. My heart thumped louder as someone yelled *no*, then *stop*. Then I heard a thud, like something hitting the floor. Then there was silence.

"Who is this?" A new voice on the phone. Not Luis. "Who the fuck is this?"

I hung up.

"We need to go," I said to Amanda. "We need to go now."

Stepping out of the subway into the night, the sirens

seemed to have grown louder. I told Amanda what Luis said. How we needed to find this package. And how we were being hunted.

"So how's this guy Gustofson connected to Michael DiForio?" she asked.

Sighing, I told her what I'd known as soon as Luis dropped the name.

"Hans Gustofson was a photographer," I said. "When Luis told me that, something clicked. I knew I recognized the name. Gustofson was one of Helmut Newton's protégés. He made his name as a wartime photojournalist—Vietnam, Kuwait—then decided to get artsy. He said the human body was more beautiful in the nude than in the grave. You can figure out what happened next."

"Let me guess...he went to the dark side."

"Like Darth fucking Vader," I said. "When I was a kid, I read every newspaper I could get my hands on, every one that the public library carried. Searching old microfiche to see what the greatest journalists ever wrote about the most important events of the last half century. I saw a lot of Gustofson's work, especially during the Gulf, and then in Sarajevo. When you want to be a journalist, you get to know all the names associated with the industry, and he was a big one."

"So what happened?"

"He got hooked on heroin and started believing he was one of the models instead of the person photographing them. Thousands of dollars in debt later, he started taking sleazy pictures, naked celebrities on vacation, things like that. Soon the mainstream papers wouldn't touch him, but the tabloids were more than happy to pay his salary."

I continued. "Every photo tells a story. It's a snapshot of a moment in time, a context in and of itself. But the pictures Hans ended up taking were a sham. That crap isn't a portrait of time, it's a bastardization of it. A quick fix with no relevance. Anyway the press dragged him through the mud until there was no digging himself out. Word was he'd become a recluse, burying himself in heroin and alcohol and women, mostly at the same time."

"So the question is," Amanda said, her sentiments echoing mine, "how is Gustafson involved with Michael DiForio?"

"Only one way to find out," I said. "We need to find Hans." Amanda nodded in resigned agreement.

"If he's living in New York, he must have an address."

I nodded again. "Time to find our old buddy Mr. White Pages."

We walked another five blocks and found an all-night diner. Fire burned through my leg with each step. Stepping inside to the welcome smell of grease and grilled meat, I asked the chef for the pay phone. He nodded and used his spatula to point us toward the restrooms.

Tattered copies of the yellow and white pages sat on a small desk beneath a soiled phone. I flipped through the white pages until I found a listing for an H. Gustofson, then glanced over my shoulder. I made a violent coughing noise, and simultaneously tore the page from the book.

Hans Gustofson lived just ten blocks away. My wobbly legs could handle it, barely.

"You think we should call ahead?" Amanda asked, grinning.

"Now what would be the fun in that?"

We made the walk in fifteen minutes, our bodies hunched over as though straining against tremendous resistance. We were no longer concerned about being inconspicuous. The last few days had sapped our energy to the point where we actually were relying on the wind to propel us.

Gustofson lived in a brick town house on 90th and Columbus. Upper West Side. Pretty decent neighborhood. Like all good brownstones there was no doorman, only a buzzer-based security system. These things were tough to crack, only done so by the most daring and intuitive thieves and espionage artists.

Or a college graduate who'd spent his entire freshman year breaking into said buildings to surprise his girlfriend for some late-night sex.

I slid out my American Express corporate card, doubting that the *Gazette* had this in mind when they gave it to me.

"Watch the master," I said to Amanda, deftly slipping the plastic between the door and frame. I leaned in close and listened, sliding the card gently in a north-south direction. I heard the telltale click and the door swung open.

"Better than MacGyver," Amanda said.

We stepped into the musty lobby. Chinese food menus were scattered about the floor. A plant stood in the corner, looking like it was last watered during the Cold War. Crispy brown leaves surrounded the pot like dandruff. A black-painted staircase wound upward. The building was five stories. No elevator. Perfect.

I checked the tenant directory and found Hans. He lived in apartment 5A. Of course he had to live on the fifth floor.

One step at a time, I told myself. Not five whole flights, but one step at a time. Positive thinking. Amanda sighed beside me.

"Do we have to walk all the way up there?" So much for positive thinking.

"Unless there's a donkey attached to some sort of pulley system, I'm afraid so."

By the time we reached the third floor my calf muscles felt like they were sloughing off my body. My wounded leg had gone numb again, which scared the shit out of me. Amanda panted as she followed a few steps behind. I offered to go alone, to rejoin her downstairs when I was through. She offered a four-letter response. My kind of girl.

As we reached the third-floor landing and headed for the fourth, a foul smell caught my nostrils. Bad Chinese food, maybe. Or someone who'd worn the same pair of socks for three or four hundred years. But as we reached the fourth floor, I noticed an ominous scent lurking beneath that smell. Something sour. More sinister. I turned to Amanda. We both had the same thought. There was something rotten one flight above us.

There was only one apartment on the fifth floor. Like a penthouse suite in a town house of clogged toilet bowls. Amanda pinched her nose, covered her mouth. Several envelopes were stuffed underneath the door to apartment 5A. It had been a while since Hans opened his mail.

I put my ear to the door, listened for any sign of movement. Hearing nothing, I inspected the doorframe. It didn't look like my credit card would do the job this time. Maybe I could pose as some long lost cousin of Hans Gustofson's. Claim Amanda was the daughter he'd never met, persuade the super to let us inside.

"What's that?" Amanda asked suddenly, pointing to a deep indentation below the dead bolt. I looked closer. Someone had broken into Hans Gustofson's apartment, and judging by the depth and relatively small number of scrapes, they'd done it quickly. Perhaps while he was at home. The lock looked too damaged to close.

"Henry," Amanda said, "we should call the cops."

"We will," I said. "But I need to see what's in there."

My heart pounded as I backed up against the wall opposite the door, crouching in a three-point stance. The muscles in my legs tensed. I blocked out the pain, focused.

"Henry…"

I took three quick breaths, then launched myself at the door.

My shoulder slammed into the metal, and instead of the thick crunch and pain I expected, the door buckled inward and I fell to the ground in a heap. I was inside Hans Gustofson's apartment.

The foul odor immediately clogged my nostrils and I had to put my shirt over my nose. Staggering to my feet, I felt a sticky substance on my palms. Then I noticed my palm print in a puddle of what I immediately knew was dried blood.

Oh, Jesus…

Nausea washed over me as I surveyed the foyer. The apartment was lit only by the haunting glare of moonlight shining through an unseen window. To the left of the foyer was a short hallway. I stepped into the apartment. The entire place was littered with debris. Not garbage, but debris. Broken glass. Shredded cotton. Electrical equipment shattered. Mail strewn about.

"Henry…" I heard Amanda whisper behind me. "Oh, God, Henry, look."

On the wall by the front door was a large matte of blood about head height. Like an abstract painting, blood had dripped down the beige wallpaper and dried in ghastly thick lines. A crowbar lay on the floor, the hooked end chipped and caked with dried blood. The same weapon the intruder had used to break in had also been used to maim someone, perhaps fatally. Something terrible had happened here….

Blood spatters dotted the hallway, marking a gruesome path through the foyer down the hall and into the main apartment. I said a silent prayer.

"We should leave," Amanda said softly. "We should call the police."

"No." My voice was more forceful than I intended. "We can't leave. Not yet."

Holding my breath, I followed the blood droplets like a trail of crimson crumbs. Entering the living room, I pieced the scene together, the gruesome events that had taken place.

Someone had broken into Hans Gustofson's apartment, while he was home. He'd confronted the intruder at the door, where he'd received a vicious, possibly fatal, blow to the head. Then the apartment was ransacked. Tables overturned, books strewn about, mattresses torn apart. Camera equipment broken and rendered useless. Photo albums torn through and discarded. It was impossible to tell if the thief had found what he was looking for. Everything looked like a standard break-in, except…

One thing didn't make sense. The blood drops…they led back *into* the apartment. The assault had taken place by the door, but it looked as though the victim had crawled back inside. There was a telephone in the kitchen, but it was clean, untouched, less than ten feet away. The victim was alive, but hadn't attempted to call for help. Why?

I looked around. The living room was covered in prints and framed photographs, mostly of nude women in soft light, very artsy and subtly shaded. Beautiful. In these photographs I glimpsed a hint of the magic that had once carried Hans Gustofson to the forefront of the art world.

I tiptoed through the carnage, feeling my way in the dim lighting, and came to a hallway with a T-intersection. Both paths led to closed doors. The blood trail curved to the left, stopping at a closed door.

I stared hard at it. The blood droplets seemed to end there. I swallowed, my heart doing a drumroll.

"Henry?" Amanda had entered the living room. "Oh, my God, Henry, what is all this?"

"I'm over here," I called out. "I don't know yet."

I held my breath, reached out and gripped the doorknob. The metal was cold and I jerked my hand away. I could hear running water. I rapped my knuckles on the bathroom door. No answer.

"Hello?" No response. Just the flowing water. Blood pounded in my temples as I took a deep breath.

Again I grasped the doorknob, this time turning it. The door was locked from the inside. I cursed under my breath. I had to get in there.

I went to the door on the right. The knob turned easily, and

I entered what appeared to be Hans Gustofson's bedroom. Photos were scattered everywhere. His desk was torn apart. A cork posterboard had been removed from the wall, pushpins scattered like multicolored sprinkles over the red carpet. The bed covers were thrown about, the mattress ripped apart like a drunken medical examiner had taken his frustration out on a cadaver. Files had been emptied out of a small bureau and dumped on the floor in a heap. Other than that, the room was empty.

I slid open a closet to find clothes dumped all over the floor, pants with their pockets turned inside out. I grabbed a wire hanger and bent the metal against my shoe until I'd straightened it into a makeshift spear. Back to the locked door, I eased the metal spike into the small hole on the outside of the knob. I jimmied it around, felt it catch. Pushed lightly, then felt a pop as the lock disengaged. I looked back at Amanda.

"Henry," she said. "Please…"

The knob turned. But when I pushed, I felt resistance from inside. Something was blocking the door.

There was just enough room to peek my head in. Craning my neck, I peered through the tiny slat.

When I saw what the obstacle was, it took all I had not to vomit.

A shoe was propped against the door. The shoe was connected to a leg. The leg was connected to a man, fully clothed, his head covered in matted blood, sitting atop the toilet. It was Hans Gustofson, and he was very dead.

There was a large gash by his right temple, and his skull looked deformed, almost misshapen, like a lump of clay hit with a baseball bat.

The blood spatter by the front door. Hans had been brained there, his head smacking off the wall. But it hadn't killed him. At least not right away. Somehow he'd managed to perch himself on the toilet. Very Elvis of him.

I held my breath, feeling my stomach churn, and gently moved his leg, now captured by the prison of rigor mortis, out of the way. His body shifted.

I stopped pushing. Made sure he stayed balanced on his death throne.

Then without warning, Gustofson's body slipped off the toilet and went crashing to the ground. His maimed head smacked wetly off the tiling. I bit my fist to stop from screaming as his dead eyes stared at me from the floor, his body horribly contorted.

I closed my eyes, stepped back, felt faint.

I'd seen a body once before, visiting the medical examiner's office back in Bend for a story I was writing. I'd felt like throwing up then, too. The ME, a surprisingly young and attractive woman named Grace, had laughed.

Don't think of it as a person, she'd said. *All it is is a husk, like a snail shell. The soul is gone.*

That helped a little. But not much.

I gently opened the door. Easy, Henry. He's just a shell. Like a steak with eyes.

I looked over the prone body. Gustofson had been an amateur bodybuilder as well as photographer, always snapped at high society events with tree-trunk arms wrapped around the supermodel of the moment. I could tell from the acne scars on his cheeks and thinning hair that he'd recently been resorting to chemical enhancers. Very Barry Bonds of him.

Hans Gustofson was once one of the foremost chroniclers of the human experience and now here he was, dead in his bathroom. And for what?

I looked at the gaping wound by his temple. The death blow. Pushing the horror of the situation away, I focused on the facts. Tried to distance myself.

Strangely, the medicine cabinet was untouched. The only part of the house that didn't look like it had been ransacked. It could only mean that either the killer had found what he was looking for, or the item was too big to fit inside such a small space. But the question remained: Why would a gravely wounded man come here to die?

"Oh, Jesus fucking Christ." Amanda was standing outside the bathroom, her hand covering her mouth and nose. "Is he…"

"Yeah," I said. "He's been dead awhile."

"It's like nobody even noticed," she said, her voice remorseful, distancing herself from the crime and focusing on the facts. Just like I had. This allowed you to see the story from a more comprehensive angle and was a by-product of journalism. Right now, it was all I had to keep myself from breaking down.

"But why would he come here?" she added.

"Well, when you gotta go, you gotta…" I left the joke unfinished. This wasn't the time.

"If you're dying," Amanda said, "and your world is about to end, there has to be a reason to come here if not for help. There's no phone. It's like he was checking up on something."

"Maybe he knew whoever attacked him hadn't searched

the bathroom. Think about it. You're lying on the floor. Some guy's just bashed you with a big hunk of metal, you're laying there dying while he's tearing your home apart. What could be so important that you'd ignore medical help to find it?"

"The package," Amanda said. "What DiForio and that man in black wanted. Maybe that's what was so important. Maybe that's what the killer missed. You think that maniac who found us in St. Louis did this?"

"Maybe. It would make sense. But I honestly don't know."

The package. The reason John Fredrickson had assaulted the Guzmans. What the newspapers assumed I'd stolen. What a stranger was trying to kill me for. What the cops thought I was hiding. Gustofson had it, and whoever killed him failed to find it.

But one thing was for certain: it was here in the bathroom with us.

Amanda looked at me, and suddenly she reached forward and wrenched open the porcelain top to the toilet. We gazed inside. Nothing but water, levers and rust. She replaced the top.

"So where..." she said, thinking aloud. I maneuvered around Gustofson's body and opened the cabinet beneath the sink. Nothing but Rogaine, unidentifiable pill boxes and an unopened pack of condoms. The medicine cabinet was stocked with hair gel, cologne and shaving gear, but nothing to arouse suspicion.

I stepped back and surveyed the bathroom. There had to be something. My eyes went to the ceiling, looking for a fake smoke detector, anything. I kicked over the hamper, sifted through a pile of dirty clothes with my shoe. Nothing.

Amanda checked behind the toilet, as I silently gave her credit for being brave enough to do so. She came up, her eyes defeated.

"There's nothing here," she said. "Maybe Hans did just come here to die on the toilet. He knew he'd thrown his life in the shitter and that's where he wanted it to end."

"No," I said, still searching. "There has to be something." Then I looked at the bathtub and saw it. Tiny chips of blue paint were sprinkled by the drain. As I looked closer, tiny cracks emerged in the tiling, invisible if you weren't looking for them.

Slowly I brought my hands up to grip the hot and cold knobs. I turned them. No water came out. Amanda's eyes went wide.

I turned around, looked at her, nodded.

I yanked both knobs as hard as I could. There was a terrible crunching sound as the knobs tore away from the wall, spraying blue paint and dust everywhere. Tiling cascaded down into the bathtub as the room filled up with steam and dust. Coughing, I waved the detritus away and peered into the two-foot wide, six-inch high hole I'd created. Inside was a thick manila envelope sealed inside a plastic bag.

"Is that…" she said.

"Be some coincidence," I said. "Now let's see what all the fuss is about."

37

After freeing the plastic sheaf from the wall, I carried it into the living room. The small edgewood dining room table had been wiped clean during the break-in, candlesticks bent and twisted and dinnerware shattered. I blocked Gustofson's body from my mind, ignoring the dried blood, the acrid smell. I would have preferred to examine our finding anywhere but a dead man's apartment, but we had nowhere to go. Time was running out, each second bringing an increased sense of dread. When was the last shoe going to drop, our last free seconds melting away? This envelope held the answers to so many questions. A lot of people were willing to kill for this, and I had no doubt that what happened to Hans Gustofson could happen to me as well.

I placed the package on the table, my breathing long and slow. I gently slipped my fingers inside, finally touched what people had died for, had killed for. I ran my hand along the envelope's grainy surface, still sharp, untouched by the elements. It was fastened with a red drawstring. Unwinding the twine, I took a deep breath and opened the envelope.

A binder slid out onto the table. The cover was shiny and

black. I ran my hand over its smooth surface. Silence
drummed in my ears as I slowly lifted the cover to see what
lay inside.

There was a photo of two men mounted on the first page,
and an index card pasted below it with two names written in
thick ink. The photo looked at least twenty years old. Both
men were wearing overcoats. And they looked like they
didn't want anyone else to know they were meeting.

Detective Lieutenant Harvey N. Pennick
Jimmy "Eight Ball" Rizzoli

I turned the page. Another photo, another index card.
Another detective. Another guy with a clichéd nickname. I
flipped the pages. More photos, more cards, more cops, more
crooks. The book was full of them. Immediately it dawned on
me. I knew what the connection was. The revelation made my
head swim.

I knew how Hans Gustofson was connected to Michael
DiForio. What John Fredrickson had been looking for at the
Guzmans' house. That many more lives were at stake than
just mine and Amanda's. That I'd stumbled onto something
big, something huge, and oh, God, there was a whole lot more
at stake than my insignificant life.

Within these pages were images that could ruin a city.

Or control it.

Fear rushed through my veins like a bad drug, seizing hold
of my body. I stood up to compose myself. I felt dizzy, un-
balanced. Whispering, under my breath. Oh God, oh Jesus,
oh shit, oh fuck.

Amanda was staring at me. She was looking at the last page, the page I'd stopped on. The page that tied it all together.

"Is that…" she said, her voice trembling like she was walking a tightrope thousands of feet above ground. "Are those…"

"Yes," I said weakly. "That's Officer John Fredrickson and Angelo Pineiro."

Inside this album were pasted hundreds of photos. Policemen. Politicians. Government officials. All captured by the steady eye of Hans Gustofson. The negatives were neatly tucked away in the back for safekeeping.

In some photos they were taking money, in others they were buying or selling drugs. Some were having sex with women. Some were having sex with men. All their faces were clear as day. The subjects were all unaware. Taking bribes. Some men seemed to be playing to the camera—they knew about Hans taking their picture from the shadows. Some photos looked twenty years old, some as fresh as the moonlight streaming through the window.

Some cops were in uniform and some were in plainclothes, easily distinguishable from their posture and countenance that they knew what they were doing was so, so wrong.

The patsy's name was written on the index card. First and last, middle initial. Rank. Their office. Also listed were their associates, the men or women they were photographed with. I recognized many of them. I recognized the name Angelo Pineiro. Blanket.

The Right Hand of Lucifer.

Oh, God…

Some of the faces looked sad, remorseful. Faces that once

held dreams of nobility but had since been reduced to this. Some were happy, jovial, looking like they'd known their associates for years. Unrepentant for their crimes, or disillusioned to the point of apathy.

"Jesus," Amanda said.

"I hope he hears you," I said. "Because nobody else seems to."

We flipped through the entire book, an encyclopedia of corruption spanning a generation. And on the very last page, staring back at us, was John Fredrickson.

He looked weary, haggard. He held a wad of cash in his palm. Officer John Fredrickson. The man who'd died at my hands. The man I was being hunted for, I'd given up my life for. I closed my eyes and replayed that fateful night in my mind. The deafening gunshot that ended one life and changed the course of another.

This binder was supposed to find its way to Luis Guzman. It was what John Fredrickson had nearly beaten three people to death for. Luis Guzman was the courier for John Fredrickson. Fredrickson was working for Michael DiForio. The hired muscle. Cop muscle. The strongest kind. DiForio had the goods on Fredrickson, and was using him to deliver the very photos that possessed his soul.

But after all that, there was still an unanswered question.

Who killed Hans Gustofson?

It couldn't have been DiForio. According to the newspapers, I'd stolen the package and the maniac in black seemed to think this as well. Assuming the assassin had been hired by DiForio, there would be no sense in him killing Hans before receiving the photos.

No, Gustofson was killed by someone working outside of Michael DiForio's jurisdiction. Someone who knew about the photos and wanted them for him or herself. Someone who'd clearly left empty-handed and was still looking.

But as I stood there looking at the photos, another realization came to me.

Within this binder was the opportunity to reclaim my life. John Fredrickson had set me on an unalterable course to hell, but this album held my salvation. These photos were the story of a lifetime. A generation of corruption captured on film. This could bring down the entire criminal justice system. It could restart my career, put it back on the path I thought had been destroyed.

Here it was, perhaps the greatest story I could ever hope to uncover, the story I'd longed to write for years, sitting in front of me in literal black and white. Here was a network of corruption whose capillaries reached far and wide, whose tainted blood carried venom to all parts of the city, and spanned decades. This was my Watergate, my Abu Ghraib.

"What do we do with this?" Amanda asked. "Bring it to the cops? Burn it?"

"No," I said, my voice monotone. "I need to use it."

"Use it how?"

"This is my story." I turned to Amanda, my eyes desperately wide, hoping she'd understand the incredible opportunity in front of me.

"What do you mean, 'your story,' Henry? I don't understand."

"Amanda," I said, gently taking her hands in mine, feeling the strong pulse in her wrists. "This album, everything inside it, this could make my career right again. If I went to the *Gazette* with this story, I'd be a page-one writer in no time. This is the kind of moment careers are built on. Reporters can go an entire lifetime and not find anything close to this. I can't pass it up."

Amanda pulled her hands away, crossed them on her chest.

"I don't know, Henry. It doesn't seem right. This could single-handedly destroy the NYPD. If you write about this, it could bring down the city. Think about it. There are thousands and thousands of cops and lawmen in New York who risk their lives every day. We have pictures of probably twenty guys who are still on active duty. You'd risk everything they work and die for, just for a story?"

"You don't understand," I said. "Sometimes you only get one chance, one moment to make a difference. If I don't take this…I don't know if it will ever happen again.

"Don't you see?" I pleaded. "Don't you see what this could mean for my life? I have nothing right now. I have no name, no hope, and my future is fucked. This could bring it all back. I can expose the truth and make up for everything that's happened."

"And then what?" Amanda said, her back ramrod straight, her eyes slicing through me. "You make your name. Congratulations, Henry Parker. Then what happens to the millions of people who lose faith because you want to make your name? The thousands of cops who have to answer for the few who went bad? You're thinking how it will affect you, and that's selfish. You want to be a great reporter? You need to remember that the story isn't about you."

"Please. This is everything I've ever dreamed of. To make

a difference. To change lives." I thumped my hand on the binder, felt the shockwave rattle through my body. "This book could do that."

"Whose life will it change besides yours?" Amanda yelled. "Whose? These cops? It'll ruin them. The people? Do you really think losing faith in their protectors—most of it completely unwarranted—will make their lives better?"

"I don't know," I whispered. "But I can't just pass this up."

"Yes, you can," she said. "Why did you want to become a reporter in the first place? Really, why?"

"To help people," I said. "To tell the truth about what needed to be told. To give people what they deserve to know."

Amanda's voice grew soft as a tear landed softly on the table. Surprisingly, it had come from me.

"You can help people," she said. "You can help them by making things right. Not just for yourself. That door opens for everyone, Henry, but this isn't your time. I know you're innocent. I know you have a good heart. So use it. Make things right for these people. Help them. *Then* help yourself."

Her eyes found mine. I cursed the cold book beneath my hand, cursed that my life had been altered. That this small folder had the power to change—and end—many other lives as well. And now I was questioning something I never thought I would. Every moment I hesitated, that door would be closing. All I had to do was prop it open. But I couldn't.

"You're right," I said. "There has to be another way." I slid the album back into the envelope and sealed it. "But right now we need to leave."

She threw her arms around me. I had no energy to hug her back. "Now the front door, I'll happily walk through."

I gathered up the package. But as we left the apartment, a deep male voice called out from the stairwell. We froze.

"Hello?"

Amanda grabbed my arm, whispered, "Henry?"

Again, "Hello?"

I heard footsteps coming up the stairs. Neither of us reacted. We couldn't let anyone see us. We had to hide. Putting my finger to my lips, I ushered Amanda back inside Gustofson's apartment. I went to push the front door closed, but something stopped it. A hand. Someone was standing right outside the door.

"I heard a noise, is something broken?" The man pushed harder. There was nothing I could do. The door swung open. A Hispanic man wearing paint-splattered overalls stood in the doorway. One word flashed through my head.

Superintendent.

He glanced down at the floor, covered in dark brown pools. He saw my hands, the residue of blood from when I'd fallen. He looked up at me, his mouth agape, horror in his eyes. He backed away, arms outstretched, pleading.

"It's not what you think," I said, realizing every criminal in history probably said that. Suddenly the man turned and bolted down the stairs.

"Help! *Policía!* Somebody's been killed!"

"Oh, fuck." I turned to Amanda. "Come on, there must be a fire escape."

We sprinted through the apartment, time again being sliced maliciously thin. There was no fire escape in the living room, and no windows in the bathroom. We hurried into Gustofson's bedroom, where we found a metal stairwell outside the window, a mesh screen covering it.

I braced my leg against the wall, pain shooting through it, and yanked open the screen. We clambered onto the fire escape, towering forty or fifty feet above the alley below us. Carefully we wound our way down, gripping the rusty metal guardrails for dear life.

Down a flight of stairs, across the metal floor, repeat. A siren wailed in the distance. Within minutes I'd have another murder pinned to my chest. The scarlet *M*. My hole was growing deeper, the dirt walls caving in.

We scrambled to the bottom platform where a ladder dangled like a piece of spaghetti. There was a pile of black garbage bags below us. And beneath that, cement. Even the bottom of the ladder was a good fifteen feet from the ground.

"You go first," Amanda said. I smiled back at her.

"And who said chivalry was dead?"

I handed her the album and wiped my sweaty hands on my shirt. Gripping the metal tight, I made my way down the ladder. Hand over hand, keeping my feet even and balanced. When I reached the bottom rung, I stopped. I didn't want to land amidst the garbage bags, which were covered with broken bottles.

I leaned to my right, then exploded off with my left foot, jumping at an angle and landing just beyond the bags. My knees buckled as I hit the ground, my palm scraping the cement, tearing the skin from it.

Wincing, I gave Amanda a thumbs-up. I grabbed several garbage bags and tossed them off the pile, clearing a small landing area. She gently tossed the album to me. I set the book aside and positioned myself directly under the ladder. I cupped my arms.

"Your turn," I shouted.

Hesitant, a twinge of fear in her eyes, Amanda climbed to the bottom of the ladder.

"You sure you can catch me?" she said.

"As long as you don't weigh more than eighty pounds, no problem."

"I'll shove an eighty-pound foot up your ass if one toe touches the ground."

"Fair enough."

Amanda closed her eyes and let go. She tumbled through the air, a shrill scream escaping her lips. Then she was in my arms, her hands locked around my neck. I lowered her down and she slowly opened her eyes.

"You weigh a bit more than eighty pounds," I said.

She jabbed me in the ribs, then gave me a gentle squeeze and said, "Thanks."

I nodded, stared into her eyes. Then the sirens broke through our embrace, shattering the moment of peace.

We jogged toward the end of the alley, then headed east on Amsterdam. We hopped on the 81st Street crosstown bus, used the transfer still good from the subway, and shielded our faces behind a discarded copy of *The Onion*.

Headline: Journalist Changes Name To Hieroglyphic Symbol.

From the corner of my eye I saw a police car speed down the block and make a sharp right into the alley we'd just come from. I exhaled and pointed it out to Amanda. She took my hand, squeezed my fingers until they hurt.

We got off at the last stop, 80th Street and East End Avenue. The steel blanket of night had descended. The East

River was dark, the moon glimmering off the water like silver beads. A warm breeze blew through my hair as I breathed it all in. On any other night, the city's beauty would have been a moment to savor. But tonight it felt like a tomb.

This neighborhood was unfamiliar. Rows of expensive Upper East Side apartments ran down one side of the block. Trees with knee-high guardrails and doormen with constable caps opened the door for fashionably dressed tenants and their fashionably dressed dogs.

On the other side of the street, as though exported from another, less affluent universe, sat a squat tenement that looked completely abandoned. Windows were boarded up, bricks covered in graffiti and slime. Old, wheelless bicycles were chained to a fence. A gate opened up to a small path leading up to the building's entrance.

"So what now?" Amanda asked. She'd wrapped her arms around her delicate body, looking at me for a sign of hope. I held the album under my arm, feeling the plastic edge biting my skin, unsure of what to say, what to do.

John Fredrickson. I knew he worked for Michael DiForio. He wasn't just "in the neighborhood" three days ago, like Luis had said. He'd gone to the Guzmans with a purpose: to retrieve this album and deliver it to Michael DiForio. With these photos, DiForio had New York in a vise. Releasing the photos would damage the city beyond repair. And losing them wasn't an option he'd want to consider. And yet somehow there had to be a way to use the album, some way to set us free. Turn evil into good.

Again I tried to distance myself, cast away all emotion, look at it like a journalist.

Like a magic trick, a great story was one where you showed all the facts but gave away none of the secrets behind them. You offered the audience what they needed to see, wanted to hear, and nothing else. There were two groups of people out there: those who wanted me dead and those who wanted this binder and *then* wanted me dead. The trick was giving them both what they needed, yet making them want only what I offered.

It had to end tonight. I had no energy left, nothing else to offer Amanda in the way of solace. I was tired, cold, hungry. And finally I'd been given a small foothold that might support my weight.

I looked at the large brownstone in front of us. So strange in this neighborhood. Like one rotten head of lettuce in a well-cultivated garden. Like Henry Parker in New York.

"This has to end," I said to Amanda. Her head dipped, her eyes coming up to meet mine. She leaned into me and I wrapped my arms around her thin waist, pulling her close.

God, I just wanted to breathe her in, hold her near me, think of nothing else but her. Amanda's breath was warm on my cheek. I inhaled it, closed my eyes, pressed myself against her skin. When I opened them her head was on my chest. I stroked her hair and kissed her forehead. *Everything will be all right….*

Then she tilted her face upwards, her lips parting slightly. I leaned down and pressed my lips to hers, felt her push back. Soft and inviting, we both gave in. The hurt and pain being sucked away. For a few seconds, we were the only people in the world, and I completely lost myself in Amanda Davies. And when we finally separated, Amanda's head falling back onto my chest, I knew it was more intimate than anything I'd ever experienced. If only it were on another night, in a different world.

Then I stepped back, opened the photo album.

"I need to finish this," I said. She nodded. She was crying.

"I want to help."

"No. This is my responsibility now, and mine alone. I don't know what's going to happen or how it's going to end, but you can't be a part of it. You've already done too much, I can't bear the thought of endangering you any more."

"Please," Amanda said, tears streaking down her cheeks. She put her hand on my face, her light touch sending shivers through my body. I bit my lip, warmth spreading through me. "Henry, I'm a part of this, like it or not. Let me help you."

I shook my head. Then I opened up the binder and removed the photo negatives. I handed them to Amanda. She took them, confused.

"If anything happens to me, give these to Jack O'Donnell. Tell him everything. He'll know what to do."

"I don't understand. Why can't I help you?"

"You already have, as much as possible, more than I ever would have expected from anyone. I can't let you do any more."

Amanda nodded, bit her lip.

"What about you?" she asked.

I smiled faintly, stroked her cheek gently.

"Trust me," I said. "I'll think of something."

38

The plane touched down a few minutes after 2:00 a.m. Joe Mauser made his way unsteadily down the narrow stairs, still feeling the effects of the seemingly endless blast of turbulence the jet had hit half an hour in. He closed his eyes, thought about the millions of tiny lights scattered over the New York landscape. Soon he'd be back into the heart of New York, and hopefully Henry Parker would be ready to have his heart ripped out.

Fighting back nausea, Joe saw Chief Louis Carruthers standing on the tarmac, two steaming cups of coffee in hand.

"Agent Mauser," Louis said, offering up the java. "Agent Denton."

"Lou," Joe said. The men shook hands, a solemn gesture.

Sipping the coffee, Mauser grimaced. Louis must have poured an entire dairy farm into the cup. Damn thing tasted more like milk than coffee. As they walked toward the Crown Victoria parked in a lot near the hangar, Mauser's cell phone chirped. He took it out, found his voice-mail icon blinking. He must have missed the calls while in the air. He checked the call log and felt his heart drop.

Six calls from Linda. She'd left three messages. Joe didn't have the heart to listen to any of them. He pictured his sister at home, waiting for good news, a sign that her husband's death wouldn't go unpunished. But right now he couldn't give her that hope, and it was eating at him like acid through a drainpipe.

"Fredrickson's widow?" Denton asked. Joe could only nod.

"So fucking hard on her," Mauser said. "I wish we had something. If I could, I'd string that fuck Parker up by the thumbs and give her a key to the room. I just want this kid so bad."

"You'll get him, Joe. It's almost over," Louis said. "We've got the city locked up tighter than my sister on prom night. If he's here, he's not going anywhere."

"You know how many fucking black holes there are in this city?" Mauser seethed, forcing another swallow of the so-called coffee down his throat. He felt the caffeine settle right into his bloodstream, a surge of adrenaline coursing through him. "You know how easy it is to disappear? Parker's not stupid, but he only needs to fuck up once. Use a credit card. Make a telephone call. Cross the street at a red light. Anything."

Just then another officer, this one young enough to look like Denton's son, came running up. He held a clipboard and a walkie-talkie in his hand and spoke like the world would end if he didn't get out a hundred words a minute.

"Slow down," Mauser said. "I missed the first, middle and last thing you said."

"Sorry, sir," the kid said, grinning from ear to ear. "But we got him."

"Parker?" Joe's stomach dropped. The kid nodded, then smiled at Chief Carruthers. Goddamn police force being overrun by guys who looked like they weren't physiologically old enough to even have children.

"How?"

"Telephone call, Agent Mauser. Parker used a pay phone and charged it to the same calling card we got him with before." Joe smiled, nudged Denton.

"Who did he call?" Denton asked. The kid looked at his clipboard. Static came over the radio. Mauser couldn't understand a word of it, but the kid clicked a button and responded "ten-four."

"Parker called his parents in Bend, Oregon," he said. "We traced his call to a pay phone on East 80th Street, by the river. It was placed nine minutes ago."

"About goddamn time we had a break," Mauser said. "You have a tape of the call?"

"Absolutely."

"I want to hear it," Mauser said, making a beeline for the Crown Vic. "Lou, have them patch the recording through to my cell phone. I want to hear Parker's voice, I want to hear the phone call."

"Done. You heard him," Carruthers said. The young officer clicked the radio again.

"Uh, dispatch, can you patch through the Henry Parker call to Agent Mauser's cell phone?" Joe gave him the number. Denton stood there chewing gum, his hands fidgeting. Mauser nodded slightly, acknowledging Denton. It would be over soon. Finally the rat had nowhere else to run.

"Take care, Joe," Louis said. "Be careful."

Mauser clapped his friend's shoulder, then he and Denton hurried to the car. Denton got into the driver's seat, Mauser holding the phone, awaiting the call. He held the door open and yelled to the officer who'd delivered the message.

"Hey, kid, any way you can hook me up with a speaker to connect to the phone?" The kid gave a thumbs-up and sprinted over to a van parked on the edge of the tarmac. A minute later he reappeared with a small black speaker. He took Joe's cell phone and made sure the connection fit. He pressed a few buttons and Mauser heard a dial tone ring loud and clear. He thanked the kid and closed the door.

They took the Grand Central Parkway exit, and a minute later Mauser's cell phone rang. Joe picked up the speaker, nodded to Denton. "Let's see what our boy has to say."

Merging onto the highway, Mauser caught Denton readjusting his pants quite voraciously.

"You got crabs in there or something?" Joe asked.

"Just riding up on me a bit." Mauser nodded and pressed the send button.

"This is Mauser."

"Agent Mauser? This is Officer Pratt at dispatch. I'm going to patch Henry Parker's call through."

"We're waiting." Joe felt sweat beading on his palms. He gripped the armrest, his hands slippery. Denton remained surprisingly calm. Mauser could practically feel Parker's neck in his hands, choking the life out of him.

There were several loud clicks and then they heard a raspy male voice. The owner sounded like he'd spent too many years with his best friends Marlboro and Cutty Sark.

"Yeah, hello?" the voice said.

"Dad?"

It was Parker. Mauser would recognize that voice through a thunderstorm. The other man was Henry's father.

"Who's this…Henry? That you?"

"It's me, Dad."

"Fucking hell, haven't heard your voice in a while. Cops called here a few times, idiots thought I might actually know where you were. You in trouble, boy?"

"I guess you could say I'm in a bit of trouble. You know I spoke to Mom last Monday. I asked how you were, she said you went out that night. Not like you to go out."

"Got me a bowling league now, every Monday. Boys call me the anchorman 'cause I always pick up where their sorry asses fall down."

"Glad to hear you're getting some exercise."

"Yeah, right," Parker Senior said. "So why're you calling, Henry? I told you I got no money to just hand out. And why are these cops calling me? Do you owe money?"

"No, I don't need money or owe anybody, Dad. I have a job. A good one. The one I wanted, at the newspaper, the *Gazette.*"

"That right? Someone actually hired you?" Henry's father laughed derisively.

"I've worked hard, Dad. A lot harder than you ever did."

"Whatever. So why're you calling so late? It's almost midnight for crissakes."

A moment of silence. Mauser feared the connection had been lost, but then he heard a choking sound come through the line. He looked over at Denton, who seemed unmoved. Mauser settled back and listened.

Henry said, "I just want you to know I don't hold anything against you for the way you were when I was growing up." Henry's voice trembled, but it remained strong. "I'm not mad. In fact, I want to thank you for making me stronger."

"The hell're you talking about boy? You sound crazy."

"You know, it's funny how you remember things sometimes. I can remember almost every word you said to me—trust me, there weren't many. How you always told me I wouldn't amount to anything because nobody in our family ever did. How the night of my high school graduation you told me I'd be better off moving away because I'd only bring you and Mom misery."

"I never said that," the elder Parker said, but his voice was unconvincing.

"It doesn't matter now," Henry continued. "Because I wanted to thank you. I was able to take all that negative shit you lumped on me and turn it into something good. I used you, Dad. I fucking used your hate as my fuel."

"What's your goddamn point?" Parker senior rasped. "Did you call just to bitch and complain? I'm too tired to deal with that and I get enough already from your mother."

"No, that's not why I called. I wanted to let you and Mom know that I'm in trouble. Serious trouble, and I don't know if I'll be able to get out of it. People think I did something that I didn't. Something terrible. But I don't want your help, at least not in the way you'd think."

"So what do you want, Henry? I told you I ain't giving you no money."

There was a pause. Mauser waited, fingernails grinding into his skin.

"I want you to hate me," Henry said softly. "I want to hear that poison from your mouth again. I want your hateful bones to say everything you've said over the years, because I'm tired, too, Dad, and I need something to keep me going. I need to know that it'll be worth it to dig myself out of this hole. I want you to lay it on me, no holds barred, no punches pulled, because that's all you're worth to me now."

"You want me to say I hate you?" Henry's father said. "Fine. I hate you. You ruined my life. I had to work my skin to dust to pay for our family. We've had to wait on you hand and foot since you were a damn baby and what have I gotten in return? Worries and misery, that's all."

"Keep going," Henry said softly.

"I had to give up the life I wanted when you were born. You think that's fun? I never had a say. You think when your mother was pregnant she said 'Honey, are you sure you want a baby?' No. She never said shit. Nine months later out you came, and nothing's been the same since."

"More," Henry said, his voice stronger now. Mauser felt the venom in the older man's voice, reverberating through the speaker. Such hatred, almost unfathomable for one's child, even one on his way to hell.

"That's all you're getting, Henry. I'm tired and you're keeping me awake. What else do you want?"

"Nothing, Dad, that's all I wanted." Henry paused. "But in case you or Mom, or anyone else is interested, I'm in New York."

"New York, huh?"

"Yeah, the big city. In fact, I'm inside a building right now, on 80th Street and East End. Big brown thing, looks abandoned. I'm on the third floor. They gutted the apartments so the space is open. I'm just sitting here. The view of the water is really stunning. I'm glad I came here, Dad, because this is something I would have never gotten the chance to see if I let my genetics decide my fate."

"Well, that's just marvelous," Henry's father said, sarcasm dripping.

"Yeah, it is. Anyway, there's this thing everyone thinks I stole. Well, I didn't steal it, but I did find it. I'm looking at it right now and I can understand why people want it. And if anyone wants it, they'd know where I am."

"Don't hold your breath waiting for me."

"I won't, Dad. I won't."

Mauser heard a click and then a dial tone.

"Jesus," Denton said. "Kid just told us where he is."

Mauser scratched his chin.

"Could be a trap," Denton said. "Kid might be waiting with an AK or something. Shit, and he has the package of drugs he stole from the Guzmans." Mauser looked at him. They both knew the improbability of Parker being armed. Denton patted down his pants, again quite vigorously.

"They really driving you nuts, huh?" Mauser said.

"You have no idea."

They took the FDR exit, threading past motorists doing the speed limit. It was after midnight and the streets of New York were still packed. Unbelievable.

They got off at 96th Street, turned left and headed toward East End Avenue. Mauser could see what Parker was talking about; the river looked absolutely beautiful. Dark blue, the surface glittering like a million silver dollars were resting at the bottom. A cold fear ran through Mauser's body, but he couldn't quite place it. The hunt was almost over. John's death so close to being avenged. Parker was waiting for them, the taste sour like metal in his mouth.

"I don't want the NYPD there until we've had our shot," Mauser said. "I want a fifteen-minute lead time. Call Louis, tell them we need backup at 14:30. That'll give us some time. I don't want Parker in custody until we've seen him first."

"They're not gonna want to wait, Joe. They want blood as bad as you do."

"Tell Carruthers he doesn't have a fucking choice," Mauser spat.

"It'll only do so much good," Denton said. "They'll come whether we tell them to or not. This is NYPD jurisdiction now. Louis is keeping *us* in the loop."

"So step on the goddamn gas and get us there faster."

"You got it, Joe." Denton dialed in the order. He heard Louis's voice, accommodating. Denton clicked the phone off.

"We have fifteen minutes. They'll have a small army ready at two-thirty, but not a moment sooner. Lou understood. Said if he were you he'd ask for fifteen minutes, too."

Minutes, Mauser thought, were unnecessary. One moment was all he needed.

The car accelerated, the headlights blurring into one long illuminated strand. He looked at Denton, who smiled, spoke earnestly.

"Hey, I want my shot, too, Joe." He grinned. "Getting Parker could be my big break."

Mauser nodded as the car sped into the night, leaving only a cloud of exhaust in its wake.

39

Angelo "Blanket" Pineiro admired the room, one of the few times in recent memory he'd had time to fully soak it in. He listened closely when their man made contact, but he soon found his mind wandering. He scanned the gorgeous oil portraits of Michael's family that lined the cherry-red walls, the lineage dating back multiple generations. There was something romantic about them, and Blanket hoped one day he'd be remembered like that, having lived a life worthy of such a painting. Surely he was on his way.

With its high windows, marble columns and authentic Persian rugs, Michael DiForio's penthouse was truly a museum of modern art. Blanket watched the man himself, sitting in his Salerno leather chair, eyes staring up at the ceiling as if waiting for divine intervention. The voices over the phone were full of static, barely understandable. When the line went dead, Blanket waited for Michael's response. He received only silence.

"You hear all that, Mike?" Blanket could almost see the gears turning in Michael DiForio's head. No doubt the police would be at the scene in mere minutes, forget the fact that the goddamn loose cannon Barnes was nowhere to be found. Blanket knew Barnes as well as a man could know a ghost. The killer was a thoroughbred, unstoppable, and a hugely valuable asset when his blinders were on. But somewhere along the line he'd run off the tracks. To Barnes, recovering the package now seemed incidental, and that was the problem.

"Call the Ringer," DiForio finally said, rising up and striding around the ornate wooden balustrade. "I want to give that asshole one last chance."

Blanket could see the man's knuckles were white from gripping the chair. He knew how badly Michael needed that package, how much time and money had been spent accumulating the treasures inside. If it fell into the wrong hands, it could set operations back years, maybe decades. Michael would lose his best—perhaps his only—chance to own this miserable city.

Fucking Gustofson. Guy'd been on his last legs when DiForio bailed him out with that assignment. Then the junkie fuck went and blew it all in spectacular fashion. For whatever reason, the middleman—Luis Guzman—never received the album. Now John Fredrickson was dead and a shit storm the size of the tri-state area looked ready to rain down at any moment.

"Boss, you want me to take some guys down to that building, try to find Parker?"

Michael shook his head, his eyes still closed. "By the time you get there, the building'll be swarming with cops and Feds. If we just send Barnes, at least there's a chance for him to slip in and slip out. Your crew? Like a bunch of retarded children trying to work a bulldozer."

Blanket held his hands out, pleading.

"Mike, I don't think Barnes still has his heart committed to, you know, *the cause.* I think he wants Parker dead, and I don't think our package is on his list of priorities anymore."

DiForio ran a hand through his hair. Blanket considered Michael's thoughtfulness a source of pride for the whole organization. To have an impetuous leader was to have a leader without a plan, without a vision, and any organization led by that example was doomed to failure. And Michael, he always had a plan. This situation, though, couldn't have been foreseen.

The plan should have been foolproof. The Guzmans had never missed a drop. Hans Gustofson was a rung away from the bottom and malleable. John Fredrickson was as loyal an employee as they got. Parker was the wild card they never could have anticipated. And in good wild-card fashion, he'd fucked everything up. A precision watch smashed into tiny bits by an invisible hammer.

Michael's eyes suddenly locked on Blanket.

"Send four men to that building on East 80th. I want them to do everything possible to get to Parker before the cops do. And tell them to keep an eye out for Barnes. No telling what that man's capable of."

"You got it, Mike." Blanket turned to leave.

"Wait, Angelo."

Blanket spun around. "Yeah, Boss?"

"Make sure the four you send are expendable."

40

The Crown Victoria pulled up to the corner of 80th and East End at 2:13 a.m. There were no spots, so Denton parked next to a hydrant. The streets were deathly quiet. They had seventeen minutes before the NYPD would bust everything open. The clock was ticking.

At first Mauser wondered if they'd be able to spot the building Parker was referring to, but it was obvious as soon as he stepped out of the car. A cavity in a mouthful of pearly whites, the tenement didn't belong here. Like Parker himself.

The only entrance was through a wrought-iron gate, swung open just enough for one body to fit through at a time. Deep rivets had been dug into the ground. Clearly few people ever entered—or left—the building.

Even in the faint light of the moon, Mauser could see the dark stains on the brick, the utter hopelessness of the building's facade. Joe slipped his hand down to his holster, unbuckling his Glock. The metal felt cool, inviting, as though it had lain dormant for too long. He heard another snap, saw Denton's hand move from his hip. Finally they were about to confront Henry Parker, and both of their safeties were off.

Mauser entered first. He moved slowly, inching across the cement, listening for any movement. The gate led to a small portico. Crouching by the stone steps, Mauser pointed at the door, nodded to Denton. Leonard raised his pistol for cover as Mauser approached.

Joe tried to breathe steadily, evenly, his heart like a hummingbird's wings. When he reached the top step, Mauser looked back at Denton, then quickly peeked through a dirt-streaked window. He saw a tiny flicker of light at the top of a stairwell, but no sign of life.

Gently Mauser turned the doorknob, the wind whistling past his head. He met no resistance, and entered the darkened foyer. The air inside smelled stale. Joe slunk along the wall, his Glock raised, his pulse racing. Denton joined alongside him and they cautiously made their way to the stairwell.

The steps were worn, caked with dried mud and dirt. Crouching down, Mauser crept up the steps. Parker had said he was on the third floor, but that could have been a ruse. The kid could jump out at any moment, catch them by surprise. Mauser seriously doubted the kid was armed with anything more dangerous than a knife or a loose pipe. In the back of his mind, Mauser hoped he'd have the balls to fight.

The second-floor landing was dark. Light burst from the floor above, trickling down the staircase. Mauser cursed himself for not bringing a flashlight, but he didn't have time to second-guess.

As he took the first step up, something soft brushed by his face. Stumbling back, he felt it again.

"The fuck!" Joe cried, tripping backward over Denton's foot. A cluster of pigeons burst from the shadows, flying around the stairwell, beating their wings madly, feathers flying in the soft light. Mauser threw up his hand, tried to swat at them. "Goddamn it, get away!"

Denton joined in, both of them flailing about until there was silence. Joe wiped the sweat from his brow, looked at Denton, the man's hair disheveled.

"So much for getting the drop," he whispered.

They approached the third-floor landing. Globs of white littered the steps. They looked fresh. Bird shit. Wonderful. When he reached the third floor, Mauser swung his gun toward the light.

The room before them was empty. The only light came from a single bulb whose pull string had been yanked off. There was no sign of Parker.

Joe edged forward, forearms tensed, gun steady. The he saw it. In the center of the room, directly beneath the bulb, lay a photograph.

Mauser knelt down and picked it up. Suddenly his knees went slack, then he felt a hollowness in his stomach. His gun hand dropped. Joe recognized the man in the picture.

It was John Fredrickson.

His brother-in-law. Husband to his sister. In the photo Fredrickson held an envelope lined with cash. Handing him the envelope was a man Mauser recognized immediately.

Angelo Pineiro. "Blanket" Pineiro.

Joe stumbled back, the photo falling from his hand. Denton stepped forward, picked up the picture.

"Jesus," he said flatly. "Is it real?"

"I think so," Mauser said. Then he noticed a small black arrow on the bottom of the photo, pointing downward.

Mauser flipped the picture over and saw two words scrawled on the back.

Fifth floor.

Mauser gripped the photo, felt it crinkle in his hand. Adrenaline pumped through him. John was on the take. Was it possible? And where the fuck did Parker get the picture? Anger boiled inside him, but now Mauser couldn't focus it.

He bolted up the stairs, the birds on the stairwell below scared into a tizzy. Denton trailed behind him, but Joe Mauser could hear nothing, just the drumming in his head.

John…why?

When he reached the fifth floor, Mauser found the door was wide open. Parker was waiting for him. The moon cast a ghastly white gleam across the floor. Shadows danced in the corners. He squinted, thought he saw something move.

"Parker!" he yelled, gun erect, outstretched.

Denton strode up beside him, their heavy breathing merging into one. The room was quiet. The birds had stopped flying. Mauser stepped forward, the room blanketed in soft, impenetrable darkness.

"I have more."

Mauser froze. The voice came from the corner of the room, by the window. All Joe could see was blackness. Raising his gun to chest level, Mauser stepped forward.

"If anything happens to me, the negatives go right to the press. Lower the gun. Then we can talk."

"Joe," Denton whispered. "He could be armed. Let's just do him now before the cavalry arrives."

Parker seemed to hear this, but his body didn't respond. It was tense, rigid.

"There are more photos," Parker said. "A lot more. They're being guarded by a friend. If anything happens to me you'll see them in the morning papers. All I'm asking is for you to lower the gun."

John's face in that photo. The money…

Without thinking, Mauser lowered his gun. He placed his hand on Denton's wrist, forcing his gun down.

Out of the shadows stepped Henry Parker. He looked like a man who'd just run an entire marathon at full speed, his arms sinewy, shirt stained with dried sweat, hair unkempt. He could see blood seeping through Henry's left pant leg from where he'd been shot. The young man breathed deeply. Joe could see dark rings under his eyes. Henry Parker looked like he hadn't slept in days, and had been running from the devil the entire time. Which was probably the truth.

"You killed John," Mauser said, stepping closer. Parker didn't budge. "You killed a part of my family. You left a wife without a husband and two children without a father. You deserve to go straight to hell." Mauser felt the blood harden in his veins, and slowly he raised the gun, aiming right at Henry Parker's heart.

"John Fredrickson is dead," Parker said. "But not because of me."

"Fuck this shit," Denton said, stepping forward, his gun raised, as well. "He killed John. Look at his eyes, he knows he did. If anyone deserves to die, Joe…"

Mauser looked into Parker's eyes, the first time he'd seen them up close since St. Louis. Since Shelton Barnes.

That photo…

And somewhere, deep inside Henry Parker's eyes, Joe Mauser saw the one thing he never thought he'd see.

Truth.

"Tell me what happened," Joe said. "And don't leave a thing out. And if I think you're lying to me, I won't think twice about shooting you in the face."

Parker took a deep breath and spoke.

"It starts with Michael DiForio and Jimmy Saviano," Henry said.

Mauser interjected. "Everyone knows about their war. It's been brewing for years and nothing's ever happened."

"Until now," Henry said. "Michael DiForio owns a good chunk of real estate in the city. More specifically, he owns the building at 2937 Broadway. Where John Fredrickson was killed."

Parker took a breath, continued.

"DiForio figured an easy way to help his business, while exposing himself to limited liability, was to use indentured servants, couriers, to run his errands. Men without ties, without hope. If these couriers had records, and they were arrested or killed, the finger would point right back at them alone. No questions would be asked."

A faint breeze drifted through the room, sending a shiver down Mauser's spine.

"Come on, Joe, forget this kid, let's take him now." Mauser looked at Denton, who shut his mouth. He felt light-headed, his world turning upside down.

Nodding at Parker, Joe said, "Go on."

"Michael DiForio's associates would reach out to recent parolees. Men with no money and no job. They were offered housing on the cheap in exchange for their services. Picking up payments, running drugs, the works. And in return they got to stay out of crummy halfway homes and didn't have to bag groceries for a living." Parker swallowed. "Luis Guzman was one of those men. In fact, over the last five years, at least ten ex-convicts have lived in that very building, getting huge rent discounts in exchange for their—" Parker paused "—services."

"I'm still not seeing it, ~~Joe~~," Denton said. "The fucking NYPD's going to be here any minute and we're fucking around with…"

"Shut the fuck up!" Mauser yelled. "Shut the fuck up! This is about my goddamn family!"

Denton looked like he'd been punched in the gut. He stepped back. Parker, clearly unnerved, tried to collect himself, his voice shaky.

"Another man DiForio employed was a photographer named Hans Gustofson. DiForio paid Gustofson to take some very incriminating photographs of very important people. Photographs of cops and government officials. Just like the one he took of Officer Fredrickson."

"John," Mauser said. Parker nodded.

"Gustofson compiled a large album of these photos over the past two decades. They could have been used for any number of reasons—to blackmail city politicians, to gain better control over the cops already in his pocket, to find out which policemen were double-dipping and working for Saviano as well. Luis Guzman was a middleman. He was supposed to collect the photos from Gustofson and hold them for Fredrickson, who would deliver directly to DiForio. But the photos never made it to Luis Guzman."

"Why not?" Mauser asked. He could feel sweat pouring down his skull, warm and sticky.

"Hans Gustofson was killed before he could deliver the photos. I know this because I found the body. And whoever killed Gustofson wanted those photos, but he'd hidden them well."

"Jesus," Mauser said.

"Unbelievable," Denton added.

"Luis Guzman never received them because Gustofson was dead. Fredrickson, assuming Guzman was holding them for his own personal gain—possibly to resell to Saviano—attempted to beat it out of him. That's when I came in."

"You and John," Mauser said. "You killed him."

"Officer Fredrickson is dead," Parker said, his voice like meat through a grinder. "But I didn't kill him. I tried to stop him from hurting the Guzmans, and somewhere in the struggle his gun went off. But I didn't pull the trigger. And if you talk to the Guzmans, really talk to them, they'll corroborate my story."

Mauser said, "And this photo album, where is it now?"

"It's safe, along with the negatives," Parker said. "I don't want it to get into the wrong hands any more than you do. But I can put the pieces together and help make things right. All I want in exchange is my life back."

"That's not possible," Mauser said. "There's a whole city wants you dead."

"The city doesn't know the whole story." He paused. "What do you want?" Parker asked. Mauser lowered his head, his shadow cast long across the wall. Then he looked up.

"I want justice for my brother. I want whoever's responsible to pay."

"I want that, too," Henry said. "And I can help."

Parker took a step forward, Mauser watching, but then he heard it. A slight sound. The fluttering of wings.

The birds had been disturbed again.

Somebody was coming up the stairs.

"Get back," Mauser said urgently, shoving Parker toward the window. He and Denton whipped around and aimed their guns at the door, crouching to create a smaller target.

Soft footsteps, but Mauser could hear them clearly. More than one. More than two. At least three people were approaching. Maybe more.

Mauser felt the Glock in his hands, a trivial reassurance of protection. He looked quickly at Denton, nodded. Then a tremendous explosion shattered the silence, then another, and another. The room lit up like a firecracker had gone off, thunder echoing through the building, tortured screams from below.

"Jesus Christ!" Mauser yelled. "What the fuck is that?"

Another explosion rocked the building, and then there was silence. The police didn't fire those shots, Mauser thought. They were shotgun blasts. Four in total. And from the intervals, it sounded like one person had fired them. Then Joe heard it.

Footsteps coming up the stairs. Just one set now, deliberate. He saw Parker, fear etched on his face, backed into the corner.

A shadow crept into the doorframe. Mauser saw the barrel of the gun before he saw the man.

As he entered the room, Joe Mauser recognized his face.

Shelton Barnes.

The man's pants and shirt were dark black, but in the

moonlight Mauser could see red, like a dozen paintballs had exploded on his chest. Other men's blood. Then Barnes spoke, his voice even.

"All I want is Parker," Barnes said, his shotgun at chest level. "For Anne."

Mauser looked at Denton, then back at Barnes. Joe stood up, gun outstretched.

"You'll get nothing and like it, Barnes," Mauser said. "Now drop the fucking weapon."

Then Denton stood up, his eyes locked with Barnes. Mauser felt a shiver sweep down his spine as a cold grin spread across his partner's face. A tremor swept through Joe's body as a hard truth entered his brain, one moment too late.

"They say you gotta make your own luck," Denton said, before pumping three bullets into Mauser's chest.

41

I watched the cop go down in a heap, a stunned look in his eyes. The man in the doorway, Barnes, didn't move. The other cop, Denton, stood there staring at the body, a sick smile on his face.

The stench of blood and gunpowder soiled the air, death lingering like steam, and it was blowing my way.

"Better to take him out of the equation, leave it to the three that matter," Denton said, looking at the assassin in the doorway. "Name's Leonard Denton. Bet you don't remember me, do you?"

The assassin flinched, his shotgun wavering.

"I just want Parker," Barnes said, but his voice sounded unsure now, like he was trying to piece together a puzzle.

"Come on, Shelton. You remember, don't you? That night in your loft? That pretty wife of yours? Or maybe you'd remember better if I had a hood on. Your first and last warning, asshole."

Barnes's arm went slack. The gun dropped to his side. With his other hand he gently touched his chest, as though making sure something was still there.

"Anne…" Barnes said, his voice tremulous. I couldn't

move. Something was playing out here, an old wound being reopened between these two men.

Denton nodded. "That's right," he said.

"DiForio," Barnes added. Denton nodded.

"Sometimes you have to do whatever it takes to get ahead in this world. When I was a rookie, I said, 'Hey, what's the big deal if I take a few bucks, kill some low-level punk who needed killing?' You pissed off the wrong guy, my friend, and Michael made it my job to fix you. Problem was, Shelton, you didn't die. Your wife died like she was supposed to, bless her heart, but you didn't take the hint. You came back and killed everyone else, somehow missed out on me. My good luck, I suppose." Barnes's gun hand shifted, the shotgun stirring slightly. "Your wife—Anne was her name, right? She was a pretty thing. Shame it had to end that way for her."

Without warning, Denton raised his gun, three more explosions ripping through the room. Barnes flew backward against the wall, the shotgun coming to rest on his knee. I heard a ragged breath escape his mouth, then he lay still. I couldn't move, couldn't breathe. But then it snapped into my head. The puzzle came together.

"You killed Hans Gustofson," I said to Denton, stepping into the light. "You were the one who tried to steal the album."

"Guilty," Denton said, raising his hands above his head. "And back up, will you Parker? I need to wait until the cops get here before I do this. Can't just sit on a body for ten minutes, you know?"

"Why?" I asked. Denton sighed, but his body remained solid.

"You know, I guess I'm just like every other nine-to-five schlub. Just didn't see my career progressing the way I wanted," Denton said. There was a hungry ambition in his eyes that chilled me to the bone. All's fair, they say. No matter whose life has to be destroyed.

Or ended.

"Working for Michael DiForio has its perks, but I genuinely did enjoy law enforcement. Problem was they don't want to give you a break unless you make a major case, and I wasn't as fortunate as our friend Joe here."

"So you steal the album, pretend you're the hero."

"That's one of two possibilities."

"And the other was switching sides, bringing it to Jimmy Saviano."

Denton's smile widened.

"You're a bright guy, I'll give you that." Outside the building, I heard several car doors open and slam shut. Footsteps on the pavement. I turned to the window, saw a dozen uniformed policemen approaching the gate.

"That's my cue," Denton said. "It's been fun, Parker, but I'm tired of this. I kind of wish your friend Barnes there had gotten off a shot, but with all the shit you pulled the NYPD won't really ask questions. If only you weren't so goddamn persistent, none of this would have happened. Now the only thing I have to do is find Ms. Davies. I'm guessing she's got the album, am I right? I'm sure she won't be too hard to find or persuade."

Hate bubbled up inside me as I stepped forward. "You touch her with the tip of one finger, I swear you'll die. I'll come back from the fucking grave if I have to."

Denton seemed to consider this. "You know, let's see if that's true."

The muzzle flashed, then I heard a deafening roar, and a searing pain sliced through my chest. The blast threw me onto the floor, a burning sensation eating through my torso like scalding water. I cried out, gasped for air. It felt like a 400-pound weight was pressing on my chest, squeezing the air from my lungs. I looked up, my breathing ragged, to see Denton approaching.

"It's a shame, Parker. You probably would've made a good reporter." The gun was less than a foot from my face. I closed my eyes, waiting for the world to end.

"No!"

The scream came from the doorway. It was Amanda, and she was clutching the album. Denton turned and aimed the gun at her, and she screamed again.

Summoning my last bit of energy, the hatred in me overcoming the wretched pain, I lunged at Denton, driving my shoulder into his back. He toppled forward, landed hard on the floor.

The gun exploded again, splinters flying out of the wall. I couldn't feel my left arm, but with my right I grabbed his gun hand. I was stronger than Denton, but weakened from the gunshot. I lifted my fist and brought it crashing down on Denton's face. Again. And again, harder. I heard a snap as his nose broke, blood spurting out. Again. Blood covered my hand. I could feel nothing.

Denton yelped beneath me and we both struggled to our feet. My hand was still on the gun, holding on for life.

Like that night…

A sticky wheezing sound came from my chest with every breath. Denton took a step back, gaining leverage, and I braced myself, my legs rubbery, barely able to hold my weight. But instead of using his leverage to better grip the gun, Denton swung his leg forward and up. Right into my groin.

I fell back, pain like I'd never experienced shooting through every nerve in my body. I writhed on the floor, my chest burning, my energy completely sapped. My limbs didn't work. I looked up to see Denton standing over me, a horrible leer on his face. He wiped blood from his busted nose, laughed at it.

"Goodbye, Parker."

His gun traced an invisible line between my eyes.

Suddenly a gunshot rang out. Then another. I saw smoke curling out of Denton's chest. The man looked stunned, unbelieving. Small dark patches bloomed under his white shirt, visible in the moonlight. One more shot shattered the air and Denton fell forward, his gun clattering on the wood. His body spasmed once and then lay still. I looked to the corner.

Barnes was sitting up. His face was pale, drained, and staring at Leonard Denton's fallen body. He blinked twice, like a sleep-deprived man trying to stay awake.

Like me, Barnes was losing the battle.

"For Anne," he whispered, then his eyes closed. The shotgun fell from his grasp.

A moment later Amanda burst into the room, tears flowing down her cheeks. She knelt down beside me, wrapping her arms around my head. I felt sleepy, leaned into her, feeling my body slowly drifting away.

"Oh, my God," she said. "Don't worry, Henry. You'll be okay." Hot tears dripped onto my face, warmth like a comforting hand. I let it soak in, letting my mind fall away. "It's all over."

I heard the sound of footsteps, looked up through a haze to see a dozen policemen enter the room, guns drawn. Immediately they came to me. Two men and a woman leaned over Mauser's body. I heard a raspy breath as they placed an oxygen bag over his face, loading him onto a stretcher. Mauser's fingers twitched, and he was carried out.

I could tell Denton was dead from the way they examined him.

A mustached officer knelt down next to me. My eyelids felt heavy and I let them close. Through the darkness I heard Amanda screaming, the sound so distant, so far away. Struggling to open my eyes I saw an officer holding her back. I smiled at Amanda, fell further and further into the darkness.

"Barnes," I said, my voice merely an echo.

"Who's Barnes?" the officer asked.

"In the corner, with the shotgun. He killed Denton. Saved our lives." I could barely breathe the words out. No more energy. It was time to sleep. Good night, Henry.

The officer stood up, then knelt back down.

"There's nobody there, son. All I see is an empty shotgun and a few shells. You sure there was another man?"

A laugh escaped my lips. Through the swarm of blue jackets I was able to see the room in its entirety. He was right. There was a splash of blood where Barnes had fallen. Nothing more.

I felt Amanda's hand graze my back, her cries keeping me

awake. Several hands lifted me into the air. Two words echoed in my head before the darkness consumed me.

     It's over.

42

One month later

I never liked spiders. Don't really know anyone who does.
But sitting on a bench in Rockefeller Plaza, sipping a cup of
coffee and watching the brilliant summer sun gleaming off
those metal arachnid monstrosities, I couldn't help but think
I'd missed something the first time around.

It was late June and deliciously warm, a gentle breeze
wafting through the city. Summer nights in New York were
long, and I planned to savor every second of them. I'd been
back at the *Gazette* for less than a week, still taking my time
from the staph infection in my leg and two subsequent sur-
geries. A week in ICU, armed policemen outside my door.
My mother came to visit. She cried, then asked if I'd found
a job yet. She said my father couldn't take the time off work.

Mya visited me, too. Thankfully when Amanda wasn't
there. That would be an awkward conversation for a later
time. She said she was glad I was okay. She said she was
sorry things had ended so badly between us. She said she

hoped we could still be friends. I told her I'd like that. And I meant it. But she looked at me in a way she hadn't in a long time. And I knew friendship wasn't all she hoped for. And a small part of me wished we'd had one more chance. I would never tell Amanda that. I'm with her now. My past might never be buried, but at least now I had a future.

The docs told me to wait a few weeks before returning to the *Gazette.* Try working two or three hours a day at first, they said. Increase your hours as your strength returns. But they knew that wasn't going to happen. If I was back at the *Gazette,* I was going full bore.

So I took a few more weeks to sit on my ass, plowing through books and newspapers in an effort not to go stir-crazy, and now here I was, back where it all started. If only I'd agreed to write Wallace's story about these stupid metal bugs, I'd have one more rib, one less incredible story. And one less love.

I felt a slight tug in my chest, took a deep breath. The scar would always be visible, but the pain would eventually subside. Denton's bullet had shattered my lowest true rib, a sliver of which punctured my right lung. The doctors said when they opened me up it looked like a crumpled-up grocery bag. Tubes were inserted into my chest to siphon the air that had built up between my collapsed lung and rib cage. Before they put me to sleep I saw Amanda's face through the glass. You couldn't get a better vision before going under.

I could feel the scar tickle the skin below my clothing, like an amputee who still feels pain in a missing limb—a silent reminder of that night. Sometimes I still see the bodies, smell the smoke, hear the gunshots. And I know they'll never leave me.

Last week I visited John Fredrickson's family, to pay my

condolences to his widow, Linda. She now knew the truth. She knew why her husband was there that night. But her husband was still dead because of me.

She looked me over, her lip trembling. And then she slapped me across the face. And closed the door. I stood there for a minute and felt the pain. There were some wounds that would never heal, no matter the balm. And I'd have to live with that. Linda Fredrickson would, too.

Joe Mauser refused to die.

I visited him, too. Some movie studio paid him a bunch of money for the rights to the story while he was still hooked up to a breathing machine. Publishing houses were throwing money at him to write a book. Jack told me this stuff was common. Few cops could live on their salary alone, and most secretly hoped for the one big case that could offer financial comfort for their families. That is if Mauser lived. I knew he would.

Jack's story was a smashing success. His Page One headline read The Mark, and featured stock photos of Michael DiForio, Agents Joe Mauser and Leonard Denton, a presumed dead assassin named Shelton Barnes, and the photo from my driver's license.

The piece began with my interviewing Luis Guzman, and ended with Leonard Denton's death. The *Gazette* sold out its entire print run. There were talks of a Pulitzer. And when Wallace offered me my old job back, the first thing Jack did was make sure that at the end of the story, there was a line which read: Additional Reporting by Henry Parker.

The only photos came from police photographers and the Associated Press.

Paulina left the *Gazette* a few weeks earlier. The *New York Dispatch* doubled her salary and made her a featured columnist. Her first column was entitled How Henry Parker Ruined The News. Next to it was an article about a television star suspected of undergoing liposuction and breast augmentation.

She was slammed by everyone across the board, but it was the *Dispatch*'s most-read and most-discussed article in years that didn't have to do with a boob job or a model's husband sleeping with a teenager. If people were bashing her, it meant they were talking about her. I heard rumors she was interviewing my old classmates, my parents, and had even called Mya for dirt. She even called me, said it was only business, you can't take things personally in this industry, and...

I hung up before she finished the sentence. The story still ran. A few days later I got my first piece of hate mail.

Heartless. Spoiled. Hateful. Deceitful. Just a few of the choice words this admitted fan of Paulina Cole had for me.

But here I was, working again. Doing what I was born to do.

I was writing in my notebook when suddenly a shadow blocked the sun.

"Visiting your friends?"

Amanda was standing over me, the sun shining directly over her head. I inhaled her beautiful smell, again had to remind myself she was real. She was wearing her turquoise tank top—my favorite one—and her lovely brown hair was tied back in a ponytail. I never thought it would be possible, but Amanda looked even more beautiful now than the day I met her.

"They don't leave you alone, do they?"

She was referring to the smattering of plainclothes cops stationed around the AP building. Just in case Michael DiForio got frisky and decided he wanted payback. I'd be lying if I said I didn't wake up in a cold sweat some nights, unsure whether it was all over, whether those three days had cost me peace for the rest of my life. Then I would look at the girl beside me, and I knew she could give me whatever I might have lost.

Amanda.

"So you wanted to see me?" I said. Forty-five minutes ago, Amanda called me at the office, told me to meet her outside. She said it was important. And she didn't use that term lightly.

"So what'ya writing?" she asked. She reached for my notebook, and I tucked it away.

"Wallace gave me an assignment to write a story about these—" I pointed to the large insects swarmed by tourists "—*things*. I never got around to it last time, so I'm making amends."

"Sounds like a nice little human interest piece," she said. She wrapped her arms around my neck. I could smell her, sweet and light, a scent to wake up to forever. "Know any other humans that interest you?"

I smiled. "I can think of one, but I haven't run a DNA check to make sure she's not from the planet Melmac."

She playfully punched my arm, then lowered herself into my lap. Amanda leaned in and nuzzled her cheek against mine. I felt her lips brush my nose, my ear. I could taste her on my tongue. Amanda. The woman who saved my life.

Then I felt something kick my leg, looked up to see a young girl on the ground. She'd tripped over my foot, but jumped up like an acrobat in training, brushed off her overalls.

"Ta-da!" she squealed, like she'd meant to do it all along.

"Alyssa!" Her mother came jogging up, holding a New York City map and a Dean & DeLuca bag. "I'm sorry," the woman said. "Kids can be clumsy."

"Not a problem," I said. I leaned down so my face was close to Alyssa's, Amanda's arms still clenched around my neck. "Careful there, Alyssa, you don't want to disturb these guys." I pointed to the spiders.

"Why not?" she asked, her little mouth confused, but spread in a mischievous grin.

"Because if you don't watch out, they might…" Then I began tickling Amanda, until she squirmed and squealed out of my arms. Alyssa was clapping and jumping, giggling like a baby.

"Or else they tickle you?" she asked.

"Exactly."

Her mother smiled at me, took Alyssa's hand and led her away.

"What can I say," I said, pecking Amanda on the lips. "Kids love me."

"I think she was sweet on you," Amanda said, her jeweled eyes laying me open. "Do I have anything to be jealous about?"

"As a matter of fact, yes. I've decided to forgo my gorgeous, mature girlfriend in lieu of a much younger woman whose parents have a more stable bank account and a good sandbox."

She kissed me, placed her hand on my chest where the bullet had torn through my skin.

"How does it feel?" she asked.

"Still burns sometimes, but not as bad. Doc says it'll hurt more in the winter. That gives me about three months of summer sun, and after that you'll have to keep me warm."

"I don't think that will be a problem."

"So what's the emergency? Sounded important."

"It is," she said. She took the notebook from my hand, kissed it, then reached into her pocket. When she looked up her face was serious, more serious than I'd seen in a long time.

"I want you to have this," Amanda said. "I've never given one to anybody before, but…" Her voice trailed off. "You deserve to see it."

Into my palm, she placed a notebook of her own. The cover looked familiar. I opened it up. There were two words written at the top of the page. Carl Bernstein.

"Remember that night in my car, how you wanted to know what I could possibly have learned in such a short amount of time?" I nodded, knew that night vividly. "Well, now I want you to know what I thought about you that day. Go ahead, look."

I read it.

Carl Bernstein
Early to midtwenties. No baggage other than a backpack, all alone. There's a look in his eyes like something I've never seen, a tenderness that seems to come from out of nowhere. Like he's scared, vulnerable. He acts like I've saved the life of somebody I've just met.

I scanned the rest of the page. When I was through, I stood up, gathered Amanda into my arms and swung her around, our lips never parting, until my rib hurt and I had to put her down.

Amanda leaned down and kissed my shirt, right where the slug had entered my body. She rose back up and grinned. "I think scars are actually kind of manly. And you know what I like most about them?"

"What?" I asked.

"You never know exactly what's below them." She smiled. "Now come on, hero, you have a story to write." We both laughed and walked down the street, arm in arm. Amanda laid her head on my shoulder. Kissing her forehead, I held her tight.

Never to look back.

Epilogue

The cold wind snapped and bit Michael DiForio's face as he stepped off the curb. An aide he'd never met stepped into an ankle-deep puddle as he opened the door to the Oldsmobile. Fucking new guys, DiForio thought. All utterly worthless.

They'd had to take on extra help after Barnes massacred four men in that run-down building on 80th Street. The new faces only added to the disharmony, only made their family weaker. And over the last few weeks, Michael's family barely had the strength to continue.

In the last three weeks, nearly all of DiForio's protection had ceased communication, fell off the face of the damn earth. Most had simply stopped responding to phone calls, others would whisper *stop calling* and hang up. That's why the new faces. That's why the whole thing had gone up in smoke.

According to a Lieutenant at the 53rd Precinct, several weeks after Henry Parker's vindication on three counts of first-degree murder, every officer, politician and newsman on the DiForio payroll received a mysterious package in the mail. Inside each package was a reprint of a photograph that Michael recognized as the handiwork of the late Hans Gustofson. Accompanying these photos was a letter, warning that unless all illegal activities were ceased immediately, the pictures in question would be released to the press.

Half the cops were scared shitless. The others all had a "change of heart." The photo album had disappeared completely. And countless hours and dollars had been thrown out the window.

We can't work for you anymore, Michael. We swore an oath to the city.

Goddamn fucking saints going back on their word after they'd already taken Michael for thousands. Cut him off, just like that. That goddamn Parker was behind it. He had to be.

Michael's first order of business was to find Henry Parker and end him. The kid had ruined so much, Michael wasn't sure how much was salvageable. Regardless, vengeance had to be dealt, and swiftly. Michael had to regain control.

Blanket slid into the backseat next to DiForio. A portly driver who reeked of fried onions got behind the wheel. Blanket gestured to the new man, who gave Michael a nervous nod.

"Boss, this is Kenny. Kenny'll be driving you for the time being until we take on more help." DiForio gave Kenny a quick nod, nothing more.

Kenny turned the ignition and began to ease out of the driveway. He braked abruptly, then started up again, sending Michael lurching forward. Kenny clearly hadn't done much driving outside of the pizza truck or wherever they'd found his sorry ass. Kenny pulled out of the complex, zipping along at four miles an hour, like a teenager afraid to piss off his driving instructor.

Henry Parker. A twenty-four-year-old kid, had all but ruined him.

The album was gone. Gustofson and Fredrickson were dead, as was Shelton Barnes. Leonard Denton, a reliable soldier for years, was dead. Luis and Christine Guzman were in protective custody. So many soldiers dead. The rest deserting like rats from a ship.

DiForio had known all along about Denton's history, figured sooner or later it would catch up to him. Talk about shitty timing, even if he wanted to take out Parker right now—which he did, oh, God, how he did—goddamn video surveillance was on him like the clap on a prostitute.

The papers didn't mention a funeral for the third man, didn't even identify the man's name. Didn't matter. He wasn't worth a funeral. And for the second time, Michael DiForio had killed Shelton Barnes. And this time, he wasn't coming back.

"Hey, Ken, whatever the fuck your name is, you want to step on it?"

"Ken's new, Mike," Blanket replied. "You'll get used to him."

"I'll be late for my own fucking funeral the way he drives. Hey, Ken, you see that movie about a bomb on the bus? You go a mile an hour under fifty the rest of the way and I'll cut your fucking ears off."

Ken nodded. The mood he was in, Michael just might keep his word.

Ken pressed his foot down on the gas and DiForio watched the speedometer climb to five, then ten, fifteen. At least Ken listened. It was a start.

As the car passed through the wrought-iron gates, a tremendous explosion shattered the air, and the car erupted into an enormous, golden fireball. The detonation knocked down dozens of pedestrians, shattering windows up to three blocks away.

Orange flames shot into the sky as the fuselage caught fire, sending the car's chassis ten feet into the air. Molten debris rained across the street.

When the car crashed to earth, black smoke pouring from the windows, people gathered around the smoldering wreckage, whispering in hushed tones, hands over their mouths to stifle the horror. Cell phones were taken out, 911 immediately inundated with horrified callers. Most simply watched the car burn, gasping at the charred corpses inside. Wondering who'd fallen victim to such a ghastly fate.

Slowly one man began to make his way through the crowd. He was tall and his skin was pale. Thin, like he'd recently lost a tremendous amount of weight. His cheeks were sunken and he wore dark sunglasses, a thick black overcoat wrapped around his gaunt frame. He walked with a slight limp and held his right arm in a sling. The man stepped forward, carefully winding his way through the gaping onlookers. As he approached the twisted mass of destruction, the man removed something from his breast pocket. It was a picture, worn and tattered and smeared with red.

He pressed his lips to the photograph, then set it on the ground by the burning wreckage, just a few feet from the charred bodies inside.

Standing back up, the man coughed into his fist, and said two words.

For Anne.

* * * * *

Prologue

They say it's better to have loved and lost than to never have loved at all.

I disagree.

I've lost before. I lost my parents' affections before I was old enough to know how the rest of the world looked upon an estranged child. I lost my first love because I was too much of a coward to protect her. I nearly lost my life due to a chance encounter. All of those losses created holes in my heart and my soul. Holes I've done my best to patch up, but no matter how well I cover the holes, they'll never be whole, never be what they once were or could have been.

Doesn't mean I can't try to fill them. Through life. Through work.

Through Amanda.

If Amanda wasn't here, lying next to me in our bed, her arm draped across my body, I wouldn't be here at all. It's not that I'd be back in Oregon, working at the *Bend Bulletin*, skiing at Mount Bachelor, thirsting through thirteen inches of annual rainfall and paying two hundred bucks a month in rent (though the last part would be nice).

If Amanda wasn't with me, it would mean I was rotting in the ground somewhere. Or in jail, trying to stay alive. And if that was the case, I might as well be dead.

I know how quickly life can be derailed. How showing up five minutes too early or too late can change your fate forever. If I hadn't returned for a follow-up interview on a news story one year ago, I'd still be working my way up from the Obituaries page at the *New York Gazette*.

If I had been thirty seconds late to meet her, Amanda would have driven off without me. And my life would have been relegated to door number one or number two, both leading to different levels of hell. But she waited for me, saved my life, opened up number three, and now we're here. Together.

And God help me, I can't lose her, because I don't have the strength to patch that kind of hole.

So as I lie here, watching Amanda's chest rise and fall, all I can do is hope to witness every last breath of her life. And hope that, finally, the stories I report won't be my own.

1

The limousine pulled up to the curb outside the Kitten Club, and like a cult waiting for its leader, dozens of heads turned at once. Hundreds of eyes widened. Pulses sped up. Hearts raced.

Flashbulbs popped by the dozen as the door opened. She flashed that brilliantly seductive smile, the one that had seduced millions around the world. Stepping onto the red carpet, she couldn't help but think that she owned them all.

She waved to the dazed crowd. Stopped to sign a few autographs. Blew air kisses through ruby lips. Laughed at the chunky schlubs who would be fantasizing about her that night as they lay alone in the dark.

Despite her seeming nonchalance, Athena Paradis spent the nights in breathless anticipation of these delicious moments. Moments when all eyes would be on her. Moments when she was a goddess among mere mortals.

Athena was dropping her very first album, *The Goddess Athena,* in just three days, and her promotional tour was in full swing. She was invited to the Kitten Club to guest DJ, spin and sing brand-new tracks that had never been heard out-side the recording studio (created with the gentle touch of some very talented—and patient—sound producers, vocal coaches and technicians). But that was for the liner notes. Her fans didn't care what happened beneath the surface.

As Athena approached the club's entrance, the manager bowed and pulled back the velvet rope. Her pair of burly bodyguards, Bruise and Bounce, ushered her through. Hands reached out to touch her. Fingers came away coated with some of the body glitter she used to give her naturally pale skin an extra healthy glow, an extra sparkle.

Athena sauntered past the throng of gawking men and starry-eyed women, slipping into the pulsating darkness of the Kitten Club. Her entourage was immediately met by Shawn Kensbrook, club promoter and owner of the Kitten Club. Just three years ago, what was now the Kitten Club had been an abandoned brick-front warehouse in Manhattan's meatpacking district. It was destined to be torn down by de-velopers or vermin, whichever got there first, and was as hip as the word itself. Kensbrook created a model of his vision for the next big New York nightspot, and bought the sink-hole for a song. Through his A-list Rolodex, Kensbrook turned a pile of rubble into a nightclub that was all the rage, the most popular destination since the heyday of Limelight and, prior to that, Studio 54. Next to hopping on Oprah's couch, DJing at the Kitten Club was the best music promo-tion you could get.

Shawn, wearing velveteen Gucci pants and enough hair gel to keep bricks in place, pecked Athena on the cheek and ushered her through the crowd to the DJ booth in the back.

She shook hands with a guy Shawn introduced as DJ Stix, a light-skinned black man whose sunglasses were coated with actual diamond dust. Stix took her hands, showed her how to control the volume and base, pitch control, and how to change tracks. Athena's manager would be standing by in case she accidentally sang without proper vocal support. Bruise and Bounce would be standing by in case some guy decided to get cute and jump the DJ booth. They were as much for image control as damage control.

After the new Beyoncé song ended, Kensbrook took the house microphone.

"Ladies and gentlemen, kittens, cats and lions of all ages," he said. All eyes turned toward the back. The house grew completely silent. "It is my pleasure to introduce you to the Queen of all Media, her royal highness herself, the woman whose killer debut album drops *this very Tuesday,* give it up, show your love, for the one, the only, the beautiful, Athena Paradis!"

Suddenly a deep, throbbing base began to reverberate through the club. Squeals of joy leapt from the lips of heavy-breathing men and women. Then, after a dozen base thumps, the synthesizer kicked in, and the club came alive.

The sweaty bodies congealed into a solid mass as the expertly arranged rhythm sent ripples through them, electricity making every person sway, every person bounce, every one of them belonging to her.

Her manager handed Athena a clear glass. She drank it in two gulps. Vodka tonic. With a hint of lime. She could feel the ecstasy tab kicking in. The whole world became a velvet dream, soft, wet and inviting. She kissed the air, watched as her lips sent waves of passion through hundreds.

She knew Shawn Kensbrook was staring at her. Shawn knew that this performance, along with the subsequent press coverage, would drive the Kitten Club even further into the stratosphere. He knew Athena could create legends wherever she pleased. And after tonight, clubs would be willing to pay *her* to promote her album.

For the next three minutes and twenty-two seconds, she *was* the goddess Athena.

When the song ended, Stix took Athena's hand and escorted her back to her seven hundred pounds of bodyguard. The crowd pleaded with her to stay. More air kisses, more reaching arms. Those three and a half minutes alone would move one hundred thousand records.

Shawn Kensbrook ducked through the prying arms. Bruise recognized him and parted the way. Shawn was dripping with sweat. His eyes were twitching. She could tell through the ecstasy fog that he was on something, coke or speed. Shawn was nearly hyperventilating. Considering how big next week's crowd would be, Athena had essentially given him license to print money.

Shawn threw his arms around her. Whispered into her ear.

"Athena, that was off the *charts*. Baby, you are a *goddess*. Look at this, I mean, will you *look* at it? All these people here for you…what's that feel like?"

She smiled at him, flicked her tongue into his ear. She felt him shiver. Felt him grow hard in an instant. For a moment, she considered it.

Then she said, "Baby, you'll never know."

Shawn watched as the bodyguards whisked her away.

Bruise parted the curtains. The manager opened the doors for her. He gently brushed her arm as she passed. Eyes waiting in line widened. She could see her limo just beyond the red carpet. It would take her to Nikos's loft downtown, where he'd have champagne, strawberries and other goodies waiting. They'd do it all night before passing out naked on his satin sheets.

Athena stepped onto the red carpet and waved at her fans. Her new fans. Her old fans. Fans who would give anything for her. Fans whose hearts and loins she had filled, who would desire her every night to fill them again and again. Athena took one step onto the carpet. Smiled.

And then a crack of thunder filled the air, and a bullet smashed through her skull.

And just like that, her blood staining the carpet an even darker red, the goddess Athena died.

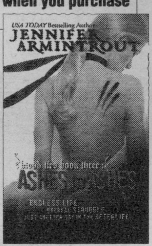

Award-winning Author

GAYLE WILSON

IDLE HANDS ARE THE DEVIL'S PLAYTHINGS.
IDLE MINDS—ESPECIALLY BRILLIANT ONES—
CAN BE MUCH MORE.

Lindsey Sloan teaches the best and brightest students at
Randolph-Lowen High School. So when brash detective
Jace Nolan arrives and accuses her kids of setting a series
of fires in local black churches, Lindsey is furious.

No matter how Jace tries to convince her, Lindsey
can't believe her pupils could do something so horrible.
But when her attraction to Jace places her in mortal danger
and people begin dying, Lindsey can no longer be sure just
what her students are capable of.

THE
SUICIDE CLUB

"Gayle Wilson is a rising star in romantic suspense."
—*New York Times* bestselling author Carla Neggers

MIRA®

Available the first week of July 2007
wherever paperbacks are sold!

www.MIRABooks.com

MGW2469

REQUEST YOUR FREE BOOKS!

2 FREE NOVELS
FROM THE ROMANCE/SUSPENSE
COLLECTION PLUS 2 FREE GIFTS!

YES! Please send me 2 FREE novels from the Romance/Suspense Collection and my 2 FREE gifts. After receiving them, if I don't wish to receive any more books, I can return the shipping statement marked "cancel." If I don't cancel, I will receive 4 brand-new novels every month and be billed just $5.49 per book in the U.S., or $5.99 per book in Canada, plus 25¢ shipping and handling per book plus applicable taxes, if any*. That's a savings of at least 20% off the cover price! I understand that accepting the 2 free books and gifts places me under no obligation to buy anything. I can always return a shipment and cancel at any time. Even if I never buy another book from the Reader Service, the two free books and gifts are mine to keep forever.

185 MDN EF5Y 385 MDN EF6C

Name	(PLEASE PRINT)	
Address		Apt. #
City	State/Prov.	Zip/Postal Code

Signature (if under 18, a parent or guardian must sign)

Mail to **The Reader Service:**
IN U.S.A.: P.O. Box 1867, Buffalo, NY 14240-1867
IN CANADA: P.O. Box 609, Fort Erie, Ontario L2A 5X3

Not valid to current subscribers to the Romance Collection,
the Suspense Collection or the Romance/Suspense Collection.

Want to try two free books from another line?
Call 1-800-873-8635 or visit www.morefreebooks.com.

* Terms and prices subject to change without notice. NY residents add applicable sales tax. Canadian residents will be charged applicable provincial taxes and GST. This offer is limited to one order per household. All orders subject to approval. Credit or debit balances in a customer's account(s) may be offset by any other outstanding balance owed by or to the customer. Please allow 4 to 6 weeks for delivery.

Your Privacy: Harlequin is committed to protecting your privacy. Our Privacy Policy is available online at www.eHarlequin.com or upon request from the Reader Service. From time to time we make our lists of customers available to reputable firms who may have a product or service of interest to you. If you would prefer we not share your name and address, please check here. ☐

BOB07

MEET THE

DEADLY
SEVEN 7

Seven titles from bestselling authors and new voices that will chill and terrorize you with their tales of murder, conspiracy and suspense.

JUNE

AUGUST

JULY

JUNE

JULY

AUGUST